Grief Encounters

Grief Encounters

STUART PAWSON

First published in Great Britain in 2007 by
Allison & Busby Limited
13 Charlotte Mews
London W1T 4EJ
www.allisonandbusby.com

A CIP catalogue record for this book is available from
the British Library.

10 9 8 7 6 5 4 3 2 1

13-ISBN 978-0-7490-8032-7

Typeset in 11/16 pt Sabon by
Terry Shannon

Printed and bound in Great Britain by
MPG Books Ltd, Bodmin, Cornwall

STUART PAWSON had a career as a mining engineer, followed by a spell working for the probation service, before he became a full-time writer. He lives in Fairburn, Yorkshire, and, when not hunched over the word processor, likes nothing more than tramping across the moors, which often feature in his stories. He is a member of the Murder Squad and the Crime Writers' Association.

www.meanstreets.co.uk

Available from Allison & Busby
in the DI Charlie Priest series

Grief Encounters
Shooting Elvis
Over the Edge
Limestone Cowboy
Laughing Boy
Chill Factor
Some by Fire
Deadly Friends
Last Reminder
The Judas Sheep
The Mushroom Man
The Picasso Scam

CHAPTER ONE

July 1978

Johnny Mathis could go to hell. The gag tightened and she wished she'd never heard of Johnny-stinking-Mathis. She couldn't understand why she'd been singled out for this treatment. The others stood around, subdued by the guns pointing at them, as her ankles were strapped to the chair's legs, her wrists bound behind her and the gag stuffed into her mouth.

Then the man who was obviously the leader of the gang produced the flat tin with the thin spout and held it above her. Seconds later the fumes from the lighter fluid were stinging her eyes as he doused her in it. They bulged in terror as she fought against her bindings. She couldn't breathe, tears were streaming down her cheeks and mucus bubbled from her nose. The warmth on the back of her thighs told her that she'd wet herself.

'Listen, you lot,' he said, 'and listen well. Do as you're told and nobody gets hurt. But any funny business by any one of you and...' he leant over the trembling girl to read the name on the badge pinned to her company-blue blouse '...and Gail here goes up like a Roman candle.' He illustrated the point by striking a match, letting it flare and then shaking it out. Gail fainted, and the gathered staff of the York and Durham Bank got the message. There'd be no heroics this morning.

'OK,' the leader said. 'Now start bringing the money out of the vault.'

Officially, the tradition of Wakes Week had died out in the wool and cotton towns that clung to the Pennines between Yorkshire and Lancashire, but the habit was as ingrained as the soot that adorned the remaining mill chimneys. In the middle of the nineteenth century the mill workers started taking a few days off in summer to break the crushing effort of work that would have had a slave owner vilified by his peers had he inflicted it on his charges. It wasn't a luxury. It was brought on by the desperation of working twelve or fourteen hours a day, six days a week, in the hammering, dust-laden atmosphere of the mills. Most of all, it was something to look forward to. A goal, however distant, that made living and raising a family just about tolerable.

The mill owners weren't happy, but began to realise that closing down completely for a week perhaps wasn't such a bad idea. Maintenance could be done. Machines could be modified without interrupting production. Inaccessible places, where the remnants of weft and weave gathered with each year's coagulated oil drippings, could be cleaned up without having to send a small child in amongst the whirring cogs, flapping drive belts and oscillating shafts. Children with arms and legs missing were a wasted resource, and a small embarrassment to the great and the good as they thanked God for their lot at the Sunday morning services. So, in a gesture of munificence that would have had a modern spin doctor blushing with shame, they granted all their workers one week's holiday, every September. Unpaid.

That week the mills fell silent and there was a mass migration to places like Blackpool, Morecambe and the Lakes. The wind blew the smog away from towns that had lived in its shadow for years, and the distant hills could be seen by anyone left to walk the deserted streets. In Lancashire it was called Wakes Week, and the name was universally adopted. Then it moved to July, to fit in with school holidays, and eventually it became two weeks until, a hundred years after the practice started, it died out. Workers wanted their time off when it suited them, not their employer.

Except that in a land of fickle weather, in an area of that land where the fickleness was taken to extremes, July was as good a time as any to take a break. The majority of workers still took their holidays then. Two weeks before, they would work as much overtime as they could to bolster their pay packets. The towns still fell quiet, but now much of the exodus was towards Benidorm, Majorca, or Cornwall. People still lived in a cash society, so off they would go, wallets bulging with two weeks' wages, plus overtime, plus what they'd drawn from the savings club that many firms operated.

It was a jolly, carefree time. It was a great time to rob a bank.

'Pile it there,' the leader ordered. They toiled for fifteen minutes, bringing the money out of the vault, until the huge safe was empty. The female members were then locked in the vault and the men worked with the gang, carrying the money upstairs. There were three flights, then it was through the hole in the wall, across the upstairs room of the hairdressing salon that was next door to the bank, through another hole in the wall and down the three flights of the next shop, which was empty and for sale.

When all the money was transferred the male staff were made to join their colleagues in the vault. A van painted with the name of a fictitious firm of shopfitters came up the back street behind the bank and parked two doors along, exactly as arranged. The gang members, all wearing green overalls, tossed the bags of money into the van as casually as if it were debris they'd made while redesigning the interior of the empty shop and they drove away. It was going to be a bleak Wakes Week for a lot of people.

CHAPTER TWO

Saturday 23rd July 2005

They were an odd couple, and it wasn't just the age difference. Plenty of men went out with women thirty-some years their junior and made brave efforts to bridge the generation gap, but in this case something had gone wrong. She was dressed in a clingy silk dress with a brief mohair jacket across her shoulders as a token protection against the evening chill; he was wearing a chain-store blue suit, with appropriate shirt and tie. She wore sling-back sandals with heels like bayonets, he, highly polished brogues. She was all Harvey Nichols and Jean Paul Gaultier, he Marks and Spencer and Debenhams.

But his happiness was clear to see. He placed a hand in the middle of her back, steering her through the throng as they exited the cinema complex and she instinctively moved closer to him. Her perfume tantalised his senses. Then there was the feel of her body, curved and alive, like a snake slipping through his fingers, and the silkiness of that dress, all conspiring against him.

'That was wonderful,' he said. 'I really enjoyed it.'

'Judi Dench always plays a good part,' she replied.

'Even if I did think the foyer was a good representation of what hell must look like.' He'd shrunk in horror as they'd entered the complex, the purple neon, strobe lights and noise battering his sensibilities. Fortunately, once inside Theatre 1, it was not too far removed from his memories of what a cinema should be.

Strolling back to the car they held hands, her fingers gently caressing his. He opened the door of his Rover Connoisseur for her and she thanked him as she sank into the seat. He walked round, slipped into the driver's seat and checked that she'd fastened her safety belt.

'Coffee at my place?' he suggested as he started the engine and pulled the gear lever into D for drive. This was their sixth date, and after the last two they'd gone back to his place. They hadn't made love, not quite, but if the progression continued, tonight could be the night.

'No, I don't think so,' she replied. 'Not tonight, if you don't mind. I'm feeling rather tired.'

'That's all right,' he said, a touch of relief tempering his disappointment. 'I'll take you home.' It had been a long time since his last sexual activity, and even then it had been all rather low key, more duty than passion, and he was the wrong side of sixty. As they left the complex he glanced across and saw the sign advertising the film they'd watched: *Shakespeare In Love*.

They drove in silence until they were clear of the town centre, her hand resting on his on the centre console, their fingers restlessly intertwining. Street lighting ended and the traffic thinned out. This was the more affluent side of town, where anything less than a Series 3 BMW belonged to the nanny. He indicated a right turn which would have taken them towards her home, but she said: 'No, Edward. Go straight on.'

He cancelled the signal. 'Are you sure?'

'Yes. I'm sorry. We should have gone for that coffee. Can we just go somewhere quiet and have a talk, please? I don't think I want to go home, yet.'

'Will he be there?'

'He may be. It's a possibility. He sometimes comes to collect things, then gets drunk and falls asleep on the settee.'

'Will you be all right?'

'I think so.'

'He hasn't been violent again?'

'No, just that one time. I think he got the message.'

'Well if he ever is, I want you to promise to call the police. Or me. Domestic violence is completely unacceptable.'

She glanced across at him, squeezing his fingers and smiling. 'I promise, Edward,' she said, then, 'Turn in here. This should be nice and quiet.'

It was a pay-and-display car park at the entrance to the Sculpture Park. Through the day visitors came from far and wide to see the Henry Moores and Barbara Hepworths in a rural setting, but parking was free after six o'clock and the clientele at eleven-thirty were students of a more natural style of anatomy. Edward was surprised to see that there was a scattering of cars dotted about the park, lights off, windows steamed, gently rocking.

'Gosh!' his girlfriend exclaimed. 'It's busy. I thought we'd have the place to ourselves. Stop over there, under the trees.'

He did as he was told and parked in the shadows, well away from all the other cars. He killed the lights and engine and pulled the brake on.

They sat in silence for a while until she said, 'I like being with you, Edward. You're so comfortable. Undemanding. I can relax with you. You're my rock.'

He reached behind her and rested his arm across her shoulders, pulling her closer. The mohair jacket fell off and he cupped her shoulder in his hand, stroking it until the strap of her dress slipped down her arm. He was confused and inexperienced, and not sure if he wanted to be regarded as comfortable. 'I...' he began, then stopped.

'You what?' she asked, gently.

'I...I like being with you, too, Teri.' It was only the second time he'd used her name all evening. It wasn't a name he felt at ease with, and far more exotic than that of anyone else he knew. 'You've given me a new life,' he went on. 'I never realised I could be this happy. If you told me that you didn't want to see me again, I'd still always be grateful to you. You'd always have a fond place in my memories.'

'Don't say things like that,' she admonished, resting her head against his shoulder. 'I won't leave you. Not unless you want me to.'

He pressed his face into her hair, saying: 'I never want you to leave me, but...'

'No buts.' She turned her face to kiss him, then said: 'Oh! This is in the way,' and banged her fist on the big car's centre console that jutted between them like a sea defence.

Edward laughed. 'We could always get in the back,' he suggested, rather daringly.

'Like young lovers,' she giggled. 'What a good idea.'

'Slide your seat forward, first,' he told her, 'to make more room.'

'How do I do that?'

'There's a button down the side.'

Teri felt for it and the seat moved forward, generating another giggle and a squeal of pleasure. The interior light came on as they opened the doors, and faded again as they made themselves comfortable in the back, laughing like teenagers as they sank into the deep seats. Teri put her arms around him and pressed her face against his chest. After a few seconds she said: 'Take your jacket off, Edward. It's like snogging with a tailor's dummy.'

Edward, eager to please, gladly pulled the garment off and moved closer to her.

'So,' Teri began, 'how much holiday do you have?'

'It's not a holiday,' he replied. 'It's a recess. It's a time to concentrate on work in one's constituency. And we still have to keep in touch. And if anything drastic happens we can always be called back and parliament reconvened.'

'How drastic?'

'Oh, a war,' he replied airily. 'Or a big tsunami wiping out the east coast. Something like that.'

'It sounds like a holiday to me. When do you have to go back?'

'You mean when do we reconvene?'

'Do I? So when?'

'The tenth of October.'

'Tenth of October!' she gasped. 'That's three months away. Who's running the country until then?'

'Oh, it's in safe hands.'

'Is it? So...does this mean I'll be able to see more of you,

Edward? Will I be in safe hands?' She took hold of his tie to loosen it, and undid the top two buttons of his shirt.

'I hope so, Teri,' he told her, his voice so gruff it was barely audible as he fought against his own personal tsunami, sweeping up his legs and engulfing his loins. 'I really do hope so.'

He was nibbling her neck, thinking of Henry Kissinger, when the camera flashed for the first time. Kissinger said that power was an aphrodisiac, to explain his success with women. Edward couldn't think of any other reason for this beautiful girl to be with an old fogey like him. The flash cut through the thought like a scalpel. He didn't know what it was. The interior of the car was there for a fraction of a second, brightly illuminated, Teri's face white as marble, her eyes closed. Then all was even blacker than before. He half turned, blinking, puzzled but not alarmed by what he thought was a natural phenomenon. Summer lightning, perhaps. The second flash told him it was a camera, pressed against the window of the car. He twisted in his seat to confront the photographer when the camera flashed for the third time. Teri had covered her face with her hands and pulled her legs up in a protective gesture, which had the side effect of exposing her stocking tops and thighs. Edward was turning away from her, his jaw hanging loose and his clothing disarrayed.

That was the shot they used.

CHAPTER THREE

Friday 12th August 2005

Detective Chief Superintendent (Crime) Colin Swainby was the ugliest policeman in the East Pennine force. I loved drawing him. The challenge was to capture the look without making him appear like a cartoon character. I'd got the shape of his face about right and was hinting at the details, smoothing out the carbuncles and assorted warts, when I realised he was addressing me. We were in the large conference room at the force HQ, at his monthly superintendents' meeting, facing each other down the length of the table. Along each side were the heads of the various specialities, plus the chief honchos from the divisions. I was standing in for Gilbert Wood, my boss at Heckley. I lifted the pencil from the pad I was drawing on and tried to look fascinated.

'Have you any comments on that, Charlie?' the super was asking.

'Nothing specific, Mr Swainby,' I replied, 'but I'd like to

have a one-to-one with Peter sometime, when he can find a window for me. We need to keep abreast of developments with HOLMES in order to maximise its benefits.' I glowed inside with satisfaction: *one-to-one* and *find a window* in the same sentence was pretty good going, not to mention *maximise*. Peter was the DI in charge of our murder-hunt computer system, and had just delivered a tedious update on its latest tricks. The DCI from drug squad sitting round the corner from me shook his head and hid his mouth behind his hand, trying not to giggle.

'That's a good idea,' Swainby said. 'I'll leave you to organise something between yourselves.'

We nodded our agreement and I resumed my sketching. The next presentation was from the female DCI who was the Force Child Abuse Coordinator, and now I dropped my pencil and listened. You see some ghastly things in this job, but we learn to deal with them. I treat it, when I can, as a pantomime, where we are all bit players with a few lines before we exit stage left. Most of the time it's not funny, but you can usually find something there to brighten your day. It might be a humorous comment from a villain, or a spark of humanity from someone who has been robbed of what little he or she had. Sometimes, you find it in unexpected places, but never in child abuse cases. We sat quietly and listened, each inwardly seething, me wondering how much worse it was for the officers who had small children.

The DCI finished what she had to say and we sat in silence for a while, absorbing her words. The super thanked her, then said: 'Item twelve. This is an extra item on the agenda I gave you at the start of the meeting. It's a personal statement that I wish to make.'

We'd all seen it: 'Item 12, Personal statement by Mr Swainby', and assumed that the old codger was finally retiring. Nobody minded. Apart from being our ugliest officer, Swainby was also the most unpopular. There'd be a collection, but it wouldn't be a record-breaker. His nickname was Bulldog, more because of his aggressive instincts than his looks, but a psychologist might have suggested that it was because of his unfortunate appearance that he was always so belligerent and hostile when dealing with junior officers.

Strange thing was, I always got on well with him. He might be a nasty bastard, but he'd done several years with the Royal Ulster Constabulary, and earned himself the Queen's Police Medal. If you worked your butt off and kept your nose clean, he'd tolerate you. I shot somebody not long ago. An hour later I was sitting in an interview room, waiting for the sky to come crashing down, when he hustled in through the door. He leant over me, gripping the edges of the table, his face inches from mine, and said: 'Just keep your mouth shut until someone's had a talk to you. Understand?'

I nodded, and he was gone.

'Ladies and gentlemen,' he began. I closed my pad and sat back to listen. He looked pale and grave, like I'd never seen him before. 'I won't keep you long, but this is important to me. On Monday I suspect I will be asked by the chief constable to hand in my resignation.' Chairs squeaked around the table as we realised this wasn't the usual retirement speech. 'He wants to see me at nine o'clock, which is always a bad sign.' He tried to smile, make light of what he was saying, but it didn't work. 'First of all,' he went on, 'I'd like to take this final opportunity to thank every one of you for the loyal service and hard work you have all given. You are as fine a body of officers as I have ever worked with. So what's it all about? I'm not going to go into details, but certain allegations have been made against me. Allegations which I totally refute. But mud sticks, as we all know, and my position in the force would be untenable if I tried to defend myself, and, if the truth is known, I don't have sufficient fight left in me to take on a long litigation. I will be asked to go quietly, which is what I will do. I admit to being foolish, but no more than that. I have done nothing illegal or anything I am ashamed of. You will hear rumours, of course. Accusations have been made against me, but I assure you that they are all totally unfounded. When you hear the rumours, I'll be grateful if you would tell your informant that I totally refute every one of them. That is all I ask of you.'

The poor bloke was close to tears. With one last effort he looked at us all and said: 'I wish you all the best of luck with your careers. Thank you,' and gathered up his papers and left.

We all sat dumbfounded until someone said: 'What was all that about?' but none of us knew.

'So is the meeting over?' I asked, standing up. I had half a mind to chase after Mr Swainby, see what I could do for him.

'We haven't discussed any other business,' one of the sticklers for protocol reminded us. Stickling for protocol can take you a long way in the police force. Sometimes I feel as if I'm submerged by sticklers.

'Is there any other business?' I asked. I certainly didn't have any.

The detective chief inspector in charge of administration and policy decided that this was one of those situations that fell into his field of expertise. He half rose to his feet and rapped his knuckles on the table. 'Do we have any other business?' he repeated.

'Um, well, I have something,' my opposite number from Halifax said, and I sat down again.

'Right,' the detective chief inspector (administration and policy) said. 'Let's resume the meeting with any other business.'

The DI from Halifax produced a pile of ten by eight photographs from his briefcase and passed half of them to the people sitting at each side of him. 'I'd like you to look at these,' he said. 'This lady's body was found in parkland just outside town last week. No doubt you've heard all about it. Unfortunately we're having difficulty identifying her. I just want to bring it to the attention of the other divisions to see if their field intelligence people might recognise her. It's a long shot: she was clean of drugs so she might not be known to us.'

The pictures reached me. I took the top one off the pile and passed them on. The woman was at the wrong end of middle aged, at a guess, with waist-length hair in a ponytail, but apart from that there was little that could be used for identification purposes. Her face was a swollen mass of bruises, completely closing her eyes; her nose was flat and her lips swollen and split like barbecued sausages. 'How did she die?' I asked, without taking my eyes off her photograph.

'She was beaten to death,' I heard him say.

Another pile of photographs arrived. This one showed her back view, covered in bruises again. Someone had really gone to town on her. 'The mark on her left buttock is a rather distinctive tattoo,' the DI told us. 'The final photo shows it in more detail.'

I waited for the next pile to arrive and took one. It was a close-up of her bum, and the tattoo was clearly visible. It said:

PROPERTY OF THE POPE

'Property of the Pope,' somebody read out.

'Yes,' the DI said, 'but I don't think we should take it too literally.'

My head was spinning. I stared at the picture and in an instant was in another, more carefree world. A long-forgotten smell stung my nostrils and my ears were filled with music. I was sitting on the bare floor, back against the wall with a bottle of Newcastle Brown in my hand, and Joan Baez was singing about the colour of her true love's hair.

'I know her,' I said. 'I know her.' I looked up and saw eighteen mouths hanging open, eighteen pairs of eyes boring into me like gimlets.

'Um, she's called Magdalena,' I told them. 'I know her. She's Magdalena.'

CHAPTER FOUR

Saturday 13th August 2005

They almost collided in the doorway in their rush to meet their visitors, he yanking the door open before the chimes had died away.

'Hello! Hello!' they all gushed as the new couple crossed the threshold.

'Have you seen this?' the female visitor shrieked, waving that night's newspaper at them. 'Isn't it wonderful!'

Her jacket was taken from her, the men shook hands, the women air-kissed each other and the two men then kissed the opposite partners, this time with more passion.

'We saw it on *Look North* just now,' the woman of the house stated, her face bright with excitement. 'Didn't you do well?'

'Teach the bastards a lesson, eh?' her husband said. 'That puts you in the lead, Teri. Well in the lead.'

'I didn't know it was a competition,' she replied.

'It isn't. But maybe we should make it one. Give the game

an edge. What do you think, Richard?'

'Um, no, I think not,' he replied. 'We might get careless. Leave things as they are and nobody can touch us. We aren't breaking the law. Well, not that anyone can prove.'

'You could be right.' He turned to the woman again and slipped his hand around her waist. 'But you did well, Teri. You did brilliant.'

The hosts for the evening were Tristan and Fiona Foyle. Tristan was old money, left a fortune by a father who despaired of his only son, but not sufficiently to disinherit him. He had been expelled by two of the best schools in the country and then amassed a further fortune of his own by cashing in early in the IT boom. In the early Eighties he developed a programme for investing in the stock market, based on following the big-name company chairmen rather than the individual companies themselves. He invested as only a teenager with a rich dad can, made lots of money for himself and other people, and sold the business for twenty-two million just before the boom ended and the markets nosedived.

Fiona was a model that he met in Bahrain, where she had gone to work on her tan. She liked what she saw there and stayed on to work behind the counter in the beauty salon of one of the new hotels, where oil millionaires came to buy presents for their wives and mistresses. She was very discreet. If she accepted an invitation to dinner she always wore the same perfume that her host had bought for his wife, earlier in the day. Tristan did not know this, of course. He met her by chance, he thought, as he came ashore from the hired yacht he was sharing with some male friends. She was a genuine ash blonde, with a figure like molten honey, and she played him like he played the marlin and yellowfin tuna he and his friends were trying to catch.

'So what is it tonight?' Richard Wentbridge, Teri's husband, asked. 'I'm absolutely starving.' They were in the art deco sitting room, with dim lights and an invisible sound system that was working its way through several hours of golden classics.

'Have you brought anything?' Fiona wondered, facing up to him.

'Ooh, I might have something for afterwards,' he replied, pulling her closer.

'We're having a takeaway,' Fiona said, Richard's arm around her waist. 'They should be here anytime.' She gave an involuntary shudder as his fingers traced a circle on the small of her back.

'Clifford and Pepe?' he asked.

'Yes.'

'Good show.'

'Come on,' Fiona said, taking Richard's arm and pulling him towards the door. 'Help me finish laying the table.'

'And make sure that's the only thing you lay,' Tristan called after them. As soon as they were alone he took his best friend's wife in his arms and kissed her, long and deep. When he came up for air he said: 'God, why do we have to go through all this rigmarole? Why can't we just get on with it like grown-ups?'

Teri laughed. 'It's more romantic this way,' she told him. 'And man cannot live on sex alone.'

'Maybe not,' he argued, 'but we could have the sex first and eat afterwards.'

'You're insatiable.'

'And what about you, on Wednesday?'

She smiled and rubbed her nose against his. 'It was rather good, wasn't it?'

'Did you tell Richard?'

'I told him I met you, yes. I presume he guessed the rest.'

'Same again, this Wednesday?'

She shook her head, slowly and solemnly. 'No-o. I think not.'

'Why not, Teri? You know what I feel about you.'

'Because it would spoil things, don't you see?'

'It wouldn't spoil things for me. I want you all to myself.'

'No you don't, Tristan. If you and I were an item, you'd be having this same conversation with Fiona and I'd be in the dining room with Richard's podgy fingers feeling all my twiddly bits. Don't you see that?'

'Mmm,' he said, breaking free from her. 'You might be right.'

'And then there's the game,' she said. 'Don't forget the game.'

'Oh no,' he replied. 'Mustn't forget the bloody game.'

The doorbell interrupted any further argument. 'Here comes the takeaway,' he said. 'I'd better get that.'

Calling a meal by Clifford and Pepe a takeaway is a bit like saying that NASA occasionally sends up a firecracker. They started with oyster ravioli with *foie gras* and rhubarb vinaigrette, served by Clifford in his athletics shorts and striped apron; then wantons with ceps and porcini in *sauce mère*; followed by sea bass with a velouté of butter beans, truffle shavings and vermicelli; venison in jalousie with celeriac and carpaccio of broccoli in *jus natural*; and finished with cassata of summer fruits with mango and papaya custard. Only Richard tried the ice cream with beetroot and anchovy, and found it not to his liking. Pepe had recommended a simple Macon-Villages white burgundy, and they took four bottles.

'Pepe! Clifford!' Tristan shouted, slumped in the captain's chair at the head of the table. 'Get yourselves in here.'

The two chefs joined them, wiping their hands on their aprons. Tristan poured two extra glasses of wine and gestured for the two men to take them. 'Your good health, boys,' he said. 'You're bloody fantastic. Another culinary masterpiece.' The others mumbled their agreement and raised their glasses.

Clifford said: 'The dishwasher's on, Mrs Foyle, and we'll come back in the morning to clear all this up. Will about ten be OK?'

'That'll be fine, Clifford,' she told him.

Clifford took a long envelope from the pocket of his apron, saying: 'And this is for you, Mr Foyle.' He delicately placed it on the table, leaning against a candleholder. Tristan gravely nodded an acknowledgement to the presentation of the bill and half raised his empty glass.

When the two chefs had gone Richard Wentbridge said: 'Right, so who's for a dab of sherbet to finish with? Do we have a mirror?'

If Foyle was old money, Wentbridge was new. His father was a carpet salesman who made a decent living when the fashion for fitted carpets started to blossom. But a decent living isn't enough for men like him, and soon he was selling inferior imports from a disused cinema, while all around him the local carpet industry was curling up and dying. Young Richard was put in boarding school while he and his wife wintered in Tenerife and that's where he came across the timeshare industry, with all its traps, temptations and opportunities. He started with a thirty-bedroomed hotel and grossly oversold it. That gave him cash to expand and soon he had a complex network of businesses all down the Costas and throughout the Canary Islands, all paid for from the life savings of countless, trusting holidaymakers. The sun was shining, he was such a nice man and it would be theirs forever. 'Where do I sign?' they asked.

In 1977, whilst under investigation by the British and Spanish fraud squads, he was diagnosed with prostate cancer. He began to systematically convert everything he had into cash. Two years later he died and left almost everything to his fourteen-year-old son.

That son, Richard, was now enjoying cashing in on his father's enterprise and other people's thrift and hard work. He'd met Tristan Foyle at public school, and had narrowly escaped expulsion for the same misdemeanour that had ended Tristan's formal education. He did a year at university before working briefly in his mother's fashionware business, modelling and sweeping up, and the two sons met again at the 1998 International Motor Show at Birmingham NEC, drooling over the latest Ferrari. They were both with their new wives and the attraction all round was mutual and intense. Since then they had done most things together.

'I'll fetch one,' Fiona said, and dashed out of the room. Seconds later she returned holding a hand mirror with a mother-of-pearl back, and a double-edged razor blade. She handed both items to Richard. He tipped the contents of a small zip-lock bag onto the mirror and used the blade to gather the powder into a pile. The other three leant forward, watching intently. With an unnecessary flourish he divided the line into two and then into quarters.

'Who's first?' he asked.

'Me,' Tristan said. His wife handed him a bendy straw. 'Is this from your courier friend?' he wondered as he fitted one end of the straw into his nose and directed the other end towards the line of cocaine.

'Mmm,' Richard replied. 'But this could be the last he can do. He reckons it's not as easy to get hold of as the papers would have you believe, unless he's just kite-flying to put the price up.'

'Probably.'

'And too much isn't good for you,' Fiona added. 'It can make your nostrils join up into one, like it did that stupid actress woman.'

Tristan pressed a finger against his spare nostril and inhaled slowly and deeply. The coke vanished up the straw.

'Ziggy-zaggy wowee-wonker!' he exclaimed. 'Struth! That's good stuff.' He shook his head to clear it and the others laughed. Richard snorted the next line, and then it was Fiona's turn.

Teri shook her head when offered a straw for her line. 'No thanks,' she said. 'It makes me sneeze. And I don't want one big nose-hole. Besides,' she went on, 'we know a different way of applying it, don't we, Tristan?' She put her arm around his neck and pulled him closer. Tristan looked momentarily embarrassed but nodded his agreement.

Her husband said: 'Well, it can do the same damage down there, you know.'

Teri looked puzzled, not sure what he meant, then exclaimed: 'Richard! That's grotesque!'

Tristan stood up and pulled Teri to her feet. 'I say, old man,' he began, 'do you mind if I take your wife upstairs? We've had the decorators in and I'd like to show her the magnificent job they've made of the master bedroom ceiling.'

'A touch of the Sistine Chapels, is it?' Richard enquired.

'No. Just a rather fine shade of magnolia emulsion.'

'Ooh! I can hardly wait,' Teri enthused.

'Oh, go on then,' Richard replied. 'Fiona and I will finish the washing up – *again*.'

Tristan gathered up two glasses and a half-full bottle of wine, and followed Teri out of the dining room. 'Be nice to each other,' were his parting words.

As soon as they were alone Richard and Fiona embraced. 'God, I thought they'd never go,' Fiona said, breaking away. 'Upstairs or the other room?'

'The other room,' Richard decided, without hesitation. 'It's warm, the lights are dim, soft music is playing, and there are no stairs to climb. What more do we need?'

'The settee's not very comfortable.'

'No, but the fireside rug is deep and soft.'

'You've convinced me. Come on.'

The settee in question was in the style of the room, all wrought iron and black leather, with infills of real zebra skin. The newspaper that Teri had brought with her hung over one arm, where she had discarded it. 'Did you manage to get some?' Fiona asked.

'Yes, here.' They sat on the settee and Richard produced a twist of silver paper from a pocket. There were three small blue pills in it. 'Two for me, one for you,' he said. He'd carried a glass of wine in with him and they washed them down with it.

'Have you done this with Teri?'

'No. She has to be careful, what with the other medication she takes.'

'Of course. I'd forgotten that. How long does it take to work?'

'The Viagra? About an hour. I'll probably be needing it by then.'

They embraced hungrily and started undressing each other. She threw his shirt over the chair arm, knocking the newspaper onto the floor. In seconds they were naked and he was pulling her towards the fireside rug. The newspaper had landed with the front page facing upwards. The lead story was the one that had created so much delight when they all met at the front door. There was a photograph of a man with an avuncular face, hair neatly combed, smiling modestly as he gazed into the distance above the photographer's head. The headline above the picture, in bold black print, read:

'MP Found Hanged.'

CHAPTER FIVE

Monday 15th August 2005

'And you expect us to believe that?' Superintendent Gilbert Wood said after I'd told him about Friday's meeting, finishing with Magdalena.

I threw up my arms in frustration. 'It's the truth. What more can I say?'

'Come on, Charlie. We're both grown up; you're a single man. There's nothing to be ashamed of in having a lover with *Property of the Pope* tattooed across her backside.'

'I'm not ashamed. Or I wouldn't be. I was an art student, she was an artist's model.'

'Is that what they called you – the Pope? Did your fellow students elevate you to the Vatican?'

'No, and we weren't lovers.'

'So it was a professional relationship. What's wrong with that?'

'Nothing, except it wasn't any sort of relationship. We used to go to Leeds College of Art for life classes. That's drawing and painting nudes, to you. Usually female, sometimes male. Magdalena was one of the regular models. To be fair, she was just about the only one any of us fancied. There was a touch of the exotic about her. The others were bored housewives who posed for a couple of hours before going to pick up the kids from school. Magdalena always reminded me of a belly dancer, or a gypsy queen. I could imagine her telling fortunes or making silver jewellery by the light of a campfire. We were all about nineteen and she was much older. At least twenty-five, I'd say. Some of the drawings we did were a bit shaky.'

Gilbert lifted one of the photographs I'd brought from the meeting and said: 'Well she doesn't look exotic now, Charlie. Somebody really did for her.'

'They certainly did.'

'Was her hair this long back then?'

'Yes.'

He was silent for a few seconds, then asked: 'Were any of these women connected, if you see what I mean, with the, um, sex trade, or anything like that?'

I shook my head. 'No, Gilbert, it was all relatively innocent, and they were probably paid about fifty pence per hour. It wasn't exactly a nice little earner by any standards. There wasn't a drug scene, although some of them, like Magdalena, may have moved in what you might call bohemian circles. There was pot about, but you had to know where to find it.'

'Did you know where to find it?'

'Pot? No.'

'Did you ever try it?'

'I had the odd puff of a joint at parties. It never did anything for me. I suspect they'd never seen any marijuana.'

'We'll strike that admission from the record. So the chief

super has handed the case to you, in your role as divisional head of HMET?'

''Fraid so, boss.'

'And you reckon the chief super will be asked to resign, later this morning?'

'His words, not mine.'

'What's it all about?'

'No idea.'

'There could be something in the air. Did you see where old Ted Goss had topped himself?'

'Mmm. No suspicious circumstances, they said.'

Gilbert looked at me over his half moon spectacles. 'That's what they said. Something will come to light, mark my words. He'll have had his fingers in one pie or another.'

'You're a cynic, Gilbert,' I said. 'His wife is an invalid and he was in a thankless job. For an MP he was a decent old cove. Last of the old-time socialists, but everything he believed in had gone out of the window. Perhaps he just ran out of the will to live.'

'And pigs'll fly. So what about Swainby? What was he? Last of the old-time coppers?'

'I don't know. We'll just have to wait for the jungle drums to start rolling.'

'Keep me informed, please.'

'Will do.' I went downstairs to the CID office and gave a collective wave to the gathered troops. I hung my jacket in my little enclave, checked for messages and joined them. Someone brought me a mug of tea. I went through the weekend's reports of crimes and allocated them to the sergeants and told them we had taken over the murder investigation they'd all read about. They updated me on on-going cases and I told them to go to it. The gift of delegation eases many burdens.

Mad Maggie Madison and Dave 'Sparky' Sparkington followed me to my office and sat down. They're the core of my murder investigation team. I showed them the photographs and told them all about Magdalena.

Dave said: 'And you expect us to believe that?'

'Wait!' I protested, holding my hands up. 'Wait! I've had this conversation once already this morning, with Mr Wood. You'd better believe what I say, because I'm not explaining again.'

Dave studied one of the photos for a while before saying: 'That's all very well, Charlie, but this tattoo is quite small and you'd be, what, about five yards back while you were drawing her? I don't think you'd be able to read it at that range. What do you think, Maggie?'

Maggie agreed with him. 'You'd have to be in much more intimate contact to make out what it said.'

'You're right,' I conceded. 'As usual, David, with your incisive policeman's brain you have stumbled upon an angle to my story that demands further enquiry. We were about five yards back, but when Magdalena was the model I usually managed to bag a seat on the front row. I still couldn't make out what the tattoo said. There were about twelve of us in the group and we were all intrigued. Tattoos weren't as common as cones on the motorway in those days. Eventually we persuaded one of the girls in the group to ask her what it said. It was a mistake. Magdalena told her to mind her own business and was obviously distressed with the question. Eventually we asked one of the tutors who we thought was having an affair with her. He used to fix her pose before we started drawing and came into much closer contact with her than we did. He told us that the tattoo said *Property of the Pope*, but he hadn't a clue what it meant.'

'OK. So we'll believe you, eh, Margaret?'

'Just about, David.'

'So where do we start?'

'We start by you two collecting the files from Halifax, go have a look at where the body was found, and set up the incident room. I'll nip to Leeds College of Art to find out what I can about Magdalena. She may be on the files or somebody might remember her.'

Maggie said: 'We need a better picture of her. Did you keep all your drawings?'

'I don't know, but you're right.'

I took three KitKats from the stash in my drawer and handed them out. Dave said: 'What did you get up to over the weekend, then?'

'Painting a couple of pictures for the police gala,' I replied. It's held every August and is mainly a public relations exercise, showing off the dogs, horses and other accoutrements of law enforcement. There's a section for cops' art and I always enter a couple of my paintings. All the other submissions are delicate watercolour landscapes or highly defined oils of hunting scenes and still lifes, but mine are always wild splashes of abstract colour, with barely recognisable form. They always arouse a great deal of comment from my peers, but they are the ones that the press like, and I occasionally sell them.

'No doubt they'll be the laughing stock of the show,' he remarked.

'Thank you, Dave. It's the lot of the genius to be misunderstood in his lifetime.'

'You wouldn't want it any other way,'

'That's true.'

'Did you see that programme on eagle owls on TV last night?'

'No.'

'Nor me,' Maggie added.

'It was fascinating,' Dave told us. 'Apparently one's been seen on the Whitby moors.'

'A wild one?' I asked. 'I thought they lived on the Russian steppes or somewhere.'

'They do. This one may be an escapee, but nobody knows. They have a six-foot wingspan and can pick up a sheep. Well, a lamb.'

'What sort of noise does it make? Sort of *too-wit too-woo-shriek*?'

'No. They just hoot.'

'It's a myth that owls say *too-wit too-woo*,' Maggie assured us. 'They just make a hooting sound.'

'Right,' I said. 'I'll try to remember that. Now how about collecting a few witnesses to this murder and seeing what sort of noise they make when we apply the bastinado to the soles of their feet, eh?'

As soon as they'd gone I picked up my internal phone and dialled Jeff Caton, one of my sergeants, who was busy at his desk in the outer office. 'Did you see a programme on TV last night about eagle owls?' I asked him.

Jeff hadn't seen it, either, so I told him all about it.

Leeds College of Art and Design is on the northern edge of the city centre, divided between two sites. One is a swish Eighties construction, allegedly designed by Lego but no doubt a joy to work in, and the other the hundred-year-old building of my student days. I abandoned the car outside the parking zone and walked back towards town, looking for the familiar façade with its fake classical mosaic that was the college's emblem. I found it hidden in a corner, surrounded by structures that were either shining new or waiting for the wrecking ball. The city was evolving around it.

Henry Moore and Barbara Hepworth are the college's most famous luminaries. From the outside it could have been a bank or the offices of an ancient firm of lawyers, with only the mosaic high on the wall to indicate otherwise. I trotted up the steps to the front door, hidden apologetically round the corner, and pulled it open.

Inside it was smaller and dingier than I remembered, like a careworn friend you haven't seen for years. No smell of turpentine or linseed oil delighted my nostrils to bring the memories flooding back; no chattering throng of students in flowing chiffon and tie-dyed shirts came flip-flopping down the corridor. A couple of girls in semi-Goth outfits clumped by and I wondered what they were studying. Tattooing and body piercing? We'd had the best of it, no doubt about it, in those golden years post the Pill and pre-Aids. I walked over to the front desk and showed the receptionist my warrant card.

The vice principal saw me. I'd hoped that his eyes would light up when I asked him about Magdalena, as he remembered hasty fondles in her changing room or the stolen brush of his fingers against her skin as he arranged her pose, but unfortunately he was far too young. He would barely have been born when Magdalena sat on her high stool, legs crossed, as a dozen dry-mouthed students struggled to capture her likeness.

He doubted very much if there would be any record of her on the files. Nude models were casual labour, paid for out of the petty cash, and most of the records were destroyed in the various moves. He could give me a list of all the teaching staff going back to about 1970, and he knew of one tutor who was still active and living not too far away: JKL Mackintosh RA RP.

'Old Mack,' I said. 'I remember him. He took us for life classes occasionally. He was a portrait painter.'

'He graces us with a visit, now and again,' the vice principal said, in a tone that implied that the visits were far too frequent and time consuming. I knew the feeling well. When I leave the station with my yellow metal Timex in one hand and the troops' bottle of Bell's in the other, I'll never make the return journey. Not ever.

'Do you have an address for him?' I asked.

He didn't, but he had a phone number and he allowed me to use his phone. JKL, as he was more formally known, was in and said I could call round. I thanked the vice principal and was soon heading past Hyde Park Corner – that's the Leeds Hyde Park Corner – out through Headingley towards Lawnswood.

Old Mack was waiting for me with a freshly boiled kettle and a plate of digestive biscuits. The years had been kind to him. His goatee was white, his lanky frame was stooped a little and the eyes rheumy, but otherwise it was the same old JKL who exhorted us to use bold strokes to capture the spirit of a subject and not just a likeness, and discussed the models as if they were unfeeling lumps of clay. The oil paintings on his walls were impressionist landscapes that shone with their own sunshine, and a couple of modern sculptures in copper and stone shepherded a family of primitive clay animals on his mantelpiece.

'Priest, did you say?' he asked, after we were seated and I'd admired his works of art.

'Charlie Priest, but it was a long time ago. We came from Batley, mainly for life classes, that's all.' As he poured the tea I remembered that the beard was more than an affectation. He had a livid scar at the left hand side, running up his neck from under his shirt collar, and he habitually turned the other cheek towards you.

He gazed up into the corner of the room and shook his head. 'No, I'm afraid I don't remember you. And you became a policeman. That's an unusual career change of direction, if you don't mind me saying so.'

'It's a long story, sir,' I said. 'I didn't want to go into teaching, wasn't good enough to make it as an artist, and my father was a policeman. I only expected to be in the force until I found something else, but here I am.'

'And you made your father happy, no doubt.'

'Yes.'

'It's strange how so many parents have an inherent antipathy to their sons going into the fine arts. I used to think it was a working class thing, but now I'm not so sure.'

I had thought it might be interesting to have a discussion about the state of the arts today, but I glanced at his clock and decided that would have to wait for a subsequent visit. 'I'm investigating the death of a woman who I believe used to be a model in the life classes you held,' I said, plunging straight into it. 'She was called Magdalena. Do you remember her?'

'Magdalena?' he repeated. 'Magdalena Fischer?'

'I don't know her surname. Fisher, is it?' I'd been expecting something more exotic, with perhaps an apostrophe in it. D'Auberville, or something.

'Fisher with a c in the middle,' he told me. 'Was she murdered?'

That was more like it. 'Thanks for that,' I said. 'It's a big help. At the moment it's just a suspicious death, but it could be murder. When did you last see her?'

He thought for a few seconds. 'It doesn't seem long ago, but when I put it into years it's frightening. It must be nearly ten years ago. I used to bump into her occasionally down Headingley Lane, out shopping. I don't get down there so often, these days, what with the traffic and all the riff-raff. We didn't speak. Just acknowledged each other with a smile. She was a good model, no doubt about it. Long hair, down to her waist. That was her most impressive feature. Does she – did she – still have it?'

'Yes, she did. I don't suppose you know where she lived?'

'No, I'm afraid not. Somewhere down in bedsit land, near Hyde Park Corner, if I were to hazard a guess. If she owns a house down there she'll probably be the last of the owner-occupiers. All the others have been bought to let.'

'I don't suppose you still have a painting or drawing of her?' I asked. Sometimes you get lucky. The secret is to keep asking the obvious questions.

'No. I donated all my old stuff to the college.' He chuckled, adding: 'They probably made a bonfire of it.'

'Was there anybody – I'm thinking of tutors – who was close to her, do you know?'

He shook his head. 'You mean having an affair with her? No, sorry. Not that I heard about.'

'Do you still paint?'

'I try, but the eyes are not what they were. Do you?'

'Now and again. I'm working on a couple at the moment, for an exhibition of policemen's art. They're after the style of Kandinsky, and should make a nice contrast with all the other stuff on show.'

'Ah ah! I bet they will.'

We shook hands and I gave him my card and told him the usual: 'If you think of anything else…' and thanked him profusely for his help. He asked me to let him know how the investigation progressed and I said I would.

I turned right at the Corner, into Hyde Park Road, with the open ground of the university campus on my left and endless rows of Victorian terraced houses on the other side. At Brudenell Road I made a right, then turned into another street and drove round in a big square. Almost every house had a couple of estate agents' signs planted in the front yard, sticking out like prayer flags in a stiff breeze, announcing rooms to let. The student population would be returning in the next few weeks and the last of what was once a community would retreat to their cellars until the blessed relief of the Christmas recess. If Magdalena wasn't on the electoral roll, finding someone who knew her would be as hopeless as looking for a matching pair in a mushy pea factory.

The troops were sitting round in a big group when I arrived back at the nick, either gossiping and telling dirty stories or discussing various cases, depending on who you asked. I made myself a mug of tea and joined them.

'Everything moving smoothly, Jeff?' I asked.

Jeff Caton takes on all the other stuff, mainly burglaries,

when I'm diverted to a murder case. 'All in order, Chas,' he replied, desperately trying to suppress a wicked smile.

I told Dave and Maggie about Magdalena Fischer and they said they'd booted up the HOLMES terminal down in the incident room, had a quick look at the crime scene and fetched the files from Halifax. Dave was sitting with his chair the wrong way round, hunched over with his elbows resting on the chair back. When the boring stuff was out of the way Jeff said: 'Did anybody see that programme on eagle owls the other night?'

'I did,' Dave replied, immediately sitting up.

'It was fascinating,' Jeff told us. 'They have a six-foot wingspan.'

'And they can carry a sheep,' Dave added.

'Well, a lamb.'

'That's right. A lamb.'

'And there's one loose on the North York Moors.'

'Has anyone actually seen one catch a lamb?' I asked.

'Not on the North York Moors, but they can, in their native land.'

'What sort of noise do they make?' asked Brendan, one of my DCs.

'They just hoot.'

'What, like a train?'

'No, like an owl.'

'Perhaps sheep are smaller where they come from,' somebody suggested.

'Sheep are the same size everywhere,' Jeff assured us. 'A sheep is a sheep.'

'African elephants are bigger than Indian elephants,' John Rose argued.

'Surely they can't lift an elephant,' I protested.

'Well, not an African one,' Jeff replied.

'Are you lot taking the piss?' Dave wondered.

After that the meeting broke up and we went home. I dined on lamb chops done in the slow cooker with all the vegetables, and frozen Yorkshire pudding. Frozen Yorkshire puddings are a gift from God. After I'd finished I went up into the loft and started exploring. There were two tents up there of an ancient design, with all the other camping gear necessary for a summer break not too far from the creature comforts should the weather turn nasty. I smiled at the memories. After college I married the best-looking girl there, and we had a couple of camping holidays down in Cornwall. It was all we could afford. Two were enough for Vanessa, though, and she moved on to somewhere with room service. I realised that I'd been doing quite a bit of reminiscing lately, and wondered what it was a symptom of.

There was enough paint up there to paint a mural on the Great Wall of China, in tubes, jars and tins, plus a couple of easels and assorted works of art that would never see daylight again. I remembered each one, where I was, who I was going with, when they were painted. I had to keep reminding myself that I was up there for a purpose.

All dad's power tools were in boxes on the floor, where I'd left them after he died. Everything was ancient, long ago superseded by cheap, and better, imports from the Far East. And DIY had never been my strong point. They, and all the camping gear, could go to the dump. My old uniform, with spare blue serge trousers, was in an old suitcase, and I found my big hat in a plastic bag. I tried the hat on and it was like meeting an old friend. The badge on the front was for Leeds City Police, where I'd started my career. That's where I first met Sparky, and that made me pause in my search. Of all the stuff up here, of all the paraphernalia of my life and the people it represented, Sparky was the only continuous thread. I put the hat back in the bag and continued the search.

There were two thick A2-sized books of them, sandwiched between stiff backs. My portfolios. I loosened the tapes holding the first one together and let the pages flop over, one by one. It was a journey through my aspirations, from raw beginner with a talent to draw, through pretentious student phase to the finished product three years later – an arts graduate with no marketable qualifications.

The drawings of Magdalena were in the first few pages of the second book. When I mused over them and compared them with the other nude studies, it was evident that poor Magdalena had captured my youthful imagination far more than any of the other models. Some of them were mere caricatures, cartoon drawings, because I was bored. Being in a room with a nude lady was the stuff of my fantasies, but not with several other people and a pencil in my hand. But Magdalena was different. With her I'd gone for gold. Every line counted, and I'd delicately used the edge of my thumb to soften the contours of her body and catch the highlights in her hair as it tumbled down over her left shoulder. At the end of the session the model would often have a quick look at our drawings, and I'd done my best to impress her. Now I was being called upon to do my best for her again. I opened the portfolio to its fullest extent and carefully removed her picture.

I drove to the nick and took a photocopy of the top half of

it. Then, up in my office, I used a pencil to sketch in the collar of a dress around her neck. I gave it a few stripes and buttons, carefully *Tipp-Ex*ed out her right nipple, and *voilà*, we had a perfectly respectable representation of Magdalena Fischer. I ran off ten copies, blew a kiss to the afternoon shift in the charge room and went home. It had been a busy day, and I was doing what I did best.

Richard Wentbridge wasn't listening to what the girl opposite him was saying. So far he'd heard about a Robbie Williams concert, the problems of having a social life with two toddlers to look after, a long saga involving the electricity board and a dodgy washing machine, and what a bastard one woman's ex was. This one, number eight, was telling him all about the super holiday in the Dominican Republic she'd just had with a group of friends. Except that she called them her 'team of mates'. Her hair was streaked with blonde and a magenta colour and she had a stud in her nose. How she came to be left on the shelf he could perfectly understand. In fact, that went for all of them, including the men. A weirder set of oddballs he'd rarely seen outside a secure home. And this was supposed to be where the upwardly mobile came to meet prospective partners. 'Earnings of over £50,000' the advert had said. This lot didn't look as if they could feed themselves, let alone hold down a decent job. Except, perhaps, for number nine, the next woman along.

She was tall and well built, but not in an unattractive way. Sort of well fed without looking overweight. Her suit was tailored and her hair was cut in layers with subtle highlights. The whole look was understated and elegant. He was imagining that she was something in high finance when he realised that number eight had stopped talking and was waiting for a reply.

'Really!' he said with feigned interest.

'Yes. And the drinks were cheap, too.'

'What language do they speak there?' he asked, leaning forward, until her perfume caught him like twin pencils up his nostrils and he leant back again.

'Dominican, I suppose,' she told him. Then the bell went, saving him from further boredom.

As he approached number nine he held his arms open in a what-am-I-doing-here gesture and grinned at her. Wentbridge had been told many times by different women that his grin always gave them the hots. They smiled at each other for a few seconds, then the smiles broke into laughter. It was instant attraction.

He sat down, looked at her name and number badge, and said: 'Hello, Gillian. I'm Richard and I'm afraid I'm completely out of chat-up lines.'

'Thank goodness for that,' she replied, and he noticed that the corners of her eyes wrinkled as she smiled. 'So far I haven't been swept off my feet by any opening statements. That last one asked me if I was a Gemini. I said no, Virgo, and he was crestfallen. Now I'm wondering if he was a genuine astrologer or if it was some sort of code they use in places like this that I've never come across.'

Richard shook his head. 'Not that I know of,' he replied, 'but there again, I'm no expert. So you're a Virgo and you have beautiful hair. What else do I need to know about you? Let me see… Do you pull the wings off flies?'

'No, I spray them with hair lacquer and watch them suffer.'

'Do you do the lottery?'

'I wouldn't know how to.'

'That's good. So far you are in the lead. Who's your favourite football team?'

'Would that be soccer or rugby football?'

Richard's eyes opened wide. 'You mean you know the difference?' he exclaimed.

'We teach both...' Gillian stopped, mid sentence. She'd been determined not to tell anyone her true occupation, to hold something back, but it had just slipped out.

'You're a teacher?' Wentbridge picked up.

Gillian blushed. 'Um, yes, I suppose I am.'

'What is there to suppose?' he asked. 'Either you are or you aren't, aren't you?'

'I'm an administrator.'

'But you were once a teacher?'

'Yes.' What the heck, she thought. It's no big deal. 'I'm a headmistress,' she confessed. 'Of a primary school.'

'Fee paying?'

'Well, yes, actually, it is.'

Wentbridge shammed disappointment. 'That changes everything,' he said, his mouth down-turned.

'In what way?'

'I was going to ask you to marry me, but I'm not sure if I want to be married to a headmistress.'

Gillian blushed even more. 'I think I need to know something about you, first,' she said.

'Fire away.' He'd been leaning forward, their knees touching under the table, but now he leant back, open and expansive, inviting interrogation.

'I'd want to know if you could support me in the manner to which I'm accustomed, so what do you do for a living?'

'I drive Formula One.'

'That's what I would have guessed.'

'Next question…'

'Do you like dogs?'

That threw him for a moment. His usual expression for anything with four legs and a wagging tail was *shit-and-bark*, and he hated them. 'Love 'em,' he lied. 'I had to have my Old English sheepdog put down three weeks ago. Nearly broke my heart.'

'Oh, I am sorry.' Gillian reached forward, put one hand on his for a moment before withdrawing it. 'Had you had it long?'

'Twelve years. Still, I try not to be sentimental about animals. He had a good life. Any further questions?'

'Just one, Richard. I can't help but notice that you're wearing a wedding ring. Are you married?'

Wentbridge looked down at the tabletop for a few moments as he fingered the broad band of gold. Eventually he looked up, his cheeks sucked in, and said: 'I'm sorry, Gillian, but that question is out of bounds.'

'I…I didn't mean to upset you,' she said.

'No, you didn't. I'd just rather not talk about it.' He smiled again and steered the conversation to safer ground. 'What sort of dog do you have, Gillian?'

'A golden retriever called Biscuit. He's wonderful.' Her face lit up as she talked about the dog, and Wentbridge saw that as a chink in her schoolmistress armour. He was telling her that he might buy a Labrador next time when the bell went again.

'Boys and girls!' the proprietor of Encounters Speed Dating shouted as she bounded into the middle of the room. She had tungsten-blonde hair, was built like a Humber barge and draped in enough gold to ballast it. 'It's interval time. Fifteen minutes to replenish our glasses, and then we'll resume. Remember where you are, and back here at...nine-fifteen. Thank you.'

'What can I get you to drink?' Wentbridge asked, pushing his chair away from the table and standing up.

'Thank you. Just an orange juice,' she replied.

'Shall we stretch our legs in the other room?'

'That's a good idea.' Gillian rose to her feet and Wentbridge noticed that she was only a couple of inches smaller than him. About five ten, he guessed. Ah well, he thought, the bigger they are, the harder they fall. He stood back and held out a hand to steer her between the chairs and tables.

They were slow, and there was a crush around the bar. Wentbridge had one of those presences that earned him prompt service, even when he was three rows from the front of the queue, but he decided not to use it. 'Look, Gillian,' he said, softly in her ear, 'as far as I'm concerned there's nobody else here that I want to meet. What do you say if we split?'

'Split?' she echoed.

'Leave. We could go to a bar. Actually, I haven't eaten. How about a pizza? There's a nice Italian place almost next door. We can walk it from here.'

'Are we allowed to?' she asked. 'What will the madam say?'

'Brunhilda? She's got our money. She'd be happy if everybody split. We're grown up. You're a headmistress and I'm a big-shot racing driver, so c'mon, let's go.'

Gillian could see no harm in going with him if they were walking. If he'd suggested going in his car alarm bells may have tinkled, but only softly. 'Right,' she replied. 'A pizza it is.'

They sat at a table for two in a booth, isolated from the

other diners. Wentbridge thought that he couldn't have planned it better. They shared a *spicy pollo* and a *quatro formaggi*, washed down with mineral water and followed by coffee. Gillian stirred cream into her coffee and smiled at him.

'I've never been in a pizza parlour in this country before,' she confessed. 'It was surprisingly tasty.'

'But you've been to Italy?'

'Oh yes, but I don't remember the pizzas being this nice.'

'I suspect the recipe has been adjusted to suit the British palate. I, on the other hand, have eaten in rather too many pizza parlours.' He patted his stomach, as flat and as hard as a manhole cover thanks to thrice weekly sessions with a personal trainer, as if he were worried about his weight.

There was an awkward silence until they both spoke at once. 'After you,' Wentbridge insisted.

'I was going to ask what does a big-shot Formula One driver do for the rest of the week?'

He flapped his hands in mock embarrassment. 'Um, I was joking. I'm not really a racing driver.'

'Never!' Gillian exclaimed. 'I was completely taken in. Don't tell me – you're an astronaut.'

Wentbridge threw his head back and laughed. 'Actually, I'm something in IT – information technology. I run a couple of companies at the cutting edge, as we say.'

'Now I am impressed,' she told him. 'Did you survive the bubble bursts, or whatever they did?'

'Oh yes. The secret is to recognise when it's about to happen and get out, but always be on the lookout for the next bubble. So what about you, Gillian? Are you really a headmistress, or are you simply the caretaker's daughter on a night out with her ladette friends?'

Now Gillian laughed. 'No, I'm the boss, for my sins. One of my teachers persuaded me to come along to the speed dating. She said she'd met somebody nice there. I eventually relented, but until you came along I was wondering how to get out, fast as possible.'

'Same with me,' Wentbridge said. 'You were like a breath of fresh air. So which school do you rule over with a rod of iron?'

'St Ricarius, over in Oldfield, and we rule by discussion and cooperation.'

'Hey, I've heard of that. You take boarders, don't you?'

'Yes, just a few; mainly from overseas.'

'St Ricarius. Does that mean it's a faith school?'

'Church of England, but all denominations attend. We pride ourselves on our cross-cultural teaching. Nearly thirty per cent of our intake comes from...'

'Enough!' Wentbridge cried. 'Enough of the sales pitch. I have no kids to send to you, but I'm sure they'd be in good hands if I did have any. C'mon, let's go and see if our cars are still outside the hotel.'

He held her hand on the way back and kissed her on the cheek after she unlocked the door of her Honda coupé. 'Can I ring you at work?' he asked, stooping to make himself level with her as she wriggled into the bucket seat.

'Yes, I'd like that,' she replied.

'Do I ask for Gillian?' he asked, flashing the grin at her.

'No, we're not that progressive. *Miss Birchall* should get me, though.'

'Fine, Miss Birchall. I'll call you tomorrow or Wednesday. Are you likely to be washing your hair Thursday or Friday, or might you be free?'

'Oh, I think the hair can wait.'

'Good. Well, thanks for a pleasant evening.'

'Yes,' she replied. 'Thank you, Richard, for rescuing me. I'll look forward to hearing from you.'

He kissed her again, lightly, on the lips, then stood back so she could close the car door. As they'd walked back to the hotel Gillian had apologised for giving him the sales pitch. Wentbridge had laughed it off, and apologised in turn for his reaction.

'What about the league tables?' he'd asked, feigning an interest in the fortunes of St Ricarius's Church of England School for the sons and daughters of the good citizens of Oldfield and district. 'How do you fare in them?'

'Brilliant,' Gillian told him. 'Last year we came top of the county in the national tests. Back slapping all round and extra funding. Hopefully we'll open a new drama wing with what we receive.'

'Top!' Wentbridge exclaimed. *'Numero uno?'*

'That's what I said.'

'Hey, that's fantastic. Congratulations. You must be thrilled to bits.' He used the expression of approval as an excuse to put his arm around her waist, and noticed that she didn't object.

'Yes, we were rather pleased,' she admitted.

He watched her brake lights flare as she stopped at the car park exit. A bus went by and she pulled out into the road. 'Oh yes, Miss Gillian Birchall,' he whispered to himself. 'La-di-da headmistress, top of the table, looked up to by all those children and their wealthy parents. Oh yes, oh yes. The bigger you are, the harder you sodding-well fall.'

CHAPTER SIX

The door-knockers struck gold Tuesday lunchtime, when they broke off from door knocking and repaired to a local hostelry for refreshment. The King's Fusilier had been called that for two hundred years, until a new brewery decided that it didn't fit in with the student clientele they were trying to attract and changed the name to the Flying Pig. It had always been a place where music was kept alive. Back in the Sixties it was folk, then jazz, followed by punk, new wave, acid, reggae, garage, hip-hop and a rash of obscure sub-genres recognisable only to the most devoted aficionados. And now, to everybody's surprise, folk was making a comeback.

The landlord had survived all the changes, and he told the team that Magdalena and her partner were regular customers until about a year ago, but had abruptly stopped calling in. He did know the name of the partner, though: Len Atkins. Mr Atkins was the local plumber.

They visited his yard and broke the news about Magdalena's death to him. He said he hadn't seen her for nearly twelve months and had spent the weekend she'd died doing all the things that single, retired plumbers do to help time pass by. He'd watched television, strolled to the cricket ground to see how the second eleven were doing, cooked a meal and walked to the Hyde Park Hotel for what used to be called the last hour, but was now the same as any other hour. They reported all this to me, and next morning I made another trip to Leeds, to see him.

His son opened the door in the big wooden gates after I rang the bell, while I was still reading the fly posters. The Kaiser Chiefs were coming but I'd missed the Arctic Monkeys. There was razor wire along the top of the high wall, double bars on the inside of the gate, and a ferocious Alsatian that started barking as my finger barely touched the bell-push. It didn't used to be like this, I thought, before a university education became a right and not a privilege.

Len junior had taken over his dad's business but didn't live here, he told me, after I'd introduced myself and we'd shaken hands. The yard was filled with plumbing stuff that looked as if it had been reclaimed: toilet bowls in avocado and coral pink; sink pedestals and baths. This was bed-sit land, and who cared if the toilet didn't match the bath, as long as it worked and was cheap? Stacks of second-hand roofing tiles leant against a wall and about a ton of lead pipe was awaiting disposal. The dog, thank God, was on a short chain.

'Two officers spoke to him yesterday,' Len junior told me. 'He's a bit upset about it.'

'Were you here?' I asked. Nobody had mentioned a son.

'No. Dad rang me afterwards and told me.'

'I'm afraid there's no easy way of breaking news like that. They'd been knocking on doors all morning, looking for someone who recognised Magdalena. Did you know her?'

'Of course I did. She was like a stepmum to me. I thought she was great, and she was the best thing that ever happened to Dad. How did she die?'

'We're not sure,' I lied. 'How long were she and your father together?'

He thought about it for a few seconds. 'About fifteen years, at a guess.'

'So when did they break up?'

'Last August. Magda walked out on him. He was heartbroken, but he wouldn't talk about it. He was having a lot of trouble with his knees through years spent crawling about under floors, so he just handed the business over to me and said he was retired.'

We were standing at the door to the back-to-back terrace house, with Len junior's hand on the latch. He pressed it and pushed the door open. 'Dad. A detective to see you,' he announced.

I'd been surprised at the idea of Magdalena shacking up with the local plumber, but when I saw him it made more sense. Len senior was only about five foot six tall, but his hair was tied back in a long ponytail and he was dressed entirely in denim. He held out a scrawny, work-hardened hand for me to shake and said: 'I spoke to two officers yesterday.'

'I know,' I told him, 'but I'm the detective inspector in charge of the investigation and wanted to talk to you myself. Can we go inside, please?'

Compared to the outside of the house, the room was a revelation. It was dim inside, after the sunshine, but the glow of mahogany and the influence of Magdalena was everywhere. Decorative plates lined the walls, horse brasses shone from the roof beams and a porcelain carriage pulled by six prancing stallions held pride of place on a sideboard. Plumbing, it appeared, was a good line to be in. The gas fire was set low, which made a pleasant change, and the television was off, which was unique. Len had been sitting in an easy chair, with a small table pulled up in front of it. A pile of tobacco, some Rizla papers and a small pile of something else gave clues as to what he'd been doing. He swept everything up and pushed it all unceremoniously into the biscuit tin he kept his stash in.

When he realised that I wasn't born yesterday he said: 'It's for my knees. My arthritis. It's the only thing that helps.'

His son asked if I needed him and I shook my head. He left, pulling the door closed behind him.

'And does it help?' I asked, nodding towards the tin.

'Yeah, I think it does. Anyway, it's cheaper than beer and doesn't rot your liver. And you don't have to listen to the same bunch of brain-dead bigots every night while you're enjoying it.'

I let that sink in, then said: 'I'm sorry about Magdalena, and how the news was broken to you. I'd like you to tell me all about her.'

'What's to tell?' he wondered.

'A lot more than you'd believe,' I assured him. 'Let's start at the beginning. Where and when did you meet?'

'Up at the Oak,' he replied, naming Headingley's most famous pub. 'We used to chat, like you do. Pull each other's leg. Then I did some odd jobs for her; plumbed her washing machine in; things like that. You know how it is.' He smiled at a memory. 'We started making plumbing jokes, said it was a mutual interest in our plumbing that brought us together. Then her landlord started cutting up rough, wanting rid of his tenants, so I invited her to move in here.'

'When would that be?'

'Back in 1989. It was a funny week. Princess Anne and Mark Phillips separated and we got together. Kirsty MacColl was in the top ten.'

I remembered something from the PM report. 'Did Magdalena have any children?' I asked, knowing that she'd given birth at least once in her lifetime.

'Yeah. She had a daughter. Angela. She came to live here too, but she was a proper little madam. Wouldn't go to school, dodgy friends, answering back all the time. She was with us for about five years. Her dad had left some money in trust for her until she was sixteen. Day after her birthday she left. I was glad to see the back of her, but Magda was upset. I said she'd be back as soon as the money ran out, but Magda said there was an awful lot for her to get through. I asked how much but she just said more than I'd believe.'

'Have you heard from her since?'

'No. Not a word.'

I wanted to tell him that I'd met Magdalena, knew her slightly, but decided not to. He might not gain any comfort from learning that I'd gazed upon her naked body in the presence of several other randy students. I said: 'So when did you and Magda split up?'

He looked down at the carpet, as if contemplating the answer, although I'd gamble that he knew the exact hour and date of her leaving. It was a painful memory. 'Last year,' he replied eventually. 'August.'

'What brought it about?'

He shook his head, as if he still couldn't believe that she'd done that to him. 'I...I don't know. She just said she had to go. It was for the best. She took most of her clothes and that's all.

Hardly any money. I couldn't understand it. Something from her past had caught up with her, but I didn't know what.'

He was silent for a while, and I left him alone with his thoughts. I had dozens of questions but it's always better if the information is volunteered. And he needed to talk. We're not counsellors, but I've got a qualification in listening.

'How did she die?' he asked, turning to face me.

I held his gaze before telling him: 'Somebody beat her up. She...died.'

'It was him, wasn't it?'

'Who?' I asked.

'Was there a post-mortem?'

'Yes.'

'Were you there?'

'No. A police woman attended.' Another lie, but it might help.

'But you've seen the reports?'

'Yes, I have.'

'So you'll know about him. The Pope.'

'I've seen photographs of the tattoo, if that's what you mean.'

'It was him killed her, wasn't it?'

'I don't know. Who is he?'

He stared at the tin containing his fixings and I wondered if I ought to tell him I didn't mind if he had a smoke. Before I could get the words out he said: 'He was Angela's father.'

'What happened to him?' I asked.

'God knows, but he was a mean bastard. How Magda became mixed up with someone like him I can't imagine. She was the gentlest person you could imagine; he was a Neanderthal.'

I said: 'Some women have a talent for falling for the wrong man. Some men too, I imagine.'

'Yeah,' he replied. '"Love and Wisdom dine at separate tables."'

I recognised the quote. 'Henneman,' I said and he looked at me with a hint of a smile. He was a fan. 'So what was the tattoo about?' I asked.

'He had it done to her. Said it was a birthday present. Magda liked the idea and chose something from the tattooist's catalogue. A flower or a lizard. Something like that. He didn't let her see it until after they got home. *Property of the Pope*, it said. He told her that she belonged to him, now, and if she ever left him he'd kill her. They'd only been seeing each other for about two weeks. That was the most she ever told me about him. After that the subject was out of bounds.'

So that was it. Magda had been murdered by the Pope. Well, perhaps not *the* Pope, but someone bearing that name. All we had to do was look in the telephone directory and work our way through them all. He made coffee for us both and we chatted for another half-hour. When I could see he was growing restless for a joint I got up to leave.

At the door he said: 'Can I ask you for a favour, Inspector?'

I turned back to him. 'What is it?'

'Magda was funny about some things. She'd never have her photograph taken. I haven't got a single picture of her. That drawing they showed me yesterday. It was her to a T. Just how I remember her when she was younger. Do you think it would be possible for me to have a copy?'

'Oh yes, Mr Atkins,' I replied. 'I think we'll be able to manage that.'

* * *

Dave was holding court when I arrived back at the office.

'...and Camilla said: "It gives me terrible indigestion, doctor," so the doctor said: "Have you tried Andrew's?"'

I try not to encourage him. 'So who did it?' I asked in my best no-nonsense tone, after I'd hung my jacket behind the door, made myself another coffee and joined them. 'No doubt you have it all sorted.'

'Pass,' someone said.

'Negative,' Dave added.

'How did you get on with the boyfriend?' Maggie asked.

'Not bad,' I told them. 'He's the last of the hippies, still living in the Age of Aquarius. The only hippy plumber in Yorkshire, but he's a decent enough bloke. Write these dates down, Maggie.'

Someone slid her an A4 pad and she clicked her pen.

'Magdalena and Len Atkins met up in 1989,' I began, 'and Magda had a daughter aged...twelve, I think. Pope was the girl's father. He must be our number one suspect.'

Dave said: 'So Pope and Magdalena must have been together, however briefly, back in...what? 1977 or even '76?'

I nodded. 'Yeah, make it '77.'

'What next?' Maggie asked.

'I'm thinking,' I told her. 'OK. Magda walked out on Atkins last August. Call it 2004 – we'll stick to whole numbers. The circumstances were odd. He said something from her past had caught up with her and she just went. So what if Pope was back in town and wanted her back?'

'Do we know anything about him?' Jeff Caton asked. 'Is he the possessive kind?'

I told him about the tattoo and his threats.

'Yep,' he agreed. 'I'd call that possessive.'

I turned to Maggie. 'So how long was Pope out of her life?'

'Um, let me see. She was with Atkins for fifteen years. She was with Pope possibly twelve years before that. So she was rid of him for anything between fifteen and twenty-seven years.'

'So where might he have been for that length of time?' I asked.

They all adopted deep-in-thought poses, Dave with his fist against his forehead, Jeff stroking his chin. 'Wowee, that's a difficult one,' somebody said.

'Perhaps he's been on missionary work in Malawi,' Jeff suggested.

I nodded my approval.

'Or maybe he's been with the Antarctic Survey, and they became stranded on an iceberg and have survived on a diet of penguins,' young Brendan expounded.

'Could you live that long on chocolate biscuits?' I wondered.

'No, silly me.'

Maggie started to speak. 'Charlie,' she began, hesitantly, 'I know this might sound outrageous, but please don't laugh. When you're dealing with people whose behaviour deviates somewhat from the norm, you sometimes have to expand the envelope. You don't think, do you, that it's just possible that our man may have been, so to speak, living off the hospitality of Her Majesty?'

'In jail, you mean?'

'Well, yes, if that's not a dirty word.'

'No,' 'Nah,' 'Never,' came the disagreement of everybody else.

'The girl's got a point,' I declared, holding up a restraining hand. 'Perhaps he's been out of circulation. So how far have you got?'

Dave produced a list. 'Nine Popes in Heckley, Chas. Fourteen in Leeds. Similar numbers in neighbouring towns. We haven't checked them all against the PNC but they appear to be a remarkably law-abiding lot. Must be something to do with the name.'

'Any who stand out?'

'A couple, but nothing special. We'll see them first.'

'What about the prisons?'

'Haven't looked, yet. If he murdered Magdalena and he's been inside for a long term he could be a lifer, in which case he'll be easy enough to pick up.'

'A lifer who came out to kill again,' someone suggested.

'Which is hardly unknown,' I admitted.

The average lifer serves about twelve years, but is only released on licence. That's the life bit. His address would always be on a file somewhere. I had a three-egg omelette for tea, with curly oven chips and marrowfat peas. I brought my easel into the kitchen and ate the meal while studying one of the nearly finished paintings. Abstracts aren't as easy as people think. There are no rules, no guidelines. You aren't striving to make the picture look like something. It's all down to personal taste.

Kandinsky is a hard act to follow. He came to Germany from Russia and became one of the pioneers of pure abstraction. I love his paintings. He wasn't the typical artist of the time, having trained as a lawyer and dressing accordingly in sober suit and tie. His orderly lawyer's brain tried to put some discipline into his art, tried to lay down rules. He wrote articles about his theories in which he gave meaning to colours and related them to different musical notes. There's a name for it, but it escaped me. You play a note, or make a sound, and some people, one in a thousand or so, see a colour. Or they say they do. Connections in their brains are cross-wired, and one stimulus produces more than one response. Kandinsky claimed he was like that, and the experts say that it's a gift rather than a handicap.

Me? I can't tell one musical note from another, and they never look like colours. All I know is that I look at one of his paintings and something inside me goes: *Pow! I like that. It pleases me greatly*. Not all of his paintings, but some of them. And I still couldn't think of the name for it.

I made a few decisions about the painting as I finished my meal. After I'd loaded my plate and cutlery into the dishwasher I made the changes, altering colours, adding some black contours and hard edges here and there, and decided that it was as finished as it would ever be. The final touch was a stylised *CP* in the bottom corner, more as an indicator of which-way-up rather than a claim of ownership. It's hard work, so after I'd washed my brushes I pulled a couple of cans of lager from the fridge and settled down in front of the television, watching a video of *A Beautiful Mind* that Dave had loaned me. Towards the end of the second can, just as I was realising that all was not as it seemed, I thought of Len Atkins and wondered if he was pulling on a joint, sharing the mellowness.

The waitress lowered the tray containing four large gins and four small bottles of tonic until it rested on the table, and Tristan Foyle placed one of each in front of his wife Fiona and Richard and Teri Wentbridge. He thanked the waitress and cast an approving glance after her as she walked away.

'How was your quail?' he asked his wife as he poured tonic into his glass.

'Delicious. How were the steaks?'

The restaurant was famous for its steaks, and the other three voiced their approval. 'And cooked just right,' Teri Wentbridge added. 'Neither burnt to a crisp nor still in its death throes.'

'Did you know,' Tristan asked, 'that a chef somewhere has invented a device that cooks steaks to perfection, every time? It's a bit like a toaster, but for steaks.'

'And I suppose you have part of the action,' Teri said.

'No, I missed that one.'

'Gosh, that's unlike you, Tristan.'

'This wine is rather good,' Richard asserted, tipping his glass to show the last few drops. 'Where did you find this one, Tristan?'

'A client recommended it, last week. He's an importer, good man to know.'

Fiona said: 'What does he import?'

'Wine, dumbcluck,' her husband replied with a smile. He was sitting next to her, opposite Teri, whose leg was stretched out towards him under the table, her shoe-less foot resting on his thigh, making circular movements against it. He reached under the tablecloth and stroked her ankle.

'Well I didn't know,' Fiona protested. 'He could have imported jellybeans for all I knew.'

'No, darling, he imports wine.' He sipped his g and t, then said: 'So, let's get down to business. I believe you have something to report, Richard.'

'Yes, I think I have,' Richard affirmed, sitting more upright. 'I think I have,' and he told them all about his encounter with Miss Gillian Birchall.

The others listened in silence until he'd finished, when Tristan said: 'And she's the headmistress?'

'That's right.'

'Of a fee-paying Church of England school?'

Richard tipped his head to one side. 'Right on.'

'Wow! That could be quite a comedown, Ricko. The boy done good.'

'I think so,' Richard agreed. 'The complacent Miss Birchall is heading for a mighty fall, no doubt about it, but I'm just not certain how to pull it off.'

'Have you been to bed with her yet?' Fiona asked with a giggle.

'Good God, no,' he replied.

'Well I would have thought that would be your first objective. Don't you think so, Trist? It has a certain poetic justice. Getting one's own back, and all that. It was people like her that blighted our lives right from the beginning, so do unto others as they did unto you. You should give her one, Richard, and think of England while you do it.'

'I'll consider it,' he replied, 'but how do you think we should hang her out to dry?'

'What have you come up with?' Tristan asked. 'You must have thought about it.'

'Mmm, a little. Are we going to Cannes again in September?'

'We'd better be,' Teri asserted.

'OK. Good. I was wondering about inviting her down for a couple of days. We could put her in the apartment. I'd take her out on the yacht and we'd do some topless sunbathing. You could take pictures, Tristan, with a long lens. I reckon the redtops would be interested in them.'

Tristan thought about it, then said: 'That would be embarrassing, but it's not a disgrace.'

'Yeah, I suppose so,' Wentbridge agreed. 'I'd have to be in

there, too. The married man. That might do it.'

'And where am I while you're cavorting with Miss Wonderful?' Teri demanded. 'And what if she refused to take her shirt off and show her boobs? I think it's a daft idea.'

'OK,' her husband replied. 'You think of something better.'

'A hotel room,' she stated. 'Good old-fashioned divorce photos. You and her in bed, or better still, on the bed. Tristan does the private detective bit, with the camera. Bang, flash, Bob's your uncle, send them to the tabloids.'

'I suppose so,' he reluctantly agreed.

Tristan said: 'How would you lure her into a hotel? We all have perfectly suitable houses.' After a silence he continued: 'Do women download pornography? Are there female paedophiles?'

'There could always be a first time,' Wentbridge replied.

'No, we've done that,' Teri objected. 'Let's try to be original.'

'Yeah, Teri's right,' Tristan said. 'If we stick to the same formula someone will rumble us. And it's too easy and impersonal. Ideally, we'd be there to see the expression on her face as her world turned to ratshit. We need a new approach.'

'I've got it,' declared Fiona, and the other three turned to face her. 'Drink driving. Richard gets her drunk one night, when she's in her car. The police breathalyse her, she gets banned, end of a beautiful career, lots of broken-hearted kiddy-winkies. Serve the bitch right.'

'She only had an orange juice, Tuesday evening.'

'Then you'll have to work at it, won't you?'

Technology has made us all change the way we work. Sometimes the changes were evolutionary, at others they were violent U-turns that hurled established practices into the hedgerow and caused new ideas to be taken on board with unseemly haste. For three hundred years clocks and watches relied on springs, cogs and balance wheels to keep them accurate, but in the space of a couple of decades these were replaced by vibrating crystals, digital displays and atomic accuracy. Almost overnight the mobile phone has created a world where it is theoretically possible for everyone in it to talk to everyone else in it. And then there are computers...

Thieving cars has evolved alongside everything else. A handful of years ago it was a brick through the side window, smash the steering lock with the same brick, short circuit two wires and you were away. It was upsetting and inconvenient for the car owner, but nobody was hurt.

The car manufacturers have done their bit to improve things, fitting immobilisers and alarms, remote control locks and even keyless systems that unlock the door and switch on the ignition as the rightful owner approaches the vehicle and slides into the driver's seat, which has automatically adjusted itself to accommodate him.

The brick through the window no longer works. Now, before you can steal a car you have to steal the keys. Searching for a brick has been replaced by an act of burglary or robbery. Sometimes it is as simple as fishing through a letterbox to hook the key for the desirable 4x4 standing in the driveway; sometimes it involves kicking the door down and terrifying the woman and her children cowering in the house. In the league table of violence, car theft has moved up into the play-off zone.

Next to his wife and daughter, Jimmy Johnson's Subaru Impreza was his pride and joy. It was the WRX model, but he'd equipped it with Speedline wheels and Milltek exhaust, and polished it until it glowed. Jimmy was a self-employed CORGI gas fitter, and was regularly on standby through the night for any reported gas leaks or heating failures. Thursday evening he'd put his daughter to bed and read her a story, then settled down with his wife to watch *Big Brother* on TV. When the phone rang he knew it was a call-out and leapt to answer it with undisguised eagerness.

Five minutes later he had reversed his work van out of his driveway and sped off towards a reported gas leak. Five more minutes later Mrs Johnson, her wide-awake young daughter resting on her hip, answered a ring of the doorbell. It had been a sunny day and was still broad daylight. The birds were singing and someone not far away was having a barbeque.

As the door swung open Mrs Johnson was knocked back into the room by a burly man who was pulling a stocking mask down over his face. She screamed and clutched the child closer to her. There were two of them, carrying steel jemmies that they used to smash a glass fruit bowl and attack the crockery on the table in a deliberate show of violence.

'Don't hurt us! Please don't hurt us!' Mrs Johnson pleaded. She fell gasping to the floor, her face growing pale as she fought to force the air out of her lungs, her arms protectively enveloping her daughter.

'Where are the keys?' one of the men shouted into her face, his voice blunted by the mask. 'To the car.'

Mrs Johnson nodded towards a drawer. Her lips were blue and her breath rasped out at irregular intervals as she huddled over the child. He found the keys, then pulled the drawer right out and let it fall to the floor.

'Good for you,' he told her. 'Now don't call anybody for twenty minutes. Understand? If you do we'll be back for the kid.'

Mrs Johnson nodded again as she struggled to breathe. She was still nodding, her back bent double to take the strain off her ribs, as the men reversed the noisy car out into the street and drove away. She didn't phone for help. It was her three-year-old daughter who found the mobile, pressed the pre-set key for her daddy and told him: 'Mummy poorly.'

CHAPTER SEVEN

My last girlfriend was an athlete. She would have made our Olympic team if it hadn't been for injury, but she was still pretty good. We used to go running round the golf course together, and through the woods, but there was a twenty-year age difference and it soon started to show. I didn't enjoy the running overmuch but I liked being fit, and as they say, it feels good when you stop.

I was reduced to Thursday evenings and Sunday mornings, and was enjoying the self-righteousness that punishing yourself to the edge of exhaustion induces when the phone rang. I was languishing in the shower, trying to decide between my usual chicken jalfrezi or something different from the takeaway, but the warbling reminded me that I hadn't been out for a pint with Dave this week, and it sounded like his ring.

I jumped out, rubbed off the surplus moisture, and spoke into the phone: 'Some pubs are far away, some pubs are near. If you're offering to take me to one I might even buy you a beer.'

'Evening Charlie,' the duty sergeant replied. 'I take it you were expecting somebody else.'

'Oh, hello Arthur. I thought it might be Sparky offering to take me out. Go on, what have we got?'

'Sorry to bother you but it's a bit garbled and Davy Rose is attending a burglary at Sylvan Fields. A GP in the Westwood estate received an emergency call about a woman having an asthma attack. She went off in an ambulance but he's rung us to say that there were signs of violence in the room where he found her.'

'Does the woman have a husband?' It's usually the husband.

'He was miles away but he raised the alarm. I think the woman must have managed to ring him.'

It wasn't the husband. 'OK. Give me the address. You got me out of the shower so I'll pull some clothes on and ring you from the car in about three minutes. See what else you can find out.'

I dressed again in the clothes I'd worn all day and gave a hungry look at the takeaway menu as I left home. The duty sergeant didn't have anything to add to what he'd already told me except that the woman was called Johnson, her three-year-old daughter was with her and her husband was on his way to Heckley General, where she'd been taken. I rang Maggie Madison and asked her to go there and handle that end. There's a law against using the phone whilst driving, but what the heck, everybody does it and it makes you feel clever and important.

The sun had set but there was no cloud cover and the sky was still light when I arrived. It was a tidy, detached house on the edge of the estate. One of our panda cars had made the initial response to the call, and they were waiting for me. A neighbour had explained what Mr Johnson did for a living and told them that it looked as though his Subaru Impreza had been stolen. I glanced through the open door and saw the damage inside. It looked senseless, but it wasn't. They'd done it to instil terror in the poor woman, make her compliant. They wanted the keys to the car, not a conversation. A quick glance around supported my initial conclusions: none of the other rooms had been turned over and it wasn't the sort of house that would have a Turner hanging on the kitchen wall or a few emeralds in a drawer. Their most expensive possession was the car, and it had gone.

Motive: theft of motor vehicle. I was sure of it. It happens all the time. I rang Maggie at the hospital and she had to come outside to use her phone.

'Ask Mr Johnson if there should be a Subaru standing on the drive, Maggie.'

'He's here,' Maggie replied, 'outside the hospital. His daughter is with him so he's had to bring her out. Hang on, I'll ask him.'

There was a long silence, then: 'Are you there, boss?'

'I'm listening.'

'Affirmative the car. Looks like they stole it.'

'It's a vehicle theft, then. How's Mrs Johnson?'

'She's in a bad way, in intensive care.'

'Right. I'll protect the scene, then, just in case. Can you ask Mr Johnson if his car is fitted with a Tracker, please?' *Just in case* meant just in case she dies. If she did, I'd launch a murder enquiry and the purse strings would be loosened. We'd test for footprints, DNA, fibres and anything else we could think of. Much of the testing for DNA would be speculative, because you can't see the stuff. Swabs would be taken in likely places and all the tests run on them. Most, nearly all, would be a waste of time, but sometimes you get lucky. For a simple car theft the SOCO would fit the case into his workload and come along when he had the chance. He'd dust around for fingerprints and that would be it. Except...

'Boss...'

'I'm here.'

'Negative, no Tracker fitted.'

'Thanks. That means we'll have to find it the hard way. Ask him the number.'

I telephoned HQ and had an APW put out for the Subaru and asked for all units to look for it. It could have been stolen to order, in which case it would be spirited far away, as fast as possible, or it could have been taken to use on a job. If the villains were planning a job, we were in with a chance. That was the *except*.

I found a fish and chip shop open and had a special and chips, washed down with Tango. I ate them from the paper, sitting on a wall outside the chippy as it grew dark around me. As soon as reinforcements arrived to preserve the crime scene I went home. It had been a long day.

Through the night they stabilised Mrs Johnson's breathing and took her off the critical list. They increased her medication but decided to keep her for another day as a precaution. Half an hour after starting work, the six-to-two shift found the Subaru parked innocently in a street of domestics just outside the double-yellow zone, barely a mile from the Westwoods. It was in the end parking place, ready for a quick getaway. I learnt all this as I hobbled into the station at seven, the night before's jogging making itself felt.

'It's all yours, then, Jeff,' I told Jeff Caton, up in the office, trying to hide my reluctance to hand the case over. Mrs Johnson's recovery had taken the pressure off me, but the Magdalena murder was bogged down and the thought of dashing all over town after more obvious criminals had great appeal. 'Let me know if you need any help,' I added as I accepted a mug of coffee from Maggie.

'Ooh, I think we'll be able to manage,' he replied with a grin, reading my mind.

'So what's a corgi fitter?' somebody asked.

'They work for the gas board. Everything you have done to your gas has to be done by a corgi fitter.'

'So what's corgis to do with it?'

'It's like canaries down a coalmine,' Brendan explained. 'Every gas fitter has a corgi in a little basket. If there's a gas leak it keels over.'

'It stands for something...something...Registered Gas Installer,' Dave informed us.

'*Council of* Registered Gas Installers,' another added. Individually we might be rubbish, but between us we know everything.

'So why did they name a dog after a company that looks for gas leaks?' Maggie asked.

'Because the Queen keeps corgis,' Brendan informed us. 'They used to be called something else, but one day there was a massive gas leak in Buckingham Palace and this brave little dog dashed into the State Room, where the Queen was about to give somebody a knighthood, and grabbed the train of her frock and started to drag her towards the door. The Queen didn't realise what it was all about and, as she just happened to be holding a sword in her hand, she chopped off the dog's head. "There, you little bugger," she told it, "that'll learn you," but then she smelt gas and realised what the dog had been trying to tell her. On the spot she decreed that they be known as corgis for ever after.'

'And she vowed never to smile again,' Jeff added.

'Oh aye. I forgot that bit.'

I shook my head and stood up.

Villains are unable to tell if a car has a Tracker device fitted, so they can't take it to a secure hideout in case it has. They just leave it at the side of the road and wait. If we don't collect it within hours they assume it's safe, and pick it up at their convenience. Jeff would have the Subaru watched all day. They didn't steal it to save a mile walk home. He'd also ask the mobiles not to stray too far away from Heckley, and ask for the chopper to be standing by with full tanks. We both had a feeling about the car, suspected it was all part of a bigger plan.

Maggie and Dave joined me in my office. They were about halfway through the Popes who lived within East Pennine division, and Leeds were similarly placed. We were having to ask neighbouring divisions to help in the trace, interview and eliminate process because we didn't have the manpower and my HMET authority cut across boundaries.

When we'd finished discussing the case Dave said: 'Did you hear about DCS Swainby?' It had been exactly a week since he dropped his bombshell at the meeting and the rumour machine had been as quiet as a dead sheep on valium.

'No.'

'Well, it appears that vice have taken an interest as his name came up in the Operation Swampland disclosures. They've found thousands of obscene images on his computer.'

Maggie said: 'Swampland? That was the paedophilia enquiry, wasn't it?'

'That's right,' Dave replied. 'They busted a major player and came up with all these names, and vice are slowly working their way through our quota.'

I remembered what Swainby had told us. 'When I saw him at his meeting he said we'd hear rumours. He asked us to give him the benefit of the doubt; claimed they were without foundation.'

'I bet he did.'

'Well I'll not be listening to them. So what are we doing?'

'More Popes,' Maggie said.

'Right. Keep at it. Any worth me doing a follow-up on?'

There were, so that's what I did, but it was a waste of time. There was a couple who had convictions for receiving stolen property, one burglar with a single conviction eight years previously and one who had defrauded the DSS of several thousand pounds until an investigator caught him on video laying a block paving drive for a neighbour. None of them appeared to be related, all had wives who gave them alibis, none knew of anybody with that name who had been away from Heckley for several years. It wasn't conclusive, but the slippers by the hearth, the half-finished ship in the bottle and the racing pigeons down on the allotment all conspired to tell me I could be better employed. Mid-afternoon I called it a day and went back to the nick. The temperature had dropped and thunder clouds were building up in the west.

Jeff was all alone there, at his desk, waiting for the phone call. He hadn't learnt that it never rings when you're waiting for it. You should immerse yourself in something fascinating, or put a pan of milk on. *Then* it rings.

'Any action?' I asked, after I'd made us both a coffee and collected two KitKats from my private stash. Before I sat down I walked over to the door and switched on the office lights. All over town people were doing the same thing, lighted windows spreading like a rash ahead of the storm.

He shook his head. 'And you?'

'Nope.'

'Perhaps we'll be lucky and have a quiet weekend.'

We both took big bites of the biscuits, and that's when the phone rang. Jeff swallowed first. 'DS Caton,' he spluttered into it as the first flurry of rain rattled against the glass.

They'd knocked over a security man delivering cash for the ATMs in the wall of the supermarket just off the town centre, and escaped with two cash boxes of money. He'd been bashed on the helmet with an iron bar, and one of the robbers may have been armed. He had something 'like a shotgun' wrapped in a plastic bag and they both wore stocking masks. They'd driven off in a dark blue saloon, possibly a Ford Escort. The standard procedure is to flee from the scene in one vehicle, which will probably be seen by witnesses, and switch to a waiting vehicle that has been left somewhere quiet, like in the middle of a housing estate. We went downstairs to the control room and the duty sergeant handed Jeff a headset.

They were amateurs, or thick. Professionals would have done the deed in the highly recognisable Subaru and had the innocuous Ford waiting nearby for their ultimate getaway. But because of its superior performance and reputation as a rally car the ringleader no doubt had romantic notions about outrunning any pursuers, but not many cars can outpace a 170mph Eurocopter or jump roadblocks.

Jeff told the cars ringing the Subaru to stand by.

'It's howling down with rain,' came the reply. 'I'm having to use my wipers, which gives the game away, somewhat. Otherwise I can't see out of the windows.'

'Blimey, we have a cloudburst,' someone added.

'It'll be the same for them,' Jeff said.

'Headlights approaching from behind. Coming past. It's a Ford Escort. Dark blue, must be them.'

'You're in control,' Jeff told the sergeant on the scene. 'Repeat: you're in control.'

'Understood.'

There was a silence as we imagined the Ford pulling in behind the parked Subaru, then: 'Roadblocks go for it. Moving in. Go! Go! Go!'

'Jesus! It's a monsoon.'

'They're legging it.'

'Which way?'

'Through the gardens.'

'Towards you.'

'We've lost them.'

'No we haven't.'

Garbled messages came through, interspersed with bursts of static as the thunderstorm passed over, followed by a long silence. We waited.

Nearly ten minutes later a voice said: 'Two suspects arrested; bringing them in,' and we breathed again.

Saturday morning we caught up with the Popes who had been unavailable through the week. I went to see one in Marsden who kept koi carp, or living jewels, as he called them. Fish should be silver and slick, I thought, not bedecked like the flag of an African republic, but he obviously disagreed. The sky was clear as I drove up there, and the moors steamed like smouldering leaves.

The would-be robbers were called Wayne Rodway and Joseph Clark, both aged twenty-two, and early Sunday morning we had to let them go. After a chase through several gardens they'd been arrested in the house of Clark's ex-wife, sitting watching *Ready Steady Cook* on TV with their hair plastered to their heads and pools of water forming around their feet. They'd been there for at least an hour, they claimed, and the ex-wife's flaxen locks nodded in confirmation.

We needed forensic evidence to put them in either of the cars, but the Subaru's doors had been left wide open and the downpour had done a decent job of sluicing out the interior. They'd worn cotton gloves, which they'd thrown off as they fled, but the masks weren't found. They must have discarded them earlier. All the money was retrieved, which was little consolation. After thirty-six hours it was muck or nettles. Jeff had to either charge them or let them go. It was no big deal. They were released on police bail but we knew where to find them and we'd be keeping an eye on their movements.

I made myself a chicken sandwich and flask of coffee and went for a walk up Signal Hill. It's about three miles to the top but I followed the canal for a while to lengthen the walk. The fishermen were out in force, their poles impossibly long as they screwed extra sections on to them, reaching out across the water to where they hoped the fish were waiting. Some nodded a hello, most were too absorbed to notice me. Mr Wood is a fisherman, but he prefers to go for salmon or trout, not what are known as coarse fish. There's a pecking order amongst anglers as with everything else. A heron flapped over, wings like barn doors, looking down in dismay at the crowded towpath. He'd probably go hungry today, I thought.

Sonia and I had jogged to the top of Signal Hill many times, when she was recovering from injury. There's a big flat rock there where she would sit cross-legged waiting for me, grinning like an urchin as I came puffing up the track. I ate my sandwiches sitting where we used to sit, facing the sun. She was in South Africa, which is more or less due south of Britain, so there's little time difference. She could have been sitting facing the same sun.

I took a circuitous route back, adding another mile or so to the walk, but as I dropped into town I realised I wasn't very far from where ex-Detective Chief Superintendent 'Bulldog' Swainby lived. I wasn't dressed for a social call but I decided to risk it.

He was in the garden, attacking a patch of grass with an electric mower. It was a detached bungalow, quite small, with overcrowded borders and a weeping cherry tree that desperately needed pruning. A *For Sale* sign stood near the gate, leaning outwards.

He turned the corner with the mower without glancing up at me. At the next pass I shouted: 'Afternoon, boss. Keeping on top of it?'

The sun was low and behind me. He looked puzzled, then shielded his eyes for a better look. Dressed in casual clothes he looked more natural, not as ugly as when wearing a suit and tie. The mower whined to a standstill and he said: 'Charlie Priest. What do you want? Come to gloat?'

'Nobody's gloating,' I replied. 'Least of all me.'

'Aren't you? You haven't heard the rumours, then.'

'I've heard them. That's all they are, aren't they? Rumours.'

'There's no smoke without fire, they say.'

'They say all sorts, Mr Swainby,' I told him, 'but most of it's bollocks. They say the early bird catches the worm, but there again, it's the second mouse that gets the cheese.'

'Mud sticks, Charlie. You'd best not be seen with me.'

I said: 'Are we going to stand here swapping parables all night, or are you going to invite me in for a cuppa? It's been a long, tiring walk.'

He pulled the cable from the mower and started to coil it round his arm, like my mother did with the washing line. 'You'd better come in then,' he replied. 'I think I've earned myself a drink.'

He took me round the back to show me the extent of the garden. The bungalow was built when people still wanted gardens, but Mr Swainby wasn't a gardener and it showed. Like me, he belonged to the *hack it down twice a year* school of agriculture. He had a compost heap the size of Snowdon and another, smaller, patch of grass, but the rest was given over to fruit growing: apple trees; raspberry canes and rhubarb. Short of paving the lot, it was his attempt to make it easy to maintain. He should have known that it's an impossibility.

We went inside, into a tiny kitchen overloaded with all the stuff of modern living: microwave; knives for carving everything; a tower of pans; racks of implements and two days' crockery in a washing-up production line. The evidence told me that there wasn't a Mrs Swainby.

'Are you on your own?' I ventured, adding: 'Like me,' as a softener.

'Wife walked out on me eleven years ago,' he replied. 'The job.'

'It's a lot to answer for.'

He found two mugs and made us coffee and we took them into his front room, where several Sunday heavies were scattered about. 'Find yourself a seat,' he told me.

I moved the business section of one of the papers to one side and sat down. It was open at the share prices page. If he'd lived as modestly as it appeared he'd be worth a few bob, not to mention his pension. 'Are you thinking of moving?' I asked.

'Thinking about it,' he replied. 'There's nothing to keep me in Heckley. I've been through all the options: Portugal; France; somewhere here but on the coast. I've a daughter in Plymouth, married a sailor. Might move nearer to them. It'd be good to see more of the grandkids.' He was quiet for a few moments, then went on, almost absentmindedly: 'I don't know if they'd mind. The kids are grown up, now.'

Another long silence, his eyes staring out of the window then flicking uneasily around the room as if looking for a subject to discuss, but finding nothing. I kept quiet, letting him decide if he wanted to talk. He scratched his arm; I took a sip of coffee. Swainby had spent almost his entire working life in a position of authority, working with some of the most recalcitrant characters you could find. The criminals he met weren't too obliging, either. He'd ruled his domain like an emperor, but overnight it had been snatched away from him, and it must have hurt. His warrant card would have been confiscated and he'd have been given ten minutes to pick up his personal belongings. We didn't strip disgraced officers of their insignia in front of the gathered ranks, but it was almost as bad. He'd have been escorted from the premises while his staff watched in disbelief, some of them shocked, others laughing up their sleeves.

'I don't think they'd mind,' he reiterated.

'Have you told your daughter that you've retired?' I asked.

'No.'

A glass-fronted drinks cabinet stood in a corner of the room, and I could see a bottle of Laphroaig inside, forward of the other bottles. On top was a photo of Swainby as a young man, proud as a turkey, taken when he'd graduated from police college. It was the only piece of memorabilia in the room.

'So what are they saying about me?' he asked.

'That they found obscene images on your computer,' I replied.

'Well that bit's true,' he admitted. 'Paedophilia, not simple pornography. The images were there, all right. They showed me them. Insisted that I look. I was horrified. Sickened. I've seen some sights in my time, Charlie, as you have, but how anybody can do that...' He let the words hang there, no doubt reliving the moment when he had to admit to the vice squad officers that they were there, on his computer.

'But you didn't download them.'

'No. Never. I can't even say that I had a look for professional reasons, or just curiosity, or stumbled on the site accidentally. I'd never been anywhere near it.'

'Was the computer new when you bought it?'

'Yes. The vice people asked me that. Brand new.'

'And nobody else had access to it?'

'No. There's just me.'

'So how do you think they got there?'

'I haven't a clue. Can you download things like that onto somebody else's computer?'

'No idea, but I wouldn't have thought so.'

I'm not proud of being computer illiterate. I've never understood people who claimed to be hopeless at mathematics, as if it were a badge of honour. It wasn't much different from being unable to read or write. But here I was, left far behind by the new technology, baffled by the basics.

'At the meeting,' I began, 'when you told us you were leaving, you said something about being foolish. What did you mean?'

He looked at me and some of the old aggression was back in his demeanour.

'You don't miss much, do you, Charlie?' he growled.

I shrugged my shoulders. 'Tell me it's none of my business...'

'No, you're right,' he said. 'Maybe I should have kept my own counsel.' He remembered the coffee he was holding, took a sip and decided it was too cold. 'Want another?' he asked, nodding towards the empty mug I was holding.

I shook my head.

'Something stronger?'

'No, not for me, thanks.'

'It's a bit early for me, too. So where was I? Oh yes, being foolish. Last February, it was. I'd been to a meeting of the so-called Community Forum, answering charges that the force was being heavy-handed in dealing with the youths who gather in the mall car park after closing. You know the sort of thing, Charlie: well-meaning people who believe that if you offer the kids the hand of friendship they'll cease behaving like feral animals and become responsible citizens. Little do they know that if you offer the hand of friendship to some of them they'll break your fingers and steal your rings. I came out with the usual but they gave me a pretty rough ride. I needed a drink afterwards and called in the Poste Chase. It's only half a mile away, and quiet in the cocktail bar. I don't like noisy places, and when it's busy some plonker always collars me and starts grumbling about traffic-calming along their street.'

'I know the feeling,' I told him.

'I bet you do. So I was just savouring my drink, starting to unwind, when this woman spoke to me…'

'Are you here for the speed dating?'

Detective Chief Superintendent Colin Swainby – 'Bulldog' to his staff – lowered his single malt and turned towards the woman who was addressing him. She was about five-foot two, whichever way you took the measurement, with bouffant peroxide hair that you could have rubbed down a fence with. Gold hung from her like Christmas decorations and her perfume was applied by a spray gun.

'I'm sorry…' he said.

'The speed dating, love. Are you here for the speed dating?'

He shook his head and glowered at her. 'I haven't a clue what you're talking about.'

'Encounters Speed Dating. Tonight is our evening for more mature clientele, better known as sugar daddy night. Isn't that why you're here?'

'Sorry love, not my scene.'

She gave him a smile like a white shark approaching a meal and moved closer. He leant backwards to escape her perfume, blinking to clear his eyes. 'I'd say it was meant for you,' she told him, looking up into his face. 'Good-looking fellow, smartly dressed, drinking alone. Don't tell me you wouldn't like to meet someone to share the good times with. Perhaps even create some good times of your own. Why don't you give us a try, eh?'

Human nature was something she knew about. She was lying like a cheap watch about his looks, but she hit the spot with the *drinking alone* comment. Since his wife left him Superintendent Swainby had immersed himself in his work, leaving as few opportunities as possible for the paralysing loneliness he felt whenever he was forced to spend time away from it. Evenings he drifted through in an alcoholic haze, Sundays were as welcome as dental appointments, holidays were ignored.

'I'm afraid I'm not much wiser,' he confessed.

'You've never heard of speed dating?'

'No. Should I have?'

'Never seen our Encounters adverts?'

''Fraid not.'

'OK. So let's educate you. Speed dating is a simple way of meeting like-minded people of the opposite sex, designed for anybody who is too busy or too shy to frequent the normal meeting places, like pubs, discos, gyms, yoga classes, what-have-you. In that room' – she pointed to a door – 'are fifteen attractive ladies just waiting to meet eligible gentlemen like yourself. If you come in you'll be given a number. I explain what happens and then you sit down at the table with your opposite number. You have three minutes to chat to her. After that time I ring a bell and you move on to the next table and the next person. And so on. You tick off on your speeding ticket the number of any person you would like to meet again. At the end of the evening you hand your ticket in and I then match up all the clients who have ticked each other. I let you know and from then on it's up to you. Want me to give you a number?'

'And presumably this will cost me,' Swainby stated.

'Of course. It's £24.99. Cheap at half the price, as we say. You don't have to meet anybody again if you don't want. It's not heavy. We have regular clients who come along just for a chat and a fun evening out.'

You mean ugly sods like me, he thought, who couldn't pull in a Thai brothel. 'I'm sorry, but I don't think I'll bother.'

'OK. Special introductory offer. Twelve pounds only to you, but don't let on to the others.'

'It's still no thanks.'

'What's your name?'

'My name?'

'Yes.'

He almost had to think about it. He hadn't been addressed by his first name since his wife left him. 'Um, Colin.'

'Right, Colin. First of all, I think speed dating is meant for you. I really mean that. Secondly, we're a bit short of men, tonight. Women throw themselves into it, but men take a little persuading, which is a win-win situation for the men. How about if I let you in for free, this time, to help make up the numbers? I can afford to do that because I just know you'll want to come back again, but next time it'll be full price. What do you say to that, Colin?'

His natural cynicism was yelling 'No!' to him, but something inside was telling him that it might be an interesting experience, and his daughter was constantly nagging him to make more effort to meet people. 'Well, that sounds very generous,' he replied.

The woman detected the uncertainty in his reply and latched onto it. 'So pick up your drink, Colin, and come with me.' She took him by the elbow and steered him towards the door, and Detective Chief Superintendent Colin 'Bulldog'

Swainby, holder of the Queen's Police Medal, one-time scourge of the IRA, felt himself being propelled towards the Encounters speed dating sugar daddies meeting. It would change his life, but not in any way he could have predicted.

His number was eight, but there were fifteen women of assorted appearance and age. Good odds, he thought, as he slowly warmed to his plight. The men were a mixed bunch. The first one who acknowledged him as he was led to the bar was elderly but fit looking, with a complexion that owed more to *Clinique* than natural weathering. Swainby could imagine him on a cruise liner, employed to dance with the wallflowers. Another, sporting stubble, jeans and a leather jacket, could have been a barrister or an unemployed bricklayer. These days, he thought, it was hard to place a person. He finished his whisky and ordered a half of lager.

The hostess and sole-trader manageress of Encounters rang a little bell and gave a welcoming speech, explaining the rules as she had done earlier and apologising for the shortage of male members. 'But,' she hastily added, 'the quality is as high as ever, ladies, so let's see you all enjoying yourselves.' She rang the bell again and the business of the evening began.

Swainby had already noticed where the number eight female was sitting, all alone at a little table. She was about half his age and as unprepossessing as he was, but he didn't hold that against her.

'Hello,' he began, pulling the chair out from under the table and lowering himself onto it. 'I'm called Colin, and you are...' he leant forward to read the name on her badge.

'Davina,' she replied, 'but everybody calls me Vina.'

I bet, he thought. 'I've never done this before,' he began. 'I only came in for a quiet drink, but madam collared me in the bar and here I am. I'd have practised some chat-up lines if I'd known.'

'You'll soon get the hang of it. I found it a bit scary the first time I came. What do you do for a living?'

Policemen are supposed to have an ability to hold someone in conversation and learn everything about them without giving away anything about themselves. He'd established that she was a regular, which was no surprise, but now she had taken the initiative. He decided to have some fun.

'I'm a slaughterhouse manager,' he replied. 'What do you do?'

'I'm a supervisor at a care home.'

'That sounds interesting. Does it pay well?'

'Not really, but we do meet some interesting people. Last year Mollie Turnbridge came to open our new day room.'

'Really!' The *slaughterhouse manager* had gone in one ear and out the other without meeting any intervening brain, and he'd never heard of Mollie Turnbridge. 'And what about speed dating? Do you meet any interesting people here?'

After Davina it was two sisters who only came for a laugh, they said. He thought it was an expensive laugh but eventually concluded that one of them was married to a thicko and was looking for a way out. He said he was a refuse collector and they lost interest in him. The bell rang and he gratefully moved on.

This time the woman was sensible and more circumspect in her conversation. She was a widow and, like him, had never been speed dating before. Swainby said he was a paint salesman, and he thought that perhaps at the end of the evening he might be tempted to tick her number on his speeding ticket. Long experience had taught him never to admit to being a cop. He gave a rare smile and realised that he was enjoying himself more than he'd done for a long time, away from the job.

After her it was two more desperate Dollies, and he became an inspector of council litter bins and chief pilot for a company that supplied wing-walkers for air shows and charity events. They were unimpressed. The bell rang and he looked round for number fourteen. This time, he thought, he'd be a consultant brain surgeon. After that there would be number fifteen, then one to seven to get through before he could go home for a decent drink. It had been an interesting experience, but he should have followed his instincts and fled when he had the chance.

Fourteen was sitting in a corner, with her back to the room. He edged round the table, checking the number on her badge, and twisted the chair opposite her so he could sit down. When he was comfortable he said: 'Hello, I'm called Colin,' and looked into her face for the first time. The ceiling fell in on him.

'Hello Colin,' she said, with a smile that jolted his chest like a defibrillator. 'I'm called Teri. How are you?' She was small and dark, with short hair and the biggest eyes he'd ever seen. Her dress was brown and clingy, and never had a brown dress looked so perfect.

'Um, I'm fine, just fine. I, um...' he dried up, like a bad actor in a village play.

'You what?' Teri encouraged.

'Oh, I'm not sure. It's just that...'

'Just that what?'

What the heck, he thought. Let's cut the bullshit for once. 'It's just that I didn't expect to meet anyone so attractive. I can't imagine what you're doing here. I thought it was only for ugly old so-and-sos like me.'

'You're not ugly or old,' she protested, tipping her head to one side and gazing intently into his eyes. Her lips were full and reminded him of strawberries. 'You're distinguished, and interesting. I'd say you've had an exciting life. It's written in your face.'

'I suppose you could say that,' he agreed.

'So what do you do for a living?'

'I'm a cop,' he confessed without hesitation. 'A policeman. Detective chief superintendent, responsible for criminal investigations. I chase murderers.'

It was his best line, and this time it was true.

For once the bell came too soon. After Teri, fifteen came and went without making any impact on him and the others went by in a blur. When the bell rang for the final time he said a hasty goodnight to the ex-model and dancer with the Fifth Generation who reminded him of Marge Simpson and looked round for Teri, but she'd left earlier, when the male numbers ran out.

Madam gave a little farewell talk, told them to hand in their speeding tickets and wished everybody a safe journey home. As he passed her at the door she asked if he'd enjoyed himself.

'Surprisingly, yes,' he replied.

'So have you marked your ticket?'

'No, I don't think so.'

'What,' madam demanded. 'Nobody at all you'd like to meet again?'

'I don't think so.'

'Go on, be a devil. You never know, it might be your lucky night.'

'Oh, if you insist,' he said, pulling the ticket from his top pocket. She handed him a pen and he studied the numbers. The likeable widow had been number eleven, he remembered. The pen hovered, then drew a firm, deliberate tick in the box. Next to number fourteen. Just so there could be no confusion he wrote 'Teri' against it, in brackets. Madam gave him a conspiratorial smile and placed the ticket in an envelope with all the others.

'And you reckon that's how it all started?' I asked.

'It must be,' the ex-DCS replied.

I was lounging in an easy chair, a glass of his lager in my hand. He was on the settee with a Laphroaig big enough to anaesthetise a buffalo. I couldn't see why he was so certain, but I left it for the time being. I said: 'And what happened next?'

'The organiser woman emailed me the next day to say three women wanted to meet me again, and one of them was number fourteen, Teri. Number eleven, the widow woman, wasn't amongst them. I was amazed, Charlie, amazed. First of all, that there were three of them, but mainly because Teri had put me down. She's a stunner, Charlie, a stunner. One of those women you see every once in a while who takes your breath away. She had this glow to her, and her eyes...' He stopped, drowning in her eyes, then said: 'How does it go: there's no fool like an old fool. Is that it?'

'That's it, boss,' I said. 'But what's wrong with making a fool of yourself now and again? I do it all the time. Presumably you emailed her to make contact.'

'No. I did nothing. I dismissed the other two because I couldn't remember who they were and most of the women there were no-hopers. They probably ticked every box. As for Teri...I thought she was just being kind, or had made a mistake. She's probably about thirty years younger than me, and, well, it's a big gap. I have no illusions about young women finding me attractive. I thought warm thoughts about her and tried to forget we'd ever met.'

I still didn't understand. It didn't make sense. I said: 'So how do you make a connection between her and the stuff on your computer?'

He took a long sip of the Isle of Islay's finest export, then told me: 'Three weeks later I found an email from her waiting for me. Gave me a phone number. Said she was separated from her husband and had been trying for a reconciliation, but it wasn't working. She told me what time to ring and said she'd like to meet me again. Said I was...'

'Go on.'

'Said I was a rock, and she wanted some stability in her life. Not what I'd hoped for, Charlie, but I'd settle for it. I rang her and we met for lunch.'

'Was she everything you remembered?'

'And more. As well as being gorgeous she was funny and intelligent. We talked about everything. I got the impression that she and her husband are quite rich. She's travelled a lot, spent holidays on yachts off Cannes and places like that. Best I could do was boast about murder cases, most of which I'd had nothing to do with. I probably stole some of your thunder, there, I'm afraid.'

'Be my guest,' I said. 'So did she have access to your computer?'

'I don't know, I'm a novice with them,' he admitted. 'We once looked up some theatre times on it, but that's about all. Could she have learnt anything from that?'

'I wouldn't have thought so. She obviously knew your email address.'

'That's right.'

'What about somebody breaking into the house and using your computer?' Keep it simple; that's my motto. 'Have there been any signs of that?'

'No. I went over that with vice. I've a burglar alarm and decent locks everywhere. Nobody's been in.'

'OK, so it's back to the computer. Did she ever send you any attachments?'

'Just the once. No, twice.'

'Did you open them?'

'She said they were photographs of her. What do you think?'

'Do you have a copy?'

'No. I never ran one off, and vice have the disk now. And the computer. They've promised to search for viruses, but haven't come back to me. I'm not holding my breath. They've screwed the most unpopular DCS in the division, so it's grins and handshakes all round.'

'I'll have a word with someone,' I told him. 'See what she could possibly have done. Is there anything else I should know?'

'Don't go to vice,' he insisted. 'I don't want that lot gloating over me any more.'

'Don't worry, I have my own experts, but I'm still not convinced it was her. How do you know it wasn't some disgruntled bobby you've sent down the river taking his revenge on you? I hate to be the one to tell you this, but you've never shied from making enemies.'

'I hear what you're saying, but I'm still convinced she's behind it. Let's be honest: she didn't go out with me for my good looks or my sparkling banter, did she? So why did she go out with me, eh? Did somebody put her up to it? My private email address is known only to the family, and Teri, of course, and since the problem came to light she's vanished from my life. The mobile number she gave me is no longer recognised. We didn't fall out, or anything, she just didn't turn up, one evening.'

'No blackmail threats?'

'No, not yet.'

'But you think there might be?'

'I think that was the intention, originally, or perhaps somebody was out to discredit me. Like you said, I have enemies, inside and outside the force. We're cops, Charlie, and like to think we can read people. All the time I was with her there was something false about her, as if she were acting a part. I didn't mind – I was acting one myself.'

'It was an acceptable risk.'

'Highly acceptable.'

'OK, let's say she's the one. Anything else?'

There wasn't, so we shook hands and I thanked him for the lager. My legs had stiffened up and I was still nearly three miles from home. I wondered if buses ran on Sundays, but it was unlikely, so I pointed myself in the right direction and strode out.

Wayne Rodway and Joseph Clark coshed the deliveryman outside a busy supermarket, in broad daylight, and there were no eyewitnesses that were worthy of the title. Plenty of people watched the action unfold, nobody could describe the villains or thought they might recognise them again. The consensus was that they were of average height and build, wore jeans, dark tops and stocking masks. A blind woman, walking with a white stick, had blundered into the action and been pushed to the ground.

'It's slipping away, Chas,' Jeff Caton admitted, Monday morning. 'They're going to walk if forensics don't come up with something to link them to the cars.'

'And they'd be crowing like bantam cocks if they had found anything. What's your next move?'

'Apart from slashing my wrists? I'll have them in again, create some smoke and fog. I'd say Rodway was the instigator, and Clark is the weak link. We might be able to turn him against Rodway.'

'It's worth a try. What about the blind lady? Is she OK?'

'Yeah, she's as hard as nails. I've sent Serena to have a chat with her, make her feel we care.'

'Which, of course, we do.'

'Of course we do.'

Dave lumbered across to join us, steaming mug attached to his hand. 'Hi, Pancho,' I said. 'Where are we with the Popes?'

'Maggie's gone to see the last local one. Then we make the next tack.'

'I haven't got another tack to make,' I confessed.

'Well you'd better think of one.'

I sauntered over to my little office in the corner and opened the window. There was the usual pile of papers in the *In* basket: mainly policy documents; minutes of meetings and notification of amendments to various sub clauses and paragraphs. All really, really interesting stuff. I riffled through it, ticked against my name on the distribution lists and dumped the lot in my *Out* basket.

One sheet of paper was left, sitting there like orphan Annie. It was a message note, timed at Saturday morning and addressed to me. We'd circulated every division of every force, asking them to look at their Popes, and Greater Manchester J division had come up trumps. George Pope was fifty-eight years old, had done time for ABH and supplying a class C drug, and, much to our delight, had lived in Australia for several years, returning to England in 2001. I rang my opposite number in Stockport and he agreed to invite Pope in for a chat. He rang me back within minutes, saying that our man would see me at home. I told Dave to drop what he was doing and we drove over the tops into bandit country.

We went in Dave's car because he has satellite navigation, and you need all the help you can get, over there. On the way I said: 'Do you mind if I ring Danny sometime for some information about computers?' Danny is his son, and my tame expert on such matters.

'Help yourself, and don't let him charge you.'

'Isn't he at college?'

'In August?'

'Of course not.' I looked at my watch. It was nearly eleven. 'Will he still be in bed?'

'Probably. Give him a wakeup call.'

I dialled him on his mobile, thinking that he probably kept it under his pillow, and he answered within seconds. 'It's your uncle Charlie,' I said. 'I want to tap into your extensive brain power and draw upon your inestimable knowledge of computers.'

'Hi Charlie,' he replied. 'No problem, but it'll cost you.'

'Normal rates?'

'Minimum wage.'

'OK.'

'I'm eighteen now, so it's gone up.'

'Fair enough.'

'One hour minimum charge.'

'Right,' I told him. 'But there is one thing.'

'What's that?'

'If this is a strictly business relationship you call me Mr Priest, not Charlie.'

'OK, Mr Priest, what do you want to know?'

'There's this policeman,' I began, 'who's in trouble because some, er, rude images have been found on his computer...'

'Paedophilia?' Danny wondered.

'Um, yes, paedophilia. He says they were planted and he knows nothing about them.'

'Well he would, wouldn't he?'

'Perhaps, but let's suppose that he was telling the truth. Could an outsider download images like that onto his computer?' *Download* is about as technical as I get.

'Is it you?' he asked.

'No, it's not me. Can it be done?'

'It's possible, if you know what you're doing. Presumably the sender would want to stay anonymous.'

'I imagine so.'

'In that case they'd have to use a public IP address.'

'You mean like an internet café?'

'No, like AOL or Virgin or Freeserve.'

'I see. Go on.'

'Then you'd send him an email with an attachment that's important or interesting enough for him to open. The attachment contains a Trojan horse virus which starts working as soon as the attachment is opened. It uploads the dirty pictures onto your friend's hard disk and hides them somewhere really obscure, amongst his files. You then send him another email to uninstall the Trojan. The Trojan vanishes but the uploaded files stay.'

'What if the cop's computer has virus protection?' I ventured, as if I'd understood everything I'd heard.

'It wouldn't recognise the Trojan, first shot, and you'd be in and out before it registered. It would be as good as impossible to detect.'

I said: 'So he could be telling the truth.'

'Yep, he could be.'

'Thanks, Danny. I'll mention you in despatches.'

'So is it you?'

'No! It's not!'

'I'll believe you.'

'Thanks for your help.'

'You're welcome, Charlie. I'll send you a bill.'

'He's a bright lad,' I told Dave as I slipped the phone back into my jacket pocket.

'He gets it from me. We're here. What's the number?'

CHAPTER EIGHT

The reason Pope wanted to see us at home and not at his local nick was because he was decorating. The house was in the middle of a long row, with a small garden at the front and plastic window units that were out of character with the Victorian terrace.

He wiped his hands on a J-cloth and led us through the front room with its bare walls, dust-sheeted furniture and smell of paint. In the kitchen he asked if we'd like a coffee, but we declined.

I let Dave do the talking. Gradually we learnt that Pope had emigrated to Australia back in the Eighties and had returned to England four years ago. He was suffering from heart problems, he said, and couldn't afford the medical bills over there.

Dave developed a sudden interest in DIY and soon had Pope swapping hints about property development with him. If it counted as your main dwelling place, we learnt, you could sell without incurring capital gains tax, as long as you kept it down to one per year. He'd worked, he told us, as a roofing contractor, but was now retired due to ill health.

He'd never heard of Magdalena, never been to Headingley and had only visited Leeds when Manchester City played United, back in God-knows-when. He'd seen the match but not much of the town because he'd kept his head down to dodge the missiles bouncing off the coach windows. On the weekend Magda died he'd drunk himself rat-arsed on Fosters and Blue Mountain Shiraz; a habit he'd developed in the Antipodes.

It wasn't a completely wasted journey. We stopped at my favourite truckers' café just off the M62 and had steak and kidney pie. The café should have died when the motorway opened, but quality sells, and now the clientele are more likely to be pensioners from Blackburn, Burnley or Bradford than lorry drivers on the Liverpool – Hull run. Dave wiped his chin on a napkin and rang his wife, told her he'd eaten.

'So what do you think?' I asked as he watched me tuck into a portion of apple pie and custard.

'I think that if I ate as much as you do I'd weigh a ton.'

'I burn it off; nervous energy,' I explained. 'It's a curse. I have to keep eating to keep my blood sugar level up. You don't know how lucky you are, having a weight problem.'

'I think Mr Pope has a cushy carry-on,' Dave reckoned, coming back to the subject. 'He's almost certainly on the pancrack, sells his house every year or two for a nice profit, after making a few modifications to bring it up to date. Nothing too strenuous, just a bit here and there, while living on the job. I think I could manage that.'

'You couldn't knock a nail in straight.'

'I can. I got a C in woodwork.'

'Did you? I thought it was religious instruction. C'mon, take me back.'

In the car I reclined my seat and closed my eyes. Dave said: 'Blood sugar level troubling you?'

'Something like that,' I replied. I was thinking about being a roofing contractor in Australia. The weather was hot, but you were on the roof of someone's bungalow, in the breeze, wearing shorts and stripped to the waist. It sounded fun. Then you come to Lancashire, where the ancient houses are three storeys high and the wind whips across them and eats into your bones like a gnawing rat. It was no contest, medical bills or no medical bills. Didn't Australia have a National Health Service? I'd check it out, but for now, Georgie Pope was still in the frame.

Serena, one of my DCs, was in the foyer as we entered, and she fell in step with me as we climbed the stairs.

'Did you go and see the blind lady?' I asked. She was working on the hold-up, with Jeff Caton.

Serena smiled as only she can. 'Yes, boss. And guess what? She says she can recognise the man who pushed her to the ground.'

'Can she? So is she only partially sighted?'

'No, she's as blind as a bat, but she says she would recognise his voice again.'

'Oh. So what does Jeff say to that?'

'He says it's worth bearing in mind, but not enough on its own.'

I hung my jacket behind the door and looked at the fresh pile of paper in my *In* basket. There was a conspiracy to swamp me in paperwork; I was sure of it. One day, deep inside the pile, there'd be something incriminating. I'd miss it, and the next thing I knew would be the rubber heel boys lifting me off my chair and throwing me out of the front door. It reminded me of the paedophilia, hidden deep in the folders on Superintendent Swainby's computer.

Jeff came in and I confessed to him that I'd quizzed Serena about the blind woman. 'You're the boss,' he conceded. 'Apparently she told Serena that the person who knocked her over shouted "Get out of the effing way" at her in a green voice. Except he didn't say effing.'

'A green voice?'

'That's what she reckoned.'

That thought triggered off images of Wassily Kandinsky and his paintings. He claimed that he saw musical notes as colours. 'Am I right in believing it's the gala on Sunday?' I asked.

'It is,' he confirmed.

'Crikey. I'd better do some work tonight, then.'

'Are you putting something in again?'

'If they're dry in time. It wouldn't be the same without my contributions.'

I made a coffee, took it into my office and dialled a number. I was about to put the phone down when Len Atkins answered.

'It's DI Priest from Heckley CID, Mr Atkins,' I said. When I was sure he remembered who I was I went on: 'Did Magdalena ever mention anyone in Australia that she knew?'

He said: 'No, never.'

'Did she ever express a desire to go there?'

'No, not to me.'

'Did Angela ever mention it? Did she ever threaten to join her dad in Oz, anything like that?'

'No.'

'OK, Mr Atkins. Thanks for your time. I'll keep you informed.'

Next I rang ex-DCS Colin Swainby. 'It's Charlie Priest,' I began. 'Just a quick question. Did the young woman – Teri, was it – did she have a knowledge of computers? Not just a bit on how to use them. Did she know about software and viruses, that sort of thing?'

'No, I doubt it. She was a hairdresser, once upon a time, and eventually owned a small chain of beauty salons. I doubt if she knew one end of one from the other.'

'Ne'er mind,' I said, 'it was just a thought.'

'Except...' he began.

'Except what?' I encouraged.

'Except...I think her husband might have been au fait with them. He was something in IT, she told me. That's computers, isn't it?'

'Yes. It is.'

'What have you found out, Charlie? Could someone have put those images on my hard disk?'

'According to my information, yes they could, using something called a Trojan horse virus. It would be undetectable.'

'So that's it, then. The husband...'

'It's a strong possibility.'

Swainby started to laugh. I thought he was choking, at first, then I realised he was laughing. It was an admission that he'd been well and truly caught. 'That's perfect,' he said. 'Just perfect. He stitched me up, good and proper.'

'It's probably illegal,' I said. 'There are laws about these things.'

'No, I'll take my medicine, Charlie. At least I'll have something to tell people, now. Those I want to tell. She told me they were separated, but obviously he didn't think so. Thanks for your trouble, Charlie. I feel better about it, now, knowing that there's a plausible explanation.'

'Enjoy your retirement.'

'I think I will.'

Having Swainby off my back rejuvenated me, and for once I didn't hang about in the office. I collected the frames for my pictures from the PC who made them and went home. They always look better with a frame, no matter how simple. I fitted them loosely and studied the finished works for about ten minutes while I ate a bowl of tinned pears. The organiser of the gala had rung me to confirm I'd be entering, and had asked what the pictures would be called, for the programme. I usually say: 'Untitled One and Untitled Two,' but he asked me to call them something more interesting.

Dylan was singing on the music system, all about his 'Visions of Johanna'. The paintings lacked something, I decided. A motif, or a cipher, to lift them, provide a theme, and link them together. The words of the song provided it. I scratched a hint of an electricity pylon into the still-wet paint of one of the pictures and painted a short row of them, green on red, on the second one. That was it. They were finished. Titles: *The Ghost of Electricity, One* and *Two*. Being metaphysical is easy once you realise it's ninety per cent balderdash.

I was sealing the backs of the pictures with masking tape when it came to me. Synaesthesia. That's the medical condition of seeing colours associated with sounds. I rang Jeff Caton and spelt it out to him before it fled from my memory again. He said he'd check it out on the Internet.

The Magdalena enquiry wouldn't go away. We looked for the tattooist but drew a blank, and started tracking down the student population who lived in the vicinity. This meant talking to their landlords and asking for a forwarding address, which would be the parents in the majority of cases. Most of the landlords were helpful, some were downright liars who were abusing the system. Not a few of the students had told their parents they were staying on for a variety of reasons, but were nowhere to be found. The ones we did locate were scattered far and wide. We forwarded pictures of Magda to the local forces and asked them to do the interview. It was a waste of time: one of the most distinctive characters of my era had become the Invisible Woman.

So we went national, and my drawing of her was shown on *Crimewatch*. Nineteen people rang in to say they'd seen her, of whom sixteen were evenly spread throughout the country but three were in a cluster around Pontefract. We were in business, or so we thought.

Dave and I made the drive and spoke to the Ponte Three. One had a stall in the market selling pet food and the woman she'd seen on television was a regular customer, buying food for a dog and a parrot, but she hadn't been in for at least a fortnight. Number two had seen her in town, whilst shopping, but couldn't add anything to that. Number three was a bus driver. The woman, he told us, caught his bus once per week into Pontefract to do her shopping. She got on and off at Little Smeaton, but he hadn't seen her for a couple of weeks. Buses to and from Little Smeaton were about as regular as solar eclipses, so it looked as if she'd changed her routine. We hotfooted to the village.

The first door we knocked at and showed the drawing elicited a shake of the head. The second and third pointed down the main street, the fourth one said: 'Next house down.'

Dave knocked and we waited, looking up at the windows, peering round the side of the house, listening for noises. The grass in the lawn was just a little too long, the windows grubby and a vase of flowers in the downstairs window was long past its best. It was beginning to look as if we'd found Magdalena's last place of residence.

I knocked again while Dave walked round the back to see if any windows were open. Breaking the door down seemed unnecessary but we needed to be inside.

'I wonder if any of the neighbours have a key,' I said.

'I doubt it,' Dave replied.

'Haven't you one of those sneaky little implements in your pocket that will unfasten any lock devised by man?' I asked.

'You've been watching too much TV.'

'Let's talk to the immediate neighbours,' I suggested. 'See what they can tell us.'

'If this were one of the Gaitskell Heights flats you'd have had the door kicked in by now.'

'No, I wouldn't.' I lifted the brass knocker one last time and rat-tat-tatted it against the door while Dave leant on the bell-push.

A voice inside said: 'All right, all right, I'm coming.'

I looked at Dave and we pulled approving faces at each other. A bolt slid back, a key turned and the door opened. Dave had delved into his pocket for his ID and he was already holding it at arm's length as the woman appeared before us.

'I'm DC Sparkington and this is...' His words trailed off. She was about sixty, with a pleasant, rounded face and greying hair that hung in a thick ponytail down the front of the dressing gown she was wearing, almost all the way to her waist. She could have been Magda's sister.

'...DI Priest,' I said, finishing Dave's introduction and producing my own ID. 'Heckley CID. We're sorry to trouble you but do you mind if we come in for a talk?'

We should have known it was too good to be true. Her son was a session musician in America, and he'd had a contract in New York so she'd flown out to spend two weeks with him, doing the shows. We'd awakened her from twelve hours' jetlag-induced sleep. I told her about Magdalena and why we were there, but she couldn't help us. We had a cup of tea with her, proffered our thanks and apologies, and drove back to Heckley.

'Ask the local forces to talk to the other sixteen?' Dave suggested as he pulled into the yard.

'Can't think of anything else, squire,' I replied, 'unless you fancy driving the length and breadth of the land and talking to them yourself.'

'No, we'll let them do it. What about the serious crime whatsit at Bramshill?'

'I've asked Brendan to prepare a résumé for them.'

'Sorry Chas. I'm not trying to tell you your job.'

I gave him a sideways look as I released my seatbelt. 'That's OK, David. You keep me on my toes.'

Jeff Caton was itching to speak to me. 'It's looking good, Charlie,' he enthused, in my office a few minutes later. 'Apparently this synaesthesia is a pukka-gen complaint, except it's not a complaint at all. Mrs Dolan – the blind lady – assures me she can pick him out from his voice. She said he has a green voice, with a bit of brown round the edges.'

'What colour voice did she say you have?' I asked.

'I didn't ask.'

'Come off it. What did she say?'

'Um, I'm not telling you.'

'Go on. I won't laugh.'

'She said I'm pink.'

'Ah ah! That's what I'd have said. So what's happening?'

'I've had a word with CPS,' he told me, 'and they've spoken with Rodway and Clark's solicitors. They think we're mad and would be laughed out of court.'

'Which is what we want them to think.'

'Exactly. They're happy to go ahead, if it's all done properly, and I've fixed it up for eleven a.m. Monday morning, if that's OK?'

'It's fine by me, but let's discuss the best way of doing it.'

We decided to run it like a normal identity parade, with extra safeguards. We'd supply four voices, the defence could provide another four if they wished, and we'd make it up to a dozen by inviting two in off the street, like we used to do. I went with Jeff to see Mrs Dolan and she was delighted that we were taking notice of her at last. I told her about Kandinsky and she said that Jimi Hendrix was a synaesthete, too. Apparently his Purple Haze was so-named because that's what he saw when he played the chords. She was a small, attractive woman, with a happy smile that radiated warmth you could almost feel, and lived in a specially adapted ground-floor flat in a sheltered complex near the town centre. She worked part-time at the supermarket, and found her way there and home again with only the help of a white stick. Although she'd been roughly handled and knocked to the ground she thought blundering into the robbery was a hoot.

That night ex-DCS Swainby rang me at home. He didn't apologise for the late hour but he did introduce himself as Colin Swainby, which was a first.

'What's the problem?' I asked, thinking I'd seen and heard the last of him.

'He's not satisfied, Charlie,' he began. 'He's not satisfied with losing me my job – the bastard's twisting the knife, now.'

'In what way?'

'I just had a phone call from the deputy editor of *Britain 2000*. He wanted to know if it was true that I'd resigned to escape prosecution for having indecent images on my computer. He said they'd be running an article next week but wanted to offer me the chance to give my side of the story.'

Britain 2000 is a weekly rag that usually promotes raving right-wing views, but isn't averse to taking a swing at the police when it suits them, and everybody, just everybody, hates a paedophile. Castration is *Britain 2000*'s way of dealing with that little problem.

'That's big of him. I don't suppose he said where the story came from.'

'I asked, but he wouldn't say. A source, that's all.'

'I'm not sure how I can help, Mr Swainby,' I said. I'd done what I could and as far as I was concerned he was on his own. I believed him, but he'd been the ruin of many an officer's career, including plenty of innocent ones. Now he knew how it felt. 'Your first step is probably to take out an injunction against them publishing.'

'I will, first thing in the morning, but it will only be an interim. I was just wondering if you had any other suggestions.'

'Confess to the affair,' I told him, 'and lay it on about the jealous husband and his knowledge of IT. That's about all you can do, I'd say. Some will believe you and some won't. You won't come out of it lily white, but nobody cares about extra-marital affairs, these days. These days you're the odd-man-out if you're not having one. Call it damage limitation.'

'And what if they took it to court? In today's climate nobody would believe me and they'd be free to print what they wanted. I could face prosecution. If it went to the CPS they'd be over-eager to appear fair and even-handed. They'd love to put me in the dock.'

'Yeah, you're right. In that case, boss, all I can suggest is having a word with the NARPO rep and asking them to recommend a solicitor.'

'I'm not a member.'

'Well you'd better join.'

'I suppose so. I'll keep you informed.'

Thanks a bunch, I thought, as I replaced the receiver. For once, I'd have preferred being kept in the dark, and I hoped I'd heard the last of him. I'd enough to worry about without taking on his problems.

'Do you remember old Leach's dog?' Tristan Foyle asked, laughing so much he almost spilt his drink.

'You mean the first time or the second?' Richard Wentbridge wondered.

'Oh, God, not the dog again,' his wife protested.

'I'd forgotten all about the first time,' Tristan said. 'That was somebody else's show, though. Not ours.'

They were seated in an alcove at the Wool Exchange restaurant, favoured haunt of Heckley's wealthy locals, visiting pop stars and footballers, and the TV crews that proliferate in the southern Dales. They'd dined well, paid the bill and Richard had asked a waiter to order a taxi for them.

'It was a good stunt, though,' Richard admitted.

'What happened?' Tristan's wife, Fiona, asked. She'd heard the story a dozen times before but her attention span rivalled that of a tadpole and she found it fresh and funny with every telling. It was Saturday night, and she was looking forward to finishing the evening with a snort of coke and rough sex with her best friend's husband, as they had done every weekend for several years. To her, all else was filling in time. She stroked the back of Richard's hand as it rested on her thigh, and smiled at his wife.

'Old Leachy took us for Latin,' Tristan began.

'Greek,' Richard corrected him.

'Was it? They were all fucking Greek to me.' He laughed again and burped. 'Anyway, old Leachy had this little dog. Horrible thing it was, fat as a barrel, always scrounging food. We used to sneak stuff out for it and it would eat everything and anything. Then, about once a week, we'd give it a load of laxative chocolate and it'd be crapping all over the place, inside and out. The stair used to stink of dogshit and disinfectant.'

'I thought you drowned it,' Fiona stated, her voice tinged with disappointment. The dog-drowning story was her favourite.

'That was later, after we started the Moonlighters Climbing Club. One night we'd been up the South Tower. Hillary

Stoneleigh-Palmer was leading. He's a friggin' neurosurgeon at St Bart's, now. Anyhow, the clumsy sod dislodged this bloody great gargoyle and it fell to the ground. It was like a force seven earthquake going off. The whole place shook. Nobody came, so we climbed down and wondered what to do with the gargoyle. It was a griffon's head; something mythical like that, except it was as real as anything could be. We decided to dump it in the fountain and hope nobody would notice it was missing. So we lugged it across the lawns and were just about to roll it into the water when Leach's bloody dog arrived on the scene, wagging its tail and hoping for food, scaring the living daylights out of us. Without a second's hesitation Stoneleigh-Palmer hooked its collar over one of the griffon's ears and rolled them both into the water. It never made a sound. Just a *plop*, and that was that. We thought we were safe, but things looked different in the cold light of day. We'd left a trail of footprints from the tower to the fountain and to our stair and there was a bloody great hole where the gargoyle should have been. Old Leach blamed me and gave me six of the best. Then he added four more because I didn't admit it. I tell you, he laid them on with all the venom he could muster. I couldn't sit down for a week.'

He stopped talking, the memory of those cane strokes almost as painful as the real thing had been.

'But we got our own back, didn't we, Trist?'

'Oh, yes, Ricko old boy, we got our own back.'

'And the game was born.'

'Yes, the game.'

Teri said: 'But you were expelled.'

'I was,' Tristan admitted. 'But it was a relief. Best thing that happened to me. What about you, Teri? You were playing the game before we met you.' He reached across the table with the wine bottle and poured the last few drops into her glass.

'I suppose I was,' she agreed. She'd been seventeen, making her way in a tough business, and had just started a sexual relationship with a potential business partner. Except that when he met one of Teri's trainee beautician colleagues he decided to pursue her, too. Teri realised she was being exploited and the business deal was going down the pan so she casually remarked to him that Debra, the girl he was hoping to seduce, was upset because she'd been told that she could never have children. To Debra she confided that Guy, the wayward partner, had been rendered sterile by a dose of shingles.

'The twins will be, what, ten or eleven years old, now,' she told them as she finished her story. 'Another six and he might be able to stop paying child maintenance.'

A waiter caught Tristan's eye and indicated that their taxi had arrived. As they filed out he said to Richard: 'We haven't talked about your schoolmistress friend, yet. Have you thought any more about her?'

'You bet,' Richard told him. 'I saw her last Tuesday for a quick drink, just keeping up the acquaintance sort of thing. I've worked it all out. I'll give you the nitty-gritty at home, but keep next Thursday free. It's her birthday, and I'm planning a little surprise for her.'

CHAPTER NINE

I definitely need less sleep than I used to. I've always been an early riser, but when you have a blackbird in the garden that greets each new dawn with a fanfare to rival anything Aaron Copland wrote, plus a family of collared doves in the rhythm section, sleep is difficult to achieve. Add the bloke down the street who works Sundays and has a dodgy exhaust, and difficult becomes impossible. Never mind: like I said, I don't need much sleep.

I pulled on jeans and shirt and opened the curtains. The sun was shining and had driven away the morning mist. It looked like being a scorcher, which was good news for the organisers of the gala. I breakfasted on flakes and banana, with copious tea, and loaded the paintings into the car. A tentative touch with a finger told that they were dry enough. They looked good in the bright sunlight. I was pleased with them. I'd suggest a price of about £50 and donate any proceeds to the Lord Mayor's appeal. If they didn't sell I'd hang them in the hallway and probably paint over them for next year's show. They usually sold. £50 isn't much to ask for a modern masterpiece.

At ten o'clock I drove to the showground and off-loaded them. A woman I'd seen before was taking a collection out of a battered transit and arranging them on the scaffolding erected to display the paintings. I left mine in the hands of the organiser, who said words of approval when she saw them. She gave me a programme and I drove into town. Sainsbury's do a decent brunch, so I had one to set me up for the day, and I called in the nick to tidy up a few loose ends.

When I was up to date with the reports I pulled the programme from my pocket and looked for the important bit. There I was. It said:

THE GHOST OF ELECTRICITY ONE   C Priest
THE GHOST OF ELECTRICITY TWO   C Priest

Fame at last. I looked down the list of entries and saw all the usual suspects. One or two of them do cracking watercolours; a sergeant at HQ specialises in Western art, all injuns and horses; a PC does portraits of rock musicians and another does pencil drawings of old street scenes. I'm always amazed by how much talent there is, where you don't expect it. Another list was new. The Association for Prisoners' Art was there in force, with twelve exhibits by unnamed artists. I'd look forward to seeing them but knew what to expect: crucifixion scenes and pictures of Mum.

I had a snooze at my desk, luxuriating in the familiarity of my own domain while nobody else was there and the phones were silent, then went downstairs to chat to the duty sergeant for half an hour. When we'd put the force to rights I went back to the gala.

The horses were being paraded and the dogs were impatient

to do their stuff. I watched for a few minutes before wandering over to the art section. My pictures had two red dots on them, indicating they'd been sold. I was chuffed to bits. Next year I'd put up the price.

The prisoners' contributions were better than I expected, and I made a silent apology to the artists. There was the usual maudlin stuff, but what can you expect from someone who's banged up for years on end? Two were a revelation. They were abstracts done in the style of Paul Klee. They didn't quite work for me, but they were brave attempts, obviously both painted by the same person. I looked closely at one of them to see if there was a signature. There was. It said *Ennis*.

Never heard of him, but maybe I'd see what he was in for. Then again, maybe I wouldn't. The woman who brought the paintings was nowhere to be seen, so I wandered back to the main arena, looking for Dave and his family. A police German shepherd was wrestling with a handler with a padded arm, and a five-aside football match was just starting in the next field. All around me small boys, and a few girls, were thinking that they'd like to become policemen. Sadly, it wouldn't last.

Monday morning the phone interrupted my breakfast. It was Mad Maggie. 'Are you going in to the office this morning, boss?' she asked.

'That was my intention, Maggie,' I replied. 'Unless you are about to make some revelation that will take me elsewhere.'

'No. I want to see you at the nick. I've a present for you. Bought it at the gala yesterday.'

'What is it?'

'Can't say. I want to see your face.'

'I'm intrigued. It's not a leaving present, is it? Have you heard something that I haven't?'

'When you leave, Chas, we'll push the boat out. You'll know all about it.'

'OK. I'll see you after morning prayers.'

Morning prayers comprised of me confessing to Mr Wood that we were at a standstill with the Magdalena case and were hoping for some revelation about the MO from our serious crime analysis section, which wasn't forthcoming. He pointed out, unnecessarily, that our time was up and HQ would take over the investigation if we didn't make some progress soon. He was wearing his funeral suit, because later that morning our ex-MP, Ted Goss, was being remembered in a service at the cathedral. Gilbert knew him through various committees and was a fellow-Rotarian with the MP's local agent.

'It should be you going to the service, not me,' he protested.

'How do you work that out?' I asked. 'You're our figurehead.'

'Because he was one of your lot, that's why.'

As I was leaving his office he said: 'And Charlie...'

I spun round. 'Yes, boss?'

'Get your hair cut. You look like a travelling Romanian knife-sharpener.'

First thing I saw in the CID office was that young Brendan had joined the shaven head brigade. His head glowed like the dome of the Golden Mosque of Samarkand in the desert sun.

'Listen up,' I shouted, and the hubbub died down. 'Mr Wood has just had a word with me about haircuts. I see Brendan is the latest to join the bullet-headed boys. It has to stop. You lot are beginning to look like a private army.'

'It's this weather, boss,' Brendan protested.

'Not good enough. You're supposed to be plain-clothes detectives, not a band of mercenaries, so let's have some variation in styles, eh? No more shaven heads unless it's on doctor's orders, in which case you'll have to have it painted with gentian violet as well.' I turned to Maggie and put on my best couldn't-care-less voice. 'So where's this present, Maggie?' I asked. I knew it was some sort of leg-pull and I was due for a disappointment, so there was no point in putting it off.

'Right here, Chas.' She rose to her feet and reached down the side of her desk, producing what was obviously a painting wrapped in tissue paper. She stood behind it, made a noise suitable for an unveiling and pulled the wrappings off.

It was the Paul Klee painting, done by one of the prisoners. I said: *'Pour moi?'* and stabbed my chest with a forefinger.

'Just for you,' she replied.

I hadn't a clue what it was all leading up to, but went along with it. She's not known as Mad Maggie without reason. I said: 'Correct me if I'm wrong, Margaret, but wasn't there a £125 price tag on it?'

'You're worth every penny, boss.'

'Have you borrowed it?'

'Commandeered it might be more accurate. I had to do some leaning.'

'Can I ask why?'

'What do you think of it? Is it any good?'

'It has a certain merit,' I replied, 'but I thought the other one he did was better.'

'Which other one who did?' Maggie asked.

'He's called Ennis,' I told her. 'There were two of his paintings in the exhibition.'

'This isn't by Ennis,' she replied.

'It is,' I assured her. 'The style is unmistakable. I'd gamble money on them being by the same person.'

'This one isn't signed Ennis.'

'Is it signed?'

'Have a look.'

I walked over to the painting and stooped to see if anything was written in the bottom right-hand corner. That's the usual place for a signature. I couldn't see one at first, because it was green on green, but it soon became apparent to me. In small, loopy letters was a clue to the identity of the man who'd executed the picture while locked up in one of Her Majesty's prisons for God knows how long.

He'd signed himself *The Pope*.

CHAPTER TEN

'He's called Ennis,' I told them again. 'Take my word for it, both paintings were done by the same person.'

'So why did he sign them differently?' someone asked.

I shrugged my shoulders. 'Why not? Maybe it was just a whim. Maybe the pictures were done years apart. I wouldn't attach any importance to that. What we need to know is who he is and where he is. I'll make some phone calls. Meanwhile, Maggie, you're excused from coffee duty for the rest of the day. Brendan can be coffee monitor,' I turned to him, 'but don't get any hairs in it.'

First stop was the organiser of the art exhibition at the gala. Her number was printed in the programme, which was still in my pocket. Her elderly mother answered the phone and gave me her work number. Eventually I tracked her down – mobiles do have their good points.

We only meet once per year but she greeted me like a long-lost friend. I said I needed to know about one of the prison artists, and could she give me the name of the person who had arranged for the pictures to be there?

'She's called Sam Spencer,' I was told, 'and she teaches art for the Workers' Educational Association. She also goes into prisons and does a lot of work with them.'

'Great. Do you have a number for her?'

She did, and fifteen minutes later Maggie and I were on our way, on the pretext of returning the painting Maggie had commandeered.

Ms Spencer and her partner were living the good life, or as near as you can get to it up on the moors. They had an end cottage in one of those terraces that are dotted arbitrarily about the place, where toilers in some long-forgotten industry once raised their families in the hostile climate up there. They had an acre of land and were making raised beds in which to grow their own organic produce. I hadn't the heart to tell them that only potatoes and sprouts would thrive at that altitude, and when theirs were ready to harvest the price in the supermarkets would be down to about fifty pence a ton. No doubt they would have hit back with a diatribe about flavour.

After a quick look around we left the partner manoeuvring old railway sleepers at the far end of the plot and sat in a garden area while Ms Spencer fetched us iced lemonade. It was idyllic, and I felt a small pang of jealousy, then remembered that the road became blocked by snow every winter, and the wet-fish man probably didn't deliver up there, either.

'He's called Peter Ennis,' she told us, after overcoming her early cautiousness. Part of her mandate was to befriend the prisoners, which put us in opposing camps. I told her about Magdalena, even asked if she'd known her while at college, and she soon decided to cooperate.

'Where did you meet him?' I asked.

'He was in Bentley prison.'

'Any ideas what for?'

'No. I never spoke one-to-one with him outside the class.'

'You said *was*.'

'That's right. He was released about a year ago. He left his paintings behind, said I could have them. I put them in the show for a bit of variety. They were the only abstracts there apart from two done by a policeman.'

We sat silently for a few seconds, wondering if she was about to make some killer criticism of my work, until I said: 'He signed one picture *Ennis* and one *Pope*. Any ideas why?'

'Not really, except he was probably embarrassed by his name.'

Maggie and I looked puzzled, until Ms Spencer spelt it out: 'P. Ennis.'

'Oh, I see,' I said. 'What did the other prisoners call him?'

'Some called him Pete, some called him the Pope. He's a big man, has a lot of authority. I think he liked being called the Pope.'

'Is he religious?' Maggie asked.

'Not so you'd notice,' she replied, 'but I believe Ennis is an Irish name.'

'Is he Irish?'

'He doesn't have the accent.'

I drained my lemonade, which made by standing a lemon next to a glass of water, but still most welcome, and said: 'Did you ever feel intimidated or threatened by him?'

'No, never,' she replied. 'He was always courteous and considerate.'

'What about his pictures? Was there anything in them to suggest a violent nature?'

'I'm not a psychologist, but I wouldn't say so. They were the usual stuff, like landscapes. The abstracts were an expression of his mood, but I wouldn't regard them as having a violent origin. Would you?'

I shook my head. 'No.'

We thanked her for her help and the lemonade. As she saw us into the car I said: 'Are you still in contact with him?'

'No, Inspector,' she replied. 'He wasn't my type.'

'You're not on each other's Christmas card list, then?'

'No.'

On the way back to the nick Maggie said: '*Always courteous and considerate*. Sounds like a typical manipulating male.'

'Tell me,' I began, 'does a woman like Sam get a feeling of power, standing in front of a class of rabid, testosterone-loaded men, knowing that she'll be fuelling their fantasies as they lie in their bunks that night, and the next, and the next?'

'*Touché*,' Maggie replied.

The nick was buzzing with strangers when we arrived back, and two uniformed officers armed with Heckler and Kochs were guarding the entrance. I told Maggie to write up our morning's work and went straight to the conference room where Jeff was holding his ID parade.

He was deep in conversation with Rodway and Clark's briefs and the CPS solicitors, explaining how he was proposing to run the show, giving them the chance to make amendments. Mrs Dolan, the blind witness, was sitting in a chair with Serena next to her, holding her hand. Jeff introduced me to the briefs and they said they were happy with the arrangements. The whole thing would be recorded on video. Jeff looked at his watch and said: 'Right, then. Let's get on with it.'

The ten innocents were lined up and the briefs inserted their two clients randomly into the line. Jeff then gave each one a numbered card, one to twelve, from left to right. He said: 'Right, gentlemen. When I put my hand on your shoulder I want you to say: "Get out of the fucking way" in your normal voice. Understand?'

They mumbled their agreement and Jeff placed his hand on the shoulder of number one.

'Get out of the fuckin' way,' he delivered as if he were auditioning for *King Lear*.

The briefs made notes and the camera rolled. Jeff said: 'Could the witness please tell us what colours that voice reminded her of?'

This worried me, and was a departure from what we'd agreed earlier. I thought Mrs Dolan would just pick out the person who'd knocked her over, but when she was told this she'd insisted that she could give colours to the full line-up, and what she saw was consistent and wouldn't change.

'Yes. He's a very dark blue.'

'Thank you.' Jeff placed his hand on the shoulder of number two.

'Get out of the fucking way.'

'Yellow fading to orange.'

'Thank you.'

'Get out of the fucking way.'

'Darkish blue again, but with some pale bits.'

'Thank you.'

Wayne Rodway was at number six. He spoke his lines and Mrs Dolan said he was two shades of green, one mid green, one more viridian, and she added: 'He's the person who knocked me over.'

We continued to the end and had a break for coffee. Twenty minutes later we did it all again, with the subjects in a different order, chosen by the defence solicitors. Mrs Dolan scored one hundred per cent. Then it was handshakes all round; I told Jeff 'Well done,' and the briefs said they'd be having a word with their clients. In other words, they'd be recommending guilty pleas. One of them suggested that Mrs Dolan go on the music halls.

I went for a pee and washed my hands and face. As I walked into the office Maggie said: 'How'd it go?'

'Perfect,' I told her. 'Mrs Dolan did Rodway bang to rights. Serena's taking her home.'

'Here's the report for this morning.' She handed me a single typed sheet.

'That was quick. Thanks.'

'Um, Charlie...'

'Yes, Margaret.'

'You know when you asked Sam Spencer if the Pope was on her Christmas card list...'

'Ye-es.'

'Well, you weren't just making small talk, were you?'

'No, Maggie.'

'You were wondering if he knew where she lived.'

'Something like that. Prisoners get funny ideas about women visitors. I didn't want to alarm her, but it would scare the willies out of me, living up there.'

'Do you think she's in danger?'

'I doubt it.' I pulled my big diary out of the bottom drawer as Maggie turned to leave. 'Don't go,' I said. 'Let's make a call.'

Gwen Rhodes is the governor of Bentley prison, and an old friend. She's big and handsome and we hit it off right from the start. I've never taken her out, but we've fought the same corner a few times on various committees and share an interest in sport. Gwen played netball for England and I had trials in goal with Halifax Town juniors. As Brando nearly put it: I could've been a defender. I found her number and she answered third ring.

I said: 'Hello Gwen, it's Charlie Priest. Sorry to come through on this line but I'd like a word, when you can.'

'Hello, Charlie,' she replied. 'This is a surprise. Can I ring you back shortly?'

As I put the phone down Maggie asked: 'Who's Gwen?'

'Gwen Rhodes. Governor of Bentley.'

Her eyes widened. 'You have a private line to the formidable Miss Rhodes! You never cease to amaze me.'

'Yeah, well. I've known her a long time. She has a bit of a crush on me.'

'And what have you on her?'

'Nothing. She's just a friend. But who knows, one day...'

Three or four minutes later she rang me back. 'How are you keeping, Charlie?' I switched the phone to loudspeaker, so Maggie could listen.

'Not bad, Gwen, but working hard, as you are, no doubt.'

'Yes, you're certainly keeping us fully employed. As the old lags say: "Three to a cell, luxury!"'

We chatted about the perils of growing older and the merits of retiring to a place in the sun, with Maggie rolling her eyes at me across my desk. Eventually Gwen said: 'So what can I do for you, Charlie? I presume it's not a social call.'

'Peter Ennis,' I said. 'Does the name mean anything to you?'

'Of course,' she replied. 'Peter Paul Ennis was our longest serving inmate. What's he done now?'

'Peter Paul,' I echoed. 'Is that his name? I suppose that's why they called him the Pope.'

'Yes. And his initials are PPE, so he just had to stick an O in there.'

I said: 'Wait a minute, Gwen. Did you know he called himself the Pope?'

'Of course. Everybody called him the Pope.'

'Jesus!' I exclaimed. 'We just spent a month looking for the Pope and you knew who he was all the time.'

'Well you should ring more often, Charlie. I've no sympathy. So what's he done?'

I told her about Magdalena and she was silent for a while. Eventually she said: 'He was a model prisoner, but we fool ourselves, don't we? We find it difficult to believe what some of our fellow men are capable of.'

'Give me some details, please,' I asked. 'What was he in for?'

'Bank robbery. Let me look him up... Here we are...July 1978. He pulled off the York and Durham bank robbery on the Thursday before Wakes Week. Got away with nearly half a million. Don't you remember it?'

'Hmm, vaguely, but I'd be in Leeds, then. So how long did he serve?'

'He was sentenced to twenty-five years. It was a particularly nasty robbery – he doused a bank clerk in petrol and threatened to ignite her – and none of his share of the money – which was most of it – was recovered. He pleaded not guilty, refused to cooperate and settled down to serve his full term, without remission. Now he's a free man and we have no idea where he is. He didn't leave a forwarding address.'

'And there's still the half a million spondulis somewhere,' I added.

'Quite.'

'Blimey.'

'Anything else I can help you with?'

'I'll be grateful if you can email me the relevant stuff, please, Gwen. And there is one other thing.'

'What's that?'

'You're right. We should talk more often. How about dinner one night next week? Somewhere a bit nice; my treat? What night would suit you?'

'Sorry, Charlie,' she replied. 'Friday I fly to Canada. Taking the train ride through the Rockies. I'll be gone three weeks.'

Across the desk Maggie was nearly choking.

'Now I'm green with envy,' I replied. 'Can I see your photos when you come back, then?'

'Yes, Charlie. That's something to look forward to. I've bought a new camera especially for the holiday. Look after yourself.'

'And you, Gwen. 'Bye.'

As I pressed the loudspeaker key to break the connection Maggie said: 'That bit about men in prison having funny ideas about women visitors. Do you think the opposite is true?'

'I don't follow you.'

'Well, do men on the outside have funny ideas about female governors?'

'Haven't you anything to do?' I demanded.

* * *

I was putting details of Maggie's report in my murder log when Mr Wood came in, fresh from Ted Goss's memorial service. He looked as if he'd lost a tenner and found a teapot lid. I kicked the spare chair out for him and asked if he'd like a coffee.

'No thanks, Charlie. I'm OK.'

'We've got developments on the Magdalena enquiry,' I said. 'We know who the Pope is, now all we have to do is find him.'

'Good. Good.' He sat down and ran a hand through what was left of his hair.

Services for suicide victims are always extra-harrowing, even when you don't know them too well. I said: 'You look knackered, Gilbert. Was it a bad do?'

'Oh, so-so, Charlie. There were a couple of lighter moments, but it makes you think, doesn't it? A man like him devotes his life to the community and all he gets is a recycling bin named after him. It's not much for a lifetime's work, is it?'

'It's more than we'll get.'

'You can say that again.'

'Footprints on a frosty lawn, Gilbert. That's all we'll leave behind. And they'll disappear as soon as the sun rises.'

'That's a good one. Who said it?'

'Dunno. I must have read it on a calendar. So what's brought this on? You didn't know Mr Goss all that well, did you?'

'It's turning into a bloody mess, Charlie. That's what.'

'How do you mean?'

'I got collared at the bun-fight by Edwin Turner. Do you know him?'

'I know of him. He was Goss's agent, wasn't he?' I'd seen his photo in the *Gazette* dozens of times, usually alongside his master at the opening of a skateboard park or cancer clinic.

'That's right. He'd been going through Ted's papers. As you can imagine, there's a whole load of stuff to be attended to. He's left a right mess behind. He's been sifting through his papers for weeks, shredding most of it. All the constituency business, stuff like that. Some of it's confidential, some highly personal.'

'I can imagine,' I said. 'People turn to their MP as a last desperate resort.'

'On the day he found the body,' Gilbert went on, 'he came across this.' He reached into his inside pocket and handed me a folded letter.

I recognised the Union flag logo instantly, and written underneath it in Roman type was the name of the august journal that had sent it: *Britain 2000*. I checked the date and saw that it had been sent about five weeks ago. Ted Goss had been dead for a month. It was addressed to the Hon Edward Goss, MP, at his home in Heckley, and said:

Dear Mr Goss

We have in our possession photographs of yourself, whom we understand to be a married man, in what can only be described as a compromising position with a young woman. Up to now we have hesitated to use this material. However, it has recently been brought to our notice that you are in the habit of downloading paedophilic images onto your computer. We have therefore reconsidered the situation and decided that it is our duty to bring this information to the attention of the public and any other interested authorities. With this in mind we will be publishing details of your activities in a future issue of Britain 2000. *Meanwhile, we would like to give you the opportunity of putting your side of the story forward.*

We look forward to hearing from you in the next few days.
Yours faithfully

It was signed with a cross by the editor.

'He hanged himself, didn't he?' I asked.

'With a belt, from the stair rails.'

'You'd have to be desperate to do something like that.'

'Yes. It's hardly premeditated. He left a couple of notes, in one of which he said all allegations against him involving downloading indecent images were untrue.'

What was it Mandy Rice-Davies said during the Profumo case: 'Well he would, wouldn't he?' And young Daniel had said something similar.

'What does he want you to do?' I asked.

'Buggered if I know, Charlie. Hush the whole thing up, I suppose. I don't know where they get their ideas from about how much clout we have, especially these days.'

I said: 'Superintendent Swainby had similar allegations and threats made against him. There's a lot of it about. So why haven't *Britain 2000* published the story?'

'Edwin has discovered that Goss took out an injunction against them publishing, a couple of days before he died.'

'I told Swainby to do that. How have you left it?'

'I haven't made him any promises, Charlie. Said we'd look at it, that's all.'

'OK. Leave it with me.' I wasn't making any promises, either. All I could do was have a word with the agent, tell him the bit I knew and suggest he issue a strenuous denial. Mud sticks, but dead men don't bleed.

* * *

'OK, listen up,' I began, Tuesday morning, to the gathered troops. 'Thanks to the diligence of one of our number we now have a name for the Pope, plus his fingerprints, DNA and mugshot. He's called Peter Paul Ennis and was released from Bentley a year ago after serving twenty-five years for armed bank robbery.' A murmur of astonishment ran through the room at the sudden leap forward we'd made in what was beginning to look like a hopeless case.

I told them that the focus of our activities was now on finding Ennis. The file from Gwen Rhodes had arrived on my computer and I'd run off several copies. One item of interest was next of kin. He had a younger brother living near Doncaster. I delegated six officers to mount round-the-clock surveillance and sent them off: two to Donnie, four home to get some rest.

In my office I rang my opposite DI in Doncaster just to clear things and then looked for numbers for the ex-prisoners' associations. Thanks to the Internet I soon had about a hundred to look at. Liberty couldn't or wouldn't help me, and neither could the Howard League. I was the enemy. The National Association for the Care and Resettlement of Prisoners were sympathetic but disinclined to turn their database over to me. I rang a friendly probation officer and he suggested contacting the Blue Sky Trust, who touted themselves around the northern jails, and I eventually found myself talking to someone who said he was the regional coordinator.

Unfortunately he wasn't inclined to coordinate my enquiry with his list of names and addresses, so I told him in full Technicolor and blow-by-blow detail about Magdalena's injuries and said we were only interested in eliminating Peter Paul Ennis from our enquiries.

He agreed to look.

He looked.

No, sorry, they didn't have him on their books.

Big deal.

Gwen had included a list of his associates in prison, and the names of the six others in the gang. They'd served terms up to eight years and were paid £10,000 each for their help, most of which had been recovered. Ennis's share, £370,000, had never been found. I wrote addresses down, sent officers off to locate them, requested other forces to keep a weather eye out for him. According to the file he was an occasional follower of greyhound racing, so I looked up the local tracks and asked about their next meetings.

I tried to estimate what I was earning in 1978 and compared it with my present salary. Some rough mathematics told me that Ennis's haul was now worth in the region of £2,000,000. Unless, of course, it was hidden in a suitcase under the floorboards, in which case it would still be worth £370,000. In 1978 it would have made him a rich man, now it would just about buy him a decent house. Did he lie in his bunk for twenty-five years worrying about inflation? Probably not.

Edwin Turner arranged to meet me at Ted Goss's house and was already there when I arrived. It was on the end of a three-story terrace that had been renovated at great expense, with most of the ground floor given over to office space. The size of the room puzzled me for a few seconds until I realised that a wall had been knocked through and it incorporated next door's front parlour, too. There were two workstations with flat screen monitors, and all the other paraphernalia associated with a busy office, including a bank of filing cabinets and a small meeting room with a table and six chairs.

Turner himself was a fussy little man with bottle-bottom spectacles and a pale, scaly complexion. He blinked constantly behind the thick lenses, as if he'd just been released from a cupboard. I could imagine him printing posters for the current regime and distributing them door-to-door, along rain-swept streets.

'What happened to Mrs Goss?' I asked, after he'd given me a brief look-around.

'She's in long term care,' he replied. 'Alzheimer's.'

'That can't have made things easy for him.'

'No.'

'What about secretarial help?'

'Part-time, but we've laid her off.'

'So what have we here?' I asked.

'This is the secretary's desk,' he told me, 'where all the party business was conducted. That one was reserved for Ted's personal stuff and low-level constituency business.'

'Where did you find the letter from *Britain 2000*?'

'In a drawer.'

'Which drawer?'

'Hmm, the middle one.'

I sat in the MP's chair and pulled the appropriate drawer open. It was filled with envelopes of various sizes, plus a box of stamps and a ream of posh headed notepaper. A Montblanc fountain pen lay on it, ready for the quick, impressive signature.

I said: 'That seems a strange place to leave it,' and he cleared his throat and looked awkward.

'You're right,' he admitted after a long silence. 'It wasn't there. I was waiting for the police and ambulance to arrive when I saw the notes he...Ted...had left. The letter was paper-clipped to one of them. I read it and…removed it.'

'You decided that the world wasn't ready for that revelation.'

'Something like that.'

I'd have probably done the same. 'You found the body.'

'Yes. When Ted was home I usually came round, about ten o'clock. Sometimes we had business to attend to, others it was just social. I liked to keep an eye on him, see he was all right.'

'It must have been a shock to you.'

'It was.'

'How long had you known him?'

'All our lives. Sixty years.'

'You were fond of him.'

The magnified eyes blinked several times. 'Yes, I was. And I admired him.'

'How'd he been before he died? Was he depressed or anything?'

'No. Just the opposite. He'd found a new friend. A female friend, and she'd put a new spring in his step.'

'Maybe she'd finished with him,' I suggested.

'Possibly, but when he'd mentioned her, rather obliquely, he told me not to worry. He said it couldn't last, it was just an enjoyable interlude, and he wouldn't be doing anything stupid.'

I wondered how much an average, left-wing, backbench MP might know that could be useful, commercially or otherwise, to an interested third party. There was bound to be something, but would it be enough to set up a honey-pot sting against him? I hadn't a clue.

'Where does he keep confidential papers?' I asked.

'There's a safe upstairs.'

'Have you been through it?'

'Yes.'

'And found nothing?'

'No.'

'Have you looked for these indecent images?'

'Briefly. I haven't had the time, what with all the other stuff that needed attending to, plus the service to organise.'

I knew the feeling. I explained about Trojan horses, sounding like an expert, and said that any photos would be buried deep in his system, somewhere. We'd need to go through his files, one by one.

We started with *My Documents* and opened the first folder, called *Corresp, Constit*. There were two screens full of them, with several sub-folders. Then it was *Corresp, Edwin*, right through to *Corresp, PLP*. It was going to take months.

'This is hopeless,' I said, after a few exploratory glances at documents. It meant double clicking on the chosen file, waiting for it to appear, double clicking on a document, clicking to close it and moving on to the next document. It took time, and there were about ten thousand items to inspect. I wondered about using the computer's search facility, but couldn't imagine what to tell it to look for. We needed help, but I couldn't really ask Daniel, and if I brought our experts in they'd play it by the book and it would become public knowledge. I was beginning to whiff some sort of conspiracy and didn't want to go public, yet.

I turned to Edwin Turner. 'Let's narrow it down,' I said. 'Only look at anything dated this year, and over 100 kilobytes. That should make it easier. Make a list of what you've done and be methodical. I'll try to help you when I can.'

With that, I fled. I had a murderer to catch.

* * *

Ennis's brother, James Francis, was a bus driver in Doncaster, my men on the job informed me. He started work at five a.m. and finished in the late afternoon. I wondered if deep vein thrombosis was an occupational hazard for bus drivers. No doubt some union solicitor was already working on it. Ennis's wife was employed in a local bakery, also starting ridiculously early in the morning, and there was no sign of a lodger. I said we'd change the habits of a lifetime and give him an early evening knock at the door. Dave wanted to be in on the action, so I let him pick me up and we headed south to Doncaster.

He didn't look unduly surprised to answer the door and find four detectives standing there. Having a brother in jail for the county's biggest-ever bank robbery probably conditions you to expect anything. I asked if we could come in and he nodded and stood to one side.

The room was bulging at the seams with furniture before we arrived, and at bursting point when we crowded into it. Brendan was left standing in the doorway. I went straight to the point.

'We're looking for your brother, Peter Paul,' I said. 'Have you any ideas where he might be?'

'Haven't a clue,' Ennis junior replied. 'Last time I saw him he was in Bentley prison.'

'He was released last August. You haven't seen him since then?'

'No. I haven't seen him since our mother's funeral in 2002. They let him out for that because he was near the end of his sentence and considered a low escape risk. When Dad died, back in 1993, they refused him permission to attend. I guessed he'd be free by now, but he hasn't been in touch.'

'What's he done this time?' Mrs Ennis asked. She was seated next to her husband, holding his hand.

'Did you ever meet a girlfriend of his called Magdalena Fischer?' I asked.

They both shook their heads. 'No, never heard of her.'

'We weren't close,' he explained. 'Pete's ten years older than me. We drifted apart.'

'Magdalena was murdered,' I told them. 'We're calling on all her old acquaintances. We think they were living together at about the time of the robbery.'

'I was only eighteen,' Ennis said. 'Pete had left home years earlier. There were lots of rows with Dad, and one day he just left.'

'Any ideas where he went?'

'Leeds, we believed. He had friends there.'

'Anywhere else where he might have an affection for, where he might choose to live now he's free?'

'Not really. Mam and Dad used to like Scarborough, took us there when we were kids. That's about it.'

'Do you mind if two officers have a quick look around?' I asked. 'You can accompany them, Mrs Ennis.'

'Do you have a warrant?'

'No.'

'You think we might be hiding him?'

'We have to consider every possibility.'

'Come on, then.' She stood up and Brendan and Dave followed her out of the room.

As they clumped up the stairs I asked if he'd visited his brother in jail. He had, in the early days, and written, but Peter had stopped sending visiting orders and things just fizzled out.

'The money's still missing,' I said. 'I don't suppose he ever asked you about investments or anything like that?'

'No. We never talked about what he'd done. He'd denied it, pleaded not guilty. That's why his sentence was so stiff. That and the thing with the petrol. The subject was never raised between us.'

Dave and Brendan came back and Dave gave me a tiny shake of the head. We thanked them and stood up to leave. We'd entered through the kitchen, and as we left I said: 'Something smells good.'

'It's bread,' Mrs Ennis told me. 'I always bring some home, fresh every day, for our supper.' She indicated a plastic bag sitting on the worktop, with two large bread cakes in it. I gave her husband a card, told him to ring me if he thought of anything that might be useful and thanked both of them for their help. If there'd been three bread cakes in the bag I'd have been suspicious. As we approached our cars I asked if anybody fancied a curry, but nobody did.

Edwin Turner had spent all day going through Ted Goss's computer files without any success. On my way home I drove round to see him at his ex-boss's house. He looked more desiccated than before, and had even removed his jacket as a concession to the effort he was putting in to the search. I noticed that he wore armbands to keep his shirtsleeves under control. I hadn't seen a pair of armbands since my granddad died. He removed his spectacles and wiped his eyes on a linen handkerchief, and I had a little bet with myself that he tucked his shirt into his underpants.

'Anything?'

He shook his head. 'Nothing.'

'Did he keep a diary?'

'No. Well, not a personal one.'

'Any idea where he met this woman friend?'

'Sorry. I presumed she was one of his constituents. Some of them fussed over him, liked to mother him. Being an MP isn't like being a doctor. You're allowed to...you know...'

'You're allowed to cultivate friendships within your electorate,' I said.

'Yes, something like that.'

I asked him to have a look through Ted's address book, see if he could find any names for these worthy ladies who pampered their representative. With his permission I collected all the diskettes and CDs that had information on them and took them home. If I found anything, I'd let him know. If he found anything, I presumed he'd delete it all. This wasn't a criminal enquiry, yet. I collected a ready meal from the supermarket, put it in the microwave and shoved the first diskette into my A-drive. Three hours later I logged off and went to bed with a headache and a renewed respect for my late MP. If he understood all the legal mumbo jumbo involved in getting a piece of legislation through all its stages, he was a better man than me. Except I suspected most of it went over his head. It's the judges who make the laws and rule the country, not the MPs, most definitely not the people.

Rodway and Clark changed their pleas to guilty and were remanded to Bentley prison. I thought about Gwen Rhodes, sitting in the observation car as it meandered through the Rockies, watching out for elk and bear. We found the girl who'd been tied up and threatened during the bank raid back in 1980, and tracked down four of Ennis's accomplices. The other two of them were dead. There's a high attrition rate amongst villains.

The girl was called Gail and I took Serena to interview her. I'd told myself to expect a 43-year-old, but the woman who opened the door looked nearer sixty. She lived in one of the towers on the project, and the years hadn't been kind to her, whichever way you looked at it. We sat down in a typical room – TV on, gas fire on, curtains only half open, canary in a cage – and I let Serena tell her that we had reopened the robbery case because the money was still out there somewhere.

She told us her side of the story. It was all still churning around inside her, and there was no stopping it coming out. Ennis had picked on her because she was the youngest and prettiest. He'd doused her in petrol and threatened to ignite her, and it had been all downhill from there. She'd been a bright girl and had hoped for a career in banking, but she'd had no support from the bank, and counselling didn't exist in those days. At the end of her probationary period they'd fired her for bad timekeeping, and she'd existed on a series of nondescript jobs since then. She'd been married to a waster who'd left her with two children, and now the kids had moved on. The doctor was treating her for agoraphobia.

It was a horror story, and I wished Ennis and his gang were there to listen to it. What had been a big, get-rich-quick adventure to them had ruined her life.

I said: 'Weren't you a bit young and inexperienced to be opening up, early in the morning?'

'Yes, but I'd asked for it. Two key-holders started at seven-thirty every morning. They'd lock themselves in and do a quick check of all the rooms. If everything was satisfactory they sorted the mail and distributed it to the appropriate desks. At about half past eight, as the others started to arrive, they'd change the date on a calendar in the window as a signal that all was OK, and unlock the front door again.

I said: 'What happened on the morning of the raid?'

'They were waiting for us, on the staircase. They made lots of threats and seemed to know about the calendar signal. Philip – he's the man I was on with – just said to do as they told us, no heroics. I didn't feel very heroic.'

I was looking for the right words when Serena said: 'You haven't told us why you volunteered for the early shift.'

'Johnny Mathis,' she replied. 'Mum was his biggest fan. He was on at Batley Variety Club that night, and she'd bought us two tickets. She'd never been to anywhere like that before. I asked to start early to give us more time, that's all.'

'But your mum never got to see him.'

'No.'

I said: 'Was there any talk of it being an inside job, Gail? When you were tied up did you notice if any of the employees might be just a little bit familiar with the gang? Eager to help, that sort of thing?'

'No, but I was probably too hysterical to notice. In court he said it was water he splashed over me, but it smelt like petrol.'

Serena asked: 'I don't suppose any of your colleagues bought a posh car shortly afterwards, or moved to a bigger house?'

Gail shook her head but we already knew the answer. The staff would have been monitored for years afterwards, and a discreet watch kept on their financial affairs.

She said: 'What happened to him? I expect he served about ten years and is now living in luxury in Spain or somewhere.'

'No,' I replied, and told her he'd served the full sentence. There'd been nothing in the papers linking Magdalena with Ennis, but there soon might be, and I'd wanted her to be forewarned. I assured her she was in no danger and told her to ring Serena if she needed to talk.

There was a message waiting for me when we arrived back. 'Please contact Edwin Turner.' The troops were returning, grumbling about the kettle being empty, complaining about the heat, so he'd have to wait. One of the gang was in jail for supplying a class A drug, and had refused to see an officer. Talking to a cop would have ruined his credibility. Two of the others were unemployed and said they'd kill Ennis on sight if they ever met him again. The fourth one thought it was all a big hoot. He regarded himself as one of the nation's great villains, and intended to write a book about it, one day. He refused to give the interviewing officer a preview of the book, 'because of all the revelations', but had failed to arouse the interest of any publisher or newspaper.

'Did we ought to pay him another visit?' I asked, meaning armed with a warrant.

'No, boss. He's a tosspot. He thinks the Great Train Robbers stole trains.'

I went upstairs and brought Gilbert up to date with things. HQ were off our backs for the moment, so we'd give it another week and then go public with our search for Ennis. *Crimewatch* would find him, but we all have a sneaky desire to do things our own way. We're supposed to be detectives, not media researchers.

When I'd finished he said: 'And what about Ted Goss? Where are we with that?' so I told him that Agent Turner was busily scouring Mr Goss's hard disk, looking for indecent images or anything else of interest.

'Let's do our best for him, Charlie,' Gilbert said. 'His politics were a bit loony, but he was a decent chap. I hate to think of his reputation being destroyed by a rag like *Britain 2000*.'

Right, I thought as I trudged back down the stairs. Anything you say. Just give me a thirty-hour day and don't complain about the dip in the clear-up figures. Edwin Turner's note was still on my desk, so I rang him on his mobile.

'I've found some photos,' he said before I'd finished telling him who I was.

CHAPTER ELEVEN

'How many?' I asked.

'Two.'

'Two? Is that all?'

'They're not pornography. One is of him with a woman, in what you might call a compromising position; the other is of the woman.'

'Where did you find them?'

'In a drawer in his bedside cabinet. They're paper copies, printed off. I knew he had some stuff up there, documents he was working on, things he had to read, so I had a look. He was a great one for reading in bed.'

'Where are you now?'

'At his house.'

'I'll be with you in fifteen minutes. But before you go...'

'What?'

'Did Mr Goss ever say where he met this woman?'

'No.'

'That's a shame. Fifteen minutes.'

He was sitting in his boss's executive chair, idly spinning

one way and then the other. I'd knocked and he'd shouted for me to come in. I flopped into an easy chair as if I were a regular visitor and loosened my tie. One VDU was dead and the other showed a firework display screensaver. The room smelt of sweat, and a bluebottle was driving itself demented against the window.

'Did you find anything on the disks?' Turner asked.

'No, except that I probably need spectacles. Did you find anything on the computer drive?'

'Not a thing.'

'So where are these photographs?'

'Right here.' He stopped swivelling from side to side and handed me a manila envelope. I took it and pulled the contents out.

They were A4 size, colour printed on normal paper, but still high quality. The first one showed Goss looking bemused into the camera, his mouth open, his tie unfastened. He was obviously sitting inside a car. Behind him, hands over her face, was a woman with her legs drawn up, revealing her preference for stockings over tights.

The second one was almost a formal portrait. It showed a woman's face, front on, smiling straight into the camera. She was dark, probably tanned, with black hair in an expensive style. But it was her eyes that beguiled me, took my breath away. They were like limpid pools of milk chocolate, with green flecks in them, and I knew exactly what Superintendent Swainby had felt when I asked him if he'd opened the attachment she'd sent him. 'It was her photograph,' he'd said. 'What do you think?'

I was convinced it was the same woman as had befriended him. I didn't know what it was all about, but it had to be the same woman.

'It's the same woman,' Turner said, breaking into my thoughts.

'Sorry…'

'In both photos. It's the same woman.'

'Oh, yes,' I agreed.

'You can see her hair. It's the same woman.'

He was right. Her hands covered her face but enough of her distinctive hairstyle was visible to say it was the same person in both photographs. It wasn't enough to hang someone, but I was convinced.

'Have you ever seen her before?' he asked.

'No. Never.'

'Will you be looking for her?'

Oh yes, I thought, we'd certainly be looking for her. I didn't know or care who she was or what she was playing at, but I was certain that I wanted to meet her, needed to meet her. Of that I had no doubts. It was written in the stones.

Her name came to me in the middle of the night, when ghosts walk the streets and invade the brains of those who have no defence against them. Usually it's a man called O'Hagan and another called Stanwick. They stand there, laughing at me, shafts of light pouring out of the bullet holes that I put in them. I shield my eyes against the glare and their faces become visible. They have dogs' heads.

But tonight it was a woman called Teri. That's what she'd told Swainby her name was. I lay naked on the bed, the duvet on the floor and the window open, willing her to go away, wishing she'd stay, cursing her for leaving, laughing when she comes back. She smiles at me and I have the falling dream again, waking with a start when I hit the bottom, somewhere on Jupiter. When the collared doves start cooing, monotonous as a Philip Glass record stuck in the groove, I get up and have a shower.

'You're early, Charlie,' the desk sergeant greeted me as I walked into the nick.

'Can't sleep, this weather,' I replied. That, and it's a good time to do some work, before the hurly-burly of the day begins. I'm on the first rung of the stairs when he calls me back.

'Charlie…'

'Yes, Arthur.' I turned, smiling, hoping it's a joke. I feel in need of a joke. A day that starts with a good joke is like a day on holiday.

'There's this woman,' he begins, and my brain runs through the repertoire to see if I've heard it. 'She's in the cells. Bumped her car in the early hours and she's OPL.'

'Go on.'

'She's distraught. Her name's Gillian Birchall. Reckons she was set up, somehow. Any chance of you having a word with her?'

It isn't a joke. 'Me?' I said. 'Nothing to do with me, Arthur. Has the doctor seen her?'

'Yes. No problems there. She's forty-five. Your age.'

'And a bit. So what's so special about this one?' Claiming that your drinks were spiked is a standard defence against drink-driving charges. It rarely works.

'Well for a start, she's headmistress of that fancy private school in Oldfield. St Somebody's.'

'So she should have known better. How much over was she?'

'Fifteen micrograms. Apparently yesterday was her

birthday and a boyfriend that she didn't know very well took her out for a meal. He drove. Afterwards he took her home and she invited him in for a coffee. He didn't stay very long, but when he went outside his car had been stolen. He then persuaded her to run him home, back to Heckley, and on her way back to Oldfield she says she was driven off the road by a Range Rover.'

'Bang to rights, Arthur,' I said. 'Sad and unfortunate, but that's the law. Did the Range Rover stop?'

'No.'

'There you go, then. She was out with the girls, got pickled, drove off the road. Tough luck. Twelve months' ban, £200 fine, loss of credibility. Is that her fancy Honda in the visitor's spot?'

'Mmm.'

'In that case, her insurance premium will double, too. That'll learn her.'

The day shift sergeant had arrived and had listened to most of the conversation. 'What's her level now?' he asked. Arthur told him that she was down to 35 micrograms and could probably go home in about another hour. He wandered off to take a look at the only prisoner we had.

'She said her boyfriend drove a Mazda RX8 and reported it stolen at about ten minutes to midnight,' Arthur told me. 'I've checked, and there wasn't a car like that reported stolen last night or any other night. Not for over a week.'

'Because she's a lying toad. You're going soft in the head, Arthur.'

'I know, Charlie, but my granddaughter goes to that school, and Miss Birchall works wonders with them. We went to the end-of-term plays that the kids put on, and they were marvellous. She's a brilliant teacher. This could ruin her. I don't think she's making it up.'

'So why didn't you just cook the figure on the Alcometer?'

'Because the doc was here. I sounded him out but he came on all holier-than-thou.'

I was wavering, not wanting to be involved. I didn't like the thought of diverting resources, namely my time, to protect a foolish woman who'd flouted the drink-driving law. When I applied Dave's Gaitskell House test – would I do this if she lived in the Gaitskell House tower block – the answer was a resounding 'no'.

The day shift sarge came back. 'She'd like a black coffee,' he said, then, to me: 'She's a good-looking woman, Charlie. Would you like to take it to her?'

I shook my head in disbelief at my own folly. 'You know how to manipulate a vulnerable single man,' I said. 'Give me the key, Arthur, and twenty pence for the machine, please.'

'It's not locked,' he replied. 'And the coffee's your treat.'

Gillian Birchall wasn't at her best, but she looked OK. Her mascara had run and her eyes were red, but the figure was well-proportioned and she had no carbuncles or other serious disfigurements. She was wearing a blue dress that showed her knees and had draped the blanket she'd been given over her shoulders. Her shoes were sensible granny's lace-ups with scuffed toes, and didn't go with the dress.

'My name's Charlie Priest,' I told her after I'd rapped my knuckles against the cell door and pushed it open. She took the coffee from me and whispered a thank you.

'I'm a detective inspector. The sergeant has told me your story,' I went on, 'but I'd like to hear it from you. I warn you, though, that if it's just a fanciful attempt to justify your behaviour, I shall be mightily displeased.' I savoured the moment. It's not often one has the chance to chastise a headmistress. I sat on the plastic chair. She was on the edge of the bed.

'It's not a fanciful tale,' she replied. 'I'm convinced I was set up.'

'Tell me about it.'

He was called Richard and was polite, handsome and quite sophisticated. He'd had a public school education, was an NS and had a GSOH. It was only the third time she'd met him, but when he learnt she had a birthday coming he'd insisted on taking her out for a meal. They'd dined well, at the Wool Exchange, and her story was more or less as Arthur had related it to me.

'I don't socialise much,' she confessed. 'I work hard and most of my friends are married. I was rather pleased to be invited out by a respectable, attentive male who wasn't football mad and didn't appear to have any hang-ups. Especially when he said he'd drive.'

'How much did you have to drink?' I asked.

'More than I ought. Normally I only ever have the odd glass of wine. He bought a bottle of an Australian Shiraz, of which I think I had more than half, and after that we each had two orange juices. I suspect there was a vodka or perhaps something more sinister in mine. He assured me it was straight orange juice, but they went down extraordinarily well.'

'Did he order them from a waiter?'

'No, he went to the bar for them.'

'Is that all you had?'

'Not quite. At my house I poured us both a small brandy.'

'It sounds as if you pushed the boat out.'

'I know. I've had a few problems lately with a certain section of the school governors. It was a nice change to let my hair down. I thought: what the heck. I was enjoying myself and school's out, so a hangover was a small price to pay.'

'Weren't you suspicious of him at all? Or of his intentions?'

'It crossed my mind. We had a quick coffee at my house, and the brandy, and I was expecting him to…well, you know…make a move. Suggest staying the night, or something. But he finished his drink and announced that he had to be on the seven-twenty train to London this morning, and better be off. On one hand it got me out of an awkward situation, on the other, I felt just a small tweak of disappointment. It would have been nice to be asked.' She smiled at the confession and sniffed.

I could imagine the scene. She'd give him a goodnight kiss, which would develop into an embrace, and her principles would start to wobble like a trick cyclist in a crosswind. I'm forty-five, she'd think to herself, and I'm missing out. My life is slipping by. She might even plan what she'd write in her diary: *My birthday; got laid.*

'So what happened then?' I asked.

'His car had gone. We saw that from the doorway. He had a quick look around and then came back in. He phoned the police and reported it missing and tried for a taxi. They said they'd be half an hour, so he persuaded me to take him home. He said the wine would have worn off by then. He needed to be in London for a ten o'clock meeting, otherwise it would cost him thousands. Stupidly, I fell for it.'

'Did he use your phone?' I asked.

'No, his mobile.'

'And you only heard one side of the conversation?'

'Yes.'

'Where did you drop him off?'

'Outside the gates of one of those riverside developments in Heckley. He watched me drive away. Whether he went inside or not I don't know.'

'And then what happened?'

'I was going down the hill, towards the Five Lane Ends Road crossroads and there were these headlights behind me. Suddenly I didn't feel sober any more. I felt decidedly squiffy. It was a 4x4 and it came up behind me, dazzling me. I slowed down because I thought it might be the police. Near the crossroads it suddenly shot past, pulled in front and braked hard. I hit the back of it and swerved off the road, into the ditch. He just drove on.'

'And it was a Range Rover?'

'I think so. I remember seeing the little green Land Rover badge as I hit it, but it was quite a swish vehicle, not one of those that looks as if it's made out of Meccano.'

'Who called the police?'

'I don't know. I phoned the AA but the police came first, and here I am.' She gestured with her arms. 'God, what a mess.'

I could imagine how she felt. The arresting officer would have treated her with practised disdain as he breathalysed her and brought her to the nick. Then it would have been a blood test and the taking of fingerprints and DNA samples. Mugshots would have been fired off, standing in front of the same wall as a long procession of killers, rapists and burglars. She'd have had her rights thrown at her and been questioned about her lifestyle until she felt like someone in a Kafka novel. Or like a criminal. And now she was in a tiled cell with a bunk along one wall and a stainless steel toilet in the corner, and I was her one hope of redemption.

'You need a solicitor,' I said. 'You're bailed to appear in court one day next week, but he can ask for an adjournment. Has it all been explained to you?'

'Yes, Inspector. *Ad nauseam.*'

'Meanwhile, I'll have someone try to find this Richard. See what he's all about. No Mazda RX8 was reported stolen last night. Can you definitely say that his car was a Mazda?'

'Definitely. I admired it. Truth is, I'm a bit of a petrol head. It was an RX8 all right.'

'Well that should make him easy to trace. Is his wine glass still standing unwashed on your kitchen table?'

'Um, I imagine so. And his coffee mug.'

'Good. Pick them up carefully and put them somewhere safe. Then, if necessary, we can check his fingerprints. I'm afraid I haven't anybody to send over at the moment.' And, of course, it gave me an excuse to renew our acquaintance at a later date.

'Do you think he spiked my drinks, Inspector?'

'Only with alcohol. Rohypnol, the date rape drug, is a bit of a myth. As far as I know there's never been a proven case of its use in this country. The preferred drug of the date rapist is alcohol. Some of those Australian wines are quite strong, and you were mixing them.' I thought for a few seconds, then said: 'You mentioned something about having trouble with the school governors. What's that all about?'

'Oh, you may have read about it in the papers. We have the usual fundamentalists on the panel and they want creationism to be taught as an alternative to evolution. I've said over my dead body.'

'Intelligent design?'

'And that.'

'Good for you. Do you think they could be behind this? Wanting to discredit you?'

'Not really. They're a couple of old dears, but are still living in the seventeenth century.'

But, I thought, they could have friends, be members of a church that had strong views about these things. Strong enough to take violent action. I hoped that Christian fundamentalists weren't behind it. I'd have prayed they weren't behind it if it hadn't seemed so hypocritical.

I said: 'Fair enough. Finish your coffee and then you can leave. The car's outside so it must be driveable. Sorry I can't be more helpful but that's how it goes.'

She said: 'Well, thanks for listening to me. I'd never felt so lonely until you came in. I'm very grateful.'

I smiled at her. 'That's all right,' I said. 'I'm a sucker for women with runny mascara.'

She wiped under her eyes with her fingers. 'Uh! I hardly ever wear it. So do you believe me?'

'Oh yes,' I told her. 'I believe you. Those are very sensible driving shoes you're wearing, but I can't see you going on a special date in them.'

She lifted her feet to look at them, toes pointed inwards, and gave me the nearest thing to a smile she'd managed all night. I waved a goodbye and stood up to leave. At the door I said: 'One last question, Miss Birchall. Where did you first meet this Richard?'

'Oh God,' she said, putting her hand to her head. 'Yet another embarrassment. I was hoping you wouldn't ask that.'

CHAPTER TWELVE

The top-of-the-range Rover 75 in Ted Goss's garage was almost certainly the one he was seated in when the compromising photo was taken, so I had a SOCO go over it for samples. We'd keep them on file for future reference, if required. The coroner had declared his death a suicide, but he was an MP and there were the inevitable questions asked about his dealings, both financial and political. For some strange reason they'd kept off the sexual possibilities, but the press would have a feeding frenzy if they ever saw the photo. Fortunately only Edwin Turner and I knew of it. And, of course, the photographer.

The nearest Mazda dealer was in Huddersfield, and only nine RX8s were registered to owners who lived in Heckley, just one of whom was called Richard. Richard Wentbridge lived at the Flour Mill, Hunter's Valley, on the soft, southern edge of town. Gillian Birchall had blushed like a navvy at an ante-natal clinic when she confessed that she'd met her Richard at a speed-dating agency. Now where have I heard that before? I thought. The Flour Mill had been just that a hundred years ago, but now it was a desirable residence suitable for a captain of industry, a cancer surgeon or a TV weather girl. I drove by, now and again, and saw the Mazda and a brand-new Series 1 BMW on the drive a couple of times, but no people.

Philip, the other early starter when the York and Durham was raided back in 1978, was now assistant manager at their Burnley branch. Brendan and George went to interview him and reported that he was married with two grown-up children and lived a lifestyle appropriate to his earnings. He remembered Gail fondly, said he fancied her like mad back then, and was heartbroken when she left. He didn't realise she'd been fired. They told him that she wasn't doing too well and he said he might try to contact her.

We tracked down a few more students and a couple of them recognised Magdalena but had nothing to offer about who her friends were. The hole-in-the-wall gang were interviewed again and leant on fairly heavily, but none of them had any idea where Ennis might be living. *Crimewatch* showed a 25-year-old photograph of him and a computerised morph of what he might look like today. Thirty-two people phoned in, and during the following week every sighting was traced and eliminated. We showed his photo at Doncaster, Sheffield and Belle Vue dog tracks, but only received shakes of the head. We'd have been better employed showing it to the dogs. Their wagging tails would have told us if they were hiding anything.

Gillian Birchall's case was adjourned on the grounds that there might be mitigating circumstances and I received a postcard at the nick showing canoeists disturbing the reflections on Lake Louise, near Banff, and signed with a G. Then the breakthrough came.

'DI Priest,' I said into the phone. It was Thursday afternoon, my feet were on the desk and I was about to go home early for once. The sun was shining again after a couple of days of showers, and my grass desperately needed cutting.

'Oh, hello, could I speak to DI Priest, please?' The voice was nervous, and sounded like a schoolboy.

'This is DI Priest. How can I help you?'

'Oh, hello. This is the Blue Sky Trust. We're a multi-ethnic, non-religious, non-sectarian charity that works with ex-offenders; trying to help them re-integrate with society.'

'Uh uh.' I swung my feet back onto the floor.

'I'm assistant to the regional coordinator, standing in for him while he's on holiday.'

'Ye-es.'

'Well, earlier today I took a call from a man called Peter Ennis. He sounded desperate, wanted our help.'

I sat up, swept the papers on my desk aside and grabbed a pen. 'Go on.'

'So I told him we were understaffed at the moment but if he'd come back in a week's time we'd arrange an appointment. I started to make a file out for him, on the computer, but then I saw that there was already one there, presumably done by my boss. It didn't have much on it. It just said: "If makes contact tell him that a DI Priest, Heckley CID, is trying to find him". So that's what I'm doing.'

I thought about explaining that he was supposed to warn Ennis that I was after him, not the other way round, but decided not to. He was probably on work experience during his uni's recess, and finding it difficult in the big, wide, bewildering world.

'Cheers,' I said, airily, as if I couldn't care less. 'He left a couple of rather good oil paintings behind when he was released, and we want to get them to him. Do you have a forwarding address?'

'Primrose House, Primrose Avenue, off Lumb Lane, Bradford. It's a squat. There's no postcode, I'm afraid.'

'We'll find it. Thanks for your help.' I put the phone down, picked it up again to confirm that the connection was broken then punched the air. 'Yes!' I shouted. 'Yes!'

Dave and Maggie saw my jubilation and came to investigate. 'That's his address,' I told them. 'Ennis's. Also known as the Pope. Ring Bradford, Dave. Tell them we're a-coming.'

There are squats and there are squats. Some are sordid, stinking houses with no facilities, lived in by society's misfits who have no respect for anything and are happy to live in their own muck. They strip the plumbing out, burn the floorboards and live in conditions that the RSPCA would find intolerable for pigs. These are the lost generation, and the next fix is as far as their universe stretches.

Some, a few, are more responsible, and for them squatting is a political statement, a defiant gesture against capitalism. They see big, fine buildings deserted and falling into decay because the absentee landlords want to develop the site some time in the future, and they move in.

Primrose House was in-between. The intention of the original squatters may have had a touch of the noble about it, if living rent-free in somebody else's property can be regarded as noble, but because of the location next to the red light district they were soon swamped by runaways and dropouts of both sexes, happy to sell their bodies for the price of a hamburger. Now, the goodies had retreated to the upper floors and abandoned the ground floor to the junkies. Ennis, an informer told us, dossed downstairs, and slept with his eyes open. He'd tried to move upstairs but they had children and didn't want him near them.

Because of the kids we decided against an early morning raid. We watched the house over the weekend and he was seen twice, going for a walk into the town centre, where he busked with a penny whistle. He performed in Forster Square on Saturday and in the cathedral precinct on Sunday, and barely made a couple of pounds each time. We knew he hadn't signed on for the dole, and had presumed this was because he had access to the proceeds of the bank raid. It looked as if we were wrong.

Monday morning we lifted him. It was all very civilised. The sun was shining and we were in our shirtsleeves, some wearing shades. We approached him from four directions, just as he was about to launch into Barbara Allen, his party piece, for the eleventh time.

'Peter Ennis,' I said. 'I'm DI Priest from Heckley CID, and I'm arresting you on suspicion of murder.'

He stood transfixed for several seconds, the flute halfway to his mouth, then said: 'Thank God for that,' and offered his hands for the cuffs.

We fed Ennis, let him take a shower and found some clean clothes for him. Prison reduces a man. It takes him and wears him down, in his head and in his body. But Ennis had survived twenty-five years of it, kept going, we believed, by the knowledge that a fortune was waiting for him when he was released. But the money hadn't been there. Gwen Rhodes told me that he was an authoritative figure, commanded respect from the other prisoners, but the twelve months or so that he'd been free had eroded all that. All I saw when we arrested him was a stooped old man whose clothes hung on him, with sunken cheeks and dark, darting eyes. He'd been living on his wits and it had scoured him to the bone.

'You were released towards the end of August last year,' I told him. 'Where have you been living since then?'

We were in interview room number one, the tapes were running and he'd adamantly refused a solicitor. Dave was sitting next to me.

'Here and there,' Ennis replied.

'I believe you knew a woman called Magdalena Fischer.'

'What of it?'

'Did you know she was dead? That she'd been murdered?'

'Yeah.'

'When did you last see her?'

He didn't reply. Just sat there, his mind racing like a runaway engine, his eyes flicking from me to Dave and back to me.

'Have you seen her since you were released?'

No reply.

'How did you learn of her death?'

'Read it in a paper, didn't I.'

'Did it name her?'

'No. There was a picture. A drawing, done when she was a lot younger.'

'And you recognised her from it?'

'Yeah. It was her all right.'

'Memories play tricks sometimes. Especially to someone who's locked up, I imagine.'

'She came to visit me inside, didn't she.'

'Often?'

'As often as she could. It wasn't easy for her.'

'Because she was living with someone?'

'Maybe she was. I don't know.'

'Living with someone and spending all your money. Was that it?'

'What money?'

'You know what money. You didn't spend twenty-five years in jail because you liked the food. You're what? Fifty-four? That's a good age to retire at, with a nice little nest egg to help you along. Except, there doesn't appear to have been any nest egg, so what happened to it?'

'I don't know what you're talking about, do I.'

'Had she spent it all? Did she and her lover spend all your money? That'd be a disappointment for you, wouldn't it? Twenty-five years in the slammer with nothing at the end of it, when you could have been out in ten with a bit of cooperation. If it were me I'd have been annoyed. Were you annoyed, Peter? Or were you raving mad?'

He didn't answer, picked up his coffee beaker, realised it was empty and put it down again.

'Tell us about Magdalena,' I said.

'What's to tell?'

'Where did you meet her?'

'In a pub in Leeds. The Coburg, I think.'

'A good pub,' I said. 'Jazz nights, would it be?'

'Yeah, I suppose so.'

'Did you go for the jazz, or was it for the university talent?'

'Bit of both, I s'pose. And the beer.'

'She was there and it was love at first sight.'

'Yeah, something like that.'

'I'd have thought Magdalena was just a little too sophisticated for a piece of rough like yourself, Peter.'

He gave a little 'huh' with a hint of a smile, and said: 'Yeah, so would I.'

'But she fell for you?'

'Yeah, in a big way, didn't she.'

'Tell us about it.'

'What's to tell? We moved in together. A year later we had a little girl. Angela. Then I got banged up for...you know...the bank job. Magda came to see me for a while, with the kid, but I asked her to stop coming. It upset us both too much. I told her to tell Angela I was dead. She could wait for me, if she wanted, but to stop coming to the prison. So she did.'

He stopped there, but for me that was only the beginning. I said: 'What happened when you were released? You met up again, didn't you?'

'Yeah,' he admitted.

'Who contacted who?'

'She wrote to me. She'd been counting the days until my ERD. I thought she'd gone for good but she was waiting for me, after all those years. She met me that first morning, and I moved straight in with her. They were the best days of my life, from last August until...until...'

He couldn't get the words out. 'Until she was murdered,' I prompted.

'Yeah, until she was murdered.'

'Tell me about that.'

'What's to tell? One morning, about six weeks ago, she told me she had to go to Leeds, on business, she said. A Saturday, it was. She never came home again. I hung about in the flat for as long as I could but I only had a few quid. Couldn't afford the rent and the landlord wanted rid of us. Had to get out, didn't I.

'Where was this?' I asked.

'Beverley, East Yorkshire.'

'She'd moved to Beverley?'

'Yeah. Magda found this place. Said it would be a new start for us.'

'And where was Angela during all this time?' According to Len Atkins sixteen-year-old Angela had withdrawn the money held in trust for her and moved on.

'She'd left,' Ennis replied. 'Didn't get on with the bloke Magda was living with, did she. Magda lost touch with her.'

'I'm told she had a substantial amount of money in the bank.'

'Yeah, well, I sent her what I could. It all adds up.'

Not long ago prisoners were on about five pounds per week. Magdalena had told Len Atkins that Angie had more money than he'd believe. It didn't add up to me.

'Where did you go?' I asked.

'Leeds.'

'Why Leeds?'

'To look for her. But it had all changed. I hardly recognised anywhere. The pubs had all changed, too. It was like being in a nightmare. Then I saw in a paper this picture of Magda. An artist's impression, it said. She was dead. I drank myself stupid for two, maybe three days, didn't I. Woke up among the dustbins at the back of that shopping place where Merrion Street used to be, without a penny in my pockets.'

'Why didn't you sign on the dole, or ask one of the prisoners' aid societies for help?' I asked.

'Freedom,' he replied. 'Magda had filled my head with a load of cuckoo nonsense about freedom. I'd had twenty-five years of being a number, and now I wanted some freedom. It sounded good to me. When it all went down the pan I thought I might sign on, but then I saw you were after me, so I kept my head down.'

'How did you get to Bradford? And why Bradford?'

'I walked it, didn't I. Took me two days. I was sleeping rough, stealing stuff from the bins behind bread shops and sandwich shops. There was this other prisoner came out same time as me. Lived in Bradford. He was the only person I could think of. We were big mates in prison. Thought I might find him. I couldn't though. Then we had some bad weather and someone took me to the squat. It was terrible, full of dope heads, but warmer than a park bench in the rain. I'd had enough, was wondering what to do, when you arrested me.'

I turned to Dave and asked if he had any questions. 'Just a couple,' he replied, and twisted in his chair to face Ennis more squarely.

'It's a good story, Peter,' he began, 'but it leaves out one important item. The money. What happened to your 370,000 smackeroos? Tell me that.'

'There wasn't any money. I didn't do the job.'

'Your mates grassed you up, Peter. One of them couldn't hold his booze and took the easy way out when we arrested him. He turned informer and received a light sentence. All the others fingered you as the brains behind the raid. What's the point in denying it? You served your time. We can't touch you. Or do you still live in the hope that the money's somewhere, waiting for you?'

Ennis sat looking down at the Formica tabletop and didn't

reply. He'd probably lived so long denying the story that he really believed he hadn't masterminded the job.

'Perhaps Magdalena was looking after it for you,' Dave went on. 'Is that it? What would she do? Bury it in the garden or invest it somewhere? Or maybe her and her lover just slowly went through it. These days it's not such a big sum. If you're interested it works out at under £15,000 per year for the time you were inside. A reasonable salary, but not extravagant. Is that what happened, Peter? Did Magda let all your money slip away?'

'No,' he replied, his voice a croak.

'Did you knock her around when you found out? Is that how it happened, Peter? Did you lose your temper, in the red mist we hear so much about?'

'No, it wasn't like that.'

'So tell me how it was.'

'I loved her. And she loved me. I told her to let me go, but she wouldn't. I said she'd be better off without me, but she said we were soul mates. She used words like that all the time. Sometimes I didn't know what she was on about.'

'It all sounds lovey-dovey,' Dave said.

'Yeah, well,' Ennis replied.

'So tell me about the tattoo.'

'What tattoo?'

'The tattoo on Magdalena's arse.'

Ennis jolted upright. 'You know about that?'

'We've seen it, at the post-mortem. Tell me about it.'

'It was a sort of present, that's all. She came home one day and said she had a surprise for me. Led me upstairs and stripped off. I thought she wanted to make love – well, she did – but that wasn't it. She slowly turned round and there it was.

She'd had a tattoo. I asked her why she'd had it done and she said rings could be taken off, but a tattoo was forever.'

'You're saying she had "Property of the Pope" tattooed on her arse to please you?'

'Yeah. That's the sort of person she was.'

'And you're the Pope?'

'That's right. It started at school. I didn't mind. It's better than Pennis.'

'Magdalena told her boyfriend a different story,' Dave declared. 'She said that you knocked her about, and had the tattoo done to her because you were jealous and possessive.'

'Yeah, well she would, wouldn't she,' he replied. 'To save his feelings. She couldn't tell him that as soon as I was released she'd be off back to me, could she?'

He had a point, I thought.

Dave said: 'I'm inclined to believe her story. I think you used to knock her about. We haven't forgotten that you poured petrol over that poor bank clerk's head and threatened to set her alight.'

'It was…' Ennis began, then closed his mouth.

Dave pounced. 'It was what?' he demanded.

'Nothing.'

'It was what? Come on; get it off your chest. We can't touch you. You know that.'

Ennis sighed and shrank even more. 'I was going to say that it wasn't petrol. It was carpet cleaner. It doesn't burn, does it.'

'Big deal. Try telling that to the girl you tied to the chair. She wouldn't believe you and neither do I.'

'Well it's the truth.'

'I think you've forgotten what truth means. Magdalena lost you your money, didn't she? You turned violent towards her and there was a struggle. Your hands were around her throat and you were shaking her. She struggled, fought with you, and you kept pressing and shaking, until, suddenly, she went limp. You'd killed her. That's what happened, isn't it?'

Ennis's eyes darted between us and I saw his Adam's apple jerk as he swallowed. 'Yeah,' he said, very quietly, after a long silence. 'That's about it. I killed her.'

I adjourned the interview and Dave and I went over the road to a little café we use. We sent an egg and bacon butty in for Ennis and I had two hot jumbo sausage rolls with lashings of brown sauce and tea. Dave had a cheese salad in panini. Sometimes, he worries me. Gareth Adey, my uniformed counterpart, came in for a sandwich to take back to his office, but I encouraged him to join us and let the office look after itself.

'How's it going?' he asked, pulling out the bentwood chair opposite Dave. 'You're interviewing someone for the Magdalena murder, aren't you?'

'We were,' I said, 'but old clever clogs here has sorted it all out.'

'Really! How's that?'

'Tell him, Dave.'

'Oh, it's nothing,' he replied. 'I just applied the skills I've honed after God-knows how many years in the job, plus remembered some of the techniques garnered on several training courses, usually centred around the policeman-villain relationship, and that was that. I manoeuvred him into a corner with faultless logic and finished him off with a sabre thrust of unanswerable argument. In the face of that he had no other option than to admit that he'd enclosed her delicate neck between his hands and throttled her. Bang to rights.'

'Well done!' Gareth proclaimed, his face glowing with approval. 'Well done, David. You must be really pleased.' He reached across the table and shook Dave's hand.

'Um, yes I am,' Dave agreed, 'but there is one small detail we need to clarify before we can take him to court.'

'Oh, what's that?' Gareth asked.

'Well, she wasn't strangled, she was beaten to death. Our man is lying like a Tunisian camel dealer.'

CHAPTER THIRTEEN

'He could be selling us a double bluff,' I suggested as we walked back across the road.

'I know,' Dave agreed.

'Fancy a pint tonight?'

'What a good idea.'

Ennis had had a long time to ponder on things; spent a few thousand sleepless nights on his bunk, running his story through his mind; planning what he'd say or do when accosted; how he'd handle situations. Did he know that the money was lost before he came out and had he plotted what he'd hope was the perfect murder? Was confessing to the non-existent strangulation all part of that plot? Had he fallen into Dave's trap or had we tumbled head first into his? Don't ask me, I'm only the investigating officer.

'OK, Peter,' I began, after I'd reminded him that he was still under caution, 'we don't believe you, so it's time you did some straight talking. Let's start after breakfast on the day you were released. Where did you go and when did you meet up with Magdalena?'

Dave had made us three mugs of proper coffee, not the gunge from the machine, and brought three chocolate biscuits from the café. Ennis wolfed the biscuit down, keeping the uneaten portion concealed in his hand between mouthfuls, as if hiding it from predators.

He swallowed and took a sip of coffee, then said: 'The probation officer took me and this other bloke into Halifax in his car. Magda had said she'd see me in the bus station, near the newsagent. He couldn't park, so I jumped out and they both wished me the best of luck. It took me ten minutes to cross the road. Everything was so fast and noisy. I followed some people across. It was the scariest thing I'd ever done. I didn't expect her to be there. I had an address of a prisoners' aid society in my pocket, and a card from one called Blue Sky, just in case. The probation officer put me onto them.'

'Weren't you offered any away days before you were released?' I asked.

'Yeah, they offered me them, but I said no thanks. I couldn't trust myself to go back. When that gate shut behind me it would be for the last time. I'd made up my mind.'

'So was Magda there?'

'Yeah. I heard her calling my name, *Peter, Peter*, and turned round and there she was. It was...It was...'

It was all too much for him, or he was a good actor. He rocked forward, head in hands, and stared down at the table. After a minute he straightened up and wiped his eyes with the back of his hand. During the silence Dave said, deadpan, for the tape: 'Mr Ennis is overcome with emotion.'

They caught a bus into Leeds and then one for Hull that took them to Beverley, where Magda had recently found the flat. I let him skip over the intimate details of their reunion and asked for the address of the flat. I had a feeling we'd be doing some checking out.

'11A, Laundry Street,' he replied.

'What happened next?'

'Nothing. It was, like, living in a dream. Magda took me places. Down by the river to feed the swans, in the Minster, looking at all these old places. It was a new world to me, wasn't it. I'd wake up in a panic, scared stiff it was all a dream, until I felt her there beside me.'

'And what about the money?'

That ended the reverie. He clammed up, drummed his fingers on the table, fiddled with his coffee mug.

'C'mon, Peter,' I said. 'You were doing so well. You've admitted you poured carpet cleaner over that girl's head, so it's safe to assume you were there and you took at least a cut. Was Magdalena supposed to be looking after your share?'

'Yeah, you're right,' he admitted, after churning it over for a minute or so, 'but I was only one of the troops. I took a cut, same as the others, that's all. Magda invested it for me. Badly. She had a couple of thousand of her own, which she said I could have, but the rest was invested and it looked as if it was lost. She apologised, said she'd make it up to me. She'd been cheated, she said, but was trying to get some of it back. There was still a chance of something, she reckoned.'

'And what were these investments?'

'I don't know. She wouldn't tell me; said I'd only get into more trouble if I knew. Truth is, I didn't care, did I. I was as happy as a pig in muck. Happier than I'd ever been in my life. I told her it didn't matter, but she said it mattered to her.'

'So you lived a life of bliss for what? Eleven or twelve months? And then what happened?'

'There was a phone call one day. This bloke. He said he had something for her. Wanted her to go and see him. Next day she told me that she was going to Leeds, to do some shopping and see a girlfriend, but she went to see him, I'm sure of it. She said she might have a present for me, but she never came back.'

'Who was he?'

'Dunno, do I.'

'Did you ask?'

'No. I wasn't supposed to know about him.'

'But you think it was to do with the investments?'

'I hoped it was.'

'So you went to Leeds to try and find her.'

'And him. I thought that if I went to her old haunts I'd find out who her friends were, but it had all changed. Then I went to Bradford and you found me.'

We had him before a magistrate and didn't oppose bail, but we asked for conditions. He had to stay in a Heckley bail hostel, report to the nick every day and keep away from Leeds. He was our *numero uno* suspect for Magdalena's murder, and his confession was on record, but we were still looking. I reported his arrest in my murder log, but I didn't draw a line across the page.

Edwin Turner rang me as I was gathering my thoughts, wondering about my next move. Poor Ted Goss hadn't been part of the equation and things had been quiet for two weeks but it looked as if he wouldn't go away.

'I've found something,' Edwin told me, his voice a conspiratorial whisper.

'What this time?' I asked. I'd assumed he'd stopped searching, given it up.

'You know…What we were looking for.'

'Images?'

'That's right. Images.'

'How many?'

'Hundreds of them. Thousands, even.'

'Are they as horrible as we were led to believe?'

'They made me sick.'

'What have you done with them?'

'Nothing. I hoped you'd tell me.'

'What was the file called?'

'Something like Letters J – Z. It was a sub-folder of a file called Statutory Instruments, inside another called Safety at Work. It was well hidden. Do you want to see them?'

'No. You did well to find it, Edwin. I can't tell you what to do with it, but I know what I'd do.'

'Delete it?'

'That's right. Then delete it again from the recycling bin.'

'Shall I keep looking?'

'It might be a good idea.'

'Have you found anything?'

'Nothing definite, but I have a few leads to follow.'

It was only a little lie. Ted Goss had found himself a girlfriend and somebody had uploaded indecent images onto his computer. The same with Colin Swainby. Swainby met his girlfriend at a speed dating meeting, which is where Gillian Birchall met her date. Something was going off but I hadn't a clue what it was. It didn't make sense. I found a telephone number in the Police and Constabulary Almanac, picked up the phone, put it down, picked it up again and dialled the number.

* * *

Richard Wentbridge watched his wife walk into the hotel and fast-forwarded two hours to when they'd be having rough, clumsy sex on the passenger seat, in the Scammenden Dam car park. The thought did things to him. He was seated in his Mazda RX8 outside the Palatine Hotel and would follow her inside in a few minutes. From now on they would pretend not to be together. A black Jaguar swung into the car park and nosed into an empty space as he twisted to watch it. He liked the Jag, had considered buying one, and wondered who came to speed dating meetings in Oldfield in a car like that. It was even the XKR model, faster off the line than a Porsche 911.

It was a man, he noted with some disappointment, as a tall figure swung out, legs first, and uncoiled into the upright position. The indicators on the Jag flashed as the doors were locked, but the man went through the procedure again, and then tried the driver's door. When he was happy that the vehicle was secure he ambled towards the hotel.

The careful type, Wentbridge thought. Let's see what we can find out about him. He swung out of the Mazda and followed the tall stranger into the hotel.

'Nice car,' he said as he found a place at the bar next to his quarry. 'How do you like it?'

'I'm sorry?' the stranger responded.

'The Jaguar,' Wentbridge explained. 'I saw you arrive in it. Been thinking about one myself. Do you like it?'

'Oh, yes, it's fine. Lovely to drive.' He reached forward to take his change from the barmaid and thanked her.

'What is it? The four litre V-eight?'

'Um, yes, I think so.'

Wentbridge laughed, open and friendly. 'Oh, what a shame,' he said. 'A beautiful car like that and it's wasted on you.'

'I'm afraid it is,' the stranger confessed. 'Actually, it's not mine. It's one of the company's pool cars. I'm only borrowing it. I haven't a clue what half of the things are for. I'm much happier in one of the the Vectras.' He took a long sip from his pint of lager shandy and licked his lips.

'Wait a minute!' Wentbridge proclaimed. 'Wait a minute. You work for a company that not only has Jaguar XKRs in the car pool but that lets you out in them at night. Have you any vacancies?'

'One Jaguar,' the tall stranger admitted. 'And I'm the boss, so I have first pull on it. Boss's perk.'

'I'm still impressed. What line of business are you in?'

'It's what's commonly called a quango.'

'Quasi autonomous, non-governmental...'

'Yeah, you've got it. I'm the CEO, for my sins.'

Wentbridge grinned and shrugged his shoulders. 'The popular opinion is that it's not for your sins,' he said, 'it's a reward for scratching the right backs. You must be doing all right: decent package; good pension; *and* they let you use the company Jag. What more does a man need?'

'Well, for a start, some time off would be useful,' the stranger told him. 'I work bloody hard to earn my package.'

'I'm sure you do,' Wentbridge agreed. 'Times are tough, and nobody's throwing their money around, these days. So what exactly does this quango do?'

The stranger took another sip of his drink. 'Look,' he began as he lowered his glass, 'don't think I'm being rude, but to be honest, I came here tonight to try to get away from the job for a couple of hours. Can we change the subject, please?'

Wentbridge raised his hands in an apologetic gesture. 'Forgive me,' he said. 'It's me who's being rude. I see a nice car

and lose all sense of proportion and discretion. I take it you're
here for the speed dating?'

'That's right. Thought it might be interesting. I've never
done anything like it before. What's the routine?'

'I've only been once, myself. See the fat woman with the
bleached hair and the kaftan near the door into the other
room?'

'Dripping with bling bling?'

'That's the lady. Register with her. She'll tell you the carry-
on. And good luck. Tell them about the car and you'll pull like
a magnet.'

The tall stranger picked up his glass and walked over to the
woman. Beaming with delight, she ushered him into the
adjoining room that she'd hired for the night and asked him
to sit down at the table just inside the doorway, where her
paperwork was set out.

'Where did you hear about Encounters?' she asked.

'A friend told me about you.'

'That's what I like to hear. Personal recommendation is the
best way of advertising.' She explained about speeding tickets
and how the evening would progress, and started to fill in an
adhesive label. The tall stranger looked around the room,
which was rapidly filling, and saw that everybody was
wearing a label.

'You're number fourteen,' she told him. 'What name will
you be using?'

'You mean, my Christian name?'

It was an invitation to use subterfuge, if he wished.
Encounters didn't care who or what you called yourself as
long as you kept coming. They dealt in fantasies, and fantasy
started at the door.

'Or anything else you'd like to be known as.'

'I'm called Torl.'

She sat back and blinked. 'Tall?'

'T-O-R-L. Torl. My mother was Norwegian.'

'Oh, I see, It suits you. You are tall. It's a good job we don't all have names that describe us. I'd have to be called something like Dumpy.'

More like Dump Truck, he thought, but he said: 'Oh, Cuddly might be more appropriate.'

She giggled and would have blushed if she had the blush gene, but she hadn't. 'You'll go down well,' she told him. 'That'll be £24.99.'

The next hour was amongst the most tedious he had ever spent, ranking alongside being caught in the queue for Ikea on a bank holiday Monday or watching cricket on TV once when he took a day off work with a nose bleed. He tried to make the best of it, sorting the liars from the desperate, but decided it was unkind and generally just went along with what they said. He knew all about the difficulties of meeting people once you'd reached a certain age. His contribution rarely got beyond explaining about his Norwegian mother, then the time was spent listening to their stories. One woman in a pinstriped suit aroused his interest and she said she was an IC nurse at the General.

'Do you use strepto traps at the General?' he asked.

'Um, no, I don't think so,' she replied.

'They're what you catch streptomycin,' he told her, losing interest again as he registered her blank look.

He'd seen number twelve almost as soon as he'd entered the room, but had to go through the full quota before he was allowed his three minutes with her. She was wearing a silk dress in a mustard colour, and a shawl in a matching green was draped over the back of her chair. Torl looked into her face as he sat down opposite her, and his mouth felt dry.

'That colour suits you,' he said. 'Not many people can wear it, but on you it looks great.'

'Thank you,' she replied. 'I like a conversation that starts with a compliment.' She leant forward to read his badge. 'Torl? Is that your name or a badly spelt description?'

He reached out and pressed an imaginary button on the table between them. '*It is Norvegian*,' he said in a tinny, robotic voice. '*My mother vos Norvegian.*'

She laughed. 'I'm sorry. I guess you've been asked that before.'

'About twenty times. But what about you? Is Teri your real name, or are you really a Gladys or a Dorothy?'

'It's my real name now,' she replied. 'I adopted it for business reasons, a long time ago.'

'What line of business was that?'

'Hair and beauty. I opened a salon, eventually had ten dotted around West Yorkshire. Sold out when I got married. What about you? What do you do?'

He explained about the quango. 'We're called LINDI,' he said. 'Local Industry Development Initiative. I'm boss of the north-east section. We look for companies that are struggling through lack of capital and help them out. We also give early stage funding to venture investors, if we think they may be on to something.'

She smiled at him and his stomach tied itself in a knot. They were both leaning on the table and he could feel the heat of her legs close to his, or was it just his imagination? She said: 'You mean, you look for these companies and give them money?'

'Well, yes, more or less, but they have to go through a fairly intensive vetting process.'

'How much do you give them?'

'We have a maximum grant of £700,000.'

She opened her eyes wide and silently mouthed the sum back at him. 'You give them all that?' she said.

'Not all of them. Most grants are quite modest.'

'But you spend your working day looking for someone to give money to. Are you sure you're not called Santa Claus?'

He laughed. 'Some companies think we are. We have an annual budget of thirty million, and last year we helped nearly four hundred of them.'

Again she mouthed the sum back at him. *'Thirty million!'* Her lips were full and her eyes hypnotised him. He'd never seen such eyes. The lights played in them as she smiled at him and the pupils were blacker and deeper than the spaces between galaxies. Even the creases in the corners highlighted their perfection. Teri reached across and placed her hands on his. 'I've made up my mind,' she said. 'I want to be your friend. Can I be your friend? One of your elves would do.'

Torl turned his hands over to hold hers and thought that she could be his slave mistress if she wanted. He bit his bottom lip and tore his gaze away from her face, struggling for the right words. He wanted something frivolous and snappy, to break the spell, but the muse had deserted him. He opened his mouth to say he'd love her to be his friend, that he might even find a vacancy for another elf, but the bell rang and all the men stood up to move round one place.

CHAPTER FOURTEEN

Dave and Maggie were walking away from the coffee-making table with steaming mugs in their hands and big grins on their faces as I entered the office after seeing Mr Wood. 'What's the joke?' I asked.

'No joke, Chas,' Dave said. 'We were just talking about coincidences.'

'Do you believe in them?' Maggie asked.

'Coincidences?'

'Hmm.'

'Do you know, Maggie, you're the second person to ask me that this morning.'

'So do you?'

'No.'

'Coffee?'

'Please.'

'I'll bring it to you.'

I read the quotation on my calendar before tearing the day off, and opened the window. I have a desk down in the incident room but I prefer all my correspondence to come to my upstairs office, where I can sort it myself. The most interesting item was a lab report on the samples taken from the back seat of Ted Goss's car, showing that Ted himself had spent some time there, and so had a woman. Her DNA was obtained from hair found on the back seat headrest, but it wasn't on our database. Fingerprints on the passenger's safety belt buckle were probably hers, too, but they hadn't done the tests to prove it. These things cost money, and I didn't have a case to charge it to.

Maggie came in with my coffee and I told her to fetch hers. I was glad of the interruption. The Swainby-Goss soap opera was consuming my waking hours, and I was supposed to be looking for a murderer.

'OK, Maggie,' I began, 'it's 1978 and you've robbed a bank. The proceeds of your enterprise come to £370,000 and fill half a dozen suitcases.'

'That many?' she interrupted.

'Going on for that, I imagine. Remember that it was in fivers, oncers and coins, not nice crisp twenties, ready to be made up into wages by the various mills and factories. So you've got away with the money and paid off your accomplices. What would you do next?'

'I was thirteen, so I'd probably have blown it on lipstick and David Essex records, but I'll try to put myself in the robber's place. How would he invest it – is that what you're getting at?'

'It's a starting point.'

'There wouldn't be much point in hiding it. Not for twenty-five years, unless he was planning to escape. For a start, he couldn't be sure that the currency would stay the same. What did fivers look like in 1978?'

'I think they were blue.'

'There you are, then. He could have put it in a building society, or several building societies. We didn't have ISAs and TESSAs back then, but there must have been something similar. Then there's the stock market...'

'Do you think he'd know how to invest in the stock market?'

'Hmm, perhaps not. Not individual companies.'

'Let's keep it simple,' I said.

'OK. I'd go for several building societies. There was no such thing as a suspicious cash transaction that far back. They'd accept money from anyone. They'd accept money filled with bullet holes and bloodstains, and stay open late for you if the sum was big enough.'

'You're a cynic, Margaret,' I said. 'So how long would you sit on the money before you started salting it away in building societies?'

'Ooh, I'd probably start out with good intentions. Maybe to hang on for a year, but as soon as the heat died down I'd change my mind. Villains are usually the impatient type, especially when they're in the money. I can't see Ennis being any different.'

'He claims he was only one of the foot soldiers.'

'He's a lying toad.'

'Would you trust the money to anyone else?'

'No.'

'Not even your Tony?'

'Well, yes, I'd trust Tony. But I wouldn't trust any of Ennis's accomplices as far as I could hurl them.'

'What about Magdalena?'

'Ah,' Maggie began, 'the fair and voluptuous Magdalena. I wondered when we'd get round to her.'

'Have you ever considered having a tattoo?' I asked.

'Never. But my sister has one. A ladybird on her shoulder. She thinks it's wonderful, I think it's ghastly.'

'Did she have it done to please her husband?'

'No, and he doesn't like it, either. I think she had it done because she fancied the tattooist.'

'Ennis said Magdalena had the tattoo done to please him. Len Atkins reckons he forced it upon her to demonstrate his hold on her. If Len was right I can't imagine her running back to Ennis as soon as he was released, can you?'

'Not really, except she might have liked a man who pushed her around a bit. The assertive kind.'

'Are there women like that?'

'So I'm told.'

'Magdalena wasn't one. I'd describe her as a proto-feminist.'

'So maybe she gave as good as she received. Maybe they couldn't live without each other.'

'You mean...like Burton and Taylor?'

'Why not? What's Len Atkins like?'

'He's...a plumber. A hippy plumber. Len's idea of a good time is to grout a shower cubicle.'

'There you go, then.'

'So you reckon she was Ennis's woman all along, and she was just passing time with poor Len?'

'It looks that way, don't you think?'

'Hmm. And it follows that he would trust her with the money.'

'That's right, although he probably had little option.'

'So she put some in an account for their daughter and invested the rest.'

'And lost it.'

'And lost it.'

'Which would leave the aforementioned Mr Ennis mightily annoyed.'

'You can say that again.'

Brendan is my youngest and newest DC. He's been with us for nearly a year and is still eager to please. We gave him a series of tedious but essential jobs, like sitting in a Transit all night with a pair of binoculars and a notebook, checking out nightclub bouncers who were dealing in ecstasy, and he came back smiling every time. His sense of humour is best described as creative, and he's in love with Julia Roberts, but we don't hold her against him. Yesterday I'd given him a job to do and now he was knocking on my door.

'Richard Wentbridge,' he said after I'd told him to sit down. 'I've done a PNC check and he's had three speeding tickets, going back fifteen years. He's currently driving a Mazda RX8, as you thought, and he's been clean for the last six years. According to the electoral roll he's married with no children. Date of birth, oh-four, oh-two, sixty-four, which makes him forty-one. His house must be worth a million and he appears to have a lavish lifestyle with no visible means of support.'

I said: 'Forty-one, a great age to be. I can hardly wait. Stick it all on a piece of paper and put it in my bottom drawer, please.'

'Already done.' He passed me an A4 sheet with a few lines of typing on it. 'Will that do?'

'Yeah, that's fine.'

'So what's it all about, boss?'

'I'm not sure, Brendan,' I replied, and told him briefly about Miss Birchall and her birthday antics. 'It might be nothing but it smells fishy. Meanwhile, it might be worth keeping a weather eye on Mr Wentbridge. Tell you what: let's make a phone call.'

I dialled the number for our asset recovery team and spoke to the DCI who set the whole thing up. They work anonymously from a suite of offices in one of the new business parks that are sprouting up all over the place. Nobody's building factories any more, but we have warehouses and offices a-plenty.

'Wentbridge...Richard,' he said as he typed the name into his database. If somebody has a rich lifestyle but cannot or will not explain the wherewithal to pay for it, the asset recovery legislation assumes that his wealth is ill-gotten and available for confiscation. In some ways it's as important a tool as DNA profiling in the war against major criminals. Not all crime involves knocking someone on the head or climbing drainpipes in the dead of night. Asset recovery goes straight to the big boys who don't get their hands dirty.

'Sorry, Chas,' he came back. 'He's not known to us. Did he ought to be?'

'I'm not sure, yet, but I'll keep you informed.' I thanked him and put the phone down. 'Right, then,' I said to Brendan. 'Here's another one for you,' and I told him about the Range Rover that had allegedly forced Gillian Birchall off the road. 'It must have suffered some rear-end damage,' I said, 'so have a word with the main dealers to see if anyone has brought one in for repair since then. Start at the top and work your way down to the smaller paint shops. I know it sounds trivial but there may be more to it.'

Brendan grinned and said: 'Great,' as he stood up to leave. He likes working on his own, I'd noticed.

Big Dave arrived and stood in the doorway. I gave him a quizzical look and he said: 'Peter Ennis failed to report yesterday. He's back in Bentley.'

'Best place for him,' I said, and picked up the sheet of paper Brendan had given me. 'Brendan!' I called as he pulled the door closed behind himself.

He opened it again and poked his head round it. 'Yes, boss?'

'Richard Wentbridge's wife,' I said. 'You haven't given her a name.'

'Haven't I?' He checked his notebook. 'Sorry, boss, I must have overlooked it. Is it important?'

'No, I don't suppose it is,' I said. 'Concentrate on the Range Rover.'

Fiona Foyle's eyes widenened. 'Monte-Carlo!' she exclaimed. 'On Sunday! Yippee! You're a darling, Tristan.' She turned and gave him a noisy kiss on the cheek. 'Did you hear that, Teri? We need to do some serious shopping before the weekend.'

'The people who've rented the apartment don't want the boat,' he explained, 'so we might as well use it. We'll be roughing it, but we'll survive for a week.'

'Silly them,' Richard Wentbridge declared.

'That's what I call roughing it,' Fiona said.

'What about the plane?' Wentbridge asked.

'Available Sunday morning for an early flight to Nice. It's all taken care of, if that's all right with you two.'

Richard looked at Teri. 'Ooh,' she said, 'I'll need ten new bikinis and a gallon of factor 25, but I think it will be all right. Don't you, Ricko?'

'You bet.' Images of himself smearing his friend's wife with suntan oil, back and front, on the mahogany deck of the private yacht, were already flooding his mind.

'Will we be able to go to Cannes, to that restaurant we found?' Fiona asked.

'And St Tropez,' Teri added. 'I love St Tropez.'

'We should be able to squeeze them in,' Tristan replied.

'And the casino!' Fiona insisted. 'We must go to the casino.'

'Definitely the casino,' Richard agreed.

It was their regular Wednesday evening meeting, and they'd dined again at the Wool Exchange. This time they'd returned to the Flour Mill, home of the Wentbridges, for the usual postprandial delights.

'What did you reckon to the meal tonight?' Foyle asked. He was sitting on a leather settee, between the two women. Wentbridge was pouring drinks at a cabinet in the corner, below an original watercolour of a Dales scene. It used to be his favourite painting, not because of its artistic merit but because he owned the pub it depicted. Now, pubs were being boarded up all over the place, and this one had become a liability.

'It was horrible,' Fiona replied.

'My sole was fine,' Richard declared, sinking into an easy chair after he'd supplied everybody with a drink.

'It's the best restaurant in Heckley but I think it's growing a bit stale,' Tristan stated.

Teri, sitting next to him, put an arm around his neck and pulled him closer. 'I hope you don't think we're growing stale,' she said.

'Nuh-uh,' he replied, shaking his head and engulfing her in an embrace. Fiona, sitting at his other side, glanced across at

Richard and they held each other's gaze for several seconds.

'So where are we with the game?' Fiona asked, and Tristan broke away from Teri.

'Yeah,' he said. 'It's all gone a bit quiet. Cost me £400 to fix the Rangey and we've had nothing to show for it. She hit me a lot harder than I expected.'

'You must've braked too hard,' Richard told him.

'It's not something I practise regularly,' he replied. 'So why hasn't she been in court?'

Richard said: 'I went down there and looked at the list and she wasn't on it. Apparently her case has been adjourned, so I'll just have to keep looking out for her. It's disappointing, but that's life.' He turned to his wife: 'Teri might be onto something, though, mightn't you, kid?'

'It's looking good,' she replied, and told them all about her meeting with Torl, the previous evening.

'Torl?' Tristan echoed with disbelief. 'He's having you on.'

'I don't think so,' Richard replied. 'I had a chat with him before the session started and he told me the same thing. And he was in fifty thousands' worth of XKR.'

'He could've hired it.'

'To pull totty at the speed dating? Come off it – he could do that with a Ford.'

'Well he sounds dishy to me,' Fiona said. 'You're only jealous because he's taller than you. Presumably you ticked each other on your cards, Teri?'

'That's right. Encounters emailed me late last night, but he hasn't rung me.'

'It's only been twenty-four hours.'

'They usually ring after twenty-four minutes.'

'He could be playing hard to get.'

'Well he's no business to.'

Richard coughed and said: 'I hate it when people play hard to get. Don't you, Fiona?'

'I don't know,' she replied, standing up and pulling him to his feet. 'It's not something I've ever experienced.'

A few seconds later they were in the master bedroom. Richard, still thinking about the following week on the yacht, threw the pillows off the queen-sized waterbed and started to unbutton his shirt. Fiona said she needed to use the bathroom.

'Have a look in the cabinet,' Richard told her. 'There should be some Johnson's baby oil in there. Bring it back with you.'

Something didn't make sense but I couldn't pin it down. There were too many distractions in the office so I took a wander around town and bought a sandwich and a bottle of flavoured water. There were plenty of distractions in town, also. The local shop and office girls were out in force, minimally dressed, all spare tyres and bra straps, as they shopped for bargains in the cut-price stores that always proliferate in towns struggling to recover from mass job losses. I amused myself checking out their tattoos, guessing between shoulder blade or small of back, between butterfly or Celtic symbol. The men were displaying, too. They wore singlets to show off their artwork, and trousers cut off below the knee to reveal elaborate patterns on the outsides of their calves. I could have been an anthropologist in a Brazilian jungle, writing a thesis on Amazonian body art.

I strolled down to the canal and sat on one of the new benches on the revitalised waterfront. A glut of narrow boats were tied up, almost as far as the eye could see, painted in traditional colours – red, green, black and yellow. A woman on one of them gave me a friendly wave as she watered her geraniums. The boats came from Stoke, Stafford and Nottingham, spending time in Heckley instead of simply passing through because the drought was causing the water levels in the canal system to fall low. You can't please all the people all the time. After a ten minute struggle I successfully extricated my cheese and Branston sandwich from its plastic box and settled down to enjoy it.

Sonia, my last girlfriend, had a tattoo. Just a tasteful butterfly, low down her spine, out of sight except under the most intimate circumstances. It hurt me, for a while, that she'd had it done for someone else, but I soon recovered. There were a dozen reasons why she may have had it done, but she was with me then, in my arms, and that was all that mattered.

Magdalena Fischer had her tattoo done back in 1977 or '78, when punk was at its height and tattooing was ceasing to be a man thing. Whether she'd had it done herself, or had it forced upon her, was something we'd probably never know. Certainly Ennis's story was more plausible, that she'd had it done to please him, and fobbed poor Len Atkins off with a lie to save his feelings. Ennis had changed, that was for sure. Not changed by twenty-five years in jail. He'd survived that, although it must have had an effect. No, it wasn't prison, it was freedom that had crushed him, reduced him to a husk of the man he'd been. Magdalena had filled his head with romantic notions, but it's easy to be a freethinking, freewheeling hippy when you've the safety net of a social security system to protect you from a fall. What was it Karl Karlson sang: *Freedom is the poor man's solace*? I was beginning to realise what he meant.

Ennis said that Magdalena told him she was going to Leeds on business. A man had rung her but Ennis didn't know who he was. Why hadn't he asked? Why hadn't he demanded to know who he was? I ran through the interview in my head. Twice we'd touched upon the phone call but it didn't make sense. Magdalena told him she had to go to Leeds, on business, or to do some shopping, or to see a girlfriend, and she might bring a present back for him. That's all, so how did Ennis know that this mysterious man had phoned her? That he existed? I cursed myself for a sloppy interview and reached for my mobile.

Towering pine-clad mountains; rickety bridges over terrifying gorges with nameless waterfalls; pancakes and maple syrup. Gwen Rhodes was in Canada, tucking into her breakfast as the train meandered through the picture-book scenery, but she had a deputy and he'd be trying her desk for size. He answered the phone second ring.

Prisons guard their charges jealously. Deputy governors with an eye on the top job more jealously than most. Eventually he agreed that Ennis could be supplied with a phone card and asked to ring me during association, which started at two. He would be offered the services of a solicitor or the probation officer, and told that he was perfectly within his rights to refuse to talk to me. I said I appreciated it was most irregular, and thanked him profusely for his cooperation.

'One last thing,' I said before ringing off. 'Have you had a postcard from Miss Rhodes?'

'No, not yet,' he admitted.

Well ya-boo sucks, I thought as I broke the connection.

* * *

Ennis rang me at twenty past two, just as I was beginning to think the worst. 'Thanks for ringing, Peter,' I said. 'Do you have a solicitor or probation officer with you?'

'No,' he replied. 'Did I ought to have?'

'I doubt it. I won't be asking you anything that could hurt you. First of all, why didn't you report to the nick?'

'Because I couldn't hack it in the hostel, could I. Load of tosspots and stupid rules. Do this, don't do that. You know where you are in Bentley.'

'It was your choice. I want to know a bit more about this phone call that Magdalena received, that sent her dashing off to Leeds. Did you discuss it with her?'

'No, not at all.'

'So how do you know it was a man and about the money? It could've been her previous boyfriend for all you knew.'

'Because I listened to it, didn't I.'

'You overheard the conversation?'

'No, I listened. It was one of those phones that takes messages. A day or two after she'd gone I was messing with it, wondering if there was anybody I could ring, if her friends' numbers were stored in it, when I made it repeat his message. He just said he wanted to see her, had something for her. I could hardly make it out, but that's what he said. That's all.'

I was silent, wondering if there was any relevance in this, until he asked if I was still there. 'Yeah, I'm still here,' I said. 'What did you do with it?'

'With what?'

'The message. Did you delete it?'

'No. Wouldn't know how to, would I. I just left it.'

'Was it a modern phone or one that takes a little cassette, do you know?'

'No idea.'

'Let me get this straight, Peter. You're saying that you didn't know this man had rung her until after she'd been missing for a day or two.'

'That's right.'

'OK. Thanks for ringing me.'

'Does this mean you believe me, Mr Priest? That I didn't kill Magda?'

'Let's say we're still looking. I don't suppose you remember the Beverley number, do you?'

'No, sorry.'

'I'll find it. Thanks again.'

I listened to it ringing, over and over again until the answerphone chimed in, for at least ten minutes. Telephone numbers are available on CD, these days, which is just as well because the Directory Enquiries system is a mess since it went public. Terrestrial numbers, that is: mobiles are something else. I'd nothing more important to do so I kept on dialling. Maybe the apartment hadn't been re-let, I thought, or perhaps it had and the new tenant was out at work.

'Hello,' a voice said.

I clamped the phone to my ear. 'Who's that, please?' I asked.

'It's the builder.'

'The builder?'

'Yeah. There's nobody here 'cept us.'

'Oh, right,' I said. That explained the delay in picking up the phone. That explained why his voice was booming and echoey, as if he were speaking from inside a million-gallon water tank. The place was having a makeover. 'I'm DI Priest, from Heckley CID, I wonder if you can help me. That phone you're speaking into: is it the type with a built-in answerphone that has a cassette, can you tell?'

'Have you rung about the phone?' he asked.

'That's right.'

'I thought you were coming to move it.'

'Was I?'

'Yeah.'

'When?'

'Today. We could do with it moving.'

'Does it have…?' I began, but he'd cut me off. What is it about builders? They show their arse cracks to the world like displaying baboons and think that gives them a licence to treat the rest of us like morons. I reached for the Almanac and tried to think of who I knew in the East Riding. I needed help there, and fast.

Nobody. The best way to get a favour done in this job is to call one in. I'd trained more detectives than most people have had sore heads, but as I ran my finger down the Humberside page I couldn't recognise anyone who'd graduated in the Charlie Priest Academy of Sleuthing. My influence was fading; things had changed.

I rang a name that sounded vaguely familiar but he wasn't in and the person who answered the phone had better things to do than help me. I looked at my watch: a quarter to three. I might just do it.

I guessed it to be about seventy, seventy-five miles to Beverley, and sixty of those would be on motorway. I scrawled a note saying where I'd gone, left it on my desk under the stapling machine, and hit the road.

The M62 suffers major gridlocks but I hit a lucky patch and

settled in the fast lane, between the BMWs and white vans, until we were clear of the A1. Then it was pushing the ton all the way to North Cave. At five past four I was driving over Beverley racecourse with the Minster hovering in the distance, directly ahead, caught in the afternoon sun. Beautiful.

I suspected that Laundry Street would be in the old part of town, within the walls, and after driving round the one-way system and asking a woman pushing a bicycle, I found it and saw the tell-tale skip and builder's van outside 11A. It was the narrowest street in Beverley, with long terraces of period houses crowding directly over the pavement. I didn't intend staying long so I parked alongside the skip, blocking the road.

The front door was wide open and the air inside hung with plaster of Paris. Everything was white, like being inside a glacier, but strangely gloomy until my eyes adjusted. A wooden ladder was laid the length of the hallway and some steps leant against the wall. The floor was covered with a dustsheet that had once been white but now displayed evidence of a thousand colour schemes, every one a variation of magnolia.

'Anyone here?' I called, my voice hoarse with the dust in my throat, echoing as if in a cavern. No reply. I moved further into the gloom and called again.

A little rotund man appeared, carrying a sheet of plasterboard. He was wearing overalls in the same colour scheme as the dustsheet, and spectacles spattered with paint and plaster, and looked harassed because the walls were built before the invention of the plumb line. 'Have you come about the phone?' he demanded.

'Yes.'

'In there.'

I went through the doorway he'd indicated, into an empty room with a bare patch on one wall where a fireplace had stood until earlier in the week. No doubt, in fifty years or so, a different tenant would try to uncover it. The telephone sat in a corner, on the floorboards.

It was a BT Response 150, in cream plastic that had discoloured with age. A red light with *Power* written next to it was glowing, and a green one, called *Messages*, was blinking. Next to the handset cradle was a cover with a small tab indicating where to lift it. I fell to temptation and lifted the tab. There, underneath, was what I'd come for: a tiny cassette.

I was reading instructions under the cover when somebody outside started blowing their car horn. I had the road blocked. I unplugged the phone and its power supply, bundled the cables around it and carried it out of the room.

'I've got the phone,' I shouted. No reply, but the car horn sounded again.

'I'm going. Where are you?' No reply again, except for another, different car horn.

Ah well, I thought, I've got what I came for, and walked out into the street. I waved an apology to the first car in the queue and started my engine. As I looked in my mirror before pulling away I noticed that the second vehicle was a BT van. I'd just made it.

CHAPTER FIFTEEN

The journey back wasn't so straight forward. I caught all the traffic and it was nearly seven when I parked in my spot outside the nick. Upstairs I plugged in the phone and its power supply and read the instructions under the cover. *Press Play/Pause*, it said, *and the unit will announce how many messages you have.*

There were ten messages, but nine of them were silent, presumably made by me earlier in the day. Number ten was a real call, but barely decipherable. The tape was worn out and the quality hopeless. After several plays I'd decided it said: *It's me. I've something for you. When can you come?* The voice was male, but any accent or other characteristic was unintelligible. He sounded as if he had a duvet wrapped around his head and a small furry animal in his mouth. I felt certain it was Magdalena's killer doing the talking, and was therefore a step forward, but how big a step was anybody's guess. I put the phone in the bottom drawer of my filing cabinet and went home.

* * *

The tall stranger stepped out of the shower and pulled a towel off the rail. He dried his hair and worked his way down, rubbing his back with a sawing motion then attending to his middle regions and each leg. He brushed his teeth, making growling noises at his reflection in the mirror, then flexed his muscles in a parody of a bodybuilder working out, while trying to decide whether to eat Chinese, Indian or Italian. It had been a long day, and his shoulders ached. He rotated them one way and then the other and decided on fish and chips, in the restaurant, with a gallon of tea. Then home to a welcoming, if lonely, bed. He pulled on a pair of jeans, matched them with a blue check shirt and was looking in his sock drawer when the warbling of a mobile phone came whiffling up the stairs. He dashed down and pulled a phone from the pocket of his jacket, hung in the hallway, but the warbling continued after he pressed the button to accept the call. It was the wrong phone. He delved into the pocket again and retrieved a different one, one that he'd not used before. He looked at the caller's number, pressed the button and put the phone to his ear. 'Hello,' he said.

There was a silence and he could hear the pulse near his ear booming and whooshing, until a tiny voice said: 'Is that you, Torl?'

'Ooh, it could be,' he replied, 'is that you, Teri?'

'Yes, it is. You don't mind me ringing you, do you?'

'Of course not. I've got your number here in front of me. I was wondering whether to ring it but you beat me.' He seated himself on the bottom step and brushed his hair back with his free hand.

'Were you going to ring me?' Teri asked.

'I'm not sure; I hadn't decided. I wanted to but wasn't sure if I ought. I'm glad, though, that you rang. It's been two days since I saw you. Two long days.'

'I know,' she replied, 'and I'm going away at the weekend. I wanted to see you before then.'

'Where are you going?'

'The boring old south of France. I'll tell you about it if I see you.'

'When will that be?'

'It's up to you. I'm not doing anything now.'

'Tonight it is then, but I need something to eat. Where can I pick you up?'

Teri gave him directions to a block of apartments that had once been a woollen mill, down by the canal. He found a pair of clean socks, buffed his shoes with them before giving each a squirt of aftershave and pulling them on, and collected his second-best jacket from the wardrobe. Pity I'm not in the Jag, he thought, but never mind.

She answered immediately he pressed her entryphone number and was there opening the door within seconds. Everything he'd remembered about her was true, but more so. If anything her impact was greater than before. She was wearing a short skirt and a bolero jacket, with a white blouse that emphasised her tan. He told her that she looked beautiful, but stumbled over the words.

'Thank you,' she said, looking into his face with a smile that sent his nervous system into meltdown, 'and you look handsome.'

'Oh, one does one's best,' he replied with a grin, wrestling his feelings under control.

He took her to an Italian restaurant that had a good reputation, a few miles out of town, and they had the chef's speciality seafood pasta dish. Torl cleared his plate, explaining that he hadn't eaten all day, while Teri barely touched hers. He resisted the temptation to ask her to pass it over to him.

'So tell me about the south of France,' he said as he topped up her wine.

'Thank you. What's to tell? It's my husband's idea. Some sort of reconciliation. We fly to Nice Sunday morning, then on to Cannes. I don't want to go, but I suppose I have to.'

'Most people would leap at the opportunity,' he told her.

'They don't know my husband,' she replied. 'He's a control freak. This is typical of him. He doesn't ask, just assumes it's all right. Sometimes he frightens me.'

'He's not violent towards you, is he?'

'Not really, but it's not far under the surface.'

'Are you living together?'

'No. He bought the apartment as an investment when they were first built, and I've moved into it. He's living in the house.' She could have added that he'd masterminded and financed the development of the whole mill, but didn't.

'So where's the house?' Torl asked.

'Heckley,' she replied, which didn't enlighten him at all.

They had coffee and he paid the bill. In the car she said: 'I can't invite you in because he might come. Sometimes he does. He gets drunk and falls asleep on the settee.'

'Don't stand for any violence,' Torl told her. 'Go straight to the police if he's ever violent, or if he threatens you. It's completely out of order.'

'I feel safe when I'm with you,' she said. 'Can we just go somewhere quiet and talk?'

He drove up onto the tops, to a place where the council kept a big pile of grit in a roadside lay-by for when the snows came. In daylight it looked like what it was, but after nightfall, with the lights of the valley spread out below, there was a magical feel to the place. As if specially requested, a three-quarter moon hung low in the sky. Torl yanked the handbrake on and killed the lights and engine. Teri shuffled in her seat and moved closer to him. He reached his arm across her back and squeezed, feeling the bones in her shoulder, as delicate as a sparrow's.

They sat like that, her head on his chest, for several minutes.

'That's called a gibbous moon,' he said, breaking the silence.

'Gibbous?' she replied.

'Mmm.'

'What does that mean?'

'I don't know, but that's one. I ordered it. Send me a gibbous moon, I said, for a rather special lady.'

He felt her chuckle to herself and she wriggled closer. He wondered about suggesting the back seat, but resisted the temptation. How long he could continue resisting, he knew not.

'What did you think of the speed dating?' Teri asked.

'I thought it was wonderful,' he replied.

'So did I,' she agreed. 'I'd never been before, but I'm glad I went. The woman who organises it is a character, don't you think?'

'She's certainly larger than life.'

'A big lady.'

'With a figure that lunched a thousand chips.'

Teri sat up and stared at him. 'Did you just make that up?' she demanded.

'It came to me, out of the blue,' he told her.

She snuggled back against him. 'You're clever, aren't you? And funny, too. I wish I wasn't going to Cannes.'

'It might be for the best,' he said, his voice a whisper.

'Why do you say that?'

'I'm a married man, Teri. I have a wife in Notting Hill. I work up here through the week and dash off back to her every Friday night. I get a bit fed up with my own company and don't like pubs all that much. I was just looking for someone to go to the theatre or cinema with, or out for a meal. That's all. I never expected...' He let the words trail off.

'You never expected what?' she asked, softly.

'I never expected...to meet someone like you.'

'I'm sorry if I'm not what you were looking for.'

'You're more than I was looking for. Far too much more. Somebody would get hurt, and I don't want that.'

Teri reached around him and stroked his neck. 'If nobody knows, nobody gets hurt, do they?' she said, her voice soft and low. Tiny electric shocks were flickering up and down the back of his head, numbing his jaw muscles. He craned his head back to signal how much he was enjoying the attention, and half closed his eyes.

'Truth is, Teri,' he began, turning to face her, 'I've a confession to make.'

She pulled her arm back and sat up. 'What's that?'

'Well, fact is, I'm a minister. I'm a minister in the Methodist church. If I had an affair with you it would be against everything I've ever believed in. Can you see that? I'd be the biggest hypocrite in the country. I think you're a wonderful girl, Teri, and I'd love to see more of you, but I'm not sure it would be wise.'

'Right,' she said.

'I'm sorry.'

'Nothing to be sorry about.'

'Are you mad at me?'

'No.'

'Honest?'

'Take me home, please.'

Torl started the engine and drove back into town. He held her hand all the way, stroking her fingers, but she hardly responded until they were approaching the canal. Her hand started to rhythmically squeeze his, gently at first, then harder until it almost hurt. He glanced across at her but she was staring straight ahead. He dragged his hand away to change gear and felt her roll from one side to the other as he turned off the main road. He looked again and saw that her head had slumped forward, chin onto her chest, and she was making noises in her throat.

He pulled off the road and unfastened his seatbelt so he could move closer to her. Her teeth were rattling and jerky movements shook her body. Torl pulled her closer and enclosed her in his arms.

'It's all right,' he said. 'You're safe. It's all right.' Now her whole body was convulsing and she kicked her bare feet against the car's bulkhead. He unfastened her seat belt and held her tighter, pressing his face against the top of her head, her perfume adding to the confusion of feelings that assaulted him as he tried to reassure her.

'It's all right,' he repeated. 'You're safe. It's all right.'

Slowly she recovered, her breathing becoming more rhythmic and the convulsions ceasing, until he thought she was asleep. 'Take big, slow breaths,' he told her. 'Through your mouth. Nice and slow. That's the way.'

She shook her head and stirred. 'Take it easy,' Torl said. 'Everything's all right. You've had a little blackout, that's all.'

'I'm...sorry,' she said, allowing herself to sink into his embrace.

'Nothing to be sorry about.'

'Was I unconscious long?'

'I'm not sure. A second or two, perhaps. Just sit quietly. You're quite safe.'

'I'm ever so sorry.'

'It's OK. You've nothing to apologise for.'

'Oh hell. Poor you. What must you think, being lumbered with me?'

'It's just one of those things,' he replied, his arms still around her. 'Has it happened before?'

'Yes.'

'Recently?'

'About six years ago. I take something called an AED for it. That's an anti-epileptic drug. I haven't had a seizure since then, once we'd found an AED that suited me. A couple of weeks ago the doctor suggested that I might be able to stop taking the pills, so I did. He was obviously wrong.'

'There's doctors for you,' Torl said.

She shrugged herself out of the embrace and dried her eyes on a tissue. 'I must look a mess,' she said.

Torl reached across and took hold of her chin, turning her face towards him. The illumination of the streetlamps showed that her hair was mussed up, her mascara smeared and her lipstick smudged. 'No,' he said. 'You look just as beautiful as ever.'

'Uh,' she snorted. 'You're a poor liar. I...I...'

'You what?'

'I was going to say that...well, I wanted tonight to be special. I was looking forward to seeing you so much. Now, I've blown it. I don't suppose you want to be seen with someone who suffers from *le petit mal*.'

'It doesn't make any difference,' he said. They sat in silence until he asked: 'How long will you be away for?'

'Just a week. We come back the following Sunday.'

'If...you know...if you and your husband are not reconciled, if it doesn't work, will I be able to see you when you come back?'

'I'd like that,' Teri replied. 'Will you give me a ring?'

'It's a promise.'

Torl put the car in gear and drove the rest of the way in silence. He parked outside the apartments and asked Teri how she was feeling.

'I'm fine,' she replied. 'Just a slight headache.'

'Did you ought to see a doctor?'

'No, it's not necessary.'

'OK. I'll wait until you're inside. Which is your window?'

'The end one on the top floor. Will you wait until I'm up there, please? I'll give you a wave.'

'No problem. Goodnight, Teri.'

She leant across and kissed him on the cheek, then briefly on his lips, and opened her door. 'Thanks for a lovely evening,' she said, 'until I spoilt it.'

'You didn't spoil a thing,' he assured her. As she turned to shut the car door he called after her: 'Don't forget to take your pills,' and immediately realised the ambiguity of what he'd said.

Teri ducked to look inside at him, her face perfectly

composed, and replied: 'No, I won't forget,' and slammed the door.

Two minutes later she opened the curtains and waved. Torl flashed his headlights and drove home. Upstairs, Teri stripped off all her clothes and lingered under the shower, enjoying the pulsing of the jets of water against her skin. She dried herself and pulled an upholstered buffet out from under her dressing table. Lulu Guiness cosmetics were her current favourites. She selected face cream and body cream from amongst the selection of lotions and spent fifteen minutes pampering herself by applying copious amounts of the unguents to her already-flawless skin, all the time going over the evening's conversations in her mind and wondering what Torl would be like in bed. She rubbed the surplus cream into her hands and opened the drawer of her dressing table. From it she selected a silk pyjama top, then felt further back, behind the night- and underwear, until she found what she wanted. She withdrew her hand, holding a plastic sex toy that Richard had bought her two Christmases ago. Pressing the button resulted in a violent buzz and vibration, indicating that the batteries were in order.

Lying on the bed, propped up by all the pillows, she dialled a number on her mobile phone. Richard answered almost immediately.

'You're home early,' she said.

'I know. Where are you?'

'I'm in bed.'

'Yes, but where?'

'The flat, cheeky. Where do you think?'

'Just checking. Is he with you?'

'No! It was our first date.'

'So how did it go?'

'All right. He took me to that tacky Italian we tried a few weeks ago. It hasn't improved.'

'So has he offered to give you one of his grants to enable you to open another beauty business?'

'No, we didn't discuss it. Softly, softly, catchee monkee.'

'That's the spirit. Are you coming home?'

'No, I'll stay at the flat tonight.'

'Do you want me to come round?'

'No, I'm all right, thank you.'

'Won't you be lonely?' Richard asked her.

'No,' Teri replied. 'I've got Freddie to keep me company.'

'Freddie? Who's Freddie?'

She held the vibrator against the phone and gave it a short burst on *maximum*. 'Freddie,' she repeated. 'My little friend. You bought him for me.'

'Oh, him. Now I'm jealous. Jealous of five quid's worth of plastic and wire, assembled in Taiwan. So how did you leave it with Torl? Was he eager to see you again?'

'No, just the opposite. I'll tell you about it in the morning, but he wasn't going to ask. I had to resort to feminine guile; to plan B.'

'And what exactly was plan B?'

'To arouse his protective instincts. I just happened to have a slight seizure.'

'You're kidding! And did he fall for it?'

'Oh yes, he fell for it. Like a lamb to the slaughter.'

CHAPTER SIXTEEN

We had a big meeting Friday afternoon and I did a lot of writing on the whiteboard. I was having trouble compartmentalising the separate cases, so it helped clear my head. Magdalena was beaten to death and Peter Ennis was the main suspect, but we didn't have a case until we eliminated all the other possibilities. There was always the chance that a total stranger had murdered her.

We knew who'd killed Ted Goss, though. He'd done the deed himself, but who'd driven him to it? He'd been flattered by the attentions of the woman we knew as Teri, the same woman who had insinuated herself into the affections of the bombastic Colin Swainby, and obscene images were found on both their computers. Were they guilty of downloading them, or was she in some way responsible?

And then there was Miss Gillian Birchall and Richard Wentbridge. Had he really wined and dined her, at considerable expense, just to have her prosecuted for driving over the limit? It seemed unfeasible.

I'd sent the troops home and was sitting sprawled in a

plastic chair, my feet on another, looking at the board. I was enjoying the quiet, thinking about the cases, separating one from the other. Magdalena was a straightforward murder. Man kills woman, sex or money, QED. But the others were baffling. The victims were people of stature in the community, namely an MP, a headmistress and a police superintendent. The two men were linked via Teri, and Miss Birchall to Swainby through the speed dating. We didn't know how Ted Goss met Teri. There's this new crime, called happy slapping, where you beat somebody up and video the whole thing on your mobile phone, for later enjoyment. It usually involves down-and-outs and drunken youths of either sex, but was this some sort of high-class happy slapping? Or even anarchy? Did we have an anarchist cell in Heckley, working to destroy the credibility of our movers and shakers?

It had been a good exercise. I'd sorted things out in my head. I'd been juggling too many balls, but now I realised that there were only two. Then the door flew open and Brendan burst into the room and into my reverie, waving a sheet of paper like Chamberlain after the Munich conference.

'Boss,' he said, his face red because he'd run down the stairs. 'I'm glad I caught you. Two messages waiting for me when I went upstairs. That Range Rover you asked me about. A man called Tristan Foyle took one into Heckley Motors on Monday the fifth, damaged in exactly the right place at the back. Cost him £350 to put right. He lives at Home Farm, Biddle, which is on the Penistone Road, and his wife is called Fiona, maiden name Jones.'

'Well done,' I said. 'We'll have him checked out, but Monday will do.'

'I haven't finished,' Brendan went on. 'You remember that

I forgot to ask about Richard Wentbridge's wife?'

'Mmm.'

'Well, I thought I'd do the job properly. Somerset House got back to me while I was down here.'

He handed me another message sheet. Someone had written on it: Teri Wentbridge, DOB 3rd March 1977, married Richard Wentbridge 1st March 1998, actual given name Angela, maiden name Ennis

'She's really called Angela Ennis,' he explained. 'This woman called Teri is Ennis's daughter,' and the balls I was juggling came tumbling down around my ears.

Maggie had asked me if I believed in coincidences. They could happen, I suppose. Of all the billions of events that occur every day, some are bound to be duplicated, but I doubted if this was one of them. She had to be someone's daughter. Trouble was, I couldn't see if it had any relevance. Saturday morning I put my walking boots in the car and didn't dally at the office after completing my diary and logbook. I headed towards Ilkley Moor and did a short walk that took me past some of the cup-and-ring and swastika stones that litter the moor. It was a warm day, and walkers were out in force, but I didn't mind. It's the tradition in Yorkshire to speak to everyone you pass while out walking, so it was a succession of 'How do' and 'Good afternoon' with like-minded people all the way round the circuit. I do my thinking when up on the moors, and managed to fit some in between the interruptions. Principal subject was the bank raid money, and how I'd invest it. I came up with a few ideas. After a late lunch at Dick Hudson's I changed out of my boots and headed into Leeds.

JKL Mackintosh looked confused when he opened the door,

until I explained who I was and told him that I'd interviewed him several weeks ago over the death of Magdalena. He invited me in and asked if I'd like a drink of any sort. I declined.

'Are you any nearer finding Magda's killer?' he asked.

'We have someone in custody,' I told him, 'but we haven't completed our case against him, yet.'

'So how can I help you, Inspector?'

The pictures above his fireplace were the same landscapes and I wondered how much they were worth. A bob or two, for sure. In the middle was a figure I didn't remember. It was a primitive red clay woman with pronounced breasts that reminded me of Henry Moore's early works. I asked about it and he told me it was a Nigerian fertility figure, the genuine article.

'There's a period in Magdalena's life that is blank to us,' I said. 'We have no trace of her between about 1980 and '88. Was she still posing for life classes in that time, do you know?'

He thought about it, long and hard. The secret of being deceitful is to only lie when it's critical. Tell the truth at all other times, otherwise you might be caught out on something irrelevant. Mackintosh either knew the rule or he had nothing to hide. 'Um, yes,' he said. 'She was still with us then.'

'Did you know her during that time?'

'I suppose I must have done, yes.'

'Did you know she had a daughter?'

'No. I had no knowledge of her personal life.'

'Was Australia ever mentioned in your conversations with her?'

'I wouldn't say I had conversations with her, but no.'

'Or a man called Ennis?'

'No, I'm afraid not.'

I wasn't bothered. I sat there and looked at his collection of works, at the primitive figurines, the watercolours and the modern sculptures. 'You have eclectic tastes,' I said.

'I know,' he replied. 'It's not exactly a collection, more a few pieces from various periods. I had a clear-out a few years ago, when my contents premium went through the roof, and just kept a few diverse pieces for myself. They're my favourites.'

'No conceptual art,' I said.

He laughed, his face turning pink, and the laughter turned into a fit of coughing, reminding me that he was an old man. As he struggled for breath the scar tissue on his neck showed livid white against his flushed skin. He apologised as he wiped his mouth on a coloured handkerchief and said: 'Conceptual art is an oxymoron.'

'I thought you were a fan,' I said. 'Wasn't Leeds in the forefront of the movement, back then? I seem to recollect a couple of students who hit the big time with some outrageous pieces. Didn't you write an article for the press defending them?'

'My darkest hour,' he confessed. 'They were good students, with some original ideas, and I tried to protect them from a savaging by the tabloids.'

'What happened to them?'

'They faded into obscurity, as did their so-called works.'

'Well,' I said, 'the money they made out of it will have softened the blow.'

He was silent for a while, as if his mind had wandered off, then he shook himself back into the present and said: 'Yes, I suppose it would.'

I drove home trying to remember the names of the two artists who's flame had burnt brightly and briefly, dividing the world into violently opposed camps. One, the man, had produced a sculpture made from bakelite telephones glued together. About a hundred of them. He called it the Tower of Babel, something like that. The woman's contribution was a barrel containing, allegedly, a million pounds, buried somewhere on Woodhouse playing fields. The point was that it changed our perception of the fields, added value to the view even though it was invisible. There were other pieces, too, usually of a sordid, sexually explicit nature, involving urinals, condoms and dead fish. I'd looked, listened to the arguments, and decided to stick with oil paints.

Sunday morning I rang Miss Gillian Birchall from the nick and told her that I'd like her to come over to Heckley and see if she could identify the block of apartments where she'd dropped Richard off. She was in the middle of revising the syllabus to fit in with new directives from the latest Secretary of State for Education, and glad of the interruption. I offered to pick her up but she insisted on driving over in her newly repaired Honda.

'Bring the glass and coffee mug with Richard's prints on them,' I told her.

We met in the car park and she suggested we go in her car, to which I readily agreed, although I nearly slipped a disc threading myself into the passenger seat. She was wearing camouflage cargo pants and a Rupert Bear T-shirt, and her hair was cut like Princess Diana's used to be. I hadn't noticed that when I saw her in the cells.

'Wow, this is sleek,' I said, pulling the seat belt across my

shoulder and looking for the place where it fitted. 'How fast
will it go?'

'My one indulgence,' she admitted. 'I enjoy owning a decent
car.'

I knew the feeling. Single, with a reasonable disposable
income and nothing to spend it on. My pleasures come cheap,
and I don't even mind what sort of car I drive, as long as it
starts on cold mornings. I could've blown my money on
paintings, I supposed, but, short of spending millions, I
preferred my own.

'Left out of the gate,' I said, 'through the middle of town.'
I gave her directions through the deserted town centre and
took her south, towards Hunter's Valley. She drove smoothly,
but stayed legal because it's nerve-wracking to have a police
inspector in the passenger seat. When we were clear of town
she sped up, snicking the Honda through the gears like a rally
driver. As we approached I said: 'Slow down. Take this left
turn, then the first right. That's it. Your friend Richard –
Richard Wentbridge – lives in a mansion called the Flour Mill
towards the end of the development.'

'Wowee,' she said, quietly, as she glanced sideways and saw
glimpses through the trees of the houses at the end of their
long drives. 'These are some mansions.' We were in football
manager territory. New money, but modest with it.

'They probably send their kids to your school,' I ventured,
but she didn't rise to the bait.

She glanced nervously at me, saying: 'He might recognise
my car.'

'He won't,' I assured her. 'It's on the right, past the big tree.
Slow down.'

The gates were closed and there were no vehicles on the

driveway. The house was well back from the road but the few windows we could see were all firmly shut. Not so with the next door neighbour. He was wearing check trousers and unloading golf clubs from the back of a Porsche Cayenne 4x4, but the most noticeable feature about him was that he was black.

'IC3,' I said as we cruised past him. 'Definition of a cool Yorkshireman: one who wears his flat cap back-to-front. I wonder what the good people of Hunter's Valley think of having him for a neighbour?'

'It's...' Gillian began, her voice touched with excitement. 'Don't you recognise him?'

'No, should I?'

'He's a pop star. He was on children's TV for years, then graduated to being a DJ and rap artist. The kids think he's wonderful. Zed Boogey, that's his name. Zed Boogey.'

'Zed Boogey,' I repeated. 'Never heard of him.' In my book, rap was the musical equivalent of conceptual art. Back in the Sixties Dylan wrote two rap songs and completely exhausted the genre he had created. 'Well now you know where Richard lives,' I said. 'He's the only Richard with an RX8 within miles and miles. We presume he's your birthday date.'

'Don't remind me,' she replied.

'Keep going,' I told her. 'Follow the road round until it rejoins the main road. Then turn right and I'll show you where Tristan Foyle lives. We think he's the owner of the Range Rover you dented. How much did it cost to repair this one?'

'Just over £900.'

'It cost him £350.'

'Uh!'

Foyle lived out of town, on the Penistone Road, in the home-farm house of what had once been a big estate until death duties caused it to be broken up. I directed Gillian down a narrow lane with passing places, between fields of newly cut corn, to a hamlet of about ten upmarket houses, built to raise cash for the old landowners and ease them out of genteel poverty. Home Farm, Foyle's house, stood slightly separated from them, with a five-acre paddock behind. I told her to park across the gateway and we looked down his drive at the triple garage and stable block, which hadn't seen a horse since the invention of the Chelsea tractor. Again, the gates were closed and there were no vehicles in sight.

'And here we have the home of Tristan Foyle,' I said. 'Range Rover driver.'

'It doesn't look as if he's in, either,' she observed.

'No,' I agreed. 'Back into town, please, then follow the brown signs for the canal basin and see if you can find the block where you dropped Richard off. It'll look completely different in daylight.'

It did look different, but the second block we looked at was confidently pronounced the one where she'd dropped Richard off. 'I turned round here,' she said, pulling into a cobbled lay-by. 'I couldn't make it in one because of that lamppost, so I had to reverse. This is the place. Definitely.'

'Right,' I said. 'Now take me back to the station, please.'

'Will you be able to prosecute what's-his-name, Foyle?' she asked.

'No. He'd say he braked for a cat or a fox, and didn't realise you'd hit him.'

'Great! And what about Richard Wentbridge? Do I have a defence against the drink-driving charge?'

'To be honest, Gillian, I don't know. There may be a defence of mitigating circumstances, but it's not straightforward.'

'So what's the point of this morning?' She obviously had better things to do than swan around with a tired old cop who didn't have better things to do.

'Putting it bluntly,' I told her, 'Wentbridge got you drunk. Then, in a separate incident, you had an accident with Foyle. If we can link Wentbridge and Foyle we may be able to show that there was a conspiracy.'

'Why would they want to conspire against me?'

'I don't know. Do you?'

'No. So can you link them?'

I looked at her. A wisp of hair had fallen across her eye, and I couldn't understand why it wasn't irritating her. I said: 'I'm working on it. Let's leave it at that.'

The private charter Lear 55 had them in Nice in two hours, and not many minutes later Richard, Fiona and Teri were nibbling a *salade Niçoise* outside a restaurant on the *Promenade des Anglais* while Tristan went off to look for their motor yacht. He owned a quarter share of the sixty-foot long *Amelia Rose* but rarely used it. He'd investigated buying outright, then considered chartering as and when necessary, but had settled on a compromise when a business associate invited him to join a syndicate. When none of them was using the yacht a management company let it for them at €4,000 per day, which just about covered the mooring fees.

'So where do you girls want to go this afternoon?' Richard asked.

'Shopping,' they replied in unison.

'Where?'

Teri: 'St Tropez.'

Fiona: 'Monte-Carlo.'

Tristan appeared, accompanied by the skipper of the *Amelia Rose* and the chef to help with their luggage, although they were travelling light. After handshakes all round they made their way down the waterfront and along one of the network of piers to where the yacht was moored. Fiona twisted this way and that as they passed the bigger boats with their helicopter pads and parked Maseratis, remembering the days in Dubai when this was the norm and not a treat. Signs on the gangplanks indicated that stiletto heels were discouraged, and she noticed the Jimmy Choo slingbacks lying on the decks where they'd been slipped off. Teri kept her eyes on the captain as she followed him. He was younger than she remembered, and had good shoulders and a firm backside. She could see his underpants through his snow-white trousers.

They went to St Tropez, with Tristan steering when they were in open water, and moored at the Marines de Cogolin. It was hot and busy, so the two men were content to follow their wives into the cool of the boutiques on rue Henri Saillon and ogle the beautiful shop girls. High on the list of must-haves for the two women were handmade sandals from Keklikian, as worn by everybody who mattered on the Cote d'Azure. Richard weighed the flimsy footwear in his hand, looked again at the price ticket and wondered how many humming birds were killed to make a pair. Never mind, he was thinking, tomorrow we hit the casino.

I sent Serena round to forensics with the answerphone tape, for them to work whatever magic they could on it. But most of all I needed a copy on a regular-sized tape or disc.

When she came back with it I told her to contact Mrs

Dolan, the blind lady, again, and invite her to assist us. Mrs D finished work at twelve, and was delighted to help, so Serena went to collect her.

'Does your gift work over the telephone?' I asked, after reminding her who I was. We were in my upstairs office and Serena had made us coffee. I watched her place Mrs Dolan's carefully in front of her and touch her fingers against it.

'Of course I remember you,' she replied. 'Red and grey. Yes, it works with all sounds, choose where they come from.' She ran her fingers round the rim of the coffee mug we'd given her, felt for the handle and raised it to her lips.

'I see you quite often,' I said, 'coming across the square. You amaze me with your confidence. I follow *you* across the road.'

'It's probably misplaced confidence, Inspector. I don't see the danger all around me. If you're going to go blind, do it when you're young, while your powers to learn are at their height. What is it you want me to do?'

'Listen to this,' I said, 'and tell me if you would recognise the voice elsewhere.' I pressed the *play* button and the muffled voice filled the room for a few seconds. I rewound and played it another twice. 'Is it any use?' I asked.

She shook her head. 'I'm not sure. It's a bit woolly, isn't it?'

'Like a sheep shearer's jumper,' I replied. 'Our forensic department are trying to clean it up, but they take their time and I'm impatient. Do you see anything at all?' I rewound the tape and played it again.

'I see something, but it keeps changing. It's as if the colours are all mixed up and muddy. I see a colour, but it's unstable and keeps sliding into another colour. What do you want me to compare it with?'

'Some phone calls, see if a voice matches the one on the tape.'

'Right. I'll try. Play the tape to me again, then play the others, one at a time.'

'We don't have them on tape, I need to ring them. This is a live show.'

'Oh. So how do I listen?'

'It's a loudspeaker phone. And we can record the whole conversation.'

'So I'll be hearing it through a telephone line and a cheap loudspeaker.'

'I'm afraid so. Do you think that would change things too much?'

'It's a lot to ask for.'

'You could always listen on a party line.'

'I'm still not sure. It would pick up more outside noise. The colours I see are strong but they're ephemeral; they change easily, tip over into something else.'

I said: 'So you think it's a waste of time? Fair enough, but I'd like you to try again when we've cleaned up the tape, if you don't mind. You did such a good job with the robbers. Thanks for coming in, Mrs Dolan. Serena will take you home when you've finished your coffee. It was just a mad idea I had. So how old were you when you lost your sight?'

'I could talk to them myself,' she said. 'On the phone. That would cut out the loudspeaker.'

'Oh. What would you say?'

'Dial the first number and listen,' she said, so I did as I was told.

After three rings a voice said: 'Atkins plumbers.'

'Good afternoon,' Mrs Dolan greeted him. 'I'm ringing on

behalf of the Royal National Institute for the Blind. I was wondering if you would care to sell a few tickets in your area for our grand Christmas draw? The first prize is £2,000 and all proceeds go directly into RNIB funds to assist the visually impaired. May I put you down for a couple of books?'

'Um, how much are they?' young Atkins asked.

'One pound per ticket and there are fifteen in a book.'

'Just send me one book, love. I'll have them myself. I'm not very good at selling things.'

'Thank you. That's very kind of you. Can I just check your postcode?'

'LS26 7JQ.'

'Any joy?' I asked after she'd replaced the handset.

'I don't think so, but I can't be sure. I sold a book of tickets, though.'

Next it was the turn of Atkins senior. He sounded tired, or stoned, and declined with profuse apologies. 'I'd forget all about them,' he explained, 'then feel guilty when I find them, months too late.'

From there it was all downhill, and I renewed my respect for unfortunates who have to earn a living by telephone canvassing. Nobody was downright abusive, but they made it quite clear that their time was being wasted and they didn't approve of scroungers who cold-called at inconvenient times. After each call she turned her face my way and gave a shake of her head.

The last one said: 'Instead of bothering me, young lady, why doesn't the RNIB simply cash in some of the billions it already has invested?' and slammed the phone down.

'*Young lady*,' she repeated. 'The cheeky whippersnapper.'

'There's no more,' I told her. 'It might not have worked, but it's been an interesting exercise.'

'That last one,' she said. 'I can't be sure; not like with those robbers, but he was the closest.'

'Really!' I said. 'That's great. That's just great.'

'So how many tickets would you like, Inspector?' she asked.

CHAPTER SEVENTEEN

They breakfasted on the boat and meandered back along the coast, anchoring at the Iles de Lérins for a sunbathe and snorkel. Louis, the chef, made them lunch of *les petits farcis* and *morue à la Niçoise* made with fish he'd caught himself, earlier in the morning, followed by fresh fruit salad in Cointreau and two bottles of Brut Imperial. After that it was snoozing in the shade as they cruised along the coast towards Monaco and its casino.

The roulette wheel is a device for randomly selecting a number between 0 and 36. The ones in the casino in Monte-Carlo are a hundred years old, made with mahogany and lignum vitae and inlaid with brass, ivory and ebony. They run on Timken bearings and are constantly monitored for any bias towards certain numbers. If the management didn't spot the bias, the clientele soon would. The croupier spins the wheel and invites bets. The gamblers watch it rotate as if it were divinely driven, guessing which pocket the ivory ball will bless with its presence when it stops its wild dance around the perimeter. The surroundings are hushed and opulent, the clientele sophisticated, the atmosphere exclusive. God, or the fairies, or Joan the Wad, or whatever force you believe controls your destiny, does its stuff and a number is chosen. The croupier's rake reaches out and pulls in the stake money. Sometimes, but not always, it pushes a few tokens towards a lucky punter.

Pulling a ticket out of a paper bag would have chosen a number just as effectively, but a certain *mystique* would be missing, and it's that mystique that drives men to lose fortunes and throw themselves off tall buildings. It's that mystique that keeps the casino owners in Ferraris, Rolexes and Gucci shoes.

Our new Chief Superintendent (Crime) rang me. He'd been studying the Magdalena case and my reports over the weekend and decided that an unbiased outside opinion from a fresh mind was called for, meaning his own.

'It's usually the simple solution, Charlie,' he told me. 'The one that's staring you in the face. Look for the sex angle, look for the money, and what are you left with?'

I waited for him to tell me. After a few seconds he said: 'Are you there, Charlie?'

'Yes, boss. I'm listening.'

'I asked you what you were left with.'

'Oh, sorry. Um, Peter Paul Ennis?'

'Exactly! Lean on him, Charlie. It's been going on long enough. Let's have a result, eh.'

'Right, sir. Thanks for your help.'

I put the phone down. Trouble was, Ennis wanted to go to jail. It was the only life he knew. I didn't have any great objections to making his wish come true, but there was always the chance that he'd change his mind when it came to court, and say we beat the confession out of him. And when I send someone to jail I do like it to be the right person.

I jammed the phone between my chin and shoulder while I found a number in my notebook, and a few seconds later asked to speak to Miss Birchall.

'Who wants her, please?'

'My name's Detective Inspector Priest.'

'One moment.'

She sounded headmistressly when she answered, and I pictured her behind a big wooden desk like the one in my old headmaster's office, then decided she'd be more likely to have a high-tech one, with a flat screen VDU and multiple telephones dotted about. She'd have a PC World calendar on the wall and a Microsoft mouse mat. My old headmaster had a cane leaning in the corner, the end pickling in a jar of vinegar to make it sting more. It never did me any harm.

'Gillian Birchall.'

'Hello Gillian,' I said. 'It's Charlie Priest. Hope I haven't dragged you away from anything important.'

'Uh!' she snorted. 'You might not think our Christmas Nativity play is important, but believe me, on the night it's the most important thing in the world. How can I help you?'

'It's not totally unrelated. I'm looking through the file, such as it is, and I'm thinking that perhaps we're neglecting the creationist angle. Perhaps we should take a closer look at your more fundamentalist governors. Do you have a school chaplain, anything like that?'

'We're attached to St Ricarius church,' she replied, 'and the vicar takes a service for us at various festivals. That's about it. He's available, of course, if anyone wants spiritual guidance.'

'Where does he stand on creationism?' I asked.

'I've never asked him, but he's a pragmatic sort of bloke. I can work with him.'

'Give me his number, please, and I'll come over and have a chat about fundamentalists, for any general background information he can give me. I won't mention you, of course.'

She didn't suggest I call in to see her for tea and buttered crumpets while in the vicinity. I put the phone down and gathered my thoughts before ringing him. I don't lie awake at night, going through the arguments for and against evolution, but it is something I have strong feelings about. Intelligent design is something that some creationists have come up with as an alternative to Darwinism. Evolutionary theory, as defined by Charles Darwin, says that we are all descended from a common origin, our differences being caused by favourable mutations accrued over about four billion years. The creationists believe that everything was created by God one wet Tuesday morning about five thousand years ago. Intelligent design is their attempt to describe how things like, say, our eyes came about. They claim they couldn't be a result of a series of happy accidents called natural selection, that there must have been some great design responsible for them. Evolution has masses and masses of evidence to support it; everything else relies on blind faith. Creationists are down there with the flat-earthers, or those who believe that every unexplainable light in the sky is proof of alien visitors. I dialled the vicar's number.

In many ways, Monaco is totally egalitarian. If you dress the part, you're in. Paying the bill is another story. Tristan and Richard wore black suits and bow ties; their wives in dresses that would have passed muster along the coast at a Cannes opening night. They caught a taxi up the hill to the casino, and were dropped off outside its elaborate frontage. The tourists in their sweat-stained T-shirts turned away from ogling the parked Lamborghinis and Aston Martins to watch the four of them trip up the steps towards the entrance, where a doorman inclined his head as if they were old friends before they were swallowed by the thermostatically controlled gloom of the interior.

The men held back, behind their wives, steering them with fingertips on their spines through the main hall with its countless slot machines. They walked purposefully, ignoring the roulette games where businessmen from Brussels, Rotterdam and Sutton Coldfield, watched by their overweight wives, lost ten Euros a spin trying for a 35-to-1 win on a lucky number. They didn't see the elaborate rococo decoration of the opulent hall, with its gilt and mirrors, its frescoes of allegoric scenes and its historic bas-reliefs as they headed into the depths of the building, towards one of *les privés*, where the stakes were much higher. Another doorman watched them with an expert eye as they approached, was happy with what he saw and pulled the door open for them. Inside, credit cards were offered and paper tubes of coloured chips with elaborate designs were gratefully received.

There were five players at the table they chose: two Chinese; a middle-aged man straight from Sticksville USA; a Frenchman fondling his girlfriend who looked about twelve; and a woman on a high stool with more lipstick on her craggy features than the Arc de Triomphe has pigeon shit. Richard and Tristan circled the table like predatory sharks, watching the wheel's silent spin, absorbing the electricity in the filtered and cooled atmosphere, feeling for the power that all gamblers believe in. They moved into place at opposite sides and the other players adjusted their positions slightly to accommodate them.

There are two rules in roulette that ought to be self-evident, but few of the players understand them. *There is no such thing as a run of good luck.* Ignore this at your peril. The second rule is really an explanation of rule one: *What has gone before can have no effect whatsoever on what is about to happen.* They watched a couple more spins and each peeled the wrapping off a tube of chips, placing them on the table. They noticed that the Chinamen had huge piles in front of them and appeared to be doing well, concentrating hard on the wheel, betting on blocks of four numbers in two different places on the baize mat. The Frenchman pushed a couple of chips to where his girlfriend indicated, as if he were feeding a cuckoo and not expecting a return, more interested in nibbling her ear than in gambling, and the woman studied the mat as if she could read it like the tea leaves, and placed a pile of four chips on number 10. She hesitated, then split the pile between 10 and 31. The Yank said: 'That's me out,' and shambled off, poorer but no wiser, and they regrouped to absorb the space he'd left.

'*Faites vos jeux,*' the Filipino croupier said, and spun the wheel again. She was wearing a backless dress slashed down the front and little else except for hair as black as a raven's wing that reached to her waist. Falling in love with your favourite croupier was an occupational hazard for the regular visitor, and encouraged by the management. Tristan and Richard had watched a couple more spins and thought they caught the measure of the wheel. One of them put a gold-inlaid chip on red and the other put one on evens. Teri squeezed Tristan's hand and moved closer to him as the ivory ball streaked around the rim of the wheel like a wall-of-death rider, held there by centrifugal force until its speed dropped. As it came round for the third time the croupier said: '*Rien ne va plus*,' and in three more revolutions it fell into the middle and began a crazy dance, skipping and leaping from number to number, finally settling in number 21, which is an odd number and happened to be coloured black. They had each lost £500.

Jonathan Leary was intrigued and invited me over to see him there and then. Tell someone you're a cop and need some help from them and they're hooked. It works with women and it worked with the vicar of St Ricarius. Dave wasn't in the office but Serena was, so I asked her if she could tear herself away from what she was doing and come for a ride.

'Oh, it's not important,' she replied with one of her smiles, 'and I'm always ready to go skiving off.'

'We're not skiving off,' I told her. 'We're pursuing investigations. How's your mileage, this month?'

'I haven't reached my quota yet.'

'Good. We'll go in your car.'

Serena's parents came from Bangladesh when we needed workers for the wool and cotton industries who would accept low wages so we could compete with cheap imports from places like, well, Bangladesh. It didn't work, but they were an enterprising race and her father opened one of our first corner shops where you could buy a pint of milk and your cornflakes right up to midnight. Soon he had a string of them, and he became a strong voice for integration and moderation. Some didn't like it, and he suffered the usual broken windows and graffiti, but he always retained his dignity and worked hard on behalf of his community. Two years ago he was elected mayor of Heckley.

Serena is the smallest policewoman we have. I think the tape measure must have slipped when she joined, or maybe someone realised we needed her and turned a blind eye. When she was in uniform I used to see her on duty in the town centre when the pubs closed and admire her courage. She took a lot of flak, out on the streets, facing up to boozed-up racist yobs that many of her colleagues would think twice about tackling, but always came through it with a smile. Some, though, came from within the force, implying that she was our token Asian, only recruited to make us look good, and that hurt her. She started looking for another job until someone noticed the fall-off in her performance and put two and two together. They had a word with me and one day I just happened to meet her in the car park.

'How's things, Serena?' I said.

'Oh, fine, Mr Priest. Just fine.'

'Still enjoying the job?'

She hesitated, then said: 'Yeah, it's fine, sir.'

'There's an aideship coming up,' I told her. 'Why don't you put in for it?'

Her big eyes grew even bigger. 'To be a detective?' she said.

'Can't make any promises,' I told her, 'and you'd get all the shitty jobs. The rape victims, abused children and worse, you know the score.'

'I could do it, Mr Priest. I could do it.'

'I know you could, Serena. I wouldn't have mentioned it, otherwise.'

So she flew through her six months attachment to CID and

was put on the books, but never quite considered herself one of the team, always being very proper in her speech and behaviour, and taking a back seat in meetings or during lighter sessions in the office. Until her father was made mayor, and everybody started treating her like royalty. Dave and Maggie made a paper chain for around her neck, and she told them to piss off. That was the breakthrough, although she still refuses to call me Charlie. She says it's disrespectful, so I don't mind.

As we drove over the tops I told her about Gillian Birchall and the possibility that she was the victim of some sort of conspiracy to discredit her. She listened, then said: 'I haven't heard this being discussed at briefing. Have I missed something?'

'No. It's all low-key at the moment. There may be nothing in it, or she may be pulling the wool over our eyes, but her story holds up.'

'Is she a friend of yours?' Serena asked, as if that would explain everything. I sometimes wonder what they think of me.

'No, Serena,' I stated. 'She's not a friend of mine. There's a possibility that she may be a victim of a campaign by anti-evolutionists or someone, if that's the word. Anti-evolutionaries, would it be? If that's so, we've got to stifle it in its infancy.' Not the most appropriate metaphor I've ever spoken, I was to learn, but accurate.

When you're a passenger you get to see the scenery. The moors were brown and desiccated due to lack of rain, looking more like Australia or Arizona than the wet north of England. The sheep would be dying of thirst and any time now the fires would start. I could see right down into Derbyshire, mile after mile of rolling moorland that had shrugged off man's puny efforts to make some use of it, barely showing the scars of his endeavours over countless millennia.

The scars of man's endeavours over a much shorter time were plainly obvious ahead, though, as we crested the brow and looked down into Greater Manchester, sweltering under a pall of smog. Fortunately we weren't going that far. We made a left turn and dropped down into Oldfield, towards St Ricarius's, Miss Birchall and the Reverand Jonathan Leary.

Churches are easy to find. There were three spires puncturing the sky, and he'd told us to aim for the middle one.

'What religion are you?' I asked as Serena negotiated a cobbled alley that bordered the cemetery. We were in the old part of town, where the houses were made of stone, as solid as bunkers, and full-grown trees stopped what was left of the light from reaching ground level. Their leaves were already falling, victims of the drought.

'Lapsed Hindu,' she replied, stopping at the end of a row of parked cars, half on the pavement. 'Will this do?'

'That's fine.'

He lived in the vicarage, at the far end of the cemetery. We walked on the flagstone path, between the gravestones, and submitted to their fascination. Here lies somebody, the inscriptions read, who was the beloved wife or husband of somebody else, and mother or father of their children. Two hundred years later we were wondering who they were, why they were singled out for commemoration instead of the countless, nameless others who'd lived and died here? It's the children who stop you in your tracks, make you question what it's all about. Died in infancy, or aged one, two, four, and so on.

'Look at this one,' Serena said, softly. It was a previous

vicar, and he and his wife had buried three daughters before she finally died in childbirth, aged twenty-nine. He made it to eighty-four. Beyond the church was a big hall, and adjacent to that some modern, flat-roofed buildings that I imagined were the school where Miss Birchall would be hard at work on the Nativity play.

The Reverend Leary didn't answer the door when we knocked and leant on the bell-push. After a few attempts we waited a minute or two, in case he was on the toilet or halfway through some religious rite that vicars have to do, and then tried again. Still no answer.

'What did he say?' asked Serena.

'That he'd a pastoral visit to make but it would wait until after he'd seen me. I suppose he could have been called out to administer the last rites to one of his parishioners.'

'Or abducted by aliens.'

I looked at her. 'Have you been working with Brendan?'

There was a sudden burst of hammering from down the garden. We turned and saw where it was coming from: a huge wooden shed that had probably been a garage before the brick one was built nearer the house. 'Wait there,' I said, and strolled down towards it. The hammering stopped as I approached, and was replaced by a sawing sound. The door was closed. I rattled it and knocked, calling: 'Is anyone home?'

The door opened a few inches and a flustered face peered around it, through the gap. He was wearing a dog collar. 'DI Priest,' I said, 'from Heckley CID. I rang you earlier this morning.'

'Ah yes,' he replied, and squeezed out without opening the door any wider. He pushed it shut behind him and hooked the

Chubb padlock through the catch but didn't lock it. 'Sorry about that, Inspector. I wasn't expecting you so soon.' He brushed the sawdust off his hands and offered a shake.

'Speed limits,' I explained. 'We ignore them. One of the perks of the job.'

'Ah! I bet they are.' He gestured for me to lead the way towards the house. 'Let's go inside. I'm fascinated to know how I can help you.'

I introduced him to DC Gupta and we were soon sitting in his front room, sipping tea. It was cool in there, and I suspected the temperature never rose above barely comfortable. No doubt the vicarage would soon be replaced by a modern bungalow and either demolished or sold to some enterprising couple who didn't believe in ghosts, and renamed the Old Vicarage. Serena and I were in short-sleeved shirts, he was in a baggy grey suit, and I gave an involuntary shiver.

'I came over here, away from Heckley,' I began, 'to get away from the local culture, to find an unbiased opinion, if possible. Fact is, we've had a couple of crimes and the finger has been pointed at Christian fundamentalists. I'm afraid I can't be more specific than that, but I'd appreciate your views on the subject. I'm aware, of course, that you are a man of God and may have certain fundamentalist leanings yourself.'

He breathed in, puffing his chest out, gathering his thoughts. I'd asked him a big one. His lips were pursed and he gazed past me. There was a wooden crucifix above the fireplace, with a figure of Christ hanging on it. Red paint in the usual places emphasised His suffering, just in case you hadn't noticed.

'It all depends on what you mean by fundamentalist,' he eventually pronounced. 'I have certain fundamental beliefs, as do most of my colleagues, like the virgin birth, the Holy

Trinity, and that Christ died on the cross and rose again to forgive us our sins. But I don't believe in some of the more extreme views expressed in the Bible, particularly the Old Testament. It was a book of its time, and times change. We've had the good fortune to be born in a land where the rule of law is generally benign and fair, and a man is considered innocent until proved otherwise. In circumstances like that I'm happy for the law of the land to take precedence over canon law.'

'What about Darwinism,' I said. 'Where do you stand on that?'

He shrugged his shoulders. 'The glories of the universe are beyond our wildest comprehension. The fossil record supports evolutionary theory and most of us accept that. All it proves is that the work of the Lord is greater than we first imagined.'

'So you can go along with it?'

'I'm happy with the Church's stance on the subject, as recently defended by the Archbishop of Canterbury.'

'Which was what?'

'Which was as I've just outlined.'

'What about intelligent design? Where does that come in?'

He lifted the teapot, feeling its weight, and asked if we'd like a refill. I nodded and slid my cup his way. Serena declined.

'ID,' he said, when we were replenished. 'It does have certain attractions to a layman like me, but the experts that I trust say it's nonsense, and I respect their opinions. I'd guess that Darwin got it about ninety per cent right with his theory of natural selection, but there's probably a bit of room for some fine tuning.'

'But we weren't designed by some supreme being who got it right first attempt?'

'Most certainly not.'

Serena said: 'So are you happy to believe that we are descended from monkeys?'

'That's what the evidence indicates,' he replied, 'and I'll go along with it until other evidence indicates to the contrary.'

'Do you have any fundamentalists in your congregation?' I asked.

'Fundamentalists in the sense used by the tabloids?'

'Yes.'

'Yes, one or two.'

'What do you think of that?'

'It's a dilemma, Inspector. Sometimes I wonder if their faith is stronger than mine.'

'Do you discuss it with them?'

'No. These days we're just happy that they come to church. And they're harmless enough. They're not the type to take direct action, if that's what you're looking for.'

'What would you do if they were?'

'I'm not sure. Have a word with them? Discuss it with my bishop? Call the police? I don't know.'

I finished my tea and asked Serena if she had any more questions for the vicar, but she didn't. I thanked him for his time and he saw us out to the path between the tombstones. On the way I said: 'Now you can get back to your woodwork.'

'Sorry?' he said.

'Your woodwork,' I repeated. 'You were hammering and sawing when we came.'

'Oh, er, that. It's nothing.'

In the car Serena said: 'Well, I'd say he gave all the right answers, don't you think?'

'Couldn't fault him,' I agreed. She found the car keys in her trouser pocket but I put my hand on the steering wheel and said: 'Don't start the engine.' I climbed out again and stood behind the wall, peering over it towards the vicarage. After a couple of minutes he came out and vanished behind the new garage, and immediately afterwards a blue Peugeot 307 drove away.

'The main road is in front of the house,' I told Serena, bending down to speak through the half-open window. 'You brought us in the back way.'

'Sorry, boss.'

'I'll have to put it on your record. Come on. Let's have a look around.'

She scuttled out of the car like a startled rabbit and fell in beside me as I walked diagonally across the cemetery, between a different set of tombstones, through uncut grass, towards the big wooden shed. He wasn't a Catholic, but he had guilt written all over him as he came out of the shed, and again when I asked him about the woodwork.

Over the church entrance was a huge banner with red lettering on it. I said: 'Hey, look at that: *One a.m. The Resurrection*. That could be interesting.'

Serena looked from me to the banner and back at me again. 'Um, I think it really says *I am The Resurrection*, boss.'

'Does it? Shows how much I know.'

A sturdy galvanised hasp and staple held the shed door, with the lock still loosely hooked through it. I lifted the lock out and pulled at the door. It had sagged and was catching on the ground, so I had to double my efforts. When the gap was wide enough I stepped into the gloom with Serena about an inch behind me.

The fruits of his labours were all around us. He'd been cutting three-by-two softwood into three-foot lengths, and nailing a square board onto each piece. It was the wording on the boards that was most revealing. I touched one, and the paint was still wet. It said: *Abortion is Murder*, and another said: *Suffer the Little Children*.

Serena said: 'Good God!'

'Which god would that be?' I asked.

Having the captain and the chef on board was inhibiting, so Tristan told them to take two days off. The four of them were happy to stay in Monaco and the abundance of restaurants there would ensure they didn't go hungry. Tristan and Teri had gone off in a speedboat with a couple anchored nearby, and Richard and Fiona were lying on the bed in the forward cabin, having just made love. Sunlight reflecting off the waves was dancing on the roof above them, and Richard, his carnal needs satisfied for the moment, was thinking about the casino. A sports car raced along the promenade, its raucous exhaust briefly drowning out the lapping of the water against the boat's hull.

If there's no such thing as a run of good luck, it follows that the same applies to bad luck. In their visits there he'd made mainly even-money bets: either between red and black or odds and evens. It's all about laws of averages. Over a long enough period of time the house should pay out just as much on red as on black, as much on odd as on even. The casino earned its money because of the 37th number on the wheel, namely the 0. When this came up the house took all. It was a modest payment, but it swayed the spin of the wheel in favour of the house. It was the humble zero, hidden and ignored by the players, that made roulette a mug's game.

In over two hours he'd lost £2,000, and Tristan slightly more. At one point he'd been £22,000 in deficit, but by careful scrutiny of the wheel he'd turned this briefly into a £15,000 gain, then lost it all to a capricious bounce of the ball. He knew where he'd gone wrong. He *knew*, and wouldn't make the same mistake again. The money meant nothing to him, but taking on the wheel, and beating it, was the second biggest thrill he'd ever experienced.

'What are you thinking?' Fiona asked without turning to him. She was lying on her back, arms and legs spread, a fine dew covering her body from their exertions in the warmth of the cabin.

'About you,' he replied. His leg was across hers and he drew his big toe up and down her calf. 'We could go somewhere special: the Maldives; Acapulco; anywhere you like. You know how I feel about you.'

'No you're not,' she told him. 'You're thinking about the casino. I've seen that look in your eyes when we're in there.'

'Yeah, well.'

She was quiet for a while, thinking about her past, wondering how much to disclose. She said: 'Did I ever tell you about one night at the Perroquet d'Or?'

'In Paris?'

'That's right.'

'No, you didn't.'

'It was when I was in Saudi. A friend invited me to go to France with him. He was head of a trade delegation, buying jet planes. It was all very hush-hush.'

'Does Tristan know about this?' Richard asked.

She laughed. 'No. Not that bit. I've told him about the gambling, though.'

'Go on.'

'He took me to the Golden Parrot. Apparently they'd signed the contract, he'd received a colossal backhander, and now he was ready to celebrate with a night at the tables. He lost a few, won a few and was getting worse for wear on champagne. I was growing bored, and I like my lovers sober. He said just a little longer and watched the wheel spin for about ten minutes. Then he placed his bet. I was wearing a red dress. He said he'd share his next winnings if he could take the dress off me; red was his lucky colour; all sorts of stuff like that. As he'd had all my other dresses off me I'd nothing to lose, so I said yes. He put a million pounds on red.'

Richard sat up. 'A million! Jesus! What happened?'

'He won, and I kept my half of the deal. Next day we flew back to Saudi.'

'The jammy sod. Did he keep *his* half of the deal?'

She was quiet for several seconds, then said: 'No. He thanked me for going with him, told me exactly where I stood and gave me £500 to cover my expenses.'

'The bastard. Did you finish with him?'

'Not straight away.'

Richard sensed that the story wasn't over. 'Go on.'

'I kept friends with him, biding my time. A few days later he held a party to celebrate the arms deal and invited all sorts of important people. Saudi princes, ministers of this and that, the chief of police. You can imagine. I wasn't invited because he was a married man, but he asked me to supervise things at his country house outside Riyadh on the day of the party. So that's what I did.'

Richard propped himself up on one elbow and turned to her. It was getting interesting. 'What happened next?' he invited.

'Oh, I just got the drinks mixed up. I knew where he kept his hard liquor and somehow managed to fill the soft drinks dispensers in his huge American fridge with Three Barrels brandy and Bell's whisky.'

'Ha ha!' Richard laughed. 'That'd teach him. Was he arrested?'

'Yes. If any one of them had been there alone they'd have shared a drink and said nothing, but because everyone was there they had to appear to be shocked and offended. Hypocrisy isn't a half of it. He was stripped of office and sentenced to two hundred lashes, but he skipped the country and fled back to Paris. As far as I know he's still there.'

Richard said: 'And that was when you learnt that playing the game was fun.'

'Yes. It was wonderful. I'd never felt anything like it before.' She turned to him and placed a hand on his stomach. 'Shall we have another try at the casino, see how *your* luck is running?'

He nodded. 'Yes. I'd like that.'

'But not just yet, though,' she said, and moved closer to him.

CHAPTER EIGHTEEN

I couldn't remember the name of the department I needed. Once we had a murder squad, which is self-explanatory and therefore too snappy and simple for the modern police force, so they changed it to the homicide and major enquiry team. While they were at it they changed the fraud squad into the economic crime unit and the serious fraud office became the serious organised crime agency. We don't have a *trivial* organised crime agency. More accurately, these bodies became HMET, ECU and SOCA. Then there's the NACP, NBPA, NCOF, NCPE, and so on. I logged on and scoured the Home Office glossary of obscure names but couldn't find what I wanted amongst all the junk, so I rang someone.

'What do they call that lot who look into the antics of the animal rights people and the anti-abortionists and the anti-fur coats lobby and the anti-third runway pressure groups and every other anti-something crowd?' I asked.

'Is that you, Charlie?' came the reply.

'Yes.'

'It's nice to hear from you, and I'm feeling fine, in case you're interested.'

'Long time no see. How are you?'

'Top of the world. How are you?'

'Terrible, fed up, over-worked. So who are they?'

'Have you looked in the Almanac?'

'Come off it,' I said. 'It only comes out once a year. They change these names more often than I change my mind.'

'You're allowed to write amendments in the back, you know.'

'I'll bear it in mind. Any ideas?'

'Hang on…Yes, here we are: you want the national extremism technical coordination unit, known as NETCU. Self-explanatory, really, don't you think?'

'Like an Ikea instruction manual,' I replied. 'Do you have a number?' I wrote it down, then asked: 'As a matter of interest, where are they based?'

'A secret location somewhere on a trading estate in the heart of England.'

I thanked him profusely, promised to join him for a drink the next time I was in London, and rang the number. In seconds I was asking a DS if they'd ever heard of the Reverend Jonathan Leary, or if there was a cell of anti-abortion activists in Oldfield.

That drew a double negative, but I learnt that the anti-abortion movement was having a small renaissance and that an American sky pilot with extreme views and a huge television congregation was due to address a rally in Oldfield at the weekend, at the start of a UK tour. They'd tried and failed to have him denied entry, and it was feared there'd be clashes between opposing groups outside his meetings. In the US Bible Belt they shoot doctors who perform abortions, and he was vociferous in his support of this, referring to the gunmen as American heroes.

'Any talk like that,' I was told, 'and we'll have him by the short and curlies and he'll be on the next plane home.'

'But you've never heard of Jonathan Leary?' I asked again.

'He's not on our database, but we'll soon make that right.'

'Will you be having a word with Oldfield about expecting trouble, or do you want me to?'

'We'll take care of it.'

'OK. Thanks for your help.'

So that was that. The reverend was gearing up for a pitched battle in defence of the sanctity of life from what he regarded as the forces of evil, and I'd had him put on record as a possible trouble-causer bordering on terrorist. Within minutes he'd be listed by MI5 and his chances of employment in certain fields would be mysteriously blocked. I didn't know if this would mean within the Church but I wouldn't be betting on him ever becoming an archbishop. I felt a heel, wondered if I'd done him a disservice, but I could live with it.

Next I rang Gillian Birchall. 'This is coming to be a habit,' she said, after I'd introduced myself in case she didn't recognise my husky tones.

'If it's inconvenient let me know,' I told her, but she said it wasn't.

'I've spoken to the Reverend Leary,' I began, 'and I was wondering how you stood on abortion. Is there an official school policy?'

'Abortion?' she replied. 'We don't talk about it. The girls are too young, in my opinion. We only have them until they are eleven, but some more so-called progressive schools may raise the subject with girls of that age.'

'But you're not anti-abortion?'

'The school or me personally? I believe in freedom of choice, Inspector, although I'm uncomfortable with the thought of late abortions. The school doesn't have an opinion. How do you feel about it?'

'Me?' I replied, slightly off my guard. 'I feel the same as you, except I'm a man, and as such don't believe I should have a vote on the subject.'

'Can I ask what this has to do with the Reverend Leary?' she asked, so I told her that he'd given all the right answers about evolution, but I'd taken a peek inside his shed and seen the pro-life placards that he was manufacturing. Then I told her about the rally.

'Oh, that's interesting,' she agreed. 'I've never heard of him being associated with anything like that. Do you think he could be behind my problem? I'd say it was a preposterous idea.'

'Have you ever spoken out supporting abortion?' I asked, 'or had conversations about it with people you don't know too well?'

'No, never. Well, not since college, and my views on the subject aren't all that obdurate.'

'Have you ever given advice on the subject, to a former pupil, for example?'

'No.'

'Then I suspect we're looking up a blind alley. Try not to worry about it.'

'I won't, and Inspector…'

'Yes?'

'Thanks for taking me seriously. I appreciate it.'

I made myself a coffee and took it down to the incident

room, sipping it while staring at the drawing of Magdalena that I'd done all those years ago. She was handsome rather than pretty or beautiful, with a Slavic slant to her eyes that added to her exoticism. Plenty of men would want to make love to her, that was certain, but did any of them want a more permanent relationship? Bed-able but not wed-able? How many times had she woken after a night of passion to find the other side of the bed cold and empty? The sexual revolution was well under way, back then, but for some it was a hollow experience, undertaken because that's what you did, and hey, we were having a good time, weren't we? Weren't we? *Weren't* we?

Is that why she fell in with a roughneck like Ennis – because he offered her stability, something more permanent than the hippie crowd she moved with could offer? Until he started robbing banks and was put in the slammer for a third of a lifetime. The best third.

And then there was the money. Whatever happened to that? I sat and thought about it, there in the windowless incident room with the fan blowing across me every half-minute and a fluorescent light flickering above the whiteboard. We didn't allow the cleaners or the janitor in there while it was active with a case, so we'd have to put up with the flickering tube or replace it ourselves. That would involve completing a risk assessment report and a stores requisition chitty for the tube. It never ends.

A phone rang on one of the desks. It was Dave. 'Hi, Chas,' he said. 'Where've you been hiding all morning?'

'Important stuff to deal with, Dave. Any news to tell me?'

''Fraid not. The trail's colder than a polar bear's rump. Do you want a sandwich bringing in?'

'Yes please.'

'What sort?'

'Ham with the slightest trace of French mustard.'

'What do you want it in?'

'About five minutes.'

'What sort of bread, dumbo?'

'Oh. Any sort. Wholemeal. Sliced. Anything.'

'What about a pudding?'

'Yoghurt. Strawberry yoghurt.'

'Yoghurt? How long have you been eating yoghurt?'

'OK, an Eccles cake then, if asking for a yoghurt would ruin your credibility with the lady who runs the sandwich shop.'

'I don't think she sells yoghurt. Is anybody else in?'

'No, just me.'

'Right. Won't be long.'

I found the original file for the robbery that put Ennis inside and looked for the name of the investigating officer. Then I rang the national association of retired police officers and asked if he was still alive. He was, and they gave me his number after checking with him. I knew they would – there's nothing a retired bobby likes more than being phoned and asked about one of his cases. Usually we have trouble getting people to talk; with old-timers it's getting them to stop.

He listed the statistics first, making it sound like the biggest heist ever: second only to the great train robbery; biggest in Yorkshire; nearly a murder; violent; hardly any money recovered.

'But we got them all,' he went on. 'The ringleader was a man called Ennis. Peter Paul Ennis. Nasty piece of work. Threatened to set a girl alight, sprinkled her with petrol. He denied everything, but the others grassed him up when they learnt how much he made out of it. That's why the judge came down on him. He showed no remorse, the money wasn't found, and he terrorised that poor girl. Twenty-five years, he got. I expect he was out in what? Twelve?'

'He served full term,' I said. 'All twenty-five. He came out last August, and because he'd served full term he was free to go where he wanted, without leaving a forwarding address. He wasn't on licence.'

'So you don't know where he is?' There was a note of alarm in his voice, as if I was ringing to tell him to watch his back.

'Yes we do.' I assured him. 'He's back inside. He's stir-crazy, couldn't hack it on the outside after all those years, so had himself put away again. When you were investigating him did you ever meet his girlfriend, a lady called Magdalena?'

There was a long silence as he thought about it. I wasn't sure how old he was but he could have been quite ancient or not much older than me.

'Magdalena?' he repeated. 'No, I never met her. Ennis was a loner, we thought. Actually, most of the investigation revolved around his fellow conspirators. It was such a professional job that we decided that they'd be the weak link, so we looked for them. We were right. They soon started flashing their new-found wealth around and that led us to Ennis. We had him bang to rights, so the investigation was wound down.'

I wasn't sure it would stick nowadays, but I'd had an admission out of Ennis, so justice had been done. I said: 'You must have been delighted.'

'And proud,' he replied. 'It was the highlight of my career. I retired two years later, but I knew I'd never have another case like that one.'

I did the maths and decided he was ancient. Still as bright as a button, though. 'Tell me about the petrol,' I said. 'I've heard conflicting reports. Was it petrol or was it water? Ennis swore to me that it was non-inflammable carpet cleaner.'

'It was lighter fuel. If anything, more volatile than straight petrol. We took it to the fire station and they did tests on it, saw them with my own eyes. It was highly inflammable, believe me.'

'Scout's honour?' I asked. It wouldn't be unknown for the tin to be switched to strengthen the case against Ennis.

'It was lighter fuel, as it said on the tin. He even struck a match during the robbery, to frighten the girl. She was within an ace of being burnt alive. So why are you looking into the case again? What's brought it up?'

I couldn't be bothered telling him all about Magdalena, so I said: 'The money was never found so the case was never actually closed. We were hoping that Ennis might lead us to it, but he's as mad as a snake.'

He was happy with that and wished me luck. I thanked him for his help and rang off.

Dave came in, pushing the door open with his backside because he was carrying a bundle of paper bags in one hand, his car keys between his teeth and a five-foot fluorescent tube in the other hand.

'Where did you get this?' I asked as I helped him unload.

'The caretaker's cupboard. We'll all be having epileptic fits if we don't do something about that flipping light. The beef looked nicer than the ham, so that's what I've brought. Is that OK?'

A bluebottle had followed him in and was buzzing around the room, bumping into things because its compound eyes hadn't adjusted to the gloom after the brightness outside. I drew one at school, once, and remembered about the compound eyes. The biology mistress, Miss Forté, used to come and sit next to me because she liked to watch me draw. That was probably the first time I fell in love.

'I said is that OK?'

'Sorry, Dave. I was miles away.'

'I brought beef. Is that OK?'

'That's fine.'

'And, 'specially for you, strawberry yoghurt.'

'You're an angel. What say we go have a picnic in the square?'

'Is that your lucky red dress?' Richard asked.

'It's my lucky colour,' Fiona told him. She didn't disclose that the original hadn't survived her boyfriend's removal technique. They were freshly showered and powdered, tanned and perfumed, her hair floating around her face like a swirling mist, his freshly gelled and spiked, as they strode purposefully towards the casino. To the casual onlooker they were a typical, well-heeled cosmopolitan couple, out to enjoy themselves by gambling away some of their wealth.

In the casino they passed the tables where the proper gamblers played, ignored the wheels in the main hall and headed towards the furthermost recesses, where the lowering of the lights was compensated for by the raising of the stakes, and formal dress was de rigueur. The doorman outside the *salon privé* gave a smile of recognition and reached for the door handle, but Richard gave a slight shake of the head and pointed forward, towards the *salon super-privé*, where the high rollers played. The doorman gave him a look that said

'Of course, monsieur, my mistake,' and let go of the handle.

The *salon super-privé* is normally opened by appointment only, for known clients, but where money is involved rules can be surprisingly flexible. Messages were passed, some electronically, some by imperceptible gestures, and when the handsome couple arrived at the heavy door it was pulled open without any hindrance to their progress. Richard smiled an acknowledgement to the doorman and they plunged into the room's opulent gloom. Outside, they'd not noticed the two large paintings in the Romantic style depicting the muses of Folly and Fortune, gazing down on all who fell under the spell of the wheel.

The two men already at the table looked up at the newcomers and Richard gave a *do you mind* gesture, which was rewarded by a wave of the hand towards the vacant places. One of the players looked like the American they'd seen before, now resplendent in dinner suit and black tie. The other was a heavy man with a moustache and perspiration problem. The woman standing behind him with her hands on his shoulders was over six feet tall, with platinum blonde hair and high cheekbones. Fiona looked at the couple and a shiver of recognition ran through her.

Richard spread his chips on the green baize then divided them into small towers. There were nineteen at €50,000 each and a further ten at €5,000, making a total of €1,000,000. He couldn't afford to lose it, but had no intention to. If he stayed on the even money bets he'd win as many as he lost. And he had a system.

Every spin of the wheel comes up red or black, regardless of the number. The chances of it stopping on the same colour for three consecutive spins were slim. Therefore, if it came up red twice in a row, you bet on the black. Richard didn't appreciate that this broke one of the cardinal rules, namely: *what has gone before can have no effect whatsoever on what is about to happen*. It was true that the chances of three in a row were relatively slim – the same as for a tossed coin falling heads three times in a row – but that was before the first two rolls. *After* them, the odds were even money on the third roll being the same. It was written in the rules of mathematics.

He started modestly, with €5,000 on black, and lost. Then he won twice which put him €5,000 ahead. After half an hour he was €10,000 down and looking for another win. Red came up twice so he put one of the big chips, all €50,000 worth, on black. It came up, and he was well in front.

From then on he played with the big chips, rolling one between his fingers, *à la* James Bond, as he watched the ball dance across the numbers. They were made of ivory, inlaid with gold wire, and embedded inside each was a unique radio frequency ID tag that enabled the management to monitor each client's worth as well as protect against forgery. Black came up again and the male croupier pushed his annual salary towards Richard as nonchalantly as he might pass a bowl of sugar across the table to his wife.

Croupiers go to training school for six months before they are allowed on the tables. There's a popular belief that they spend most of that time practising how to make the ball land on a certain sector of the wheel, opposite any big bet. It's probably not true, but it may be. It may just load the wheel another couple of points in favour of the casino. Richard didn't believe it, but it was another good reason to stay with the fifty-fifty bets. Nobody could control them.

He was ahead, with two reds gone, so he placed two of the

big chips on black. Fiona, standing behind him, stroked his neck. He felt for her leg and traced circles on the tender place behind her knee until he felt her quiver and her fingernails dig into him. Red again. He'd lost.

A waitress who could have been Bardot's granddaughter took orders for drinks and they asked for cocktails. The Arabic-looking player was betting on groups of four numbers and losing regularly, with a rare win to keep him interested. The chips had lost any value to Richard, were merely plastic tokens, not real money, and he started gambling the smaller ones on single numbers, chosen by Fiona, while waiting for the right sequences to come along. The American was following the Arab, shadowing his bets as if the secrets of the wheel were written in the desert's sands.

Richard had a losing spell and began to panic. He was out with another man's wife, playing the high roller, which was fun, but his own wife enjoyed the casino almost as much as he did. He could afford to lose a certain amount, but he'd catch hell from Teri. The ball settled into the red pocket and the croupier pushed his winnings towards him. He was in front again, the crisis was over, and he felt as if neat adrenalin were coursing through his veins.

He played on his winnings for twenty minutes, the original €1,000,000 pushed to one side. *Gambling with the casino's money*, as the punters liked to call it. Black followed black again, so he put one of the big chips – worth €50,000 – on red, and promptly lost it.

But now black had come up three times in a row. There's another system that rooky gamblers use, known as doubling your bets. The theory is that when you lose you simply double your stake for the next bet and keep doubling until you recoup your losses. There are fancy names for it, like negative progression, or the Martingale system, but it's a dangerous strategy, smacking of desperation. Doubling up is for fools.

Richard calmly slid the last of his winnings, all £100,000-worth, onto the baize mat and waited for the capricious ball to determine whether a similar amount would come his way or if his stake should vanish into the casino's vast gaping coffers. The colours and numbers on the wheel were a blur as they sped by under his gaze, the light flickering on the centre crosspiece of the wheel like the swinging watch of a hypnotist. Richard felt himself sway as the ball began its fandango and he gripped the edge of the table.

Round and round it went as he tried to follow its progression, willing it to bounce out and find another home. But it didn't. There it was, firmly lodged in a black pocket. He'd lost again.

They'd been in the casino for nearly three hours, and Richard had on the table exactly the same amount of money as when he started. The croupier stacked the losers' chips in his rack and Richard reached out with his left hand and steered his original million in front of him. He wasn't dispirited: the previous three hours hadn't been wasted; no, they were an *investment*.

He felt as if he were breathing pure oxygen, was on a high better than anything he'd experienced by chemical induction. The colours of the table were dazzling bright – green, red, gold, black and the richest mahogany he'd ever seen, and Fiona's fingers were kneading his neck muscles, probing under his collar, finding nerve endings that he didn't know existed. He wanted her, right there and then, on the table with the American and the Arab looking on. But most of all he wanted to win, to beat the system, to prove that he, Richard Wentbridge, could walk out of the casino a winner, with the uniformed lackeys bowing their heads reverentially as he passed and the most beautiful woman in Monaco hanging onto his arm and his every word, ready to submit to his every whim.

It had to be red. Five blacks in a row were unthinkable. Fiona was wearing her lucky colour and he could see into the future. More than that: he could *control* the future. It must be red. It had to be. He had a vision of the Arab taking Fiona's dress off her and something curdled inside him, an anger he never felt when confronted with Teri's lovers. But this was his moment, his chance to steal the limelight that surrounded his pal Tristan wherever they went.

The croupier invited them to place their bets and Richard slid four of the big chips into the red diamond, nervously tapping another on the edge of the table.

Four blacks in a row, he was thinking. It might never happen again. Surely this was his time and his place. As the ball began its second revolution he snapped out of his trance and shoved his remaining chips after the others.

The Arab looked at him then courteously gathered in the chips he'd placed on various bets. 'Good luck, monsieur,' he whispered.

The American showed no similar finesse. 'Holy Moses!' he exclaimed and followed the big money, placing a more modest bet alongside Richard's.

The ivory ball appeared to defy gravity, following its orbit like a doomed satellite, soon to fall prey to Newton's laws and plunge into the Sun. Only the croupier breathed.

As it slowed the ball fell into the 12 red pocket, jumped out again, ran around the lip of the wheel for half a revolution before falling into the 21 black slot. This time it stayed. The croupier's rake shot out like a striking cobra and dragged all Richard's chips off the mat. All one million euros' worth.

'That's me done,' the American said.

CHAPTER NINETEEN

We found a seat in the square and ate our sandwiches watching the people go by, wondering what the hurry was, what was so important that they had to phone someone while on the move. I seem to be watching things go by more and more often, these days. Must be something about my time of life. I told Dave about the conversation with the bank robbery's investigating officer and his assurance that it was petrol that Ennis doused the girl with.

'Poor lass must've been terrified,' he said.

'What do they talk about?' I wondered.

'Who?'

I nodded towards a young man in a suit, striding across the square with an umbrella hooked over one wrist, phone clamped to his ear. 'Him. And her. And her.'

'They have social lives, Charlie. Friends and all that. And jobs that give them time to lead lives other than work. Did you know that...'

But my phone was ringing so Dave didn't finish his question, and I suddenly felt as if I belonged. 'This could be it,' I said, pulling the phone from my pocket. 'This could be my invitation to the ball,' but the number on the display was all-too familiar. 'Charlie,' I said, and listened.

I stood up and put the phone away. 'Message for me. Let's go.'

'Who from?'

'Graham Mellor.'

'Who's he?'

'No idea.'

Fifteen minutes later I was talking to him, learning first hand that he was a second-year chem-eng student at Leeds University. 'Chemical engineering?' I queried.

'That's right.'

'OK. That sounds a proper subject. What you've told me sounds very interesting, Graham, so do you mind if we go over it again, and I'd like to record our conversation, if that's all right with you.'

'No problem.'

'Good. Let's start with the papers.'

'Right. I sent last Thursday's *Evening Post* and a copy of the *Leeds Other Paper* to my parents for them to see what properties are for sale around here. They're not happy with my present arrangements and are thinking of buying something, moving into the buy-to-let business. They've never done anything like that before, so it's a big deal to them.'

'It's not to be undertaken lightly, Graham,' I told him. 'Where do your parents live?'

'Hucknall. It's just outside Nottingham.'

'I know it. Go on.'

'Right, well, I sent them the papers and yesterday my

mother rang me about an article in the *Other Paper* about this woman who's been murdered. There was an artist's impression of her and she said they met her when they came up here to look at a house, back in early August. I've looked in my diary and it was 6ᵗʰ August, a Saturday night.'

Magdalena's body was found on the Sunday morning. 'Where did they meet her?' I asked.

'At the Hairy Lemon.'

'What the devil's the Hairy Lemon?'

'It's a pub the students use. I believe it used to be called the Wig and Gavel. The locals had a petition about the name change, but they lost.'

I said: 'Three hundred years of history down the pan to please you lot. What did your parents think of it?'

'Not much. It was my idea we go there because a local girl called Corinne Bailey Ray was singing. Have you heard of her?'

'No.'

'You will. It was a bit crowded but I managed to find seats at a table at the back for them. I wandered off looking for my girlfriend. They left before Corinne's second set, but Mum reckons they were sat with the woman in the drawing, and spoke to her.'

I needed to know about that conversation. 'What time do you estimate they left, Graham?'

'About nine-thirty.'

Estimated time of death for Magdalena was between ten and one a.m., and her body was found lying on the grass near Shibden Park, twelve miles away as the crow flies, at seven next morning. I needed to know about that conversation more than anything else in my life.

'Do your parents know that you've contacted me?' I asked.

'Er, yeah, I made it right with them.'

'Good. I'll have to talk to them. You'd better give me their number.'

'You idiot! You bloody stupid idiot!' Teri Wentbridge tore herself out of her husband's arms and stomped out onto the deck, slamming the door behind her. The Foyles had gone for a walk, and Richard Wentbridge had taken the opportunity to confess his gambling losses to Teri.

She went to the front of the boat, stared down at the water, gripped the handrail, impotent in her bare feet to vent her anger in the midst of all that quiet, seductive wealth. She strode to the other end and looked up towards the casino and the palace; seeing only them and not the solid wall of depressing tenements, compressed together like a termite mound, that formed the Principality of Monaco. Her shoes were there so she stabbed her feet into them and walked round the deck, disappointed that her heels didn't mark the surface.

Richard's hand fell on her arm. 'Come inside,' he said, and she followed him into the cool of the main cabin, pulling away from him to show that it was her idea to go back inside, not his.

'I said I'm sorry.'

'You bloody, bloody idiot. A million pounds, just like that. Can we afford to pay for this trip?'

'Of course we can. I'll have a word with Tristan; he'll understand.'

The colour bloomed in Teri's face. 'You'd better not. It's bad enough Fiona knowing. Is there something going off between you two?'

'Well...you know there is.'

'I meant more than that. More than screwing her brainless at every opportunity. Are you two plotting something?'

'Of course not. Where did you get that idea?'

'I've seen the way you look at each other. A million pounds, up in smoke, just like that, to impress Fiona.'

'It was a million euros, not pounds. It's nowhere near as much.'

'It's not far off.'

'Listen, Teri,' he pleaded. 'I know I was out of order being there with Fiona and not you, and I'm sorry about that, but I'd have done the same no matter who was with me. There'd been four blacks. Five blacks on the trot is unheard of. The odds against it happening are ridiculous. Nine hundred and ninety-nine times out of a thousand I'd have won. Anybody will tell you that.'

'Uh!' she snorted. 'So where does that leave us? Can we still afford to have friends?'

'We'll be all right. It's just a blip in our fortunes. And I've been thinking about things, about the game. I've decided that doing it for kicks is good fun, but now we've proved how good we are we ought to start making some money out of it.'

'What do you mean?'

'Not now, kiddo. I'll tell you when we go home.'

We'd had a few days of cloudy weather but the high-pressure system came back and settled right over Sparky's house. This meant hot days again although the evenings were chilly. 'Back-endish,' as my mother would have said. Mr Wood went off fishing in Ireland for two weeks, chasing the uneatable, and Gareth Adey had a heart attack.

I'd deployed the troops and made myself another coffee, and had carried it downstairs to have with Gareth, just to be sociable. He's regarded as a bit of a pratt, because he can be, but he'd rather do you a good deed than a bad and he gets the job done eventually. I don't think he's ever been a Morris dancer, but I could imagine it. He was slumped over his desk, clutching his chest in agony.

I ran down the short corridor, flung the door open and shouted: 'Help! Gareth's office!' at the top of my voice, and dashed back to him.

He was breathing in short, shallow gasps and his lips were blue. I unfastened his tie and undid his belt and the buttons of his shirt, telling him that he was going to be all right. Figures appeared around us and we pulled his chair away from the desk and rocked it backwards to make him more comfortable. Somebody arrived with a mouthpiece for CPR and said there was a defibrillator somewhere at the front desk. Outside I could hear the ambulance's siren growing louder.

I rode with him to the hospital and one of Gareth's bobbies followed in a panda. When we'd seen him settled and been assured by a doctor that he was doing fine we went and told his wife the bad news. She was too upset to drive herself, so we took her to the hospital and left her there, sitting by his cot in intensive care.

I rang the super at HQ and apprised him of the situation. He said that I was in charge and asked if I needed any help. I didn't want some fast-track whizz kid with as many GCSEs as he had zits telling me how to run my fiefdom, so I told him we'd manage.

'What about Magdalena?' he asked. 'Are we any nearer a result?'

'I'm hoping to do a substantive interview in the next few days,' I replied. 'I may have something for you then.'

We hadn't allowed for the race riots. I was looking forward to lording it from behind Gilbert's desk, issuing directives about wearing short-sleeved shirts and important stuff like that, when a member of one of our minority groups stabbed a member of an alternative minority group. Or, to put it another way, a rasta jacked-up a paki.

That night the windows of most of the shops in what Dave refers to as our multi-ethnic quarter were smashed and there was a stand-off in the town centre between large groups from both sides. The whites demonstrated their neutrality by joining in the looting, whoever threw the brick, and it was a good time to put feelers out for a new DVD player or iPod. I cancelled all leave and prayed for rain.

I'd telephoned Graham Mellor's parents and arranged to drive down to see them, but I had to call it off when the jihad started. His mother had answered the phone, and sounded quite eager to talk, and talk, and talk. I told her that I'd rearrange a meeting as soon as I could. The stabbed youth, who was born in the town, was soon out of danger but his attacker escaped. He was stabbed in the stomach but never saw his assailant, and the twenty or thirty other people present in the youth centre all just happened to be looking the other way. I put everybody I could on the streets in the evenings, looking for the ringleaders and agents provocateurs who always flock to where there's trouble, and confiscated the films from all the CCTV cameras.

We had two days of it but Friday lunchtime, just as the media started to arrive in force, the sky darkened and the rain came. The workers of Heckley arrived in the morning wearing

T-shirts and shorts and went home under brollies and raincoats. Gullies and gutters overflowed briefly and buses ploughed on through flooded roads. Two hours later it was all over and people were remarking how it had cleared the air. Shopkeepers took the boards off their windows and normality settled like a dove on the peaceful town of Heckley.

I heaved a sigh of relief that blew the papers off my desk and rearranged the shift patterns to give some of the troops a weekend off. My team had been diverted to the stabbing enquiry because that's where the public's interest lay and where all the kudos was to be earned for the next day or two. The public interest being as defined by the tabloid press, and the kudos handed out or withheld by the self-appointed, so-called community leaders. Magdalena had been relegated to the back burner for a day or two but she stayed in my thoughts as I worked out the best way of nailing her killer.

Graham's parents lived in a detached house on the edge of town, handy for the M1 and the park-and-ride into Nottingham, as Mrs Mellor told me when I rang them to rearrange what she called 'our little talk'. It was a modest but spacious house, built of brick at a time when people wanted gardens and nobody foresaw that one day we'd all have cars. The front garden wall had been demolished and their two-year-old Vauxhall Zafira stood on a paved area where once had bloomed roses and wallflowers. Most of the neighbours had made similar modifications. The car was freshly polished, the double-glazing sparkled in the Saturday morning sun and a water feature gurgled happily under the window. Two artificial butterflies with twelve-inch wingspans clung to the upper storey wall and a small dog came dashing to meet me, held back by a gate at the side of the house.

Mr Mellor opened the door when I was still ten feet from it. I held my ID out, saying: 'Inspector Priest. You must be Mr Mellor. Pleased to meet you.'

'It's Roy,' he told me as we moved into the front room after the obligatory handshake, 'and this is my wife, Veronica.'

'Hello Mrs Mellor,' I said. 'Thanks for finding the time to see me.'

'Veronica,' she said. 'We don't stand on ceremony, here. People can take us as they find us, and that's that.'

'Glad to hear it,' I replied, 'I'm Charlie. Charlie Priest. Do you mind if I sit down?'

'Of course not. Do you like lemon cake?'

'Um, yes please.'

'I'll put the kettle on. If you're like the policemen on the telly you'll enjoy a good strong cup of tea.'

'It would be most welcome.'

She vanished backstage and I turned to Roy. 'How's the Zafira?' I asked. 'I was tempted by one myself.'

'It's OK,' he replied. 'I like it, though it's only the sixteen hundred. They were doing a special deal on them.'

Veronica reappeared in the doorway. 'It's plenty powerful enough,' she stated. 'We bought it when we learnt Graham would be going to Leeds. You know what young people are like. We expected to be carrying his stuff back and forth every term, and we wanted something reliable so we could go and see him, now and again. The Astra couldn't have coped, could it, Roy?'

'No, it...'

'It just didn't have the boot space. Mind you, we've had the Zafira loaded up like Billy Hardcastle's removal van a few times.' The kettle made switching off noises and she vanished again.

The lemon cake was fine – I could have managed another slice – but she assumed I took milk in my tea and was generous with it. When we were settled I said: 'So how's the house hunting going?'

'We've given up,' Roy said.

'It's temporarily on hold,' she corrected him. 'It's a sellers' market at the moment and they're asking ridiculous prices. You should have seen some of the places we looked at. I could tell you stories about them, Charlie, that would make your hair curl. Isn't that right, Roy?'

'Yes, but…'

'Rachmanism. That's what it is. Sheer Rachmanism. That place where Graham stays isn't fit for animals. The student accommodation wasn't too bad, but he's had to move out for this year. He's not used to living like that.'

I'd had a long conversation with Graham, and had learnt that he was shacked up with his girlfriend in a house with three other girls, and thought he'd found heaven. What he'd shown his parents I couldn't imagine. I stole a glance at the clock over the fireplace and decided I was falling behind schedule.

'You were in Leeds on the weekend of 6th August,' I said. 'Did you stay up there?'

'We did,' said Roy.

'In a very nice bed and breakfast in Alwoodley,' Veronica added. 'We've stayed there before, a few times. Almost part of the family. It's a very nice area and they don't mind dogs.'

'You take it with you?'

'Yes, but she stays in the car most of the time. She's no trouble.'

'I understand you went to a pub with Graham on the Saturday night.'

'That's right,' Roy confirmed.

'The Hairy Melon, or something,' Veronica said. 'It was dreadful. Not our scene at all.'

'Hairy Lemon,' Roy corrected her. 'It's called the Hairy Lemon.'

'I don't think it is, but Graham wanted to see this young girl singer. He said she'll be big, one day. Can't remember her name. She was all right, I suppose, if you like that sort of thing. Black, of course.'

'She wasn't black,' her husband protested.

'She was dark skinned, and they like to be called black, don't they, Charlie?'

'I...really don't know. Tell me about the woman you sat with. The one you think you recognised from the drawing.'

'She was nice, very friendly,' Roy said.

'A bit too friendly, if you ask me,' Veronica added. 'I think she'd had a drop too much to drink, but she was good company, and spoke intelligently. It's her in the paper, I'm certain of it.'

'What sort of a mood was she in?'

'Quite cheerful,' Roy thought.

'Cheerful, yes,' his wife reckoned, 'but she was more than that. She seemed slightly excited, almost high. It didn't occur to me at the time but now I'm wondering if she was on drugs.'

'That never occurred to me,' Roy said.

'You were sitting alongside her, I was facing her. You couldn't see her face like I could.'

'I don't suppose you asked her name?'

'No, sorry.'

'What did you talk about?'

'The singer,' Roy said. 'We were both reminded of Billie Holliday.'

'I asked her about her hair,' Veronica told us. 'What shampoo she used, how many times she brushed it, things like that. And about the necklace she was wearing.'

I'd picked up my cup, but put it down again. 'What necklace?' I demanded.

'The one she was wearing. It was an ethnic thing, all silver and semi-precious stones. Quite big, hanging down to her bosom, almost.'

Magdalena most certainly hadn't been wearing a necklace, ethnic or otherwise, when she was found. 'Can you describe it?' I asked.

She did her best until I pulled an A4 pad from my briefcase and started a drawing from what she told me. Centrepiece was a matchstick figure of a flute player, flanked by two crescent moons inset with amber stones. These were surrounded by pieces the size of coins, with green stones on them. The metal plates were held together with chain links and the whole thing hung from a leather thong. Slowly, we built up a picture of what could have been an Aztec or Mayan ceremonial badge of office.

'Do you think it was genuine?' I wondered as we gazed at the finished drawing.

'No. I asked. She said she used to have a friend who made them.'

I put it in my briefcase and pulled out my notebook. 'Now I've got to ask you all the normal policeman questions,' I said. 'Some of them might sound impolite, but my boss will be asking me them, and he won't accept my word that you are a nice couple and definitely not murderers. Do you mind?'

Him: 'No.'

Her: 'You've got your job to do, Charlie, and we expect you to do it well. We're all worried about the soaring murder rate, these days. If losing some of our civil liberties is the price we have to pay to make things safer, then so be it, I say.'

'Good. Thank you for being so understanding. What time did you leave the pub?'

'About ten o'clock.'

'Just before, actually. Nearly five to ten.'

'Thank you. Was the woman – she was called Magdalena – was she still in the pub?'

'No, she'd left about twenty-five minutes earlier. That would be about half past nine. She heard the singer's first show, then said she had to go. We said good night, thanked her for her company, and that was that. Are you allowed to tell us how she died?'

'She was beaten up.'

'The poor woman. Does this mean we were the last people to see her alive? Apart from her killer, of course.'

'In an investigation like this,' I told them, 'we try to retrace the victim's last movements. We didn't know she'd been in the Hairy Lemon, so you've opened up several new lines of enquiry for us. But yes, you were the last people we know about who saw her.' And the necklace, I thought. What happened to that?

'Actually...' Mrs Mellor began, 'actually, we did see her again, didn't we, Roy?'

'Did we?' He looked puzzled.

'Yes. As we drove back to the bed and breakfast in Alwoodley. She was walking along the pavement. I said:

"Look, she's there, we could've given her a lift," but you said it wasn't her.'

'I didn't recognise her.'

'Well it was her, I'm certain of it.'

I said: 'And she was walking towards Alwoodley?'

'That's right. I'm sure it was the same woman. I saw her hair.'

'But you didn't see where she went?'

'No, sorry.'

'Was anyone with her?'

'Not that I noticed.'

'Were there many people about?'

'Not many. All in the pubs, I imagine.'

'But you didn't notice if she was being followed?'

'No.'

'Which side of the road was she on?'

'The right.'

'OK,' I said. 'That's very useful. What did you do next?'

'Went back to the bed and breakfast,' Roy said. 'Went straight to bed. We'd had a long day and wanted an early start.'

'Well, not quite,' Veronica stated. 'Don't forget the dog, Roy. You took her for her walk, like you always do. Heaven knows where you went. I fell instantly into the sleep of the just and never heard you come to bed.'

CHAPTER TWENTY

Sunday evening I retraced the journey I'd taken with Gillian Birchall, stopping briefly outside the Flour Mill, where Richard Wentbridge and his wife, Teri, lived, and then near the Home Farm, home of Fiona and Tristan Foyle. The downstairs lights were on inside the Flour Mill, and Foyle's Range Rover was on the drive of the Home Farm. I sat in the car, hiding behind my shades, for about half an hour near each place, but nobody came or went.

I thought about Miss Birchall, workaholic with hardly any social life, and wondered what she was doing. Teaching was my alternative career choice when I graduated from art school, but I decided to become a cop. It sounded better when you introduced yourself at parties. *Charlie Priest, I'm a cop* was a better bird-puller than *I teach art at the comprehensive*. That's what I thought; it just hadn't worked out right. We probably earned about the same although she was a few years younger than me, and whoever heard of the art master becoming the head?

Then there was Gwen. She'd be back from Canada, editing

her photos, treasuring her memories, wanting to share them with someone. When she was on the train, up in the observation car, did she look up at the rocky peaks catching the morning sun and think: *Look at that; it's beautiful; Charlie would like that?*

I thought about one or two others, and I thought about the Mellors' Zafira, wondering if I ought to have a SOCO go over it with a microscope, looking for traces of poor Magdalena. I spun the engine and drove home.

This time, *he* rang *her*. 'It's Torl,' he said. 'Can you speak?'

'Torl! Hi. How are you?'

'I'm fine. How was Cannes?'

'Oh, so-so. The weather was lovely so we did some sunbathing, and the boat was fun. I'm glad you rang; I've really missed you.'

'When did you arrive back?'

'About lunchtime. We flew up to Leeds/Bradford.'

'That's the way to do it. So are you all reconciled, now?'

'No, not a bit. He lost a fortune on the tables and I wasn't even with him. Where are you?'

'On the motorway, at the services, on my way back to Heckley. Did just the two of you go?'

'No, we were with friends: Tristan and Fiona. You'd like Fiona. She's beautiful. It's Tristan's boat.'

'One beautiful woman's enough for me,' he said. 'What's your husband called?'

'He's called Richard.'

'I hate him.'

He heard her involuntary giggle, carried through the air by electromagnetic vibrations. 'Why?'

'Because he's got you, that's why.'

'No he hasn't, Torl. He has his friends and I have mine. It didn't work out between us.'

'Does that mean I can see you again?'

'If you want to. I wouldn't be surprised if you didn't.'

'Of course I want to see you. How are you feeling?'

'Fine. I just have to keep taking the medication.'

'Are you free tomorrow night?'

'I'm free every night, except if I go out with a girlfriend.'

'Tomorrow then. Are we eating?'

'We don't have to, but I expect you'll be hungry.'

'I certainly will. Do you like Chinese food?'

'I love it.'

'Great. Shall I pick you up at eight?'

'Yes, please. I'd like that. I'm really looking forward to seeing you again.'

'Me too, Teri, me too.' He didn't dare tell her just how much he was looking forward to seeing her again, or why.

Monday morning I rang our student liaison officer for Leeds University and asked if the students were back. 'Today,' she confirmed. 'Semester one starts today.'

'But nobody's been in to see you?'

'Sorry, Mr Priest. No one at all.'

We'd been lucky in that while they were on holiday – travelling the world or working to offset their student loans – we'd been able to identify the local people who comprised the real community. But the students had been filtering back for a couple of weeks, and the weekend had seen the final big influx. The landlords rubbed their hands and the shopkeepers renewed their orders for brown rice, Pot

Noodles and ketchup. They were back in business. The locals hadn't been much use in our attempts to find Magdalena's associates and I hadn't much hope of the students helping us, but we had to try. For a start, she'd been living in Beverley for a year, so there was no point in talking to students starting their second years – young Graham Mellor being an exception to this, of course. I had a team over there with instructions to sound out the folk music scene, but apart from developing a taste for brown ale and an aversion to Pete Seeger it was a waste of time. We didn't have much luck in the Hairy Lemon, either.

We printed off hundreds of leaflets with Magdalena's picture on them, under the caption: *Did you know this woman?* and distributed them willy-nilly, but waiting for volunteers to walk into the station and confess to knowing her was like waiting for contact from aliens, and about as likely. I found a number in my diary and picked up the phone.

'It's Charlie Priest again,' I said when the boss of the asset recovery agency answered it. 'I need some more help. Can I come over to see you?'

'Anytime, Charlie,' he replied.

'Cheers. Give me some directions and I'll be straight over.'

'Honest, you'll love it,' Torl told her. 'Just put it in your mouth; it won't bite.'

'I can't,' Teri protested. 'It's too big.' She picked up her fork and tried to spear the offending morsel, but it slipped away.

They were in the Bamboo Garden Chinese restaurant, two bowls of the chef's special wanton soup before them, at Torl's recommendation. 'You have to be brave,' he said, 'and just go for it. Cutting them in half spoils the effect. Use your chopsticks, like this...' He picked up one of the pastry parcels between his chopsticks and popped it whole into his mouth. 'Mmm, delicious,' he told her, after chewing and swallowing. 'Now you do it.'

Teri picked one up and moved it tentatively towards her parted lips. Torl watched as she opened her mouth wider to accommodate it. Their eyes met and held each other's as her lips closed around the morsel and she chewed upon it, slowly and rhythmically, all the time holding his gaze.

'You're right, that was lovely,' she pronounced after taking a sip of sparkling water. 'What's inside them?'

'Prawn meat, I think.'

'Mmm, they're nice. I'm glad you made me have it. Sometimes, it's good to be forced into something you didn't expect to like, don't you think?'

'Oh yes,' Torl replied, dabbing his lips with his napkin, his eyes still on hers. 'I couldn't agree more.'

They shared an aromatic crispy duck with pancakes and finished with toffee banana and coffee. Teri told him about her trip, and about her husband's losses at roulette, without disclosing the actual sum. She made it sound like the final straw that wrecked their marriage.

'Can he afford it?' Torl asked.

'He's got the money, but it's tied up. Don't ask me how. He'll have to sell something. An investment, I mean. Not the house or anything like that.'

'Where is the house?'

'At Hunter's Valley. Do you know where that is?'

Torl shook his head. 'No.'

'It's nice there. Our next-door neighbour is a rap artist, called Zed Boogey. Have you heard of him?'

Torl chuckled and shook his head again. 'Zed Boogey? No, he's a new one on me.'

'He's quite famous. He's just had a string of hits. I like some of it but Richard says it's jungle music. We water his plants for him when he's on tour.'

'Wait a minute,' Torl said. 'He has this bad-ass gangsta rap image but he grows pot plants in his conservatory. Is that what they are: pot plants?'

'No! They're avocados and lemon trees. And castor oil plants. Things like that. They don't need much attention. I go in every two or three days when he's not there, which is most of the time. He's gone off today, to a gig in Germany. He's ever so sweet, not at all like you'd imagine.'

Torl looked at his watch and signalled a waiter for the bill. 'Do you mind if we go?' he asked Teri. 'I need to call in the office for my briefcase. I'm going to see someone in the morning and it will save me half an hour.'

Teri looked crestfallen. 'Oh, does that mean you're taking me home? I thought we might spend some time together.'

'No, I'm not taking you home, unless you want to go home. We'll collect my briefcase and then go for a drink somewhere, or a ride up to the tops and you can show me how much you've missed me. How does that sound?'

It sounded fine, and he paid the bill. In the car she said: 'So are you seeing someone to give them a load of money?'

'Something like that.'

'What sort of business are they in?'

'I'm not sure until I read their application. They're after what we call angel money.'

'Angel money? What's that?'

'It's a theatrical term. People who give money to theatres so they can put on plays are called angels. It's a high-risk investment and there's a good chance they'll lose it all. We use it for small businesses who want some start-up capital. Most businesses that fail do so because they're under-funded. We try to help them in those critical first two years.'

'So how much will you give them?'

'It depends on the business and how many jobs they might create. Usually about £50,000 is enough to ease them through a crisis.'

'Wow!' she said, softly, and then sat silently for a while. Eventually she said: 'Torl...'

'Yes, my dear.'

'Did I tell you that I once owned a string a beauty parlours?'

'Yes, you did mention it. You said that you had ten, and sold them when you married. I was surprised. I wouldn't have taken you for a ruthless tycoon.'

'I had to be ruthless. Well, hard-headed. I wouldn't have said I was ruthless. I left home when I was sixteen and bought a half-share in a hairdressing business. Everybody was out to screw me, in more ways than one. I had to learn fast.'

'I bet you did. Dare I ask where the money came from?'

'Nothing illegal or embarrassing. My father left £25,000 in trust for me until I was sixteen.' Torl was about to ask about her father but Teri went on: 'He was a sea captain, but he died when I was about one year old. Mum told me about him. I made good use of the money. Five years later I sold up for £300,000.'

Torl turned off the main road and negotiated a roundabout with pointers labelled with unit numbers and drove slowly past a huge sign listing various companies. The buildings were glass-walled and the road illuminated as brightly as an aircraft carrier's deck.

'What about your mother?' he asked.

Teri took her time answering, then said: 'I've never seen her since I left. All I can remember is that she had a string of fellows. I never knew where home was, she changed so often. Sometimes I went home from school in the wrong direction. And then...'

Torl waited, but it didn't come. 'And then...' he prompted.

'She was going with this bloke,' she began. 'A suave sod, he was. We hadn't moved in with him completely. It was just for a few days, as a trial, I believe. Mum was out at work – she worked afternoons down at the art college. I don't know what she did. It was a warm day, like we've just had. It was games afternoon at school and we'd been playing rounders, so I came home all hot and bothered. I went upstairs and he...he...'

'Go on.'

'He followed me upstairs and raped me. I was twelve years old.'

'That's terrible. Did you report it?'

'No. I told Mum. She said I'd imagined it, persuaded me to forget the whole thing. A week or two later she fell in with another bloke and we went to live with him. He was just the opposite, but it didn't work out. Not for me. I was a trouble causer, I'm afraid. I ran with the wrong crowd, but I soon realised it. Living on a university campus is a strange way of life, with lots of temptations, especially for a young girl. Mum stayed but I split as soon as I had the money.'

'You've never tried to find her?'

'No. As far as I'm concerned, she's dead. When he was, you

know, doing it to me, he kept saying: "Don't pretend you don't like it – like mother, like daughter". When she persuaded me to keep quiet it was like giving him a licence to rape me. I'll never forgive her for that. He didn't, but only because I slept with a kitchen knife under my pillow. I told him I'd stab him if he ever touched me again.'

'I'm sorry, it must have been dreadful,' Torl said, then: 'C'mon, let's go in.'

He pushed a button below the security keypad and a voice said: 'Hello.'

'It's me.'

'One moment.'

They waited, and in a few seconds a man appeared. 'Evening, sir,' he said. 'Working late?'

'No. I just want to collect my briefcase. We won't be a minute.' He led Teri up a flight of stairs and along a corridor illuminated only by security lighting, through a door marked *EPP Marketing* into a large, open-plan office. Every desk had a computer and the air bristled with static from them as they chugged away on standby, helping burn a hole in the ozone layer. Lights on printers blinked, others stayed steady, some cast little coloured pools of light on piles of paper. Torl headed directly for another door in a corner and pulled it open to allow Teri in first, but not before she'd read the sign on it. The computer-printed notice, held on with Sellotape, said: *D. Storey, Director.*

'Here we are,' Torl said, lifting a briefcase aloft. 'This is what I want. Let's go before I find a job that needs doing.' The caretaker let them out and soon they were driving round the bypass, towards the road that led over the tops.

'Drink somewhere?' Torl asked. 'We might just make it.'

'No, I don't think so. Can we just stop somewhere quiet?'

He drove to the place where they'd seen the gibbous moon, before Teri had the epileptic fit, and parked in the same spot, overlooking the valley. The moon had progressed through its cycle and was now on the wane, high behind them.

Teri said: 'So who are EPP Marketing?'

'Ah!' Torl said. 'I wondered if you'd ask that. It's our nom de plume. We don't advertise our presence because we'd probably be overcome with applications. Also, we have been accused by some we've turned away of giving an unfair advantage to their competitors. We have to be discreet.'

'And who's D Storey?' she demanded.

'Ah ah! You've got me there. Guilty as charged, your honour. Torl's my nickname. At school my elder brother was called Short Storey, because he was six feet tall. When I went along, even taller, they christened me Tall Storey. At the speed dating the madam suggested that I might not want to use my proper name, so I said I was called Torl. I changed the spelling.'

'And your Norwegian mother?'

'Um, I lied about her. She's from Stoke-on-Trent.'

'So what does the D stand for?'

'David. David Storey. That's me.'

'Tristan said you were lying.'

'Your friend with the boat?'

'Yes.'

'Why would I lie?'

'He said, to get inside my pants.'

'That's a very compelling reason. Did you believe him?'

'A little bit.'

'Do you still?'

She laughed and smiled at him. 'Put your arm around me.'

He did as he was told, and pulled her close. 'But you don't want to, do you? Your religion won't let you.'

'What? Get inside your pants?'

'Mmm.'

'It would be a sin.'

'But would you like to?'

'That's a sin, too.'

'Just wanting to?'

'Yes.'

'So are you a sinner?'

'Up to my armpits.'

She laughed and kissed him on the cheek. He instinctively turned towards her, to return the kiss on her lips, but misjudged and kissed her nose. She stayed facing him, waiting for him to try again, but he gazed stoically through the windscreen, slowly counting to ten while imagining he was mowing the pitch at Wembley, in a downpour, with a very small lawnmower.

'Am I forgiven?' he asked.

'I'm thinking,' she replied. After a long silence she said: 'Torl? I mean, David...'

'Torl will be fine.'

'OK. Torl. When I split from my husband there'll be a heck of a row over money. He won't want to give me a penny. I'll need a job, or a little business. Would I be eligible for one of your angel loans?'

'Hairdressing and beauty?'

'Probably.'

'I would imagine so.' His arm was across her back, his fingers gently kneading her shoulder. Periodically a vehicle would pass on the road, its headlights briefly sweeping the lay-by and illuminating the interior of the car, but leaving it darker than before. A hatchback with a noisy exhaust came in with a rattle of gravel, saw Torl's car and drove off again.

'Promise?'

'I can't promise,' he said, 'but put it like this: you're a deserving cause and I'm incredibly weak-willed.' His fingertips traced circles on the back of her neck. 'I can't imagine anybody having a better chance of persuading me to hand over someone else's money. Can you?'

He turned his face towards hers and this time he didn't misjudge it. 'No,' she said when she needed to breathe. 'I can't.'

On the way back Torl said: 'This man. The one who raped you. Have you considered making a complaint against him?'

'No. And he's probably dead by now.'

'Can you remember his name?'

'He was called Julian. That's all I remember.'

'Julian. Right.'

They drove the rest of the way in silence, his hand lightly resting on her thigh, her fingers interlaced with his. Torl was wondering how much of what she'd told him was the truth; how much was lies and fantasy; and whether losing his job was too high a price to pay for what he was being drawn into. He remembered her saying that she wanted to be one of his elves and imagined her in a little costume, sitting on a toadstool, looking up at him with those doe's eyes, and nearly drove off the road.

Teri was thinking about the game and looking forward to going to bed with Freddie, but most of all she was wondering how much to take this latest sucker for.

* * *

Gareth Adey was taken off the danger list and put in a ward with that week's quota of heart attack survivors. We took turns to visit him during the day, and left the evenings to his family. I sat talking to him about the job, how we were managing, but it was a struggle, and asked his advice about my clematis. He's a keen gardener. I'd a feeling that he'd be doing a lot more gardening in the future.

'What sort is it?' he asked.

'Um, a white one.'

'When did it flower and how big were they?'

'It didn't flower, so I don't know how big they'd be, but they were white on the little picture.'

'When did you plant it?'

'Just after Christmas. It was a present.'

'Has it any leaves on it?'

'No. They fell off.'

'I suspect it's what we technically term as dead, Charlie.'

'Is that bad?'

'As bad as it gets. It's probably an armandii. They sell lots of them in garden centres but they're not hardy.'

And so on. Yorkshire had lost again and the football season had started, but I'm not into cricket and Gareth can't stand footy, so those subjects were soon exhausted. When I asked him about the food for the second time I decided it was time to flee from the place. Hospitals depress me. My parents died in hospital and I've spent some time there in my own right, after being shot. I've only to look at a cellular blanket to break out in a rash.

'It's madness.'

'No, it's not.'

The Wentbridges were sitting on the patio at the back of the house, sipping red plonk from Riedel handmade glasses as the afternoon sun dropped behind the fells. He was wearing calf-length pants and a polo shirt; she was in shorts and a skimpy top, with a Hermes scarf over her shoulders.

'Well I think it is,' Teri protested. 'He lives next door, for God's sake.'

'What difference does that make?' her husband retorted. 'We live in a global society. Burglars travel hundreds of miles to do jobs. If anything, living next door takes the heat off us. People like Zed Boogey are a target for the professionals – everybody knows that. He's stinking rich, and no doubt he creams off thousands from his concerts that he doesn't declare. He can afford to give us a million.'

'To replace the million you threw away to impress *her*,' she retorted.

'Yes, darling,' he replied. 'To replace the 700,000 *pounds* that I lost due to a cruel spin of the wheel, when I just happened to be in the company of your friend Fiona. This is a way for me to get something back; to make amends; to regain your affection.' He reached across and stroked her arm until she pulled it away.

They sat in silence for a while, until she said: 'Why can't you just download the images onto his computer from ours, like Tristan does?'

'For one simple reason, darling: I don't know how to. I'm not bad on them, but no expert. I need to be at his computer.' He picked up the wine bottle and shared the last few drops between their glasses.

'Have you forgotten that he has the most sophisticated burglar alarm that money can buy?'

'No, darling. Have you forgotten that we have a key and

the code number? You water his plants every day, remember?'

'I water them twice a week.'

'Right.'

'So won't he know it's us?'

'No. There'll be nothing to see.'

'And then we blackmail him?'

'Not necessarily straight away. We could afford to wait a year or more. It'll be like money in the bank. And even if we don't take any money from him, we can always bring him down, call it part of the game.'

Teri drained her glass. 'The game's good fun,' she said, 'but I think I prefer the idea of taking him for a million.'

'Good girl.'

'There's just one thing.'

'What's that?'

'If you download the images but hide them on his hard disk where he can't find them, when you threaten to expose him what's to stop him taking his computer to the dump and scrapping it?' She sat back with a triumphant smile, confident that she'd scuppered the plan.

'You're thinking well,' Richard replied. 'That's what I like to hear. It makes us a team. But work on it. His computer will have all his accounts on it, plus his showbiz contacts, his address book, all stuff for the Inland Revenue, not to mention his music and lyrics. His world depends on it and he'd be lost without it. He can't afford to throw it away. We bury the stuff in several places, maybe tell him where a couple of them are. Even if he buys a new one he'll have to transfer all the stuff from his hard disk to it, including the stuff we put there. He'll be shitting bricks for the rest of his life.'

'Richard!'

'Sorry, but he will.'

'What about fingerprints and DNA and all that?'

'We wear gloves, but we've a perfect right to be there. We've been in before, and you do the plants, so it's no problem.'

'It sounds as if you've thought of everything.'

'I have.'

'So when do we do it?'

'You said "We". Are you coming in with me?'

'Of course. It sounds fun.'

'It will have to be tonight. He comes home tomorrow.' He reached out to touch her again, and this time she didn't pull away.

Teri went in as normal to water the plants. She used her key and entered the code number into the burglar alarm to disable it. There was a CCTV camera watching the entrance, but she walked nonchalantly past it without an upward glance. In the kitchen she switched off two switches on the wall which Richard told her must be for the outside security lights, as per their house. She found a tea towel and draped it over the CCTV camera, sneaking up behind it as if it might suddenly whirl round to accost her. She didn't reset the alarm as she left.

They dressed like aristocratic burglars in an amateur theatrical production of something by EW Hornung: black silk polo necks; double-dyed black Farah jeans; leather gloves. The outside security lights didn't come on as they tiptoed round the back of their famous neighbour's house, just after midnight, when the street was at its quietest. After Teri had watered the plants they'd discussed the job over and over again, then watched a video of *The League of Gentlemen*.

They both carried tiny torches, Chinese copies of Maglites that Richard had bought at the local filling station. Teri unlocked the door and saw that the towel was still over the camera lens. Richard nodded approvingly. They knew that the office was upstairs, on their side of the house, because they'd seen Zed Boogey up there occasionally, working. All the houses in the square were individual, but they'd been designed by the same architect and were similar enough for them to find their way around. In seconds they were upstairs, in the computer room.

Richard closed the door and extinguished his torch. 'Pull the curtains together,' he said, placing three Maxell re-writable CDs on the desk next to the keyboard, 'and turn the light on.'

Teri did as she was told. 'Isn't it exciting?' she said, her voice low but expressive.

'Too exciting. Keep quiet.' After a few seconds with the familiar displays following each other on the screen, he said: 'No password, just as I'd hoped. That makes it easier,' and started exploring Zed Boogey's *My Documents* files.

It took nearly an hour, with Teri sitting on the floor in the corner while he transferred the images of abused children to obscure corners of the rap artist's hard disk.

'That should do it,' he said, eventually. 'He'll never find that lot in a month of Sundays. Let's go.'

They retraced their steps. In the kitchen Teri closed the switches for the outside lights. Richard went out through the door and Teri pulled the towel off the camera and hung it where she'd found it. She went out as if she'd been in to water the plants again. She wasn't worried about the discrepancy:

Zed Boogey didn't go through the video films every time he returned home.

Richard was waiting for her. 'Quick,' he whispered. 'There's a car coming up the main road. It's turning into the square!'

He dragged her by the hand round the back of the house and the security lights came on, bright as daylight. They ducked into a pool of shadow behind a yew tree and held their breath.

'Jesus, it's him,' Richard hissed as the Porsche Cayenne's xenon headlights swung into the driveway, blazing like anti-aircraft searchlights. The Wentbridges, cowering behind the tree, felt like two moths caught in a projectionist's beam.

They heard the automatic garage door rumble open, the car door slam and the garage door close behind the Porsche. 'C'mon,' ordered Richard pulling at his wife again, and they slipped across the garden into the safety of their own territory.

Inside, they flopped on the settee, after Richard had poured them two stiff brandies. 'Phew! That was close,' he admitted. 'We nearly blew it. I was going to suggest that...you know...'

'That we made love on his bed?'

'Something like that.'

'I was thinking the same.'

'Let's go over it. Did you lock the door?'

'Yes, boss.'

'Put the towel back?'

'Yes.'

'Switched the security lights back on?'

'You saw them working.'

'True. Switch the alarm back on?'

'I did.'

'And we opened the curtains upstairs, closed the doors, switched the computer off and unplugged it, so we're in the clear. A job well done and we're as safe as houses.'

'Not his house.'

'Well, no, not his house, but we've covered everything. All we have to do now is be patient.'

Teri stood up and started pulling her husband to his feet. 'Patience isn't one of my virtues,' she said. 'Come on, I'm sure our bed is just as good as his. Bring the bottle.'

CHAPTER TWENTY-ONE

The riots generated enough paperwork to fuel a small power station and enough hot air to make it redundant. By the end of the week things were settling down and I could direct my thoughts and resources towards simpler, less contentious issues, like murder. The politicians agreed that the riots were not racially motivated, which was a great relief to us all, and resumed their vacations. Those of us who thought differently were just grateful that tempers had cooled along with the weather. Serena was sitting at her desk reading something, and looked up as I walked in to the office. I gestured for her to join me in mine and she rose to her feet.

She sat in the spare chair, pushed her notebook onto the desk and looked at me. I said: 'Are you doing anything tonight, Serena?'

'Um, er, no, not really,' and I swear she blushed.

'If you're not, I've a little job for you.'

'Oh. Right.'

I spread my AA three-miles-to-the-inch road atlas on the desk and pointed. 'That's where the pub called the Hairy

Lemon is,' I showed her, 'and this, down here, right where the pages join, as always, is where Magdalena's body was found. Let me show you on the A to Zs.' I produced the books and found the pages straight away because I'd already looked. 'That's where the pub is, and...that's where the body was found. They're only about twelve miles apart, in a straight line, but as you can see, there's no obvious easy route between the two.'

'You want me to drive the route and see how long it takes?'

'In both directions, please, between about ten and eleven.'

She looked disappointed, as if she'd been expecting something more exciting, but she said: 'No problem.'

Serena was hardly back at her desk when Maggie rang. 'It's me, Chas,' she blurted out. 'I've got a positive on the necklace.'

'You have! That's great. Where are you?' I'd had Maggie and a couple of others asking round the jewellers to see if anybody had tried to off-load the necklace. Robbery is a powerful motive, and we have to follow every lead, if only to eliminate that possibility and pre-empt the defence's smokescreens when we eventually put someone before a court.

'Henderson's on Wilson Street in Halifax. Mr Henderson said a bloke came in with something like the piece in your drawing about two months ago, maybe less. He couldn't be sure.'

'Did he buy it?'

'No. It's called a torque, by the way.'

'A torque?'

'That's right. Mr Henderson said it was an attractive piece but not anything in his line. He said it was made by an

amateur and had little intrinsic value, so he told the seller to
try a pawnbroker. He said the seller looked as if he could be a
down-and-out.'

'Well done, Maggie, well done. So now it's the pawnshops.'

'Yep. No rest for the wicked.'

I looked out of the window, then at the pile of paperwork
in front of me. The ACC wanted an update, we were behind
with our budget forecast, there was a reminder from finance
that I hadn't claimed any expenses for three months and I'd
been invited to give my comments on a proposed merger of
forces. Well, Gilbert had been invited, but we had similar
views about that one. Outside, the sun was shining again and
I could hear the pigeons cooing above the rumble of the
traffic. There couldn't be that many pawnbrokers in Halifax,
I thought, and if the man was on foot...

'Where are you now, Maggie?' I asked.

'At the end of Wilson Street. Are you coming?'

'I'm thinking about it.'

'That's what I predicted.'

'Am I that obvious?'

'Yes. I need to use the loo, so I'll see you in Debenhams,
soon as you like.'

'Do you have the Yellow Pages with you?'

'Never go anywhere without them.'

'OK. See you in the restaurant. I'm on my way.'

It took me nearly half an hour and Maggie was growing
restless when I arrived, but she managed another coffee while
I ate a bacon sandwich. She'd already extracted the addresses
of the town's pawnshops and plotted the shortest route
between them.

But it wasn't necessary, because we struck pay dirt at the

very first one, just round the corner from the jeweller's. The buxom woman behind the counter, draped in the obligatory prince's ransom of gold chains, looked carefully at our IDs, listened to what we said and went away. Five seconds later she returned and laid an ornate necklace on the glass-topped counter.

'Ten pounds,' she said. 'I allowed him ten pounds against it. More than it's worth.'

'Did you take his name and address?'

'Of course.' She reached under the counter and produced a ledger. 'He's here somewhere. Do you have a date?'

'Second week in August.'

'This must be him. *Mexican-style necklace, ten pounds.*' She spun the book round so I could read it for myself. He was called F Raw and lived in town. I put my finger on the place and Maggie copied it down.

'We'll have to take this,' I told the woman. 'Do you have a plastic bag we can put it in?'

'I thought you carried them with you.'

'We do, but we had a run on them this morning.'

'I'll need a receipt for the necklace. I gave ten pounds for it.'

She didn't ask if it was stolen. She'd no need to.

We decided to go and see Mr Raw, and collected Maggie's car from the multi-storey. She knew the way and in minutes we were driving along a street of terraced houses, looking for number 52. The local primary school had just disgorged its charges and the street was filled with little groups of them, carrying impossibly large rucksacks, accompanied by their mothers. We were in the middle of the Asian community, and some of the kids wore turbans or topknots with their school blazers. The adults were in pyjama suits in bright colours and one wore a full burka. It was black and white, with just her eyes showing, and the cut of it looked expensive. She was tall and slim, and I suspected that she was fully aware of the impact she had. Another, leading a little girl by the hand, wore an eau-de-Nil suit and four-inch stilettos. The kids chatted and dashed back and forth between groups, like kids all over the world. Maggie stopped to let them cross the road and we both smiled.

Number 52 let the street down. The windows were dirty and bags of rubbish were strewn about the small front yard. 'Shall we disturb his reverie?' Maggie asked.

'No,' I said. 'Park where you can and we'll do a PNC check.' I phoned the nick and asked for it. Only certain officers have access to the computer and the data it contains, and we weren't on the list. Two minutes later the reply came back, just as the school party, or what remained of them, caught up and passed us. The woman in the burka and the one in stilettos weren't with them. Frederick Raw had convictions for being drunk and disorderly, causing an affray, assault, ABH and threatening behaviour while armed – the arm being a shotgun – and had spent a decent portion of his adult life as a guest of the Queen.

'Sh-sh-sheest,' I hissed. 'We nearly walked into that one, Maggie.'

So I did some more telephoning and thirty minutes later a familiar battered Ford Transit turned into the street and parked nearby. Maggie raised a finger off the wheel in acknowledgement and we drove back to Heckley.

* * *

'Where are you going?' Richard Wentbridge asked his wife.

'Shopping,' she replied. 'With Fiona. You know it's our shopping day, or have you stopped my credit card?'

He looked sideways at her, unsure of her attitude. 'I thought you'd forgiven me,' he ventured.

'But not forgotten,' she replied. 'Perhaps I'll find it in my heart to forgive you when we get the million off Zed Zed Doodlebug next door.'

'I told you: we have to be patient. It's money in the bank for a rainy day, which hopefully will never arrive. So where are you going?'

'Dreary old Leeds again. Fiona's choice.'

'Do you want a lift?'

'No. She's coming here and I've ordered a taxi. We can still afford taxis, can't we?'

'Somehow, dearest, I can't imagine you going on the bus, even if one ever came this way.'

'Ah! I'd slit my wrists first. She should be here by now.'

The sun was shining again and the combination of hot weather and the recent downpours had caused the plantlife to shoot up over the last few days. The Wentbridges employed a gardener for a few hours every week, but Richard insisted on cutting the grass himself because he was the proud owner of a Hayter Heritage ride-on lawn tractor and didn't see why he should employ a gardener to have all the fun. He kissed his wife goodbye and went through the inside door into the garage, where he tossed his shirt onto the bonnet of the Mazda and climbed aboard the mower. The engine started first turn of the key and he steered carefully out onto the drive and round the side of the house, towards nearly half an acre of waiting grass. Fiona had pulled onto the drive as he exited the garage and she gave him a wave. A flock of small birds flew away as he turned down the side of the orchard to make the first cut.

Their taxi deposited the two women on Duncan Street, as close to the pedestrianised area in the centre of Leeds as was practical. They turned up their noses at the fashions on offer in the Corn Exchange but had a giggle over some of the gear in the S&M and Goth shops. Fiona held a leather bustier adorned with studs and zips in front of herself and Teri nodded approvingly. Then it was to the overpriced designer ware in the Victorian Quarter.

They lunched at Anthony's and rested themselves over coffee in preparation for the serious shopping. A cursory glance around House of Fraser set the credit cards vibrating before they plunged into Harvey Nichols and their version of heaven. The liveried doorman pulled the door open with a smile and in Switzerland the Coutts Bank von Ernst cleared the decks in anticipation of some serious trading.

Richard Wentbridge parked the mower in its corner of the garage and retrieved his shirt. In the kitchen he took two bottles of his favourite Czech lager from the fridge and poured them into a pint glass. He showered, changed into freshly laundered chinos and polo shirt, and carried what remained of the lager upstairs to the computer room.

Ten minutes later he was feeling despondent but not defeated. The stock market was depressed and his various other business interests were suffering from the general fall-off in spending, while his outgoings were multiplying like rabbits. They weren't there yet, but another couple of months like this one and he could be having cash-flow problems. He'd have to off-load something, and that would be like selling the family silver. He thought about Teri, loose in Leeds with a credit card, and hoped she wasn't being silly.

A little pile of CDs at the back of the desk, behind the monitor, caught his eye, and he reached for them. There were three of them, in plastic see-through envelopes, and written in marker pen on the top envelope was the message *Ibiza 2003, Disk 1*. The second one was *Ibiza 2003, Disk 2* and the last one was, predictably, *Ibiza 2003, Disk 3*.

The trouble was, Disk 3 was missing. The envelope was empty. Richard Wentbridge had never been to Ibiza. He'd never had a desire to go to Ibiza and never intended going there. It was probably the last place on earth that he wanted to go, and watching three disks-worth of somebody's holiday photographs taken in Ibiza was about as appealing to him as spending a month living in one of the dumpsters at the back of the hospital. Amputation ward.

He'd assumed that nobody else would pick them up and want to watch them. That's why he'd chosen Ibiza as a suitable label for the disks. The disks that contained the images of bruised and beaten, ravaged and raped children that he'd uploaded onto his next door neighbour's hard drive. A freezing cold hand with metal fingers clutched at his bowels and he desperately needed the toilet.

He ran through the entire expedition, over and over again, but always came up with the same answer: he couldn't remember removing Disk 3 from Zed Boogey's D drive. He could remember inserting it, hitting the right buttons and glancing briefly at the image of a Chinese-looking girl being held down by two men, but not removing it. He'd left it there; of that he was certain.

He'd done the same thing with his own computer hundreds of times. Almost every time he logged on a message came up saying *Non-system disk error. Replace and strike any key when ready*, because there was still a disk in one of the drives. He mentally cursed himself for not being aware of the risk, but he also gained some comfort from it. Maybe Zed Boogey did the same thing. Perhaps he wouldn't look twice at the renegade disk. Perhaps...

It was all conjecture. He would deny any knowledge, if challenged, and nobody could prove otherwise. Meanwhile, he'd just have to wait and see. He took another lager from the fridge and gazed through the window across the newly mown lawn. This was his domain, and nobody would ever take it from him.

The taxi dropped Fiona and Teri off at the Wentbridges' riverside apartment and they struggled the last few yards laden down with bags bearing the familiar logo, chattering and giggling like jackdaws in a farmyard. Teri held a bag between her teeth as she typed in the number for the security door and Fiona leant against the wall, making gurgling noises. Teri had bought two silk tops, three pairs of shoes and had replenished her make-up drawer. Fiona was taking home a suit by Gaultier, a black lace teddy for a special occasion and five blouses. In the flat they dropped the bags and slipped off their shoes, still giggling. Teri slopped gin and tonic into tumblers and passed one to her friend.

'Oh, that's better,' Fiona gasped after taking a long draught.

'Definitely,' Teri agreed, licking her lips. 'There's nothing like a good stiff one after a hard day's shopping,' and they both spilt their drinks as they laughed.

'You didn't buy much,' Fiona stated when she had recovered. 'I thought you were going to make him pay for his transgressions.'

'You mean losing a million when he was with *you*?' She spat the word out to exaggerate her displeasure, as if pretending that being with her friend was her only objection. 'I haven't finished with him, yet. He'll be sorry.'

'Poor Richard. He really was unlucky, you know. Don't be too hard on him.'

'We'll see.' Teri reached for the gin bottle and recharged their drinks. They were in the kitchen, Teri leaning back against the work surface, Fiona sitting on an art deco stool from the breakfast bar.

'Thank you,' Fiona said, and placed her glass on the bar. 'So how are things with Mr Wonderful,' she asked. 'We haven't mentioned him, yet.'

'Who could you possibly mean?' Teri wondered, but her eyes lit up and Fiona was transfixed by them.

'Torl, of course!' Fiona blurted out. 'Don't go all coy on me. I want to know everything about him, starting with what he's like in bed.'

'I don't know. I haven't seen him since Monday, and we haven't, you know, done it, yet. He's nice. I like him. He's a bit weird; you're never quite sure if he's listening to what you say or far away on another planet, but he's interesting, and funny.'

'Tristan's still convinced he's a fraud.'

'Well he's wrong.'

'And he's boss of this big company?'

'Oh, yes, he's that all right.'

'So why haven't you shagged him?'

Teri pulled another stool from under the breakfast bar and placed it close against Fiona's, but pointing the other way. She sat on it, facing Fiona, and took one of her hands in hers.

'Didn't I tell you?' she said. 'He's religious. Some sort of minister. Methodist, I think he told me. Apparently, if we went to bed with each other it would be a sin.'

'Of course it's a sin,' Fiona stated. 'That's what makes it so much fun.'

'I'm working on him. I think it will only take a little push.'

'Then give him a push, for God's sake. I'm starting to worry about you.'

'There's nothing to worry about. All is under control. He's there for the taking. Money first, then sex. It will be his reward.'

'He hasn't, you know, converted you, has he?'

Teri reached out with her free hand and placed it behind Fiona's neck, lifting her tresses and letting them fall through her fingers. Fiona saw the look in those big brown eyes and moved closer, her hand on Teri's knee.

'Oh, no, my darling,' Teri said as she pulled Fiona's face towards hers. 'He hasn't converted me. You're the only person who ever converted me to anything.'

CHAPTER TWENTY-TWO

We had a prisoner in the cells. 6 a.m. Thursday morning I strode into the nick and checked the night log and it said we had one prisoner in the cells. Prisoners are a bind. We try to avoid them at all costs. They have to be fed, dressed, watched over, taken to court and generally pandered to when we could be out doing more important things, like, well, catching more prisoners.

We were in early because I wanted a little talk with Frederick Raw, and he had a record of violence as long as Heckley High Street, so it had to be done properly. It's amazing how many ex-shotgun licensees just happen to have an unregistered one lying around. The mess room was crowded with uniforms wearing body armour, carrying weapons, sipping coffee. Upstairs in CID, Dave was waiting, and one or two others.

He said: 'Morning, Charlie. There's a prisoner in the cells.'

'Mmm, I saw the log. Anybody we know?'

'The Happy Fryer.'

'Who?'

'The Happy Fryer. He's the proprietor of that fish and chip shop near the bus station. There was a domestic there last night and he assaulted his wife.'

'Right.'

'It wasn't a serious assault.'

'Wasn't it?'

'No. She was only lightly battered.'

'Have you finished?'

'Yes, boss.'

'Let's go, then.'

Unfortunately, Mr Raw didn't have a telephone. If he'd been available that way I might have rung him and invited him to come out, but he wasn't. It could have led to a stand-off, but that's preferable to sending officers into a dangerous situation. That option wasn't available, so we did it the gung-ho way.

I stood on the corner and watched as they sprung the door and poured in. The sun was already high and the sky was streaked with jet trails and smudged with mackerel clouds. Two minutes later they led Raw out and took him to the nick. Dave and I gave his house the once-over but it didn't feature in our enquiries and there was nothing in it to interest us. He lived alone, read the racing papers, lived on a diet more suitable for *Rattus rattus* and never cleaned his bath.

The street had woken up when we went outside again, and little groups of men in baggy pants and sandals stood around, watching. 'C'mon,' I said. 'You can buy me a bacon sandwich.'

The Happy Fryer had gone home so we gave his cell to Raw. We also gave him breakfast, a paper jumpsuit and a solicitor.

I kept it general at first, finding out about his background, where he spent his time, who his acquaintances were, that sort of stuff. Anything to keep him talking. He had a job, keeping the forecourt clean at the supermarket filling station, and his leisure time revolved around the bookmakers and the local Labour Club. He spent the evening of Saturday, 6th August in the club because that's where he spent every Saturday night and he couldn't remember the last time he'd missed. Dave was sitting in on the interview and he excused himself. A few minutes later he returned and passed me a note. It said that the Labour Club was about halfway between Raw's home and Shibden Park, where Magdalena was found. I already knew that he lived about a mile and a quarter from the park.

'Do you have a car?' I asked, and he said he didn't.

'Can you drive?'

'No.'

'When were you last in Leeds?' That confused him for a while, but after a long deliberation he decided that he'd last visited the city when he'd served a brief stint on remand in HMP Armley, back in 1988.

'And you haven't been back?'

'No, never.'

'Is that never to Leeds or never to Armley jail?'

'Both.'

Then we showed him the torque. He put his head in his hands and leant on the table. After a while I said: 'You obviously recognise it.'

'Yeah,' he nodded. 'So that's what it's about, is it?'

'Yes, Fred. This is what it's about. Do you deny taking this necklace to a pawnbrokers in Halifax and pledging it for ten pounds?'

'No. I mean, that's right.'

'So where did you get it?'

'Stole it, I suppose.'

'Where from?'

'From…you know, from her body.'

'Would you like to tell us all about it? Start when you left the club. No, start before that. Why do you go to that particular drinking establishment?'

'Because I'm banned from all the town centre places. Pub Watch has me listed. And they have a snooker table, big screen TV for Sky Sport and the beer's decent.'

OK, I'm convinced, I thought. 'So what time did you leave?'

'About half ten. I was skint, and I'd had enough.'

'Go on.'

'It was a nice night, so I had a walk down to the park. I like it there. It's quiet, and you can see the stars. When we were kids we loved astronomy. Dan Dare and all that. Then I studied it a bit, when I was inside. You can't see the stars nowadays, because of all the streetlights. Kids don't know what they're missing. Sometimes I sleep down there. I lie on my back and watch for shooting stars. Anywhere's better than that pigsty I live in, surrounded by chapatti eaters and towel-heads.'

'Go on.'

'This car came, driving over the grass. It was pitch black but it stopped and I thought I saw the driver take something out of the boot and leave it. It was heavy, whatever it was, and he struggled with it. I imagined he was dumping rubbish. When he drove away I went over for a look. It was a body. I could hardly see her, but I felt for her neck to see if there was a pulse. There wasn't, and this necklace thing came away in my hand. I knew I would be a suspect, and I panicked. I took the necklace because it was all separate pieces and I thought it might fall apart, with my prints on some of the bits. That's all I did. Steal the necklace. I didn't kill nobody.'

We broke for coffee and I went upstairs and kicked my chair across the office.

Dave said: 'I can't see an astronomy-loving Dan Dare fan turning into a murderer, can you, squire?'

'More to the point,' I said, 'how did he get Magdalena's body from Leeds to Halifax in the allotted time schedule, without a car? This'll make the ACC's day; I promised him a result.'

'Let him go?'

'No, not yet. I'll talk to him some more; you get down to his house and look for car keys. Tomorrow we'll check out his alibi and we'll keep a watch on him.' Raw wasn't registered as a car owner, but that didn't mean there wasn't one in a lock-up somewhere that he saved for special occasions.

Dave said: 'Fine. Fancy a pint tonight?'

'Um, no,' I said. 'Thanks all the same but I've a few things to do.'

Waiting for a phone call was the main thing I had to do, but I waited in vain. I didn't waste my time, though. I took a big sheet of drawing paper and divided it into columns and horizontal lines. At the head of each column I wrote the name of a suspect. Everybody who had been embraced by the investigation got a column all to themselves, with the end one reserved for a Mr Anybody. He was the favourite. Down the left-hand column I wrote the type of evidence, starting with things that would be admissible in court, like alibi, motive, opportunity, and whether they had a ponytail.

After that it was the more subjective stuff, and I started to flounder. I've met a few murderers and they're difficult to classify, but some fit the template. I didn't want to put *does he look like a killer?* or *are his eyes close together?* so I settled for *temperament*. Then it was *strong enough* – Magdalena was a big lady – followed by *local knowledge*, *transport* and *location*. I remembered Mrs Dolan's contribution and added *voice recognition*.

After that, working horizontally, I gave everybody marks out of ten for each question, awarding a five if it was irrelevant or unknown. I made a banana sandwich and a coffee and waited for the phone to ring, but it remained dormant, like Vesuvius, threatening to erupt any time but just sitting there quietly.

Last job was to add up the columns and give everybody a total score. When I'd done that we had a clear winner. I drew a circle around his name and went to bed.

The Valley of Desolation at Bolton Abbey is a bit of a misnomer. The Victorians may have thought it was inhabited by demons, only to be approached with trepidation and a full explorer's outfit, but on a warm summer's afternoon it's as pleasant a walk as you could wish for, and one of my favourite places. I'd soon left the picnickers behind and was enjoying the gloom cast by the trees as I headed upwards, past the waterfall, which was reduced to a trickle by the drought. Then you burst out onto Barden Fell and a different landscape. It's grouse-shooting land up there, part of the Duke of Devonshire's back yard, but the guns had fallen silent and the chief life form was an occasional lesser hairy-legged walker. The last time I'd been up there I met a girl in a downpour, and gave her a lift home. I smiled at the memory and wondered what she was doing now.

I ate my sandwich on the Rocking Stone and did my thinking. I knew who killed Magdalena, of that I was certain. Proving it was a different matter. We didn't have a witness, we'd no forensics, and I couldn't be sure of finding any. It would have to be a confession, I thought, but that would have to be carefully managed. Shock and surprise, with a subtle touch of misinformation might do it. I wondered about being wired when I talked to him, but decided against it. Then it was over Lord's Seat and down to the river again to complete the circuit.

Torl, also known as David Storey, was watching a video about cheetahs on the Masai Mara when the phone rang, and he knew without looking who it was.

'Hello Teri,' he said. 'How are you?'

After a silence she said: 'How did you know it was me?' in her little-girl-lost voice.

'I didn't,' he replied, 'but I willed it to be you. I wanted it to be you more than anything else, and it was you.' The cheetah was stalking a newly born wildebeest. He turned the volume down but stayed watching the picture.

'Did you really?'

'Yes. I've missed you.'

'And I've missed you, too. When did you get back?'

'About an hour ago. I like to drive back while it's still daylight. So how are you?' The cheetah sprang from its cover and the ten-minute-old wildebeest started running for its life.

'I'm fine. Richard's being awkward, but I won't bore you with that. Will I ever see you again?'

'I hope so. When are you available?'

'Uh. I'm always available. Will tomorrow – Monday – be all right?'

'Of course it will. Monday suits me fine. It's a depressing day and you'll brighten it up for me, plus, of course, it's only twenty-four hours away. Any thoughts about where we might go?'

'Not really. I like the cinema, or the theatre if there's anything good showing.'

'I'll have a word with them, see what I can arrange, and give you a ring on your mobile tomorrow afternoon.' The cheetah sank its teeth into the other animal's throat and the chase was over.

They said their goodbyes like star-crossed lovers and broke the connection. Torl retrieved the *Gazette* from the recycle bin and thumbed through it, looking for the entertainments page, and drew a circle round an advert for *The Caucasian Chalk Circle*, performed by the Heckley Amateur Dramatic Society, known as the HADS.

That night he dreamt he was in the middle of a tug-of-war between an elf and next door's cat. Every time the elf looked like winning the cat found some extra strength and pulled him back into the middle. At four o'clock he made some tea and read a book until it was time to go to work.

Gilbert was back behind his desk on Monday morning, looking ridiculously healthy. Sitting on a riverbank for eight hours squinting at a stick poking up out of the water, every muscle poised to react instantly to the slightest flicker, brain engaged in nothing more demanding than outwitting a fish, must have therapeutic qualities. Regular flushing of the system with large quantities of Guinness is probably helpful, too. I brought him up to date on the job, told him about Gareth and waited for his comments.

'What about the Magdalena case?' he asked.

'Ah!' I replied, holding up one finger. 'I'm glad you mentioned that. Give me this morning, Gilbert, then I might have something for you to offer the ACC.'

We'd given Freddy Raw the seven a.m. call, chosen after consultation with the country's most eminent – and expensive – psychiatrists as being the time of day when the average villain's metabolism is at its most inert. I had a theory – this one came free – that ten o'clock on a Monday morning was a pretty torpid part of the circadian cycle, too. Now was the time to put it to the test. I unhooked my jacket from behind the door and was pulling it closed behind me when my phone started ringing. I walked backwards into the office, hung my jacket up and continued in the same manner back to my desk.

'DI Priest,' I said.

'Good morning, Inspector,' replied a voice that I didn't recognise. 'This is Edward Shires of Shires and Oxley. We have met before.'

'I remember you, Mr Shires.' He was a partner in a firm of solicitors and accountants in the High Street, established by his father many years previously. They didn't do criminal work, so I wasn't sure what he wanted. 'How can I help you?'

'Can I put a hypothetical case to you, Inspector? That is, if you have the time. I realise I'm intruding.'

I said: 'I was on my way out, but go on, if it won't take too long.'

'Thank you. I've just had a phone call from one of my clients. One of my more affluent clients who has a certain standing in the public's eye. He was working at his computer over the weekend and he found a CD disk in one of the drives. Apparently people send him disks. I won't go into why, at the moment, if you don't mind. He couldn't find the box for the disk so he had a quick look at it. It was filled with pornographic images of children being abused. My client was quite upset by it. He's not sure where it came from but thinks he could pin it down to five or six possibles.'

'Is he reporting it so we can pursue them?' I asked.

'Um, at this juncture I'm not sure. His first priority is to keep his name in the clear. As I said, he's in the public's eye and he's scared stiff of being associated with anything like this. Mud sticks, as you know. I was hoping we could have an off-the-record talk about it.'

I said: 'You know the rules about off-the-record talks, Mr Shires. We can't use it to conceal any criminal activity. Where is the disk now?'

'Shall we say he's destroyed it?'

'Best thing to do with it. As your client came forward voluntarily with this information, without any duress or the inducement of self-interest, I can't see there being a problem in him retaining his anonymity. Also,' I said, 'and I'd prefer this not to go any further, we've had a couple of what may be similar cases. I'd be most interested in having a talk with your client, Mr Shires, as soon as possible.'

'Off the record?'

'You know the rules, but as off-the-record as I can make it.'

'That's all I expected, Mr Priest. When are you available?'

'Today. I'd like to see him today.'

'He's here with me. One moment, please.' The line was silent for a while, then: 'My client says he has to be somewhere this afternoon, but this morning's fine. He suggests you visit him at home, if your other appointment can wait.'

'Where's home?'

'Hunter's Valley.'

A bell started ringing in my head. I said: 'No, sorry. It'll have to be your office or here at the nick.'

Another consultation, then Shires came back. 'Here, then Inspector, shall we say in twenty minutes?'

'That's fine,' I said. 'Can you tell me what your client is called?'

'Yes. He's Zed Boogey, the rap artist.'

Now why wasn't I surprised?

The change of plan meant that I'd have nothing to show Gilbert or the ACC, but that was too bad. Sometimes, you have to go where destiny takes you. I like visiting solicitors' premises when it's not my name on the file. They have attractive receptionists and decent biscuits. I said: 'Black, no sugar, please,' and she showed me into the boss's office.

Mr Boogey was wearing lightweight linen trousers with leather slip-on shoes and a short-sleeved Craghoppers shirt. His handshake was gentle and his smile genuine. He looked less like a rap artist than I did.

'It's all image,' he said, after I'd put that point to him. 'It's amazing what a few fake dreadlocks can do.'

Shires coughed and thanked me for coming. 'Mr Priest appreciates your desire to be kept out of any publicity,' he said to Zed Boogey. 'I'm sure you can be frank and open with him.'

Boogey looked at me, saying: 'You caught that serial killer, didn't you? The one who fell off the bridge. Wow! That must make you feel good.'

'There were a couple of others involved in the investigation,' I told him.

'So did he fall or was he pushed? That's what everybody was asking.'

'He fell. Tell me about the disk, please.'

'I'll believe you; thousands wouldn't. OK. I've been away in Germany for a few days. I had a gig in Dusseldorf – I'm big in Dusseldorf, would you believe? – and a pro-am golf tournament in Bremen. I got back in the early hours of last Wednesday. Since then I've been in London, working on a new album, so I've had no opportunity to use my computer. Until yesterday. I switched it on and it came up with this error message. There was a disk in the D drive. I hadn't a clue what it was so I had a look and it had all these photos on it. They were horrible. I was nearly sick, only looked at a few. Then I spent all the rest of the day wondering what to do. I decided that whoever sent it to me needed catching, so here I am.'

'You think somebody sent it to you?'

'They must have done, mustn't they?'

The receptionist came in with my coffee and I thanked her. When she'd gone I said: 'And you put it in your machine? Don't you remember receiving it?'

'Mr Priest,' Boogey began, leaning forward. 'I do a show on Trafford Radio twice a week, where we showcase local talent between the other stuff. It's mainly hip-hop and R&B, and some funk. Every week I receive about five or six demo disks from kids who think they're the next Mistajam. It must have been one of them sent it, either accidentally or on purpose. I've a heap of covering letters, if you want them.'

I couldn't help smiling. 'But you don't have a filing system?'

'Actually, I do. I take it seriously. I'm treading on these kids' dreams, but this one must have slipped through.'

I said: 'You were on children's TV, weren't you? How did you become a rap artist?'

'I trained as a classical actor,' he replied. 'RADA, the whole works. My dream was to play Othello, but the best I did was a banana in Jelly and Co. It was a living, and I enjoyed working with the kids, but there's an age limit. I couldn't dance and I couldn't sing, I was too small to play a cop and not many TV villains are black, these days. The rapping started as a bit of a laugh and took off. I'd found my role in life.'

'Is there a message in your songs?'

'Apart from *buy the CD*? No, boss. If it rhymes, it goes in, but we try to keep them reasonably wholesome. We're not into gangsta stuff and all that.'

'I'm glad to hear it,' I said. It was interesting, but hardly relevant to the case. 'Do you have a burglar alarm on the house?' I asked.

'A good one,' he replied. 'Including CCTV.'

'Have you had a look at it?'

'No, but nobody's broken in. They can't have done. The alarm is working and there's no sign of a burglary.'

'Who else has a key?'

'Nobody.'

'Nobody at all?'

'Well, only Richard and Teri.'

'Who are...?'

'My next door neighbours. Teri comes in and waters my plants. That's all.'

I picked up my cup and drained it. 'Thanks for coming in, Mr Boogey,' I said. 'What you've told us is very interesting. We'll be looking into it.'

'Do you want those covering letters?' he asked.

The answer was *no*, but I didn't want to sound complacent, so I said: 'Yes please, if you could drop them in here or the police station I'd be very grateful. And your CCTV tape.'

'What about the CD?'

'You haven't destroyed it?'

'No.' He looked towards the solicitor, who opened a drawer in his desk and produced the offending disk.

I thought about it for a few seconds, then said: 'Well let's do it now, shall we?'

Torl parked outside the theatre and collected the tickets he'd ordered. They were good seats, four rows from the front and fairly central. He had a coffee in Burger King and used the facilities there, swishing water around his mouth and grimacing at himself in the mirror. When it was time he drove to the riverside development where he'd arranged to pick up Teri and tapped her number into the security keypad. 'Your carriage awaits you, mademoiselle,' he said, when her *hello* came crackling from the little box.

A minute later she came out, wearing a powder blue suit consisting of a skirt bordering on the illegal and a jacket held at the front with a single button. She wasn't wearing a blouse under it, just a gold chain with a crucifix, and high heeled sandals. Torl stood there, transfixed, and she noted the effect she had on him, exaggerating her walk as she approached the car.

I'm in trouble, he was thinking, feeling he'd reached the point of no return – had gone under twice and was going down again. Then: what the heck, it's life and life only. He opened the door for her, saying: 'You look sensational. I'm not sure if the HADS are ready for you.'

She slipped into the passenger seat, holding back her smile, and said: 'To the theatre, please, James.' Torl pulled his seatbelt across and twisted in his seat to look at her. She said: 'You wanted someone to go to the theatre with, so here I am.'

He leant across and kissed her lightly on the cheek. He didn't recognise her perfume. It was distilled from the pheromones of a billion butterflies, brought in from the hills of Araby by Nubian slaves who were promptly sacrificed lest they divulge its secrets. He blinked and waited for his heartbeat to settle.

The HADS – Heckley Amateur Dramatic Society – were known by rival companies as the HADN'TS, and tonight they justified the unkindness. They hadn't much talent, hadn't learnt their lines and hadn't rehearsed enough. But they had enthusiasm by the sackful. The stunned silence of the audience gradually changed to sniggers of amusement, then open derisory laughter, followed by outright enjoyment of the actors' discomfort. The cast, troopers to the end, eventually realised where things were going and started playing it for laughs. They weren't given a standing ovation at the final curtain, but nobody asked for their money back.

As they filed towards the exit Teri said she needed to use the ladies. There, she had a pee, replenished her perfume and made a phone call. In the car she said: 'That was fun. I enjoyed it.'

'Not what I was hoping to impress you with,' Torl said, 'but it was the first night, so we'll give them the benefit of the doubt. Drink, somewhere?'

'I could fix you one at the apartment, if you like.'

Bits of his body told him that, yes, he would like it and he ran the tip of his tongue along his upper lip. 'Right,' he said. 'Your place it is,' and he coughed to clear the hoarseness in his voice.

'Easy on the gin in mine, please,' he was saying, fifteen minutes later. He was standing in the kitchen, watching Teri fix the drinks after briefly admiring the German appliances and the bold décor. He'd read that some of these apartments went for a million pounds, and this one was the penthouse. They carried their drinks into the lounge and seated themselves on the settee. Teri crossed her legs and Torl took a long sip of his g and t, then found a safe place for his glass, to leave his hands free.

'This is rather magnificent,' he told her, casting his eyes around the room. 'You have excellent taste, but I already knew that.'

'I'll show you around, later,' she said.

'I'd like that,' he confirmed, trying to hide his enthusiasm for a guided tour.

'I might lose it,' she said, 'if Richard plays awkward. That's why I need an income. I've been looking at a few places and seen one or two that have possibilities.'

'In the beauty business?' he asked.

'Yes, it's all I know, but there's plenty of money to be made at the top of the range. That's where I'd aim to be, but it costs money to break into it.'

'It usually all boils down to money,' Torl replied.

'That's where you come in,' she said, reaching an arm out towards him. 'My Mr Santa Claus. Do you think you'll be able to help me?'

The doorbell rang before Torl could gather his senses to form an answer. Teri looked startled for the second or two it took for the chimes to die away, then said: 'I've been a bit naughty, Torl.'

'In what way?'

'Well, Tristan said he'd like to meet you. He likes to look after me, a bit, to make sure nobody takes advantage of me, so I've invited him over. Do you mind?'

Torl minded like Joan of Arc minded being burnt at the stake. He minded being deprived of the sole company of this woman and he minded having his credentials questioned. He didn't know which he minded most, but he minded all right, he minded like hell.

'No,' he said. 'Of course not. Wheel him in.'

Teri went to answer the door and Torl pulled himself more upright on the low settee. She returned in seconds followed by three people, one of whom Torl recognised.

Teri said: 'This is Tristan, this is Fiona and this is Richard.' Turning to them she said: 'And he's Torl, sometimes known as David Storey.'

Torl looked up at them towering over him, looking aggressive. He was a shade taller than the two men but they held the high ground and had him outnumbered. The woman was interesting. This would be Teri's friend, he thought. She was the opposite of Teri: tall, fair and elegant; where Teri was petite, dark and gamine. But just as beautiful. Every bit as beautiful.

'We've met before,' he said to the one called Richard. So Teri had been at the speed dating with her husband, all those weeks ago.

'So we have,' he replied.

'Tell us about this company of yours,' Tristan invited. 'This quango. What's it called? Local Industry Development

Initiative, or LINDI for short? Is that it?'

'That's it,' Torl replied. On the edge of his vision he could see a chair that might be useful, and some iron candlesticks that would make a decent weapon, if things went the way they were looking.

'You might be interested to learn that I've been doing some investigating,' Tristan was saying. 'I visited the premises where Teri says you took her and they've never heard of David Storey. So I've asked around. I have my contacts. There's no such quango as LINDI, giving large grants to small businesses. There are regional development agencies, but none of them has a David Storey working for them and none is based in Heckley. So who are you and what do you want?'

'You're getting things out of proportion,' Torl replied. 'I'm from out of town and I met a beautiful woman at the speed dating. That's all there is to it.'

Tristan turned to Teri. 'Sorry, Teri,' he said, 'but he's a complete fraud. He's been leading you on.'

'And that beautiful woman happens to be my wife,' Richard said.

Torl looked up at him and saw that he was now holding a baseball bat. 'So what are you going to do?' he asked.

The two men took a step towards him. 'We're going to give you a good hiding and chuck you in the canal,' Tristan told him.

'I don't think you'd be wise to try that,' Torl warned.

'Why not?' Richard asked, raising the baseball bat.

'Yeah, why not?' Tristan added.

'Because then you'd be in more trouble than you're already in.'

'What's that supposed to mean?' Richard wanted to know, lowering the bat slightly.

'Who are you?' Tristan demanded. 'Just who the fuck are you?'

Torl reached into his inside jacket pocket and produced a leather wallet that he flicked open with practised ease. 'My name's Priest,' he told them, 'as in Roman Catholic. Detective Inspector Priest of Heckley CID, and you four are under arrest.'

CHAPTER TWENTY-THREE

I pulled my mobile from my pocket and asked for assistance up in the apartment. I'd had a car shadowing me during my assignations with Teri in case she accused me of impropriety at a later date. The four of them stood there, looking shell-shocked, each wondering how to salvage something from the situation. Richard carefully stood the baseball bat in a corner.

Fiona broke the silence. 'Jesus Christ,' she said, 'I need a drink,' and headed for the kitchen.

That broke the ice and Tristan took up the challenge. 'What do you mean, *under arrest*?' he demanded. 'What are we charged with?'

I said: 'You're not charged with anything, yet,' and gave them the caution.

'So what's the offence?'

'How about conspiracy to commit blackmail, for a start,' I replied.

'We've never blackmailed anybody.'

'You tell me then. Why did you download obscene images onto the computer of Ted Goss, one of the most decent MPs in the business, causing him to commit suicide? Why did you do the same to ruin the career of Colin Swainby, a fine policeman? Why did those two break into Zed Boogey's house and leave a disk of obscene images in his computer? We've got you on the conspiracy, so if it wasn't blackmail, what was it?'

Tristan looked at Richard, a horrified expression on his face. 'You broke into next door...' he began.

His wife had returned, a tumbler of clear liquid in her hand. I'd have gambled it wasn't water. 'You idiot!' she shouted at Wentbridge. 'You fucking stupid idiot.'

Teri spun to face her. 'If you hadn't made him lose a million pounds he wouldn't have had to do it,' she shrieked.

I sat there, looking from one to the other as the relationship crumbled, feeling like an umpire at Wimbledon, developing a crick in my neck.

'Shut up! Shut up!' Wentbridge shouted, and grabbed his wife before she tore out somebody's eyes. We were saved by the doorbell.

'I'd answer that,' I said, 'or in ten seconds they'll batter it down.'

People have a perception of psychopaths as nutters who go about raping, stabbing and strangling. Some do, of course, but it could be argued that your average rapist, strangler and stabbist just happens to be a psychopath. The majority of psychos, or sociopaths as they are sometimes called, have learnt to live normal lives and have no more desire than the average man to go about raping, strangling and stabbing.

They just don't care about people. They're all around us, in all walks of life, fitting in because they have learnt how to. Millions of them. There's one in every office, several in every factory. The police force probably has as many psychos in its ranks as any other occupation.

Your friendly neighbourhood psycho is the one who laughs most when you get done for willy waggling in the park, even though he was at your barbecue the night before, enjoying your wine and admiring your block paving. He's the one who sniggers at the old woman with the wooden leg who sleeps in the dumpsters, or who is cheered up for the day if he sees a dog flattened by a car. Most of the time, he's a regular guy.

But he's an island. John Donne got it wrong. The psycho lives in his own world, immune to the feelings of his fellow men and women. He gets by. He's happy. He's often successful. There are advantages in being an island, but there are advantages in numbers, also. Sometimes psychos drift together and join up, like patches of scum on a river. Usually it's just two, and if they have evil intentions the world soon knows about them. I'd just arrested four.

I wanted them isolated from each other, so we took Teri to Heckley and shared the others between Halifax and Huddersfield. I drove home and went to bed, and slept like a puppy until my six o'clock call. I skipped Gilbert's morning meeting and held an intensive briefing with my team. When we were through I sent Dave and Brendan to talk to Fiona, and Maggie and Dave Rose to interview the two men. That left Teri for me.

'They're falling apart, turning in on each other,' I told the troops. 'All we have to do is encourage them. Fiona is the weakest link, and we've got the least on her. If she realises that, it might encourage her to spill the swill on the others.'

'Hint that she might be dealt with leniently if she cooperates?' Dave suggested.

'Yes, but subtly,' I said. 'Let her think of it herself.'

'Maybe I should let Brendan do the talking.'

'That sounds a good idea.'

'I'll say one thing, Chas,' Dave said.

'What's that?'

'You're mixing with a good-looking bunch of women, these days.'

Teri was as good-looking as they come, and a night in the cells hadn't diminished her. She'd washed her face and, unmade up and dishevelled, she still looked beautiful. Vulnerability was her trump card, her golden share, and she played it well. I said: 'Hello, Teri. Did you manage to get any sleep?'

'No,' she replied.

'Would you like another coffee?'

'No.'

The duty solicitor was sitting alongside her and we were taping the interview, so I went through the preamble. When I'd finished I said: 'Do you know why you're here?'

She nodded and I asked her to speak, for the tape.

'It's because of the game,' she replied.

'The game? What game?'

'It was Tristan's idea. He thought of it,' and she told me all about the games people play.

Teri described the rape she'd suffered as a child, and blamed that for her attitude towards men. She'd obviously decided that it would be the main plank of her defence, reinforced by her little-girl-lost act. Maybe she'd even throw in a faked epileptic fit when she appeared in court, I thought. She seemed not to realise that she'd told me – or Torl – all about it, and went through the rape in more graphic detail than before. Or perhaps she was simply rehearsing, or wanted it on tape. I didn't know.

Talking about it gave her strength and direction, and I could almost see her formulate her plan of attack. She said: 'I thought you were different. I thought I'd finally found a man I could trust. Not another who would manipulate and exploit me, like every other man I've met. I don't even know your proper name.'

I didn't say anything, just sat there, looking at her, witnessing my feelings for her turn from something out of control into icy indifference. We rode the silence, waiting for the other to speak as if it were a party game, until Teri said: 'You were special. I was falling in love with you. I should have known you were too good to be true, like all the rest. It couldn't happen to me. It couldn't.'

Another silence, until I said: 'I believe you were formerly known as Angela Ennis. Is that right?'

She twitched and looked at me, saying: 'Angela died when she was twelve. He killed her.'

'And your mother,' I went on. 'Was she called Magdalena?'

'She's dead too, or I hope she is. She wasn't fit to be anybody's mother.'

I said: 'I've some bad news for you, Teri. Or at least, what most daughters would regard as bad news. Magdalena Ennis, your mother, was found dead on 7th August. She was murdered, but we haven't arrested anybody, yet.'

Her mouth fell open and she stared at me. The big eyes had lost their glow and I held them easily for a few seconds until she said: 'What do you care? I'll add hypocrite to the other qualities you possess.'

I can only take so much. I said: 'It's not all bad news,

though. We've found your father. He's just been released after twenty-five years in jail, and he's looking forward to meeting you. He says you two have some catching up to do.'

So I invented that last bit, but I enjoyed saying it, and her face was a picture.

As I walked past the front desk I was told that Mr Wood wanted to see me. I dived into the CPS office and talked for an hour about what we could do Tristan & co for. They were at least looking at conspiracy and downloading the images – the very crime that they tried to pin on their victims. I liked the sound of that, and blackmail was still a possibility. 'Mr Wood's looking for you,' they choroused as I went in through the big office.

I rang the photographer at the *Gazette* and told him to get himself and his sniper lens down to the court. Once the story broke, Tristan & co would only be seen outside the court with blankets over their heads, but they'd be unprepared for this first visit, and shaming them was all part of the service. I wanted their mugs over all the tabloids, whatever sentences they might be given. He said: 'Cheers, Chas, I owe you one,' and dashed off to polish his tripod.

Brendan was answering the phone. He put it down and made agitated gestures. I poked my head out of the office and was told that the ACC was on his way upstairs. 'And Mr Wood wants you,' they added as I grabbed my jacket and headed for the door.

'Tell him I'm out,' I said.

'Where do we say you are?'

'Um, interviewing a suspect.'

'Where?'

'Oh, anywhere. Make something up. Use that vivid imagination of yours.'

I dived down the back stairs and was in my car heading out of town before the lift deposited the ACC on the top floor for his case review meeting.

I saw him in the street before I reached his house, strolling along with two Morrison's carrier bags dangling from his hands. I parked nearby and sat on the doorstep, waiting for him. The sun was shining again and his little overgrown garden was alive with bees and hover flies. It was a shame to spoil his day, but it's what I do.

He juggled with the bags as he let himself into the garden, carefully reset the gate latch and turned to face me. As he saw me sitting there a look of confusion, or perhaps fear, spread across his face.

'Good morning, Mr Mackintosh,' I said, rising to my feet. 'I wonder if I could have a word?'

He put on his old man act, fumbling for his keys, pretending he didn't remember me, but I suggested that we could talk at the police station, if he'd prefer it, and eventually found myself in his familiar front room. He didn't ask me if I'd like a drink.

'Tell me about conceptual art,' I said, sitting down without being invited to.

He thought about it, then switched into lecturer mode. 'Conceptual art,' he began, 'is a style of art that challenges the viewer, or participant, to look beyond the physical appearance of the work to the idea that created it. The movement began in the 1920s in a very small way, but blossomed into an accepted art form in the Sixties. It faded but was revived in the Eighties thanks to schools like Leeds.'

I interrupted him. 'I was thinking more about its investment possibilities,' I said. 'Was it a good investment?'

Sunlight coming through the bay window was lighting the side of his face and I could see the edge of the scarring on his neck. He jumped up and pulled a curtain across a few inches to make some shadow.

'As an investment,' I reminded him.

'Well,' he began, 'these things are subject to the whims of fashion, as you know. Tastes change. What is popular today, regarded as the height of good taste, may be considered hackneyed and over-exposed after a while. In the art world we often destroy that which we hold most precious.'

I said: 'I don't think the conceptual art movement collapsed through over-exposure, do you?'

He gave a brief smile. 'You know what they say, Inspector: your investments can go down as well as up.'

'And past performance is no guarantee of future performance.'

'Exactly.'

'Did you explain that point to Magdalena Fischer?'

His demeanour changed. He shrank into himself and began tapping the arm of his chair with a talon-like hand. 'I'm sorry?' he said.

I spelt it out for him. 'When you invested Magdalena's money. Did you explain that it was a gamble, that the value could go down as well as up?'

'I don't know what you mean.'

'I think you do. I think you invested Magdalena's money in so-called works of art that were inflated in price far beyond their worth. We have ways of checking these things, you know. There are records. The banks, the Inland Revenue, auction houses. If you've anything to hide you'd better come out with it, because believe me, we'll find out in the next day or two.'

'It wasn't like that,' he protested.

'So tell me what it was like.'

He gathered his senses for another lecture. 'They were exciting times,' he began, 'and we were at the forefront of things. The art world was beating a path to our door. If anything, we were victims of our own success, because everybody started jumping on the bandwagon. We had some great talent at the college, at the leading edge of the movement, but you're only as good as the critics allow you to be, and it's a London-centric world, the art world.'

'And some of them thought it was a case of the emperor having no clothes on,' I suggested.

'If you say so.'

'How much did you invest for her?'

'I don't remember.'

'She'd've had about £300,000.'

'It was nowhere near that much.'

'How many pieces did you buy for her?'

'I don't remember.'

'Who set the prices?'

He was on firmer ground with that one. 'They were bought at auction. It was all very proper. Thorneycrofts, I believe.'

'Auctions are easily rigged,' I said, and he sank in again, up to his knees. I opened my notebook at a blank page. 'Let's say you bought three works,' I continued. 'That's 100K each.'

'It was nothing like that,' he interrupted.

'Let me finish. You gave, say £5,000 to the artist. He hasn't eaten for a week and is glad of anything you throw his way. You have somebody bidding against you to take the price up to £100,000, which gives the auction house commission of 10K, leaving £85,000 to you. Three times. A nice little earner, as they say. Next day it's in the papers that Kevin Verruca's collage of stale loaves and hubcaps has gone for a record amount and all the collectors and talentless wanabees clap their hands.'

'It wasn't that much,' he said.

'I think it was. I think you cleaned her out. What happened to them?'

'The pieces? They went on show at the Lichfield gallery in London, then came back to Leeds for an exhibition at the Schofield gallery. After that they went into storage. The reviews weren't good; tastes had changed.'

'So where are they now?'

'I don't know. They were in a lock-up, but the damp got in. Then the lease ran out.'

'So they were scrapped?'

'Yes, very probably, but by then I'd lost touch with Magda.'

He shook his head as if to clear his brain, tapped his fingers, stroked the scar on his neck. 'Am I under arrest?' he asked.

'No.'

'Did I ought to have a solicitor present?'

'Probably. Do you want one?'

'No.'

'When did you last see Magdalena?'

That shook him, but he recovered quickly. 'I told you before. It was probably about ten years ago.'

'On the night she died, August 6th–7th, she was seen barely fifty yards away, heading this way. Are you saying she didn't call to see you?'

'Well, no, she didn't call here.'

'How many times did she telephone you in the last twelve months?'

'None.'

'And how many did you ring her?'

'None.'

'So you deny telephoning her at Beverley and leaving a message on her answerphone, telling her you wanted to see her because you had something for her? I have the tape, if you'd like to hear it. We're currently checking with the phone company to verify the times of your calls.'

'I...I...' he stuttered. 'I...don't know. She rang me, yes she did. She was a nuisance. It wasn't about money. She was unhappy, wanted to see me again, get her away from that jailbird she married.'

'So what did you have for her?'

He looked confused. 'I did have some money for her, but it was my own. I wanted to help her, wanted her to stop pestering me.'

'So did you give it to her?'

'No. She never arrived.'

I stared at him for a good minute, then said: 'I don't believe you.'

He said: 'I think I'd like to see a solicitor, now.'

'That might not be wise,' I told him.

'Why not?'

'I'm looking for the person who murdered Magdalena,' I explained. 'Do you remember her daughter, Angela?'

'No, well, yes. Vaguely.'

'She remembers you quite vividly. Says you raped her. Is your name Julian?'

It nearly choked him, but he admitted it was.

'She gave a good description of you.' I scratched my neck to illustrate my point. 'Like I said, I'm investigating a murder. Angela assumes you're dead, isn't looking for you. She's moved on, but I could easily talk her into pressing charges. Sometimes, murder is almost excusable, there can be mitigating circumstances, but raping a child...'

I let it hang there and watched the cogs going round as he did the maths. 'It...wasn't rape,' he said.

'What would you call it?'

'It was with her consent. She was fourteen years old, and a proper little hussy. Her nickname at school was Winmau.'

'Winmau?' I echoed.

'They manufacture dartboards. It was a rather crude comparison.'

'I see. Go on.'

'She had a shower, came downstairs with just a towel round her, looking for something or other, she said. Her hairbrush, something like that. She didn't complain or tell her mother. It wasn't rape.'

'She was eleven or twelve,' I said, 'not fourteen, and destroying a child's character is not a good way to influence a jury. You're going to jail, Mackintosh, either for rape or for murder – the choice is yours. I'm told child abusers have a tough time in prison. Let's talk about Magdalena. She did call here, didn't she?'

He didn't answer, just looked down at the floor.

'We'll be swarming over this place and your car like ants over a jam pot. If she's ever shed a drop of blood in here, or been in your car boot, believe me, we'll have you. Are you following me?'

He nodded.

'So how much were you prepared to give her?'

'A couple of thousand pounds.'

'That's not much.'

'That's what she said, but it's all I had. I didn't owe her a thing. I wanted her to have it for…for…'

'For old times' sake?'

'Yes, something like that.'

'What happened?'

'She was a big woman. Bigger than me. She grabbed me by the shirt and started shaking me. And threatening. She said her boyfriend once poured petrol over a girl and threatened to set her alight. He'd do the same to me if I didn't find some more money. I panicked. When I was young…' His hand came up and rubbed the scars on his neck. 'We were playing with petrol in a den we'd made. I was in hospital for three months. When she said he'd do that it all came back to me. The pain, the scars and the other school kids laughing at me. I threw her off and grabbed that statue on the mantelpiece. The fertility god. I hit her with it and she fell down. She was dead.'

'Then what did you do?'

'I dragged her out of the back door and put her in the car boot. I just drove. Didn't know where I was going. When I realised I was near Shibden Park I took her in there and dumped her.'

It was good enough for me. We had him cold, and as soon as it was all down on paper we'd ask him to explain how Magda's body had over fifty separate wounds on it. He'd gone berserk with her, beaten her to a pulp. The blow with the fertility god may have been the fatal one, but he'd worked her over, well and truly.

'I'm taking you to the local nick,' I said. 'Is there anything here you need to do before we go?'

'I don't think so.'

'Get your coat, then.'

'Um, can I go to the toilet first?'

'No, but we'll only be five minutes. Where are your door keys?'

I handcuffed him and sat him in the front seat of the car. Standing outside it I rang Gilbert. 'It's Charlie,' I said. 'I understand you've been after me.'

CHAPTER TWENTY-FOUR

'And she believed you?' Dave said, incredulous, when I was back at Heckley and had placated Mr Wood. They'd all been wondering how I'd managed to inveigle my way into Heckley's hedonist set and win the attention of a young woman like Teri, the inference being that she was too good-looking for me.

'Of course she did. I'm a very plausible person.'

'That you were called…what was it…Torl Storey?'

'That's right.'

'She must be as dumb as a boat horse.'

'Actually, she's quite bright.'

'So whose was the Jaguar?' Brendan asked.

'I borrowed it from the asset recovery boys. They'd confiscated it from a drugs dealer a fortnight before. I used their offices, too, but only the boss knew about that. He stayed over to let me in with Teri one evening, pretended to be the caretaker.'

'A DCI working as a caretaker! He'd be out of his depth, there.'

'So what's happening with the others?' I asked. 'Are they singing?'

'Like a choir of angels,' Dave said.

'With four-part harmonies,' Brendan added.

'That's good to hear.' I looked at my watch. 'Anyone fancy a curry? I'm famished.'

Once we had them charged we could take samples and set the forensic boys and girls loose. Richard's prints were on the glass and coffee mug that Miss Birchall supplied and traces of Teri's DNA were found in the cars of both Colin Swainby and poor old Ted Goss. I'd destroyed the CD that Zed Boogey found by drawing a ball pen across it, after carefully checking it for prints and finding it clean. It didn't matter: the tape from Boogey's CCTV showed Teri going into his house and leaving about four hours later, with some blank tape in between. It was a guess that she'd disabled the alarm whilst in there and they'd spent some time uploading the images, but when I accused them of going in they'd taken the bait.

Gillian Birchall was banned from driving for three months, with a £200 fine. The normal ban is twelve months, so she was lucky. We're hoping for decent jail sentences for the Famous Four, as Dave calls them, but they can afford good briefs and we're not holding our breath. A search of their houses revealed two CDs of paedophilic images at the Wentbridges' Flour Mill, labelled as if they were holiday snaps, and some more on his hard disk, but Tristan Foyle was too canny to keep anything like that. Unfortunately for him, Wentbridge has fingered him for downloading it originally and masterminding the whole game. They'll almost certainly have to sign the sex offenders' register, and the *Gazette* has their photos on file, which is about as much as we could hurt them. Traces of cocaine were found at both houses, but only enough to be regarded as for personal use.

The Foyles split up shortly after they were released on bail. She's moved in with a nightclub owner who owns the major share in the boat they have at Cannes. It's called *Amelia Rose*, after one of his daughters. Tristan has been converting some of his investments to cash, and we've learnt that he's been making overtures to old friends in South Africa, but we have him covered. If he tries to flee the country his feet won't touch the ground.

The Wentbridges are still together, at least as far as the outside world can see. His riverside apartments have been described in the press as their love-nest, and this has generated some much-needed interest in the unsold units. As my mother would have said: 'It's an ill wind...'

JKL Mackintosh made a full confession to killing Magdalena, making it sound as if she'd attacked him and he'd acted in self defence while in a state of panic. I've a funny feeling that the nasty old sod is going to get away with a suspended sentence and a severe telling off. Sometimes, I wonder why I bother. We even informed Teri that he was still alive so she could consider rape charges against him but she rejected the idea. She was probably advised that her own character might not stand up to severe scrutiny.

As always, the paperwork nearly swamped us. We daren't throw anything away because it might be needed at the trials, but haven't room to store everything. We'd solved two cases, but right now, right here and now, two more cases are trundling around the carousel of life, with my name, Charlie Priest, written on them.

I unpinned the drawing of Magdalena from the incident room wall and laid it on the table. This was the original, unexpurgated version, drawn all those years ago. I wondered about putting a dress on her but decided not to. What the heck, I thought, we're all grown-ups, and he might appreciate a picture of her in all her raging glory. It wasn't signed, and I hesitated. After a few seconds I scrawled *Torl* across the corner. He'd been a good friend, we'd had some fun, so it was fitting to commemorate him.

I rolled up the drawing and slid it into a cardboard tube that I'd already addressed to Len Atkins. I kissed it and dropped it into the *out* basket.

'S'long, girl,' I said. 'I hope we've done you justice.'

There were two message notes on my desk when I went back upstairs. The first one said: 'Ring Miss Rhodes, Bentley prison,' and the second: 'A Gillian Birchall wants you to give her a call. She says you have her number.'

Flipping typical, I thought. You spend half a lifetime looking for a good woman and then two come along together. I turned the two messages face down, shuffled them and laid them side by side on my desk. I placed an index finger on the left-hand one and started to recite: 'Eenie...meenie... minie...mo...'

'*A million pounds for a frozen turkey with a ribbon around it? Pull the other one. Did any money change hands? I doubt it. A handful of dealers in the art world make insider traders in the stiock market look like bungling amateurs.*'

JD Lockwood, *Where Have All the Painters Gone?*